Hippie Homeschooling

Hippie Homeschooling

Carlton Smith

BLUE WEST BOOKS

RIVERSIDE, CALIFORNIA

Blue West Books
Riverside, California

ISBN: 978-0-9859495-2-5
LCCN: 2012954453

Blue West Books is a publishing collective dedicated to promoting emerging and established authors of contemporary fiction, poetry, and essays in California and the Southwest.

www.BlueWestBooks.com

In memory of James Tilton—as eternal and vivid in my mind as Mt. Gay rum, conch salads and the long sandy beaches that were the St. Croix summer.

For Deborah Paes de Barros, without whose loving kindness there would be no direction on the long road into the unknown, as true and right as the Northern Star. Forever and always.

"It is awfully easy to be hard-boiled about everything in the daytime, but at night it is another thing."
– Ernest Hemingway, *The Sun Also Rises*

Hippie Homeschooling

FIELD TRIP: Day of the Dead

Ensenada, Mexico (Ten Years Earlier)

LATER HE remembered the far away sounds of wooden guitars and singing, the moon balanced above the dark sea so close he could lean against it if he started to fall, the salt air thick with smoke and perfume, the bones that swam in the dark. And Ethan, his son, Jerry would remember him too.

"Nothing like a Mexican holiday to make you see the world for what it is, right, pal?" he said to Ethan.

"You look weird wearing your sunglasses."

The boy slumped harder against the wooden railing where they stood on the bluff above the beach. He had a right to be tired after the long drive from San Francisco on the Volvo's hard seats, but a small body could fall through the fence slats and tumble unseen onto the sand. It made Jerry's head hurt just thinking about it. Even so, he wished he'd brought the bottle of Jack Daniels.

He sipped his beer and looked out toward the blackening sea. "Step back away from the edge. Your mom might kill me when we get home, but it doesn't mean you have to get hurt."

"I'm fine," said Ethan. "I'm grown up now."

"You and me both."

The boy stood away from him, still leaning against the slanted railing. "So are you and mom going to split up?"

"We came to see the dancers, Ethan. That's all."

"We've been gone a while."

"I thought you'd have fun."

It was just like his son to worry about his mother, Evelyn, to see right through all of his father's ridiculous plans. Jerry had promised her to quit the crazy field trips and act like all the other fools in the Haight. Why chase electric butterflies when he could obsess about retirement plans, pay attention to his cholesterol, trim the heirloom roses on weekends and go to bed at a reasonable hour?

"Throw a ball in the yard," Evelyn said. "Go to the zoo. Shit, a porno flick would be better. I'm sick of it. Act like a real father, why don't you, not his friend. No more trips. And I'm sick of you and the bars and the girls, too."

He'd been watching TV, sipping his whiskey, when the silver-haired host started talking about *Día de Los Muertos*. Something about the music in the background reminded Jerry of the moonlight over the water, the way it lingered in a line from the horizon, the way the people danced in the dark in Baja, like the old days.

"One more time with Ethan," he scribbled in a note, taping it to the fridge for Evelyn. "Gone to see the ghosts."

Now this, half-stoned in Mexico, waiting for the dead.

They could hear the bus before they saw it, from somewhere on the road behind them. It careened onto the sand, engine bellowing, stopping by the closest fire where the silhouettes of the revelers circled the raging pits. The doors opened and more dancers climbed down on to the sand, bodies almost disappearing, the white bones painted on their shirts hanging in the dark.

"They just want to see the spirits," Jerry said. "Nothing to be scared about."

"You still sick?" Ethan asked.

Still sick. Jerry knew what that meant. The words

seemed to hang in the air, fouled with the smell of burning diesel and mesquite that billowed from the fires. He needed to change, he knew that, but later, because tonight was a night to celebrate the dead.

"Your head still hurt?" his son asked again. "This really is supposed to be fun."

They walked down the path to the closest fire, the heat so near Jerry felt it on his cheeks. Ethan walked ahead. A year or so ago, when they had driven to Big Sur to see the trees, Ethan never quit clinging to his pant leg with his small hand. Closer to the flames a dark faced man knelt, jiggling tiny skeletons on strings while three or four kids stared. Ethan pointed at them.

"Go on. Just stay close," Jerry said.

He watched his son find a place between the two children about his own age, his body blending into the other shadows. Above the water the thin trail of a firework arced silently into the sky and then exploded, the shards of white light reflecting like a spider web on the slate sea. In that instant Jerry saw the faint outline of horses walking in the shallows, the shapes of two boys waving sticks alongside.

Ethan was gazing up to the sky. The crowd of dark shapes moved, dancers snaking around them. You really got to stop this, Jerry thought.

"You're from the other side," came a voice — a girl's voice.

She stood beside him, staring up at the embers going black, her curls as translucent and golden as the bottle she dangled in front of the fire.

"A fellow traveler," she said, holding up the thatched bottle. "Shit, I'm wasted."

"I'm here with my boy," Jerry told her. He made a face

towards the puppeteer.

"Cute," she said, "like his father."

"How old are you?"

"What kind of question is that on a night like this?" she asked, laughing.

"I'm twice your age."

"Maybe more," she agreed. "Age is in your head, right?"

"Right."

"What brings you to the dark side?"

"Used to come down here with my friends in the old days. Thought he should see the place. It's different now."

She held the jug out again.

Without thinking he took a gulp, the warm liquid burning inside his ribs. He took another and handed it back to her. The mescal flared inside his stomach and rose like warm water to his brain.

He closed his eyes. When he opened them the girl swayed to the music, her hips turning slowly. She held the bottle up and the ghouls cheered. "At least we're alive, aren't we?"

"My wife's really going to kill me when I get back."

"You're here now, right?"

She set the bottle down in the sand. Then she took his hands, leaned back and started dancing. Behind her a starburst shuddered against the faint veil of moonlight as she tugged him closer.

When she kissed him, her lips felt warm and strange, tasting of cigarettes and medicinal cactus and lip balm.

He closed his eyes and kissed her again as everything receded, replaced by a dull sensation he associated with long ago bottle-spins and make-out couches in spider-webbed garages, with stolen bottles of peppermint

Schnapps and the long hot nights of summers when he was a boy.

"I can't," he said, pushing her away. "I'm married."

She lifted off the long necklace of colored beads and slipped it over his head.

"Nobody's married down here." Her words slurred into the guitar chords.

"I have to go home."

Her laughter sounded like water. And then they fell, his body tumbling onto the sand with hers, all around them the sparking light from the fires. She dragged up the bottle of Mescal and took a swallow, then fumbled it over to him. He took another drink, though he knew better.

She kissed him again, this time holding on tight to his shoulders, a long and slow kiss that made him dizzy. He kissed her back, then felt a flush of embarrassment on his face.

"Come on," he said, touching her cheek. "I'm just an old hippie."

"Don't you love me?" she teased. "All the boys love me."

He pulled the beads off and helped her to her feet. When they managed to get upright, she blinked at the fire.

"Your son," she said, "he's gone." Then she turned. "Jesus. Look at that."

She was talking about the bus. It had caught on fire. The undercarriage roiled with flames that climbed up the sides. Jerry wasn't listening anymore.

He peered at the black forms retreating from the fire-pit. The kneeling puppeteer was gone; so were the kids. Everyone was moving away, pushing towards them, a mass of black heads.

One of the bone-shirted ghouls danced atop the bus,

tipping a can like a cartoon in the moonlight. In another instant the side of the bus exploded with blue and yellow flames, dispersing the crowd in all directions.

"Ethan," he yelled at the shapes. "Where are you, son?"

His voice sounded faint in his own ears, swallowed by the cheering of the crowd and the sound of the sea, but he kept on yelling. He pushed against the dancing bodies as he ran, while his feet churned the sand beneath him and his eyes burned.

Just past the last fire pit something caught his eye, something moving above the smoke, the yelling, the skeletons. He was doubled over, gasping, his breath gone.

He looked past the bus, smoldering, black smoke drifting towards him. He could make out the horses at the edge of the water and the thin shapes of the two boys.

With a hundred yards to go, he could barely breath. He ran past bodies, flailing, pushing, screams trailing, laughter, bottles and cans flying past him, until he finally got free from the smoke, just in time to see the outline of his son fall from the horse, his black shape disappearing into the sea.

The water was thick and warm. Jerry gasped, hurling himself though the shallows, the white surf curling on both sides of him. He kept moving, each step longer, the water half way up his thighs.

When he got close enough to see the faces of the boys, he dove headlong under the thick surface, skimming his hand on the sandy bottom until he finally collided with his son, the small limbs entwining with his own as he yanked the boy to the surface. Out over the sea, the moonlight looked electric as the man opened his eyes and pulled his son's face close.

"You're okay, son," Jerry yelled, getting his feet under

him.

Ethan was laughing, his black hair slick on his face in the half-light. So were the other two boys, waving their sticks at the night.

Ethan tried to free himself. "I just wanted to ride the horse."

Jerry released his hold, and they both stood in the shallow tide, the sea swelling around them. The horses, small and white, skittered away, while the two boys waved their sticks behind them. On the shore the fires sent ruby sparks into the sky and they waded towards the flames.

"You scared me," Jerry said.

"Sorry."

"Let's go home."

"Is it like you remember?"

"It was a long time ago, Ethan."

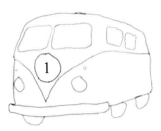

THAT MORNING Jerry steered the Jeep Wagoneer past the intersection of Haight and Ashbury, turned right, and a block later pulled to a stop across the street from his old house. He sipped coffee and looked up at the rambling, yellow Victorian, and at the enormous elm towering in the front yard. On mornings when he had the time, he liked to park and stare up at the house where he no longer lived.

He rolled down the Jeep's window and let the fresh wind blow on his face. The rain had finally stopped, and up high the clean, wet leaves of the tree glinted with light. He almost grinned, seeing the brief patches of blue sky and hearing the faint wet noise. The coffee was good too — black, slightly bitter, and still very hot. But then up above the elm tree, through the shining tops of its leaves, he made out something different, something new — a small scaffold secured beneath the upstairs window, the one he and Ethan had fitted with a stained glass image of a sunburst.

He squinted into the glare. No doubt about it, the stained glass was gone, replaced with a sliding windowpane. By now you'd think he'd gotten used to it, but he wasn't. A lot had changed since Evelyn sold the house eighteen months ago. The new owners had added French doors to the side, the green copper cornices had all been removed, and the front porch reconfigured. Would they rip out the old tree and bird-feeder next?

Jerry tossed what was left of his coffee onto the street and started the Jeep. Hell, he thought, what difference did it make, the house was gone already.

Driving along the thick canopy of trees in Golden Gate Park, he reminded himself what he had set out to do this morning, and tried to concentrate on the flat of fresh eggs he needed pick up in order to make breakfast at the shelter. Mahatma, the owner and proprietor of the Bayside Shelter, had a thing about getting eggs from the little market at the Upper Ferry Building, ever since he read an article in the Examiner about how an image of the Virgin Mary had miraculously appeared in the thin tracery of an eggshell.

By the time Jerry got to the market, he'd almost forgotten about the old house. He managed to smile when he stood at the counter, even though he saw no evidence of the divine in the surly face of the young Latino with a bald head.

"Any more of them Mary eggs?" Jerry asked.

"No man," the kid said. "All gone."

After loading the eggs into the back of the Jeep, Jerry headed down Embarcadero towards the wharf. When he reached the crest, he could look down and see the blue and waxy greens of the bay, clean and simple, until eventually the rust-colored spans of the Golden Gate Bridge and the rough hills of Marin came into view.

No matter how many times he saw it, the bay always got to him. Near the edge of the water he could see the dun-colored network of plain square buildings that made up the old Presidio, and past that the long wooden pier where the accident happened.

Now, with the sun tinting the edges of the water, he wondered again what that night must have looked like to someone across the bay. One of those rich dot-com entrepreneurs who maybe sat half-watching a late night movie in front of a bay window, and then was suddenly startled by the high-beams of Jerry's Cadillac Coupe de Ville coursing through the blackness into the bay, moving through the night like a comet.

More likely, whoever was watching figured the sight for what it was — a drunk ass crazy steering his car into the Pacific. Inside the car's cab that night there'd been nothing mystical about his descent, that he knew for sure. Just the pure line of a Muddy Water's lick on the car stereo and the darkness rushing towards the big Caddy window, then the shimmering mica and sand in the underwater slants of the headlights, the inky water rising around him.

By the time he got back to the shelter, a line had already formed near the door. He drove slowly past the storefront window and pulled around back into the alley across from the concrete loading docks of Mahatma's adjoining organic produce market. In the distance he could see Mahatma at the little card table atop the loading platform. He wore baggy shorts and a faded Hawaiian shirt. He was sipping coffee from a Dunk'n Doughnuts cup, and from his expression, Jerry could tell he was no doubt making an important point about sobriety to the two ashen-faced men sitting across from him, just as he'd lectured Jerry nearly a year before.

When Jerry drove past, Mahatma waved, giving him a thumbs up, which Jerry always felt required a reciprocal return from him. Mahatma's long gray hair, still surfer-like, framed his eager face, and Jerry lifted his thumb and waved back, cruising past.

He'd barely returned his eyes to the alleyway to negoitate the turn into the parking area when he saw a blur in front of the windshield.

He jammed the brake. Above the squeaking of the drums, Jerry heard the eggs slam against something in the back.

"Shit," he said.

At first the lank-haired kid in the window looked like the countless other misfits who hung around the shelter, but then Jerry recognized the high freckled forehead and flat nose. It was Willy, a boy who'd lived in the free housing unit a while back. He'd been into Mickey's Big Mouth and airplane glue, Jerry recalled.

Jerry opened the Jeep door and started around to the back to try and retrieve the eggs. He reminded himself about his obligation to others on the same path, but his ears were still hot.

"Didn't anyone ever tell you not to walk in front of moving cars?"

The boy laughed. "I knew you wouldn't hit me."

"Lucky for you," Jerry said. "I got to cook breakfast, Will."

At least the kid was able to walk a straight line. Jerry saw that he had something under his arm, an old shoebox or broken piece of cardboard. "You sober?"

It was a terrible question, Jerry knew. Even now, a year after his accident and the coma, old-timers still threw it at him. Still, the boy had ruined his eggs, not to mention his morning.

Will nodded. "Been sleeping in the movies."

Jerry understood. Many of the kids on the street spent

days in the cool safe confines of the skin movies, down on North Street. Jerry reached in and straightened the case of eggs. The whole top row looked cracked, the yolks spilling over the edge of the carton. Jerry handed Will the tray and found an oily rag to wipe the mess.

"What you got there under your arm Will?" He looked into his eyes. "Sometimes you just got to say it."

"Mom always said that God has a big book and writes it all down, everything — good and bad."

"I need to go cook some hungry drunks their eggs," Jerry said.

"And you being a legend and all."

Jerry took the carton of eggs from Will's free hand. "I'm no legend, kid."

He knew he had to be patient. Whatever foolishness the boy was up to, it really wasn't Will's fault. And the part about the legend, although it annoyed the hell out of Jerry, that wasn't Will's fault at all. When Jerry woke up after the accident, he looked into the mirror the nurse held and saw what everybody saw. With the medicine and the trauma, and the curly and now gray hair that covered his head, there was no denying it — he looked like the famous, deceased rock star. When they started calling him by the same name, Jerry didn't care. He'd lost everything; his son had run away, his wife left, the house was gone — even most of his memories, so what the hell did a name matter?

At the door Jerry stopped. "You know the drill, Will. I've got to go to work. You got something to tell me, better just say it."

Will held out the box. "Don't want it written down I stole from a legend," he said.

Jerry balanced the carton of eggs in one hand and took the box. The lid, bent and stained, barely covered the contents. He recognized a Lucite Buddha that Mahatma had given him, but the rest of the stuff looked like junk.

"Now it's over," Will said. "Whatever the hell else is in that book, this is too. I returned it."

Jerry pushed the door open. At least the kid got it off his chest. The boy's face even looked lighter on its bones, his eyes alert. "Mahatma's got some organic peppers I'm going to throw in with the eggs," Jerry said. "Come on in. Unless you don't like my cooking anymore."

"No, man. You take it easy, Jerry."

Inside the kitchen, Jerry quickly chopped up Mahatma's vegetables and whisked them with eggs and milk in a big steel mixing bowl. In the rectangle of the service window, past the orange glare of the floodlights, he saw Saul glance at the front door and nodded to him.

Saul slowly turned the key and let in the procession of takers. The tables filled and Jerry started sliding the plates of eggs and toast through the window. Like the others who boarded and worked at the shelter, Saul once lived in the other world. He sold insurance in the pyramid building down by the Wharf, and had a winter house in Palm Springs, before hitting bottom. Now he dressed neatly and kept his stubby fingers scrubbed, and talked in platitudes.

"Miracles happen," Saul said, clutching one of the plates carefully.

"Don't burn yourself," Jerry said, trying not to sound irritated. "Nice day, huh?"

When the breakfast service was over, Jerry pulled out the little shoebox and went into the concrete-walled room with the dishwasher and stainless counters. He liked the quiet there, the coolness.

He sat down on one of the folding chairs and set the box on the floor. Bad luck, he thought, this trash from a former life. He thought maybe he'd just toss the whole mess into the trash bin under the sink.

Jerry lifted the lid and pulled out the little Buddha that Mahatma had brought back from India, setting it on the concrete floor. He'd keep that, but the rest looked worthless, some old bills, a couple of fountain pens, an empty note pad with a psychiatrist's address. Looking at it, Jerry wondered just what Will feared about being put on some Higher Power's list for all this. It didn't seem likely that God in his white robe and long beard was busy writing Will up for this shit, but Jerry supposed that wasn't the point. Anyway, what did he know?

He went through the scraps, getting all the way to the bottom before he came to it, a postcard. Even though he couldn't see the writing, he knew at once who had sent it. He ran his finger over the glossy picture, his hand trembling.

The postcard's picture featured a salt encrusted lake, its surface dull and greenish, surrounded by bleached mountains, the sort of place he and Ethan used to like. On the edge of the lake a tiny stick man had been carved into the picture with something sharp, giving the impression of a little hieroglyph. Just like Ethan, thought Jerry.

When he turned it over and saw his son's handwriting on the back, the strand of mercurochrome light from the heat-lamps swelled somehow, making the room hot suddenly. Jerry got up and cracked the rear door, letting in some air and a smoky shaft of light.

Not quite able to read Ethan's note yet, Jerry focused on the caption — a brief description of the Salton Sea and how it was formed in 1922 when an irrigation ditch broke and flooded the valley.

Jerry barely read the words. On the opposite side from

the caption, the postmarks explained where the card had been before Will stole it. The card had been delivered to Jerry's old address, the Victorian, and then had been returned when Jerry was in the hospital. There was no explanation of how it had reached the shelter, from where Willy had evidently taken it. Had the postcard been forwarded and dropped into the mail-slot the night Will took everything?

What did it matter, thought Jerry. It had come, that was the main thing. Even so, he couldn't bring himself to read the words.

He sat quietly for a second, listening to Saul saying goodbye to the diners, eventually hearing the little bells on the front door ring. Then came the clatter of silverware and Saul carrying plates through the swinging door.

He set them down in the basin and looked at Jerry. "Still waiting for that miracle?" he said, his porcelain veneers evident in his widening grin.

Jerry sighed heavily, struck suddenly with the thought of punching him. It was an odd emotion, a bit like the old days, and Jerry was ashamed of himself.

"You never know, do you Saul? God works in mysterious ways."

"That's the spirit. One day at a time."

Jerry grabbed the Buddha and postcard and headed out the door into the clear morning. The salt smell was heavy off the bay and everything looked clean; he told himself to relax.

He found Mahatma unloading wooden crates filled with baby eggplants from a dolly cart into one of the vans. "Bro, give me a hand will you? My back's killing me."

Jerry jammed the card and Buddha into the pocket of his jeans. He felt thankful for the momentary distraction.

Mahatma's appearance up close always amused Jerry, like one of those die-hard old surfers with the long boards riding curls down by the bridge. With his bleached-out blue eyes and straggly hair, Mahatma might have been mistaken for one of the shelter's patrons if you didn't know better.

Jerry hefted one of the crates from the dolly, the case shiny with perfect purple and white vegetables.

"Come on, man." Mahatma said, staring at him.

"What?"

"I'm right here, bro."

Mahatma could always tell that something was bothering Jerry. Maybe it was because of his time in India, or just an annoying trait, but ever since he coaxed Jerry off the streets, Mahatma had power like some kind of trippy fortune-teller.

"Remember that kid Will?"

"Model cement. Right? I saw him hanging around this morning."

"He was making amends. Brought me some things he took when he lived here."

"Did you go easy on him?"

"Sure."

"What, then?"

Jerry backed away from the crate and pried the little Buddha and card out. Mahatma smiled a little.

"He took the Buddha?" Mahatma said.

Jerry held out the card. "This too."

Mahatma glanced at it.

"Ethan," said Jerry. "He sent it from the Salton Sea, maybe a year or so ago. Near the Mexican border."

Mahatma gazed in the direction of the water, the thin strip of blue you could see past the building. "I know where it is, bro."

Jerry knew what Mahatma was thinking, and stuffed the card and Buddha back into his pocket. He bent and lifted a crate from the dolly into the back of the van.

"You going to talk to me, bro?" Mahatma said. "I mean I am kind of your sponsor."

Jerry kept lifting the crates. One of the baby eggplants fell off, and its thin skin shredded on the concrete. Picking it up, he thought about how Mahatma had sat with him at the hospital, his only real visitor, and what he owed him.

When Jerry stood, Mahatma came around the front of the van, holding two cigars, presenting Jerry with one. Jerry knew that this meant Mahatma wanted to lecture, which Jerry surely didn't want to hear, but he figured he wasn't in much of a position to protest.

They sat on the edge of the loading dock and Mahatma struck a match, lighting Jerry's cigar. He lit his own and then started in.

"I ever tell you the first thing the old guru told me?"

Jerry shook his head. He tried to think about all the stories Mahatma had told about his time in India, as he sat by Jerry's bed in the hospital. All recovered drunks had stories, with beginnings, middles and ends. Mahatma's started in the seaside town of Laguna Beach, California, where he smoked pot, fried on acid, and rode big swells. The middle was Vietnam, and after that, his time with the swamis in India.

"The thing about sleeping on bones?"

"No man, before that." He puffed on his cigar. "Here I am, bro, after riding a train to the south of India for two days. Middle of nowhere — just mud and these dirt houses. I'm sick, hardly eating, flies are really bad. Train finally gets to this village where the man's supposed to be, and I get out and stumble to his little hut."

"I know the feeling."

"That's what I'm saying. So I knock on his door. And there he is, this little brown dude no bigger than a fifth grader. But I can see it in his black eyes, how far back they went. He knows shit." Mahatma blew smoke into the clear sky. "He asks me, What you want? Like that. What you want?"

"So?"

"I say, like salvation, man. The fucking truth about love and salvation and why the moon doesn't fall from the sky — shit like that."

"If he told you, I hope you're going to share it."

"You know what that little man did?"

Jerry shook his head. Obviously not.

Mahatma fixed his eyes on Jerry. "Takes my backpack and dumps all my shit on the ground. I got some primo dope and this killer blotter acid in there and he just spills it onto the dirt."

Jerry looked at Mahatma. The scene could have been yesterday. Jerry knew how that worked. Before losing it, Jerry had been a therapist, a teacher at San Francisco State. He'd read his Freud and knew that time didn't exist. Not in the unconscious. It hade been a long time, but he still knew that much. He also knew his clearest memories were of bars, and long solitary walks on the streets.

Then Mahatma said, "So he picks up the sheet of acid and runs his tongue down the whole thing — every last bit, like it's honey."

Jerry could picture the little brown man. "Jesus."

"So I'm sitting there thinking he's going to die, or go crazy. This was some good shit, Jerry."

"I know the kind."

"I know you do, bro." Mahatma was coming to his

point. He paused and exhaled for drama, then turned to Jerry again. "The thing is, nothing happened. He's fine, just smiling, his little tongue like a lizard. He looks at me and says, You no ready."

"What do you mean?"

"For truth, for wisdom, for all of it."

"What are you telling me? Sometimes I wish you'd just say it. You know? In plain English."

"Think about it, man. He was saying that the truth is harder to handle than all that acid."

Mahatma licked the edge of his cigar and gazed at the ash thoughtfully, then looked at Jerry. "I know you're thinking about going after him," Mahatma said. "You no ready."

Jerry lifted himself from the hard concrete and went back to the crates. He clamped the cigar between his lips and lifted one of the crates. He understood Mahatma's point and knew his doctors would probably agree.

"You ever think miracles might be true?" Jerry said.

"You've been hanging around Saul too much. And anyway, you're alive and sober aren't you? That's not enough of a miracle for you?"

"I don't know."

"If it's meant to be, he'll come home, bro."

"He's out there. I know that."

Mahatma shook his head and slid off the dock. Jerry loaded the last of the crates and closed the panel doors.

Mahatma stood by the front door. "I'm heading over to Chez Blue, you want to come?"

"I need to walk."

"Let me know, will you?"

"Sure."

As Jerry walked along the water towards the Presidio,

he marveled at how quickly things change. He'd known that before of course, but time stood still in the shelter. Mahatma always said, "Be here now," quoting the mantra from his old friend and New Age guru, Ram Das. But what exactly did that mean? And what did it get you, anyway? Maybe Will was right. There was no now, just a book where everything was written — your few merits and the, hopelessly long, list of demerits and personal failings.

Jerry sat on the grassy knoll, watching the crab fishers stringing nets out on the pier. A thin sheet of clouds swept past the bridge, blurring the crisp lines of the cables. Just behind him rose the mounds of ice plant and sand, the place where he'd slid down into the water and then was plucked out by one of the night time fisherman.

He reached into his pocket and pulled the Buddha out and placed it on the grass. The postcard was ragged and bent. He set it down next to it, still unable to read the words.

On the dock some boys were playing with toy sailboats, yelling as the little toys floated under the shadows of the pier.

At first he didn't know that one of the boys who'd come from the dock was talking to him. The boy was eight or nine, with gleaming orange hair and freckles.

"Come on, go get it," the boy yelled from the boardwalk.

He looked beyond the boy, staring at the tiny, toy boat that fluttered against the swimming-buoy.

"I don't like water."

"You're scared," the boy said. He made it sound like an "a" came before the "s", like Ethan used to.

"I can't swim, really, kid."

On the dock the other boys were laughing, pointing at the boat.

"Come on."

Jerry grudgingly rose and took off his shoes. He figured the water was pretty shallow. He placed his baseball cap on top of the card.

The rocky bottom hurt his feet, but he made his way slowly outward until the footing turned sandy. The pier grew closer though the position of the little boat itself seemed to be unchanging. It rose and fell on the blue sheet of water. It struck Jerry, at this moment, that he'd made a terrible miscalculation. He turned to see if the boy had perhaps grown bored and wandered off, but instead saw him hopping and pointing, guiding him outward.

Jerry lifted his arms and kept wading, the sudden idea of a gin and tonic entering his mind. But then he let his eyes take in the vast spread of water that moved out to the center of the bay, where the tourist boats and sport cruisers loomed, and he could feel all cognitive thoughts overcome by the internal swooshing of his heart. Worse, he heard Saul's singsong voice crooning foolishly inside his head, calling "One step at a time, buddy."

Ten feet from the buoy Jerry became aware he was a spectacle. All the people on the pier were pointing, even the Japanese crabbers with their cigarettes pinched in their lips. He kept moving, increasingly cold, a slow ache swelling up around his abdomen.

Jerry wanted to stop, to go back and read the postcard, to tell the kid he was right, he was a coward, but he kept moving in the cold water.

By the time Jerry got close enough to grab the boat, the water had moved up to his armpits. He could detect the eroding bottom and realized getting his hands on the boat would be risky, requiring a lunge.

After shoving off the muddy bottom, Jerry managed to

grab the toy and felt a brief surge of exaltation, giving him momentary buoyancy like a balloon. But just as quickly a cascade of freezing blue swallowed him and the sky disappeared. Desperately waiting for the bottom, Jerry clamped his eyes shut. He'd swallowed a gulp of thick water, flailed, but was still surrounded by darkness. With a hard pull of his arms, he quickly surfaced, erupting again into the sun and noise of cheering.

Back on shore, Jerry handed the kid the boat. The boy took it wordlessly and galloped back towards the pier.

Jerry sat down and pulled his hat down over his eyes, hooked the rims of his sunglasses behind his ears, and considered the card by the little Buddha. He let the cold water drip off him and dried a little in the sun. Finally he picked up the card and studied the picture.

But before he could turn it over, he felt an encroaching shadow. He lifted his eyes. A woman stood over him, her tan arm and hand holding on to a stroller.

"God, I can't believe it's you," she said.

Jerry lowered his sunglasses, gazing at her over the rims. Despite the frizzy hair and granny glasses, she wore an artfully tie-dyed shirt that looked expensive. "I'm not him," he said.

"Me and my old high school boyfriend followed you for a year. I knew you were still alive. Provincetown, the Cow Palace, Hawaii — God."

Jerry listened, aware of the real things in his life — the postcard, the idea of his son out there somewhere.

"Leave me alone, lady. I'm just some guy, that's all."

She recoiled a little, and then smiled. "I'm married to someone else," she said. "Things are different for me too. And this is Jacob," she said. "I'm going to tell him you came back, when he gets older."

"You do that."

"I love you," she said.

Down on the gravel boardwalk, she stopped pushing the stroller and turned back. "Your secret's safe with me," she said. "We miss you though."

When she was far enough away to blend into the other tourists swarming around the shops at the base of the pier, Jerry sighed heavily and glanced at the card, finally turning it over.

At first Ethan's handwriting felt ancient, like a sacred text written by someone holy a long time ago. Then, slowly, he could hear his boy's voice behind the words:

"Hey old man, Be home soon. No worries. Hooked up with some kids here. Feels like the stories you used to tell. Trying to stay good, but you know how that goes. Don't worry, okay? I like it here. We travel around, look for music and truth. Everything changes, old man. Right? Peace out, Ethan."

On the walk back to the shelter, Jerry did his best to try to stride evenly. It was an old habit, and he had years of practicing on the late night streets all over town, mostly after the bars had closed and he didn't want to go home. Then his head had been filled with the hope of pushing everything away, all the bad thoughts.

But Ethan was out there, loose somewhere in the world.

By the park, he walked past a group of elegant men in white straw hats rolling bocce balls, sipping Limonado in tall glasses. They were old Italian men who routinely gathered to talk and roll balls over the tailored grass. Sometimes their grandchildren were with them, yelling and tossing Frisbees and eating candies the old men handed to them. Jerry paused and watched one of them, a handsome fellow with coffee-colored skin and a soft white suit, roll the ball. For an instant Jerry thought about the cloudy yellow liquor in their glasses, wanting to feel the sharp taste of it in his mouth and the liquid sensation of his limbs. Slow down, he thought. You've blown that possibility. No Limonado for you, old man. Everything changes.

Back at the shelter, in dry clothes, Jerry found Mahatma in his little office. The room stirred heavily with smoke and Mahatma rested his feet on an old mahogany desk. He kept his eyes on an ancient Field and Stream magazine while Jerry took a seat.

"We should go fishing," he said. "Trout, maybe."

"I thought you didn't want me to leave."

"Steelhead — the King of fish, bro."

"I'm going."

Mahatma lowered the magazine and took a long draw of his cigar. He opened the lid to a new box of expensive Dominicans and lifted his eyebrows at Jerry.

Jerry said, "I can't just not go looking for him."

"Saul's a lousy cook," Mahatma said, gazing through the smoke towards his little shelf of mystical books and figurines. Jerry followed his eyes and found a black and white picture of a matted-haired Mahatma and the Indian.

"The postcard makes it sound like he's part of a gathering that meets at the Salton Sea and travels around."

Mahatma tapped some ash into an ashtray on his desk. "Think it might have something to do with the hippie homeschooling, dude?"

"Maybe they'll be back there, I don't know."

"Kids run away from fucked up parents."

"Take it easy."

"You no ready, man."

"I'm better."

Mahatma laughed, then coughed on the cigar. He set it down and looked at him. "Today was a good day. Why you have to go and mess it up?"

"No telling when I'll get back."

"The guru was into Shiva," Mahatma said, a note of resignation in his voice. "Shiva says destruction rules. I read that."

"I can't just leave him, all right?"

"I'll pray for you, brother."

In his little room above the shelter, Jerry gathered his dirty clothes and tossed them into the trash. He packed clean shirts and pants and his toiletries into a duffle bag, and carried it downstairs.

At the loading dock, Mahatma stood near the Jeep, holding the door open. Clouds had moved in off the bay, making the air heavy and cold. A cardboard box heaped with what looked to be oranges and Ritz crackers sat on the back seat.

"Jeep leaks oil sometimes," Mahatma said. "And watch the overheating."

"You sure about this?"

"Like old times, hey buddy? Out on the road again, running wild."

"Yeah."

Mahatma pulled back the door and waited. When Jerry got inside, he found a little statue on the dash, one of Mahatma's figurines. He didn't know much about Hindu mythology, but recognized the man with a wheel of arms extending from his torso. It was Shiva.

THE LIGHTNING started in the south, above the muted lines of the outlying hills, then moved slowly over the turgid water of the Salton Sea. Jerry awoke, sat up, gathered his bedroll around his chest and stared out the window. The charged bolts came down in branches and hollowed out parts of the night and left shadows before going dark again.

Nights when he couldn't sleep in his little room above the shelter, Jerry could look out and see the city lights cascading down the hill toward the bay. Even when it rained, or fog fell over everything, there were the lights. Here, there was only the rain coursing thickly through a solitary sphere of yellow light from a bulb atop the tourist center.

He cranked down the Jeep window, still watching the electrified currents fester over the shoreline and brooding black water of the sodden lake. From the looks of it, the Visitor's Center wasn't much — just a doublewide trailer set out near the edge of the water. It was hard to imagine what Ethan saw in such a desolate outpost, but then again he'd had a hell of a good teacher about tales of desolation.

When Jerry awoke again the storm was gone and sweat rimmed his neck. Moonlight glimmered off the edges of the dash and the little Shiva, but the water out the window still looked thick and dull as far as he could see.

He dug in the glove box and found one of Mahatma's cigars, hoping the aroma would keep down the stench of the rotting water. He'd gotten half way through his cigar when he saw something moving over the lake. Nothing, he thought to himself. Now I'm imagining things.

He took the cigar from his mouth and leaned towards the open window, then reached over and pulled on the lights and tapped the high-beam switch with his foot. The figure kept moving, getting larger. When it finally got close enough Jerry saw it was a man, a big man with a belly and beard, walking into the glare, his small round glasses reflecting light as bright as constellations.

Then the image wavered, as if swallowed up by the lake, gone.

Jerry watched the backdrop of stars twinkle against the celestial darkness and thought about what he saw, though he didn't have to. The face was unmistakable. It was Captain Trips, the old hippie musician who'd died years ago. Ghost or man, the Captain was back.

THE NEXT morning Jerry opened his eyes into the sharp light refracting off the chrome fixtures of the dash. He pulled himself up on the bench seat, expecting to get a look around, but found himself looking straight into the face of someone on the other side of the window, an old man pinching his eyes at him from under a felt cowboy hat.

Jerry stiffened, trying to look respectable. He'd forgotten what a crummy feeling it was to be greeted by a leering face in the morning, like all those times he'd wandered home from the bars and fell a little short of his destination, waking to face the critical stares of latte-toting tourists or pissed off shop owners.

The man waved a cane at the window. Jerry reached over and turned the window knob. The man stood close enough that Jerry could see his veins under the layer of sunscreen and smell his cologne, Old Spice maybe or Brut. "Ain't a trailer park, kid," the man said. "Cops come when I call them."

Better not to take umbrage at the old guy's insinuation, thought Jerry. He tried to look respectable, not like the old days when he'd make a clown face or bark at onlookers, or the moon, eventually picking himself up and heading home.

"I got in late. I'm here looking for someone."

The old man gazed morosely over the hood in the direction of the lake. "God help him if he's near this son-bitch. We got maps and such inside."

Jerry got out and jammed his shirt into his pants, then made a futile attempt to smooth back his hair with his palms. He checked his reflection in the broad side-mirror, struck once again by his own resemblance to Captain Trips, before replacing his Giant's cap.

Past the Jeep the lake looked astonishingly wide. It ran as far as he could see, a vast repository of stagnant, gray water. Along the shore, a margin of clearly visible dead fish floated on the tide, their stinking husks undulating and reflecting like gypsum.

Inside the trailer the old man squinted at something he held under a magnifying glass at arm's length. Musty light came in through the windows.

"Got some coffee brewing in the corner," the man said, not looking up. "If you can keep it down."

Jerry filled a Styrofoam cup and ducked under a spider web dangling off of a tattered seagull tacked to the wall. The ravaged bird suggested something about being blown off course that he didn't want to ponder.

"They dropped the big one out there," the old man said cheerlessly. "What do you think about that?"

"Excuse me?"

"You know, the bomb. Right out that window, fifty years ago. Is it any wonder it's a cesspool?"

The man lowered what he was holding with his pliers. Jerry saw it was a fish of some sort, its large mouth bent into a hideous scowl.

"Even used to have Piranha fish out there," he said, shaking his head. "This one here lost an eyeball." The old man cackled a little.

He pulled back the sliding door on the display case and set the fish among the other specimens. "What's so important you got to sleep in your car all night?"

"Like I said, I'm looking for someone."

"I don't get involved in affairs of the heart."

"I'm looking for my son."

"He a runaway? Lord knows, we got our share."

Jerry pulled Ethan's postcard out of his pant's pocket and handed it to the man. The old man set his coffee cup down and frowned, his eyes flickering as he examined the picture. Then he turned it over and read the note and Ethan's description of the place he was staying.

"He's a good kid," Jerry said. "It's been a while. I was hoping he might still be around here."

Out the window rivulets of tidewater jostled the fish atop the crusty salt beach. Jerry looked back at the man, waiting for him to say something.

"Bombay Beach," the man said finally, handing Jerry back the picture. "That's the place."

"Bombay Beach?"

"Just like it sounds. All sorts end up there — hole-ups, mental defectives, kids who hate mommy and daddy. Losers."

"My kid's not a loser." Jerry held his eyes on the man.

"Didn't mean nothing by it. Out east. Two miles down the road, turn right at the old resort. Keep going. It's a ghost town now. Trailers, A-frames and such. You'll see the old boat-house past the café." The old man picked up a feather duster. "I hear some kids holed up in an old equipment shed out there. Look for the shiny metal roof."

JERRY FOLLOWED the shoreline, driving past more dead fish, groves of them rimming the entire lake. He came upon a still inlet littered with broken seagulls, their ravaged husks thickly snagged on half-submerged branches.

He slowed the truck, gazing at them. The dead birds made his skin tingle, the desolate ecology, empty of any possibility. Still, Ethan was a smart boy, Jerry thought, and kept on.

He passed a deserted encampment, an old truck and lean-to. A toddler in front of a dilapidated trailer stared. No one else.

When an old shed came up in the window, the metal roof sparked above the salt flats like a tin can, just as the man said it would. Jerry pictured Ethan inside maybe playing cards with his friends, sheltered from the dust and sun.

After he got close enough, he saw what the place really

looked like. The wood-frame building's broken siding was rotted and shot through with miserable desert light. He parked alongside and got out, aware suddenly of the looming sand and endless light. It had been a long time since he'd been out of the city under such a big sky. Overhead a shadow turned, and he looked up in time to catch a black wing of some sort of bird disappearing into the white sun. The brightness stung and he clamped his eyes shut. Ridiculous to think he would find Ethan here.

A few steps further and he heard a low buzzing sound, only a suggestion of sound, a radio maybe.

Stay calm, he told himself, and slowly rounded the shed. Odds were, Ethan was nowhere around here. But hell, maybe Saul was right about miracles.

The room into which he peered was striated with long, dusty shadows. A rusted Stingray leaned near the door, one of its rotting tires spinning and creaking above the faint sound of the radio.

"Anybody in there?"

Except for the barely faint music, silence. He pushed back the door and gazed in. It took a second for his eyes to adjust. Past the shady lines of dusty light coming though the broken slats, towards the corner, tangled up in the folds of an army blanket, lay a girl.

She was young, Ethan's age perhaps, wearing jeans and a tee-shirt that rose just perceptibly with her breath. The roots of her yellow hair showed a hint of dark.

He stepped cautiously inside. The ground was littered with bent-up coke cans, melted candles and plastic medicine bottles. He knelt beside the girl and tapped her shoulder.

"Hey there," he said. "You okay?"

She pulled her legs into a ball.

"Come on, you got to get some air," Jerry said.

"I'm thirsty. Who are you?"

Her delicate eyebrows looked feral under her chopped bangs. He'd seen kids on outreach calls that weren't nearly as dead as they looked, but they had nothing on this girl.

"Sorry to barge in on you. You feeling all right?"

"I want some water. You have water?"

In the Jeep he dug out a bottle of water from Mahatma's care package. When he got back inside, she gazed vacantly ahead as he handed her the plastic container.

"You here by yourself?"

She drank some water before answering, then lowered the bottle. "Shit. I must've dozed off."

"You take anything you shouldn't have?"

"You a frigging desert narc or something?"

"Just thought you might need some help."

She looked out between one of the broken slats, then back at him. "Just smoked a little. Plus some of mom's blue pills. Shit."

Jerry watched her start to guzzle the water and thought to warn her, but she slowed, sipping. She probably had friends around somewhere, friends who might even know about Ethan. Still, being around this underage druggie hurt his temples.

She held her eyes on him. "You really want to help, I could use a ride into town."

They drove back on the two-lane, two miles back to Salton City. She rested her arm on the window frame and leaned her head back against the bench seat, squinting into the wind while it fluttered her hair back and blew on her face, looking like a girl still wasted enough to enjoy the ride.

"My name's Jerry," he said.

She rocked her head, the sun white on her cheekbones. "Lily."

"They've got a lake or something out there filled with dead fish. Never seen anything like it." He tried to make conversation.

He could feel her staring at the side of his face. "Fuck. I know who you are!" She laughed.

"You're mistaken. Really."

She pressed her face close to her window, then suddenly grew bored again, still high. "Whatever."

He clicked open the glove box and took out the picture postcard Ethan sent, tossing it on her lap. She lifted it slowly with both hands. She finished reading with a sigh, flipping the card on the bench seat and resuming her blank stare out the window.

"Not my problem."

"He's my son."

"All I want is a ride."

They drove past a succession of brick buildings, rising above the salt colored land, paled by the sun and separated by patches of lavender ice-plant and crusty sand dunes. The place had the feel of an ancient beach town, all the oxidized metal signs and pastel blue bricks making Jerry think of old people sitting around pools drinking gin and tonic highballs, listening to Frank Sinatra records on big wooden consoles and fearing the commies. The town was once a low-rent Palm Springs for all the aspiring to the middle class, square types who built the world before the 60's, who manufactured a cheap resort town where they could drown their self-doubts.

When they came upon a roadside diner, Jerry slowed, figuring she might help him if he got some food in her stomach. At any rate, it was worth a try. "What do you say about a cheeseburger?"

"I don't eat dead animals. But whatever."

Except for the two of them, the restaurant was empty. They sat in a window booth looking onto the road. Lily gulped her fries, dipping each ceremoniously into a dish of ketchup before cramming them into her mouth.

"You want to know what I'm doing out here, right?" she said. She wiped her mouth with her napkin, rolling her eyes. "She's crazy. Well, not exactly crazy, but smart. Really fucking smart. She's like this frustrated artist. Big professor. God, she pisses me off." She gave him a funny look. "Men like her, though. She's a girly-girl. Pretty. You'd probably even like her."

"Your mother?"

"Who else?"

Jerry sipped his coffee and looked past the road to where the outlying hills, sun-bleached and chiseled like rock salt, lined the blue plane of sky. He thought about his fucked up dharma, the twisted road he'd driven onto.

"This old guy told me they dropped the bomb out there. Why the hell did you want to come here?"

After a silence, she said, "Max."

"He's your boyfriend?"

"Yeah."

"Just you and Max in that old shed?"

She stopped chewing and glared at him. "Okay, others come there too. It's like a thing. You wouldn't get it. It's just music." A thin smile of amusement touched Lily's face. "Unless you're really him. Come back."

He set down his coffee cup. She was still a little high, the sideways light dull on the iris closest to the window, but her features seemed sharper, her skin pink.

He brought out his wallet, extracting the single picture

it carried and slid it across the formica counter. Ethan, fifteen, standing next to a medieval looking church, a blurred bird angling past the stained glass image of Gabriel above his head. He could have been any kid, features hidden by a round bowl of hair, his thin arms and legs, the disconnected, vacant look as he stared at his fucked up father holding the camera.

"I need your help here, Lily."

"No offense, but he looks like a retard."

"Look at his face — I think his hair is short now."

"You think?"

"It's too hard to explain. I haven't seen him for a while. You think Ethan could be with them?"

"Them?"

"Your friends."

"Look, I don't know him, okay?"

Lily swished the last fry on the salty plate, dipping it in the ketchup, her expression like a spoiled girl. He took a gulp of water, set down the glass and watched his own image in the tilted pie display. The waitress scribbled at a crossword puzzle on a folded sheet of newspaper.

"What do you say to a piece of pie before I take you back? I can't leave you out there starving."

"You haven't taken me to town."

The waitress slammed a pan.

"I think we're done here," Jerry said, wanting only to get out of there, pulling the picture back toward him.

She ate the pie quickly, scraping the last of the cherries on her plate. When she finished, she wiped her lips with her napkin and looked across the table at him.

Her smile was a little phony, even though she tried to hide it. "I was thinking, you know. Max might know Ethan." Her voice became soft, almost playful. "If you can just get me to Max, I bet he could help you."

Jerry heard the clock tick, saw the waitress look over at him. The girl was trouble, but he couldn't just drive off and leave her in the desert. She was bargaining for something, for sure, but he couldn't see any other options.

"What's so special about Max?"

"Max is beautiful. Everybody loves him. I love him."

"Some sort of leader?"

"God, like it's a cult, or something? You must know my mom. People dig his shit is all."

Right, thought Jerry, beautiful Max. "So where's this guy now?"

"Just up the road. Next bend in the river, you know."

"I need to find my boy, Lily."

"My mom's wiring some money to a drugstore in town. Take me there and then we can go find Max. You help me and I help you."

"Jesus."

An American flag billowed beside a building, anointed with big star-shaped placard, announcing the sheriff's station that sat next door to the Rexall Drugstore. Jerry waited in the Jeep across the street while Lily went inside the drugstore, and he watched her collect her money on the other side of the plate-glass window. Maintain, he thought, the old words coming back. When she finally came out, he expected her to be buoyant, having scored enough to keep moving down the road, but instead she climbed in and fixed her eyes vacantly over the hood.

"Everything go okay?"

"Last time she sent a note."

"Why don't you call her?"

"Shut up and go, all right?"

On the way back to the shed, Lily's eyes drifted to the

blanched roadside that blended into desert while she held
the green envelope of money in her lap, running her finger
over its edge. Even though he didn't feel like it, Jerry knew
he had to act like the responsible one here. Since waking up
and starting over damn near from scratch, he often felt as
feeble as a child. But he had to say something.

"You know how you can have a dream, vivid and clear
as anything, but when you wake up it's gone?" he said.

"Kind of."

"I had an accident. I got jacked-up one night and put
my car in the ocean. Except for the ocean part, it's sort of
what I did every night."

"That sounds bad."

"When I woke up, I couldn't remember a lot of what
happened before — still can't."

"Shit."

"I just can't recall much about Ethan leaving. About
him."

She looked away, her eyes following the last of the slab
encampments. "I wasn't a good father," he said.

"You seem pretty cool." Again, the sly smile.

"Sometimes cool isn't cool."

"What'd you do before you were wasted?"

He laughed a little and tried to sound more definite than
he was. "A psychology professor. But that was a long time
ago."

"Like that Timothy Leary guy?"

"Kind of."

She winced, shaking her head as if tired of the
conversation, looking away again. "Kids come and go," she
said. "I don't really know him. But Max knows everybody."

It was a bad deal she was proposing. But he'd already
driven this far down the road.

"How come your good friends left you here?" he said, still hoping she'd somehow talk him out of the plan. The girl shrugged. "I just had to pick up my mom's wire." She twisted a ring on her pinky. "I mean there's no guarantee. But if your son was cool, he went with Max."

WHILE LILY collected her things in the shed, Jerry sat against a low concrete wall across the dusty remains of a street, smoking a cigar, watching dust-devils move above the wide plane of emptiness beyond the road. Then one stirred close. At first, the dust lifting into the sky looked like a thermal kicking up, but when it got nearer the windows flashed and a minute later a small, late model car turned off the highway and sped towards the shed.

Jerry watched as the car ground over the dirt and skidded to a stop alongside the wood building.

A woman, maybe forty, maybe more — he was out of practice appraising women — got out. She scanned the horizon briefly, not seeing him. Her dark hair was pulled back into a bun, eyes obscured with dark glasses. He knew right away who she was.

He held still and watched. She wasn't so much a girlie-girl as some kind of princess. But too intelligent seeming for a princess, and self-possessed. More like a brainy princess. Shit, he thought. Shit.

The yelling echoed out of the slats. "Fuck, you followed me!" came Lily's voice. "I'm almost eighteen and you can't stop me,"

Jerry put his hands over his ears, but could still hear.

"Your father wants the police involved. Is that what you want, Lily? And you really think I'll leave you here. In this of all places?"

"Just go!"

"Who were you with? I saw you at the drugstore, Lily. You and that degenerate!"

Jerry decided he had to do something. He tapped out his cigar and walked over to the shed, pulling the door back slowly. He could have done without the drama, but standing there in the doorway like that, it was hard to avoid.

The woman turned. He was close enough that he could see the lighter gold streaks in her brown hair and detect a floral odor in the small room that hadn't been there before.

"And just who are you?" She advanced a step toward him, raising her cell phone and holding the illuminated panel to his face. "My daughter is a minor, and I absolutely will not hesitate to call the police."

"I'm looking for my son. I gave her a ride. That's all. Some water."

The woman seemed dazed. She stepped back, her face crumpling into lines. "This is not happening."

"Look, I'm sorry. My boy's a runaway too. I heard he was out here. Same thing." Out the little window the dust devils lifted white columns of chalky earth behind her. "I'll leave you two to talk."

Jerry waited outside.

Lily was crying. "Just go back to your stupid college and try to tell all those stupid college kids what to do. I'm going. You can't stop me."

"You stupid girl. Of course, I can stop you."

Jerry didn't want to hear anymore. He went back across the street and waited for it to end.

When she came out of the door, the woman bumped her leg on the rusty bicycle and wrenched it aside with a disgusted shove. The bike left a dirty mark on her pressed trousers. Lily trailed behind her, holding what looked to be a piece of blanket in her arms. Jerry walked back over.

He thought about trying to apologize again, about trying to explain, but it was useless. Her words were clipped and professional as she ran her hand over her now disordered hair. "I'm not leaving her." She glanced at her daughter. "And Lily refuses to come with me."

Lily stomped her foot in the dust.

"You can't make me. I'll just leave again. I'll jump out of the car. And this time you'll never find me."

The woman looked down. She was composed. "Lily understands that if she won't come with me, I have to stay with her." She laughed bitterly and glanced again at Lily. "She won't ride with me, and I'm not letting her out of my sight. You know what that means."

Jerry shook his head. "Excuse me?"

"You need to drive her. I'll follow. And when we get to the car rental place in Palm Springs I'll ride with you too."

"I just want to find my son." Lord, he thought, no more crazy women, please.

"It's either this or I call the police."

Jerry wasn't sure if she spoke to Lily or to him. But the woman glared at Lily, who stared solemnly at her shoes, her face smeared with tears.

"I mean it Lily."

"Whatever," Lily muttered, "whatever."

The woman turned toward Jerry. "You're going to have to help me with this." Her fingers fidgeted with her scarf and again he caught the faint scent of rose.

He couldn't believe this.

The woman looked past him, as though there might be something moving in the old paint cans at the back of the shed.

"I didn't agree to drive anyone anywhere. Or to help

anyone."

"But you want to find Ethan," Lily said. Her voice was soft, the way it was back at the diner. "This is the way."

The woman raised her chin slightly. "If she won't ride with me, you'll just have to drive her. It seems you were going to anyway. Just follow me back to Palm Springs. If I can trust you not to run off with my daughter."

"Look lady, I'm not a professional driver. This is crazy."

"So what do you suggest? That I leave her alone in the dirt?"

Lily had stopped crying. "We have to get going now," she said.

Get going now, thought Jerry. We? What was happening here? He could hear Mahatma's nasal intonations in his head about the capriciousness of Shiva, about the unforeseen detours along the Dharma highway. But then he didn't come this far just to get back in the Jeep and go home.

"I don't even know who you people are," he said, hearing the ineffectuality in his own voice.

In the silence, he glanced at Lily. She wiped her nose and sniffed in a way that suggested something heartlessly manipulative, but admirable. "They're waiting at this place near Borrego Springs. Almost everyone will be there." She looked at him. "Maybe your son too," she said. "Probably."

"That's it then," said the woman.

"Wait," said Jerry. "I didn't even say I'd go."

"What choice do you have?" asked Lily. Jerry wanted to believe he could hear something sincere in the girl's voice, but it didn't seem likely.

"Believe me," said the woman. "It's not my favorite idea either. But if you're really looking for your son — "

Mahatma had warned him, but they were right: what choice did he have? He had no other leads. Somewhere Ethan was out there and this messed up child and her brittle, angry mother just might lead the way.

"What's your name?" Jerry asked the woman. "I mean, if we're going to be driving together."

She'd already stepped into the light of the open doorway and stopped and turned. Her sunglasses sat on top of her head. The desert sun made her eyes go hazel and liquid brown, the same color of the sea glass he sometimes found on the beach by the wharf. He noticed for the first time that she was beautiful. It had been a long time since he recognized such a detail in a woman, preferring to concentrate on the more basic things in life, like holding a fork and staying out of liquor stores, walking straight.

"Talia," she answered reluctantly.

He started to reply with his own name but she interrupted.

"Lily told me about you," she said. "It's Jerry. And you're apparently some sort of revived rock person. I get it. Now can we leave this terrible place?"

3

THE STARBUCKS'S patio cooled under the shade cast by a long line of red mountains. The peaks rose spectacularly in the near distance, etched with dark fissures and ravines, and made everything else in town look small.

Sitting across from him at the table, Lily didn't seem interested in the view, or in conversation. She had contorted her torso, managing somehow to get both high-tops on to her wire chair and spent most of the time redialing a number on her cell phone while staring with exasperation at the passing cars. Jerry didn't know what he'd say to her anyway. He was just as happy to pass time pretending to stare at the mountains and watch the other people, and thankfully, he found a pair a few tables over that seemed to provide suitable distraction.

The older man wore white pants and a matching white sweater, and his tan arm fell elegantly from the loose cashmere sleeve. His platinum Rolex gleamed as he stirred his espresso. When he finished, he set the little spoon on the edge of the plate and gazed thoughtfully at his companion.

The young man adjusted his sunglasses and fingered his own coffee disdainfully. "The thing is, we have different interests."

The older man nodded. "But this is quite healthy."

Jerry detected a slight accent and considered whether the younger man was a son or lover.

"Not when we want different things."

"You don't know what you want," said the older one.

"Not opera and aged Scotch."

"No, you prefer a more medicinal aesthetic."

The younger man was irritated. "I knew this was a mistake." He stood up. "We're wasting time here. I'll call you." He walked away, not looking back.

The man in white looked after him for a few minutes, and then swallowed the rest of his own coffee. He made an entry in some kind of notebook. When he stood a Labrador with a shiny black coat emerged from under the table. He patted the dog and leashed him, before leaving the coffee shop. At least he's got the dog, thought Jerry, as the man went down the sidewalk.

It was the mountains looming above the busy Palm Springs street that had made him dizzy, Jerry decided. They looked almost three dimensional, cascading out of the sky, a trace of early spring snow glimmering on the highest peak up there, where oxygen no doubt would be thin. Meanwhile beneath them Lily kept glancing nervously across the busy street, where her mother was checking out of the terra-cotta colored hotel.

Lily rose suddenly off her hip and pulled out a pack of cigarettes. The patio had suddenly become crowded and the smoke from her cigarette drifted into the perfect blue sky and lingered above the tables.

She took a quick drag. "In your day people fucked in Parks. That's honest at least."

"What the hell are you talking about?"

"Like Ethan. I mean you've got to run away just to have a chance."

Jerry drank some iced tea and looked across the street. "How long can it take to get a room?" he asked.

"You're catching on," she said, raising her cigarette.

"Don't say anything, okay. Her freak-out list is long enough already."

"I make it a point to mind my own business."

Jerry continued to watch the front of the hotel. Lily scraped her cigarette out on the tabletop and tossed it underneath, before she dug in her pockets and pulled out a pair of mirrored Aviator sunglasses. When she put them on Jerry could see a cascading sprinkler reflected behind him, making it seem as if someone had turned a hose on his head.

Lily's expression creased as if she were listening to something only she could hear. "Don't believe her. It's not just because of Max she's here," she said. "She just can't deal with things not going according to her big plan."

"What plan's that?"

"School, a respectable boy, some kind of profession where you get paid to say smart things but don't really do anything. Like her."

Lily yanked the straw out and started chewing on it. She stirred her drink and looked at him squarely enough that he could see his own reflection in her glasses now that the sprinkler had stopped.

"Max gets impatient when he's got a show. Sometimes he goes on ahead."

"So he's a musician?"

Lily sighed in renewed irritation. "No, not a musician. Not like you're thinking. He's an artist. Performance things, you know."

Jerry shook his head, not really hearing.

"Pictures. Sounds and stuff on the radio." She looked at him almost pityingly. "You don't know anything."

Jerry shrugged.

"Anyway," Lily added, "We might have to keep going. If Max isn't there."

Jerry watched the fancy cars roll past, the sunlight strobing off the chromed and waxed exteriors. How much further was he going to have to travel with this screwed-up girl? "So how'd you and Max get together?"

"Get together? Like going to the prom or something?" There was something close to a sneer on her pretty face.

"I'm just asking how you met."

She sighed again, clearly amazed at what a drag he was turning out to be. "A Greenpeace rally a few years ago down near the border. Do you know about the shit the *micadoras* spill into the water? Max did this brilliant film."

"And now you're out in the desert trying to find him. Where are you from anyway?"

"I live on the road." She puffed on her cigarette. "I live in the now."

Jerry didn't let himself laugh. "I have a friend who says the same thing. But what about the then?"

"I lived with my mom in Santa Barbara."

She exhaled smoke and dropped the cigarette under the table, glancing once again past the cars and tourists to the hotel.

"You're not going to try and save me or anything?"

Just then Talia appeared alongside the cascading fountain, a pair of suited bellhops setting out a row of fancy bags by her feet. She raised her hand. Lily glanced up. "Shit. Here she comes." She ground out the cigarette butt with her foot.

LILY DOZED in the back while they moved toward the desert of Anza Borrego, the Jeep grinding a little on the steep hills. Talia rode up front with him, her unwavering gaze trained on the mesquite and chaparrals.

"Do we have to have the windows down?" Talia said, narrowing her eyes against the wind. "I can't stand the feel of dry air rushing by my face."

"Sorry, the air-conditioner's busted."

She huffed, crossing her arms. "Of course it is."

Jerry felt his face get hot. "Look, this sure wasn't my idea."

She unfastened her lap belt and reached back over the top of the bench seat to check on Lily. When she re-buckled, she returned to the same rigid position.

"I don't suppose she told you about Max wanting to cart her across the border to Canada and leave civilization?"

"They all make plans. You can't take them too seriously."

"I suppose your son made plans before he left."

The sun beat down on Jerry's neck. "I wasn't against him finding out who he is, if that's what you mean."

"Well forgive me if I'm not quite as philosophical."

Her tone irked Jerry. Their whole stupid arrangement was her fault. "Listen, I didn't ask for this."

"You think I did? Chasing after a daughter bent on becoming a — " Talia searched for a word. "a bum. Or a vagabond at least." She sat back in her seat. "Self destructive."

"Just because you never did anything like it."

"What? Lived in a teepee and ran naked in the woods? I never jumped into a car and drove around with idiots? Besides, you haven't an idea as to what I was like when I was her age."

She jerked down the sun-visor, her eyes darkening with disgust before resuming her watch on the desert.

Jerry considered telling Talia he knew all about her and girls just like her. Her type always set out their hand-tailored clothes on all the nights before, scrawled perfect notes in a leather day planner, no doubt with perfect hand writing mastered on three-lined paper in Catholic school. And she always did exactly as she said she would do, never hurt anyone or animals unintentionally, had her lectures neatly outlined on her laptop, praised her daughter when she dressed up as the tree in the school play, and avoided guys like him. He knew all about her type.

He knew other things too, like what it felt like to stare at the ceiling at night, an ache under your ribs, the way the mornings never really brought a new day.

But he didn't say anything.

Instead he could hear Mahatma telling him that the first rule of being a reformed fuck-up was to mind your own business, so he kept quiet and steered the Jeep down the desolate little road. Besides, he had his own problems.

The sun had crept behind the outline of hills, a violet light moving across barren reaches, and then it grew dark. The days hadn't grown very long yet.

"Doesn't look like much could live out there," he said finally, trying for small talk.

"Lily says you had a terrible accident."

"Is that all she told you?"

Her eyes moved away from him. "She said you can't always remember things, that you used to be a psychologist, and that you gave her some water."
Jerry's back ached. He tried to change his position, but the pain stayed low, riding above his hips. He was bored with this.
"Look, I'm just going to say it, Talia. I was a drunk and a pill head. I lost everything that meant anything to me. The Caddy in the water was the least of it. Like you said, we don't have to be buddies."
"I guess not."

THE LIGHTS of Anza Borrego came into view, a constellation of dim porch lights spread thin across the desert. Further ahead on the straight road a luminous haze rose up from the center of town. Jerry's temples ached, partly because Ethan might be there, partly because he might not — either way, the desert road reaching past the headlights had no turns.
"Better wake her," he said.
Talia turned back and nudged Lily. She rose sleepily in the rear-view, her face flushed in the oncoming lights. "On the other side of town," she said, pointing between them. "Past this. Further. You have to go further."
As Jerry drove, he thought about the famous magic bus, the one with "Furthur" written on the destination placard, the one he'd actually been on, if only briefly, when he was younger and braver, less weary about the other side of things. All kinds of people had ridden on that bus. Everyday people. Some who were artists, musicians, writers. Now, driving through town — a low strip of ugly stucco buildings, closed for the night — he watched the

mercurial outlines of the Jeep shutter in the storefront panes of window glass, finally buffeting and gliding off into the indigo sweep of night and stars like a phantom, and didn't feel so brave.

Back among the yuccas, a road sign came up. Lily bumped his shoulder, and he turned onto a hardpan dirt road littered with broken window glass that crumbled loudly under the tires. "Just go until there's no more to go." Lily said, flopping back.

Talia buttoned her jacket and looped a scarf around her neck. "Is it safe?"

"What do you imagine, mother? We're the new Mansons?"

"Why do you always have to deride me, Lily?"

"Because you're fucking scared of everything."

Jerry hands tensed on the wheel. Ethan might be out there in the dark. "Let's just do this."

They passed over the rise and the black incline of the road ahead gave way to more flat scrub, and then turning, then came upon a flickering electric light in the distance, the shadowy outlines of a ranch house visible behind. Closer, Jerry could make out a general commotion of bodies, pieces of music floating above the darkness between the ghostly outlines of the yuccas.

"Take a look," said Jerry, slowing.

Lily lunged forward across the seat, pulling her hair back, intently focused on the solitary house. "Jeez, they're here," she said. "He's showing one of his movies." She smiled and unhooked her seat belt. She was half standing up and bouncing a little on her seat.

Talia sighed. "One of his famous performance pieces, you mean."

"At least he's not a fake."

The Jeep reached the first of the cars parked along the road and Jerry braked to a stop. "You guys need to wait here," Lily said, looking first at him and then at her mother.

Talia stared at her. "We made an agreement, Lily. I'm trusting you."

"Hold on," Jerry said. He dug his wallet from his hip pocket and pulled the picture of Ethan out, handing it to her.

She got out and took a few steps, then spoke to him through his open window. "Don't get your hopes up," she said. "But hey, you never know, right?"

They watched her stride past two or three parked cars, then jog across the street, entering the party between more cars parked at odd angles in the wide driveway alongside the gathering.

"She's a good kid, you know that don't you?" Jerry said.

"Of course I know that. And I think I know my own daughter better than you."

"At the shelter I see all kinds. I'm just saying."

"Yes, well I'm sure you're an expert."

Lily stood at the edge of the flickering light, her dark outline as crisp as the trees. They watched while a silhouetted figure rose slowly and waded through the column of radiance, as if crossing a river.

When Max embraced her and the two shapes became one, Talia looked away.

"You can say whatever you want. He's a maniac." Then in a low voice, almost to herself, "I'm not going to let him take her."

Lily tugged at Max's arm, pulling him by the hand from the others onto the porch, where they stood in the yellow haze of the porch light. She spoke with her head down, waving bugs from her face with her hand.

Jerry kept his eyes fixed on them under the bright light. Max had a rangy build, six inches taller than Lily, with black choppy hair that fell over his ears like crow feathers. He wore tight black jeans and an open paisley shirt that hung untucked around his narrow hips, and a metal chain of some sort dangled from his neck.

"So you're the expert," Talia said again. She forced herself to laugh a little. "What do you think he looks like?"

Jerry shrugged. "He looks like all of them. Skin and bones and attitude — it works until it doesn't."

"And Ethan. Is he like that?"

"No."

"What then?"

"He's smart and a little shy, everything inward."

"Like Lily."

Two girls in matching white dresses wandered away from the larger group under the projector, their pale faces and wispy blonde hair remarkably similar. The dresses looked to be made from bedspreads, like the hippie dresses girls used to make back on the Haight. They stopped and hugged Lily, then disappeared through the screen door into the house.

"So you've met Max?"

Talia lowered her face. "Lily brought him to the house after a demonstration," she said. "When Lily told him I was an art professor, he laughed. Said I was a sellout to the man. I should have seen this coming."

"You think she really wants to run off to Canada with him?"

"She certainly seems to want to run off somewhere."

Now Lily was facing them, standing next to Max, waving her arm for them to come over. Jerry put his hand on the door-handle, but stopped.

"Are you up to this?"

Talia ignored him, pushing her door open and walking off.

When they got to concrete driveway, Lily stepped forward from the porch and pulled away from Max. He stood there stiffly, rubbing his tattooed arm as if it itched. Up close his deep eyes glistened with intensity, foreboding and dark, staring out past them as if they weren't there. Beside them, where all the other kids huddled in the darkness, the music blared out of box speakers set out on the dirt, a mix of spoken words and electronic droning that had something to do with the pictures flashing on the adobe wall through the haze of pot smoke.

Lily held the picture of Ethan. "Jerry, this is Max."

"Hello, Max."

Max nodded, rubbing his chin with his thin hand, a skull ring like Lily's around one of his fingers. He focused his black eyes on Jerry and nodded, then looked at Talia. "Talia. Been a while."

"Not long enough."

"No shit," he replied, laughing to himself. "Anyway."

"He's not here." Lily pressed the photograph into Jerry's hand. "I'm really sorry, you know."

"That's it?"

Lily smiled a little. "I told you — no guarantees."

Jerry thrust the picture towards Max. "He's older, the hair's different maybe. Look again."

Max glanced towards the party-goers stirring in the dark. What made his eyes look so black were the pupils, dilated and enormous. "What do you want from me, dude?"

"Are you wasted, Max? Meth maybe?"

He tucked his black hair behind his ear. "What the fuck kind of question's that? You're just some old man drove in out of the desert. Are you even real? I don't have to talk to you."

"Listen, Max, he sent me a card last year around this time. Just take a look, will you?"

"Anybody ever say you look like somebody?"

"I really need your help."

"Like you think I keep track of everybody who comes and goes?" He swept his arm at the kids under the streaming projector rays. "Could be sitting right out there for all I know." Max laughed a little.

"My God, how do you live with yourself?" Talia said suddenly. "He's looking for his son."

"And like that's my problem?"

Lily took a step towards Max, her face white under the lights. "Jenny and Amber might know something," she said. "They hung out last year, didn't they? Maybe they'd know something if we asked."

"Suit yourself. It's a free country."

Lily pulled back the screen door, with Max following. Jerry went in behind Talia, guiding her by the shoulder into the open room. It looked pretty much like Jerry expected, a rundown house set among the scrub and cactus out here on the sun-baked edge of nowhere — a place for hole-ups and runaways far from the law. The drapes, walls and shabby carpet all ran together, everything a kind of indeterminate brown, bleached many shades lighter from the sun.

Talia looked around. "Your uncle know what goes on out here, Max?"

He reached up and spun the drooping blade of an overhead fan as he went into the room, his tattoos high on his forearms. "He's cool with it."

The two girls had their backs to them. They sat on a couch watching wrestling on an old console television, stiff in their white dresses. Lily went around the couch and stood in front of a coffee table, its worn top covered with scraps of weed.

"This is Amber and Jenny," Lily said. She glanced up. "This is my mom and Jerry. He's looking for a boy named Ethan."

Lily took the picture from Jerry and gave it to one of them. "You see him around last year, Jenny? Maybe when you guys went up north to Oregon and Seattle for the festival?"

Jenny glanced at Max and lowered her eyes to the photograph. "No."

Handing it to Amber, she watched her sister reluctantly glance at the old picture of Ethan. "Nope," she said softly, looking back at the wrestlers on the big television.

Max spun the fan again. "Jenny was kind of out of it then," he said. "She's a good girl now, though."

"How do you find out about the concerts?"

Lily looked disgusted. "Internet, radio, texting — what do you think?"

Max reached up and slapped the fan blades. Behind him on the wall hung a rattlesnake skin, the rattle the color of toenail clippings. "Read your Tzu, dude. The tools of oppression become a weapon for freedom."

Jerry had as much as he could take. When he went out the screen door, it rattled loudly behind him. He bumped past two kids smoking cigarettes in drooping sweatshirts while they leaned on the porch railings and watched the crowd of kids.

At the edge of the gathering, what looked like twenty or thirty kids Lily's age, a dark swarm of barely visible faces, Jerry side-stepped along the adobe wall and stood frozen, the jumping light hitting him in the eyes. He waved his arms into the pieces of brilliance, blinking out at the faces underneath, while he tried to catch his breath.

"Hippie!" one of them yelled.

Jerry climbed on a chair, holding the picture of Ethan up high. Lily came up behind him.

"I'm looking for this boy," he said to the blanket of faces. "His name's Ethan and he's my son. I need your help."

As he stood holding the picture, Jerry waited for the huddled shadows to shift, but nobody moved. From somewhere among the vacant faces, the flashing beer cans and glowing cigarettes, a girl's voice said, "Is this part of the fucking show, Lily?"

To reach the driveway Jerry found he needed to put his arm on Lily's shoulder. He felt weak. When he got there, he doubled over, bracing himself with his hands on his knees. Behind him the movie started up again, the vagrant blades of light moving around his feet.

What had he expected? That Ethan would really be here, that he could put him in the Jeep and take him home, tell him how sorry he was for everything and it would be all right, the way it was before?

"You okay?" Lily said, bending so he could hear.

"Go talk to your mother," he told her. Just breathe, he told himself, pulling the cool air between his teeth.

Lily left him and walked over and stood next to Talia. He watched the shadows move around his shoes, the cracks in the concrete dancing like snakes. When Jerry finally stood tall, Max was yelling, bounding off the end of the porch into the darkness behind the garage. Then Lily ran after him, her black clothes blending into the night.

Talia walked over to Jerry and crossed her arms, staring out at the haze of stars past the Jeep. She spoke almost

wistfully, still gazing at the night. "I made another deal,"
she replied.

"Christ. What now?"

Talia unfolded her arms and looked directly at him,
then away, as if she couldn't believe what she was saying.
"They'll continue on their little adventure, and we'll follow.
You can look for Ethan, while I look after Lily. Crazy, isn't
it?"

"And Lily signed up for that?"

"I told them if they didn't I would call Lily's father, then
the police. Max is practical. He knows he'll never get to
Canada if he's in jail for harming a minor."

"What about Lily?"

She shook her head and her laugh wasn't pleasant. "She
likes you. Or she thinks you're a distraction. Besides, I
think she's amused. I had to promise not to meddle, which
means let them do whatever they do." Talia paused and
lowered her voice a little. "And I imagine they plan to ask
for money. That's why Max agreed, I think."

"And you're all right with that?"

"I don't have much choice when you think about it. If I
don't, I lose her for sure."

"Why don't you just call the police?"

Talia looked at the ground. "I did that before."

So she too was grabbing at slim chances. He knew how
that worked.

"And there's something more," Talia said. "I think she
feels sorry for you."

"You just assume I'll go along with your plan? Because
it's convenient for you? I don't think so, Talia. Go patronize
someone else."

"Ethan," she finally said, as if she needed to remind
him. He stayed quiet. "The girls think he might be

following the music festivals. If he was at the Salton Sea last year. That's where those kids went." They stood there for a while and then Talia spoke again. "You need to do this, Jerry. And not just for me."

Jerry kicked the dirt. "What the hell are we going to do for travel arrangements?"

"There's a resort nearby. After that we'll just have to see."

"And you think you can drive around with me?"

"I'm actually trying not to think about it."

They wandered back to the car, the raucous music behind drifting over their heads onto the desert. Talia walked slightly ahead, her narrow shoulders sagging. He considered Lily's condemnation of her as a cold academic, more interested in her students than her own daughter. Maybe it was true, maybe not. But what difference did it make? He remembering all the old talk about the doors of perception and how everybody was locked into their own trip. God only knew what Ethan thought of him, what drove him onto the road to escape.

At least Talia was here, willing to ride in a car with his sorry ass. She'd left work behind, trying to take her daughter home, just like he was trying to do with Ethan. For whatever reason, they were companions on Mahatma's dharma highway, a temporary alliance in a temporary world. He had to give her that.

At the Jeep though, she stood stiffly, and something about the way she icily pondered the desert with her arms crossed, set his stomach on edge. As he put the key in the door he concluded that Lily was probably right.

"I need a cigar," he said when they got to the Jeep.

"Not while I'm in the car you won't."

"I'll walk a ways. It's a clear night."

"And leave me here?"

Away from the lights of the house, the moonlight seeped over the valley, the wide spread of sand and rock and shadowed foliage like a quiet ocean. They stood on a patch of worn gravel, near a Joshua tree.

Talia gazed thoughtfully at the glittering stars. It had been a while since he'd stood sober beside a woman, looking at the night. She was sad. He could see that, in spite of his own ineptitude.

"You sure about this?" he asked again. He certainly wasn't.

"We need each other to do this," she replied. "Even if I'm not the type to travel around on a hippie bus. You need to find him and I need to stay with her."

Jerry tried to blow his smoke haze into the blackness away from her. The way she said hippie bus made him smile. She said it like everyone else who thought they knew what it was all about.

"I thought about that bus today."

"The actual one, with all the colors that those fools drove around," she said. "I know about that bus. I read a book about it. A hippie bus that roamed the country full of drugs and crazy people"

"I was eleven, almost twelve. I heard about it in the neighborhood, this far out bunch that wanted to get high and drive off and start something new. Rode my ten-speed twenty miles to take a look."

She didn't try to hide her sarcasm. "A pilgrimage."

"I get there and hide in the pines, stare out though the brambles and ivy trying to get a look. No one was around, the bus just sitting by this old wood house. I can still remember the way the light came down on the colors past the pines — crazy colors."

"Then what? A magical vision I suppose."

"Sort of. A girl, maybe twenty with white hair, pretty as anything, comes out of nowhere from behind me. My heart skipped. But she just took me by the hand and walked me over to the bus."

"I don't think I want to hear anymore."

"Nothing like that. She just sat with me and rolled a joint. We just got high, sitting in the bus, watching the birds play in the trees, the light."

"I guess you really were on the bus," she said.

"Last time I saw the damn thing it was in a ditch in Oregon, a couple years ago. I took Ethan up to see it. I remember that at least."

She shrugged her shoulders and started back for the Jeep. "Let's hope we have better luck. I assure you I don't want to end up in a ditch somewhere."

NEAR DAWN, sunlight streamed into the small room, the bright rays rising behind the low lines of sand just out the window. Mahatma answered on the third ring. "Where the hell are you, bro?"

Jerry blinked into the glare, his eyes eventually adjusting enough to find a patch of blooming, blue desert plants. Something can always grow in the desert, thought Jerry. He waited for the idea of the flowers to bloom in the hollow space between his heart and bones, but his chest remained an arid vacancy.

"I'm looking out a window at the sky — it just goes and goes."

"Bro, I hear darkness. You going to tell me what's going on or make me guess?"

"Did you know they tested the bomb in the Salton Sea? Maybe it's a good thing Ethan didn't turn up there."

There was a hesitation and Jerry could almost hear the wheels of Mahatma's mind rotating.

"So you're turning the Jeep around," Mahatma said.

"That's good news."

"There's another place a ways up the road. I've come this far."

"Hell, there's always another place."

"I'm a disappointment, I know."

"That voice. You better listen to old Mahatma, bro. Get your ass to a meeting."

Jerry heard some kind of commotion in the background, probably one of Mahatma's charity cases. Jerry never asked Mahatma for a hand, but damn if he didn't have a hold of it now.

Mahatma said, "Just what do you see happening here? You find the kid and he says all is forgiven, you win the prize as a father?"

Jerry watched the tops of the telephone poles stretching out to the highway gathering sunlight. "I'd forgotten what it felt like to set out on the road," he said. "You can damn near see the curve of the earth if you look hard enough."

"Shit, you aren't breathing from the ribs, bro. I can hear it. The tools man, the tools. You've got to remember."

In his warehouse Mahatma often made his workers — all shelter refugees — lie down on the floor and visualize heaven. He'd hover over them, stroke his beard, and ask them what they saw. For Mahatma, heaven meant a particular teenage prostitute in Saigon. Someone else would talk about the corn when they were a kid in the Midwest. Jerry always drew a blank, disappointing Mahatma to no end.

"Don't walk around all day worrying about me. You got bums to feed."

Hanging up, he figured it was just as well he didn't fill Mahatma in on Talia, Lily and the whole traveling menagerie he'd hooked up with. Some things are better left un-visualized, he thought, staring at the blue flowers.

HE REACHED the first telephone pole just as the sun touched its base. The sun illuminated each pole and gave them the appearance of a picket fence winding all the way to the distant highway, where the windshields of cars sparked past. The morning air felt more crisp than it looked from inside his room, and he bundled his coat as he walked.

He'd arranged to meet Talia in the hotel restaurant later for breakfast and he knew better than to sit around thinking. Walking under the black wires, he again pondered the creosoted poles running over the red rock and sun-baked scarp and told himself, as he had done often during recovery, "Just do something, anything." He'd scoured each and every pot in the sink, or folded an endless bin of towels. Just making the bed and scrubbing the toilet bowl could, however briefly, clear the head. He reminded himself to set tasks and do them, just like those monks in Tibet that Mahatma always talked about, the ones who courted enlightenment while sweeping sand or toiling in their gardens. It all helped, right?

At the tenth pole, about halfway to the roadway, he looked up at the sagging wires and felt whatever gripped him begin to slip away, as if seeping out his pores into the wide-open space of desert. Hope maybe, he thought.

But the last pole he came to was festooned with faded crepe paper, silver ribbon, and a deflated metallic balloon that had been tied around the trunk, all of it bobbing in the wash of dusty wind from the passing traffic. A wreathe of dead flowers and more ribbon leaned against the stanchion. Nearby, in the scrub, two white crosses poked out of the brush, surrounded by broken glass and pools of melted candle wax left after the fact. Stupid kids probably, or a stupid man. Sometimes all you could do was try.

He was about to start back, when he noticed someone ambling over the road's gravel shoulder in his direction, a man with his thumb lifted for a ride.

The man wore faded fatigues, with a face the ruddy color of the rock, but too far away for Jerry to see much else. Jerry wondered what the hell the guy had in mind, wandering out here at this hour, but then realized he was one of those wandering guys too.

A semi slowed, brakes squealing as it pulled over, and the man climbed in.

Jerry started back when the truck's horn sounded. He turned just in time to see the face of Captain Trips, sun burnt and creased behind the little passenger-window of the truck. He held his eyes on Jerry, flashing a peace sign as the truck moved down the road.

"I COULDN'T sleep last night," Talia said, as she carefully poured hot water over the tea bag in her cup, the rising steam tinged with cinnamon. "I kept imagining Lily and grizzly bears. They have them in Canada, you know."

The light through the window glistened on the side of her face and hair as she watched the sun turn the valley a shade of amber. "Just hot water," she'd told the waiter. "I always carry my own tea."

Watching her, Jerry thought he too might prefer the frigid Rockies and big bears to Talia. But if he was going to do this he had to get along.

"Does your husband teach too?" Jerry imagined a male version of Talia, all imported tweeds and clean-shaven. "Lily said something about his building pyramids."

Her laugh wasn't exactly pleasant. "He builds theme parks. And he's my ex-husband." She took a sip of tea. "He's the impresario of roadside attractions, according to one newspaper."

Jerry couldn't picture it. "You big on amusement parks?"

"Don't be ridiculous. And he wasn't always a buffoon. We met in a drawing class at Princeton. He was studying architecture."

Jerry picked up the box of tea. They looked like regular tea bags. "So what's so special about this stuff?"

"It's real tea. Imported. And the bags are actually very thin silk."

"Right," said Jerry. He tried again. "Your husband. Ex-husband. Does he get along with Lily?"

"She's lived with me since the divorce. But really, it was before that they became distant. About the time he decided to become a super capitalist and build his stupid parks. The Pharaoh's Tomb — surely you've seen one along the freeway."

"Jesus."

"Exactly."

The waiter came and took their order, more coffee for Jerry and poached eggs for her.

"Lily says you wanted to paint," Jerry said, deciding to try and make conversation.

The teacup clicked hard against the gold-rimmed saucer. "She told you that?"

"So what's the big deal?"

"I don't know that it really concerns you."

"I'm just trying to be friendly."

The waiter served Talia's eggs in small silver cups. She put her fork in one and bit her lip, beckoning to the waiter back from the other side of the room.

She smiled patiently at the poor man. "I don't mean to be difficult, but these are a bit overcooked. And they're sticking to the cups. Vinegar in the water helps."

The waiter whisked her plate away.

"What's wrong now?" She looked at Jerry. "You're staring at me."

The eggs looked just fine to him, but Jerry didn't say a word. He disliked people who sent their food back in restaurants. But it figured, he thought. Another karmic strikeout. He was stuck out in the desert with a finicky prude with a food fetish.

"Hard to poach eggs just right over a campfire."

"I don't think I'm the one to worry about. I'll get along fine." Talia raised her eyebrows in amusement.

The waiter returned and with something just short of a bow, placed the eggs in front of her. Jerry could tell she still wasn't satisfied, but he concentrated on being thankful that she'd evidently let the waiter off the hook.

She took a single bite and then turned to Jerry. "The yolks are still hard. Anyway, you know, I actually do understand romantic kids full of Jack London and Thoreau and the idea of the wilderness. But you don't know Max. Trust, me, he's not exactly the romantic type."

Jerry drank coffee, trying to see the depression in the dirt where the road left the valley. The blue flowers were nowhere in sight.

"We might need tents," he said. "And flashlights for seeing bears."

She held her cup still, staring over it at him. "Tents?"

"I doubt they have an LL Bean or Abercrombie and Fitch out here."

"Abercrombie is for adolescents." She set her fork on

her plate and touched the corner of her mouth with the linen napkin. She'd eaten about three bites. No wonder she was so thin. "One other thing — I don't have to worry about you, do I?"

"What do you mean?"

"Going crazy, getting drunk. You said you quit, but I have a girlfriend who quits Vicoden and Merlot every other week. Before I left, she ran her Volvo into a sycamore tree and the paramedics hauled her away." She reached back and put on the sweater that hung on the back of her chair. "Fine. We'll buy tents."

AT THE local hardware store, Jerry leaned over a shopping cart, following Talia down an isle stacked with brightly bundled sleeping bags. She had the air of a picky curator considering a new and largely unsatisfactory shipment.

"You ever been camping?" Jerry asked. "Form follows function, sort of."

She glanced at him dismissively. "In seventh grade Marci Wilkes and I spent the night in her backyard, which happened to be along the tenth hole of the country club. At midnight the sprinklers came on and sent us running into the living room, soaking wet. I've stayed indoors ever since."

"Can't say I've never woken up in a yard or two."

"I'm sure you have," she said, and abruptly began trying to tug one of the bags out of a pile. "All those millions of years to climb out of the primordial ooze. Why go back?"

Jerry yanked out a blue bag and threw it into the cart. They wandered over to the floor display of tents. He wondered if she meant he was primordial or if she just regarded camping in general as culturally backward.

A moment later she was peering through the yellow, webbed door of a domed tent. Her hair was pulled back and for a second she looked like a model for some yuppie camping supply catalogue, beautiful but hopelessly out of place.

"Not everyone's spent their life roaming the countryside," she said. "I imagine you went off to the woods every weekend with your father, eating nuts, chewing leaves, or whatever it is campers do."

"Only once."

"Really? You seem the rugged type to me. One of those Iron Johns who strip naked, beat drums and bay at the moon."

Jerry rested his weight on his forearms, rocking the cart back and forth. "You don't want to hear the story."

She shrugged. "I'm listening."

She might have been just being polite, but then there wasn't much else to occupy her right then. "On Sundays my old man and I used to watch that wilderness show on T.V., Mutual of Omaha, where that old guy'd wrestle crocodiles and fish for sharks. That guy loved bears, too, now that I think about it."

"Wonderful."

"It was our time together, you know. He'd sit there and tell me about fishing trips we were going take, camping in the bush. But after a while, I came to understand all my old man wanted out of the weekend was dry martinis and his recliner."

"Like father, like son."

"On Saturday my mother always went to the beauty shop. One day when she was gone he asked me if I wanted to go. Hell, I was twelve, thirteen, excited as hell. He had the car all loaded up, ready to go into the unknown."

"Sounds like a Disney film."

"We start driving, but he doesn't really tell me where we're going, we just drive. After a while I can tell something's wrong. He looks awful, pale, tired. And we're not really going towards anything. He's just driving around."

Talia started wheeling the cart forward. Plainly, she thought his story was taking too long.

"Pretty soon he just pulls the Chrysler over on the shoulder and I can see his eyes are wet — he's got his head in his hands, crying. I'd never seen him cry before."

"This is your idea of a story?"

"Said he wanted to leave my mother, but just couldn't. Made me swear I wouldn't tell. I never did."

The cart rolled forward again. "My God. Thanks for the cheery tale."

"You asked."

IN HIS room Jerry sat on the edge of the bed examining the hotel stationary and tried to compose a message for Ethan. Talia could post it on Max's Rainbow site. He thought about trying to explain to Ethan the accident and memory loss, the morning wake-ups on tilted sidewalks, the days spent working at the shelter, but staring out the window at the blue panorama of sky above the barren curve of rock, he found that actual words proved as scarce as the clouds out there in all that pale blue sky.

He decided to keep the note simple, asking Ethan to meet them at Lake Havasu, where they would arrive in a day or two for the concert. He told Ethan to look for Max's old VW bus and the skull and crossbones flag, then scribbled the words "Love, Dad."

When he knocked on her door Talia took her time before she answered. She stood in the doorway, wearing fresh clothes, staring at him as if she didn't really want to let him in.

"You want me to come back later?"

She took the note. "This is barely legible."

Passing close to her, he smelled rose oil on her skin. The room was as immaculate as she was. Her bags lay neatly on the bed, and her laptop was opened on the wooden writing desk by the window.

While she worked at the computer, a small pair of tortoise-framed reading glasses tipped on her nose, he stood by the window and watched for Max and his VW van to pull into the parking lot.

"You don't seem quite as enthusiastic as yesterday," he said to her.

She punched her keyboard. "I told you, don't worry about me."

"At least you know where Lily is."

"Right." She kept typing. "I'll add their itinerary. In case he can't make it until the next concert."

"How do you take time off from work?" He'd been wondering about that.

"Academic leave," she said as she typed Jerry's message, her clean oval fingernails clicking a little on the silver keys. Her face softened a little at the last word.

In spite of herself, she was pretty, Jerry thought again.

She looked up then, her eyes deeply brown and intense behind the small, square lenses. "You never know. This might work."

"Maybe."

She set her glasses on the table and got up, then stood

close enough that he could smell her rose oil again. She gazed thoughtfully out to the parking lot, where the spiny fronds of some palms rustled against the hills. Past the trees where he'd seen old Captain Trips, the telephone poles arced out to the highway.

"I saw you walking out there this morning. You looked, well solitary. Lonely, even."

"It's a drunk thing."

"What do you mean?" She caught her breath. "You aren't drinking?"

Jerry ignored the question. She couldn't help herself, he figured. Far away out the window the scrub and mesquite gave way to blankness. "Sometimes you just have to get out of your own way. Stop thinking so much. I go for walks."

"I sketch sometimes."

"So I guess we do have something in common."

"Does it work for you?" she asked, holding her eyes on him. "Not so much for me." Her eyes shifted away. "But I'm not much good at sketching. You seem pretty adept at walking."

"I've had some practice."

The highway had grown busier. It was a long way out there, but he thought he could see the little balloon and silver crepe paper refracting like a signal mirror.

THEY STOPPED for gas at an old Econo-Fuel, whose whitewashed exterior was flecked with rust, like the broken refrigerators and hot water tanks they passed alongside the desert road. Surrounded by mesquite and desert scrub, it sat alone on the edge of the wide flat horizon.

When Talia and the girls wandered inside the mini-mart, Jerry hung up his nozzle and walked over to where Max leaned against the van, struggling a little with the antiquated gas pump while watching the numbers slowly tick by on its oval face. It was worth giving him another try.

Jerry ran his hand along the van's curved roofline. "Spent a few nights myself in one of these. Classic cars really take you back."

Max jiggled the nozzle. "Lily says you like to drive them off cliffs."

"It wasn't exactly intentional."

"I had an uncle who talked to birds. No shit. Used to have long conversations in the backyard. He couldn't drive real good either."

Jerry shook his head. Nothing about this was going to be easy. "We keep this up Max, it's going to be one fucking long trip."

Jerry squinted out to the yawning desert, the wide-open space toward which they were headed. Max looked bored. "I thought you might have remembered something about Ethan is all."

Max laughed. "You're the broke down acid-head. I remember things just fine."

He hung the nozzle on the hook at the side of the pump. Before going inside the little office to pay, he stopped and looked out at the desert.

"Look at that shit out there. Miles and miles of it. You ever think maybe he doesn't want his old hippie dad hunting him down?"

"Forget it, okay."

Jerry could feel the concrete heat climb from the concrete into his head. He glanced toward the Valiant, where Lily and Talia stood near a cluster of propane tanks, talking to Jenny and Amber in the Valiant.

Of course, Max had a point. But Jerry felt his fists curl anyway. "Don't drive too fast, all right?" Stupid. Stupid to be here, stupid to even try.

Back in the Jeep, the desert enveloped them again. The flowers dwindled. Talia sat quietly for a while, occasionally lifting her eyes to check on the Valiant and Max's van, which sped ahead on the lonely stretch of road.

"It's a wasteland," she said almost to herself.

"Don't tell that to the Indians."

"Well, I don't live in a teepee or eat dirt."

She was truly tedious. But on the other hand, she wasn't really to blame. He had to keep reminding himself of that fact as he stared out at the rear window of Max's van. Talia had been dragged out here by circumstances too. As much as Jerry hated to admit it, maybe they weren't that different in the end. "Looks pretty empty to me."

"I was here once. Not here, exactly, but near." She became thoughtful. "Camping, if you can believe it. My freshmen year in college."

"Not in the yard this time?"

"Professor Grinde was his name. A cross between Brad Pitt and Levi-Straus, sort of. He organized a spring break trip to see the hieroglyphics. Picasso reinvented the line after he crawled into a cave and saw the drawings at Altamont."

"I studied psychology, remember?"

"The first night we were there Grinde tried to pull my roommate into his tent and kiss her. He was drunk. He had his shirt off and his chest painted." He could feel her appraising him. "I adored him, too. I'll bet you were one of those types with your students. They probably lined up for a chance at you."

"You don't let up, do you?"

Naturally she was right. At San Francisco State he'd seen himself as something of a low rent Timothy Leary who wore tie-dye and lectured students about mystic consciousness. But as his ex-wife Evelyn said when they separated, it was all an act to get laid. On more than one occasion he woke up in his office, scurrying to escort a co-ed out of the building before his colleagues arrived for morning classes. His wife would know because she'd been one of them, but Talia?

"So I never got to see the lines," Talia continued. "I jumped on the closest plane and flew home."

"Who knows," he said, "you might have been a painter

if you'd seen those lines, lived a whole different kind of life. An artist or something."

"Except for Lily charging off into the frontier with Max, I like my life just fine. Even if I could, I wouldn't change any of it. But thanks anyway for the career advice."

THEY PASSED an abandoned mining camp, the wood sluices and rusted implements wedged into the broken earth next to a sun-rotted shed. The old boards were smeared with graffiti and the hard ground littered with broken bottles and sooty boards left over from fires. Jerry made out the words, "Peace and Love and Fuck You" spray-painted on the rock atop the mine entrance as they rushed past, the old building giving way to an outcropping of black rock and a rising butte.

"There's some wall art for you," said Jerry. "Kids being kids."

Talia craned her neck to get a look. He thought she was ignoring him, but then she spoke softly. "One morning I went into Lily's room and found her unconscious, my prescription bottles all over the floor. Before she passed out, she painted her room black."

Jerry nodded, feeling foolish at this rebuke. Even ages ago when he was a therapist, he was never good at giving real advice. His favorite joke line had always been to "take two hits of acid and call me in the morning." And his parenting skills weren't rated high on anyone's list, either.

Talia leaned back now in her seat, shaking her head. "I just don't get this fascination with destruction and darkness."

And she never would, but there was no sense in telling her that.

IN THE late afternoon, the Colorado River came into view, an almost black panel of water, thick and undulating in the open cut of desert. Across the water a network of casinos rose, a line of stark square buildings whose angles disrupted the bleak earth. Then the Jeep crossed over a metal bridge and the undercarriage buffeted over the grating, with the black water churning through the slats underneath. Once across, the van and Valiant edged onto the shoulder, disappearing behind a wash of dust.

"They're turning north," Jerry said. "What now?"

"We stay at one of the hotels up there and wait," Talia said. "Max apparently is meeting some people at the campsite." She laughed a little then. "Lily said to take advantage of the last bath for a while. She'll catch up with us there in the morning. That's what she says anyway."

"It'll be O.K."

"Keep your fingers crossed."

As the two vehicles drove away from the paved road, Lily put her hand out the window and pointed at the cluster of casinos. There was a quick honk of the horn, and the van turned away. Talia followed the van with her eyes, a forlorn expression on her face as the VW receded in the windows.

Past a dismal industrial field of power boxes and transformers, with a web of wires that went back over the water, they turned and motored down the corridor formed by the ugly casinos, whose dimly lit neon borders did little to relieve the sudden dreariness of the place. The late afternoon light was fading.

Jerry drove slowly. All the buildings looked the same. "Not a 4-star hotel in sight," he said.

Talia looked down at a slip of paper and then gestured

toward the Riverview, where a sign boasted "All You Can Eat Jumbo Shrimp."

"Of course," he said. "And a river-front view in the bargain."

THEY TOOK adjoining rooms on the water side of the building, and after Jerry helped the bellhop unload Talia's bags from the dolly and carried them into the room, she walked him to the door.

"I'm thinking about trying some of those shrimp," he said.

Talia leaned on the door. "Really? You'd eat fish so far from the sea?"

Jerry smiled. "Is that another rule?"

"Actually it is. I only eat it when I'm within 50 miles of the ocean, otherwise you're certain to get frozen. Although there's never a guarantee."

Jerry tried to figure out what his role was here. Was he supposed to keep her company? "You probably should eat something," he said finally. "Dinner?"

She seemed tired, her face pale. "I think I'll stay in. Call Room Service maybe."

He hoped his own face didn't show his relief. He was tired of talking.

After cleaning up, he went downstairs to the buffet. He sat at a cocktail table and ate the shrimp, which were not particularly large or fresh, dipping them into ketchup and looking out onto the gloomy river, which looked dark and opaque from the shade cast by the casinos.

Down on the concrete boardwalk fronting the river, a man in flip-flops held the hand of a gaunt woman teetering on a pair of rollerblades, her skirt hiked up on her thin thighs.

Jerry handed the waiter money for the bill, and when he glanced down there again, he saw Max standing on the boardwalk. So much for the people at the campsite, Jerry thought. He looked on to the walkway again. Sure enough, it was Max, smoking a cigarette and listening to the man next to him.

Jerry had been around long enough to know that this guy was bad news. The man was built like a boxer, the muscles of his shoulders showing through the fabric of his cheap jacket. His hair was oiled back and his cheeks were marked with deep acne scars. The man raised his voice a little, but Jerry couldn't hear what he was saying. Max just smoked and looked at the water.

The boy was up to something, Jerry thought. But then the waiter brought his change and wanted to tell him a story about the baseball game, and when Jerry looked again, both Max and his dubious companion were gone.

With darkness falling, the lights strung on the roofs of the party boats glowed brightly on the water. Down at the river's edge, Jerry watched the hulls drift on the glacial currents and tried not to brood. He lit a cigar and halfway through, he felt himself relax.

"I think Lily smokes too when I'm not around." It was Talia's voice.

She leaned on the rail next to him.

Jerry felt like a kid busted for smoking in his room and tossed the cigar into the water, the ash hissing on the surface. "I thought you were sleeping," he said.

She gazed at the boats. "It's pretty I guess. Not exactly the Seine, but who's asking. I'm thinking of taking a boat ride."

Jerry looked apprehensively at the water. But it was

probably unlikely that he'd drown twice. "What the hell."

They took the steps to the level of the docks and walked along the sand towards one of the boats, where the surface of water glistened from motor oil and shone in the lights of the casino.

Talia studied the muddy water. "It's actually disgusting, isn't it? What are those?"

Jerry made out the fish stirring in the dirty water. "They look like carp. Mud suckers, maybe."

"That's hideous."

"Like you said, this isn't Paris." Jerry waited. "You still want to do this?"

She shrugged. "What else is there to do?"

The lone kid operating the boat wasn't much older than Lily, a smooth faced boy with tight black curls who wore matching blue shorts and a polo shirt buttoned at the collar. He winked lasciviously at Jerry as he clamped the rail-gate behind them.

The boat groaned out towards the center of the river. Jerry stood beside Talia in the stern, and soon the bridge and transformers came into view, past the neon haze from the long line of casinos and hotels fronting the river.

Talia clutched the stanchion as the boat swayed and turned in a wide arc. "I had a glass of wine," she said. "In college we called it the whirly-birds."

Jerry yelled to the boy, and he pulled back the throttle handle. They could feel the pull of the water under the hull, then quiet.

Talia shivered. "I actually hate the water," she said.

Jerry started to say that it was her idea, but stopped himself. "I was thinking maybe we should go for a swim later, get a look at those fish."

"Funny."

Though it felt like they weren't moving any longer, the road lights on the other side of the river slowly drifted past. Jerry stood beside her, his hand on the pole above hers, the familiar rose scent blending with the crisp sweet smell coming over the cactus and rock under all the stars. Drifting closer to the casinos, the hull rocked gently through smears of reflected neon blues from one of the hotels.

Talia gazed out at the water. "What's it like," she said softly. "Remembering and not remembering?"

Jerry thought about it. "Like a movie you saw a long time ago and mostly forgot. But you still see the scenes, ones that stay with you and keep you up at night."

"That doesn't sound like a movie I'd want to see."

THEY WALKED back from the dock to the hotel and Jerry felt something almost like buoyancy for a minute. It had been a while since he'd spent time with a woman.

He was about to ask her if she wanted to get a Coke or watch the roulette wheel when she yawned delicately.

"I'm very tired," she said. "Bed." When they reached the steps leading to rooms, she yawned again and gave him a congratulatory look. "Compliments," she said. "Another day. Isn't that what you drunks say?"

"It's only been a day. Give it time."

WHEN HE couldn't stop turning in his sheets, Jerry got out of bed and went back down to the bar.

The darkened room had changed. The ice trays full of shrimp and salad condiments had been carted off, replaced by a big-screen console flashing pictures of what looked like naked girls riding motorcycles, and the lounge turned with beams of colored light flooded with smoke and loud music.

He tried to find a stool at the crowded bar, then gave up and sat at a table and ordered a club soda from a girl whose breasts sparkled with spangled pasties. She knelt when she put his drink down, the pasties close enough to his face that he could see a layer of baby powder on her breastbone.

She whispered in his ear as she slipped the napkin under the glass.

"I go on the wagon sometimes, too" she said. Her vodka and cigarette breath enveloped him. "Keeps the boogey man away, right?"

When she stood up, Jerry looked at her face. She appeared about twenty, her hard features concealed by dark lipstick and heavy black eyeliner, a soccer kid or softballer who grew up to be a B-rated porn queen.

After she left his table, Jerry watched the brooding river slide by in the window. He knew this was a low place with a rotten beer stench and stale smoke, and filled with a blankness of all the hollow, fearful eyes, but it settled his bones. He knew he'd be wise to get his butt out of this place — Mahatma would have told him as much — but he found it strangely soothing.

A half hour later, when the girl sat down across from him, Jerry didn't recognize her at first. She looked different in street clothes, a short tight skirt and a bare-shouldered, orange top barely covering her breasts.

She lit a cigarette and let her eyes drift from him to the bar and then back again. "I think I said sometimes I'm on the wagon," she said, crossing her legs. "Not always. Aren't you going to buy me a drink?"

"The boss lets you sit with customers?"

"Like this is the Hilton," she said. She leaned back, laughing as she exhaled smoke. "This is nowhere."

Another bare skinned waitress brought a rum and Coke and set it down, nodding knowingly.

Jerry studied the girl's face. She had faint smile lines under the thick make-up and was older than she looked. She was trying to act cool, but the thin fingers clamped around her cigarette fidgeted too much. Her hair was jet-black, smoke-scented and shiny, and if she wasn't exactly pretty, she was something close to it.

He wondered if he looked desperate, too. "Nowhere else to go, huh?"

She flicked her ash under the table and peered at him, unconsciously scratching her arm. "You seemed nice, okay?"

"Why don't I just give you some money and you can go score."

"Like I'm a charity case? Look at these freaks, I could snap my fingers and have every bill in their wallet."

He'd hurt her feelings. He felt bad. "Look, I'm just here to watch the water," he told her. "I didn't mean anything, okay? I know how it goes is all."

"I like your hair," she said playfully. "Reminds me of my Dad's."

"What's a girl like you doing in a place like this?"

"A girl like me?"

"Forget it. I'm getting up. I need to go for a walk." Jesus, thought Jerry. He was spending the whole night walking.

He went out the exit, glad to be in fresh air, escaping to the boardwalk where he had walked with Talia earlier. The river was quiet, no more boats on the flat black currents. He lit a cigar and put his foot on the lower rung of the railing.

"Bet you try to dump all your girlfriends," the girl said. She stood beside him sipping her drink, the breeze tangling her hair in the swizzle stick.

Jerry looked at her. This wasn't good, not at all. "What's your name?"

"My real name? Katie. What's yours?"

"People call me Jerry."

"Why do you like the water?"

"It's peaceful, don't you think?"

"Go swimming down there and you'll throw up for days."

"I told you, I'm going to walk."

"Mind if I walk too?"

As the girl strolled ahead, Jerry couldn't help noticing the curve of her well defined leg. Talia had nice legs too. They walked for a while in silence down the dark sidewalk that ran along the river. Jerry thought about what he was doing.

Old timers defined insanity as doing the same thing over and over again and hoping for a different outcome, but at least watching her walk was better than thinking about Ethan. The orange top slipped down a little. Jerry thought about her skin.

BACK IN his room Jerry looked down onto the dim spread of desert across riverbanks. Somewhere a wood fire, small but intense, glowed against the dark abyss.

When he turned away from the window, Katie lay on the bed, the white sheets pulled up around her neck. Her cigarette burned in the ashtray next to her drink on the cheap bureau, a line of smoke drifting though the lampshade. Her clothes were folded neatly on the floor.

"I'm really that disgusting, huh?" she said, tugging at the sheets, looking away.

Jerry walked to the bed and sat down next to her. "My friend's in the next room," he said. "She's a light sleeper."

"You gay?"

"It's just been a while," he told her.

"Come on," she said, taking his hand. "I can be real quiet."

When he got in and felt her skinny ribs and legs next to his, the faint odor of alcohol and talc welled. Her skin tasted salty, the cheap perfume bitter under her ears. He wrapped his arms around her and he felt her fingers move around him and help him inside her warmth. Then they were pressed together, her breath pushing into his, her black eyes pressed closed. When she climaxed, her eyes opened and got wide, a stifled grin coming across her clamped lips like someone afraid of laughing in church.

Intermittently he thought about the thin wall between him and Talia. Truth be told, he was almost glad when they finished. He rolled over and looked at the popcorn ceiling, his eyes lighting on a gray water stain.

"You okay?" he said.

"God, are you crazy?"

"Probably, yes."

At the door she paused, kissing him on the cheek. "You still got it," she said. "Love the one you're with, right?"

Perfect, he thought, slipping some bills into her hand. "Don't be a stranger," he said, taking a stab at levity.

She gave him a funny look and he watched her disappear into the shadowy recesses of the narrow hallway.

Closing the door, he stood listening to the air-conditioner hum. The room was quiet, still hazy from her cigarette. As he flipped off the light switch, he heard a metal click echo in the corridor outside, the unmistakable sound of the lock closing in the room next door. Perfect, he thought, again.

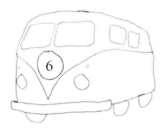

6

THE BOWLING alley near the old Harrah's Casino smelled of Pine Sol and stale beer, a scent that might have made Jerry retch if he'd been hung-over. He poured some coffee from the percolator sitting near the rack of colored rental shoes outside the lounge entrance, pulled down his cap low and waded past the faces to the tables in the back. The last time he set foot in a bowling alley was a glow-ball night for kids, when Ethan was ten, with trippy colors and music blaring. So much for life's little circle, he thought, taking a seat with his compatriots at the AA meeting.

"We're all drunks here," the guy at the lectern was saying. "But at least we're still on a horse called sober."

He wore a cowboy hat and spoke like an Indian in a movie. Jerry wondered if he had heard him correctly when he said his name was Injun Bob.

"You hold on to sobriety and she'll never buck you," he said.

Jerry glanced at his own reflection in the glass of the popcorn cart and thought, I've been thrown on my ass.

He'd imagined for a long time finding Ethan and showing him how much he'd changed since being fished out of the Pacific. Sure, Ethan knew full well his old man's capacity for excess — and not just booze and weed, but all the rest. Ethan knew about the girls, too. It was as if Jerry still lived in an endless summer of love where the sun-dappled days on the Haight never stopped shining. But Jerry hoped those times were all behind him. Last night was just an episode and besides, Katie had been a perfectly nice girl with very nice legs. It wasn't as if Jerry had commitments to someone else.

"Any newcomers to the six a.m.?" the man at the lectern asked. "People suffering?"

Jerry stared into his coffee.

Injun Bob wore deep blue tattoos up and down his arms and delivered his speech with dramatic gestures, lifting his palms at the right moments. Jerry admired his conviction.

"She lit me on fire," he said to the ten or twelve others. "Kerosene running down my face, all over my body. I just lay on my back, watching those flames rise, floating on a lake of fire."

Jerry listened earnestly but knew Injun Bob was wasting his time. As speakers went, he was good but not good enough. Even Mahatma, with his Eastern voodoo and magical thinking was way in over his head with Jerry.

"In the end I had to climb on my horse and ride out of there," Injun Bob said.

When the meeting was over, Jerry surprisingly felt a little better and wanted to thank Injun Bob. He found him by the percolator, blowing into his coffee cup.

"I kind of feel I'm riding bareback," Jerry said.

Injun Bob smiled, "You got to find the right pace, if you know what I mean."

Jerry didn't know what to say. Of course Injun Bob was right. "My sponsor back home's been to India."

"We're all the same."

"The thing is, I'm looking for my boy. He's run away."

"They do that."

"I'm hoping he's around here. At a music festival or something out at the lake."

Injun Bob sipped his coffee. Jerry saw his seriousness. "Havasu, huh? There's some bad stuff out there. Not like our day. Crank is a nasty deal."

"My kid likes weed."

Injun Bob made a fist and pounded his chest, just like a movie Indian. "Take heart, my brother," he said.

Sitting in the Jeep, Jerry rolled down the window. A breeze, edged with the hot desert smell of juniper, touched his face. He stared at the smooth curves of rock and considered Injun Bob's words. My heart really is a wilderness, he thought.

WHEN JERRY returned to the Riverview, a note wedged in his door informed him that Talia was at the pool, waiting for Lily. He studied the penmanship and the perfect inky loops for some hint of her mood, but the letters only revealed the careful correctness that must have made Lily wild.

The pool area was quiet. Jerry scanned beneath the aqueous shadows floating above the long wall of the enclosure. Talia sat alone under an umbrella at the far end.

She wore white pants and a thin blouse, under which Jerry could see the sharp black outlines of her bathing suit. She barely moved when he came in through the pool gate. Only her hair stirred a little in the breeze. Jerry sat down at the glass table, but her oversized sunglasses stayed fixed on the pages of a doubled over New York Times.

Jerry folded his hands on the metal tabletop and waited. Beyond the Plexiglas wall along the riverfront a ferryboat like the one they rode in the night before trailed a wake. In the bright sun, the boat struck Jerry as shabby, the dull hull plain and marked up in the full light of day.

When he got tired of waiting, he said, "Nice day. Warm for March."

She brought the paper closer to her face, and then raised her chin a little.

"I hope I didn't keep you up," he said.

"When I came out this morning, a snake was in the pool. Can you imagine anything more disgusting? A rattlesnake, according to the pool boy."

"You have a right to be pissed."

She nodded sharply. "There should not be snakes in the pool, yes."

"That's not what I'm talking about. Go ahead and get it off your chest. Holding back is no good."

"Still the counselor. There's fortunes in self-help books, you know." She set down the paper and looked at him over the top of her sunglasses. "We just took a boat ride, Jerry."

"I know what you must have thought, okay?"

She looked up, as if pondering his statement. "Why would I think anything, Jerry? We have no connection."

"It just happened, you know."

She put her teacup down so hard the saucer rattled. "Earthquakes, avalanches, tsunami — those things just happen. Jumping into bed with a teenage prostitute, that you did." She gazed across the pool, as if something far away in the distance interested her. "Frankly though, your habits are something I don't care to discuss."

The reflected light from the pool turned against the side of the building like a lava lamp. He was dismayed at how quickly the glow from Indian Bob's talk faded in the face of Talia's upbraiding. Nothing like a stuck-up prude to fuck it all up, he thought.

"I went to a meeting this morning, not that it's any your business. Can we just leave it at that?"

She picked up her tea with a faint sigh, her voice admonishing. "You seemed concerned whether I could make this trip," she said. "Maybe you should be asking yourself that question instead."

Thankfully, right then the girls came through the pool gate. They appeared light hearted, or at least Amber and Jenny did, wearing bright sun dresses that swirled in the breeze. Lily still had on her dingy black. Talia stood, looping her canvas bag over her arm.

"You're on your own, Jerry. The girls and I are going on an excursion." She smiled at Amber. "While we wait for Max to get ready."

Lily looked scornfully at the other girls, who smiled conspiratorially up at Talia. "Yuppie scum from Beverly Hills and La Jolla like to get their nails done and go to spas."

"Maybe so," said Talia. "But we're stuck in the desert waiting for Max. We might as well do something."

Jenny smiled shyly. "I've never been to a spa."

"Me either," said Amber, shoving Lily a little with her shoulder. "Don't be such a killjoy, Lily."

"How's the group shaping up?" Jerry asked Lily. "Anybody new come around to follow the music?"

Lily bit her nail, irritated. "It's not like I wouldn't tell you if he showed up, okay?"

Talia put her arm on Jenny's shoulder, ushering them

towards the iron-gate. "Come on, girls. He's just anxious, Lily."

Lily sighed. "Sorry. Max is just hanging out. Maybe he knows something."

"Do they do black?" Amber said. "I want black nail polish, just like Lily."

After they left, Jerry wandered through the hotel gaming area and gazed through the patina of cigarette smoke at all the tables. The room depressed him, a sea of gaudy carpet and green felt populated by old people wearing synthetic shirts. A small crowd assembled around the Wheel of Fortune, evidently waiting for a sucker to step up. Decked out in fake gold bangles, the woman spinning the wheel had on a shiny black Cleopatra wig. Her eyebrows were black and pointed at the arch and her skin was dead white. She smiled at Jerry and beckoned to him. Great. Now a corpse was flirting with him, asking for his money as she manned the gates to the underworld.

Jerry pushed his way through the onlookers. What the hell, he thought, I might get lucky.

"We got a big spender," the lady said, smiling at Jerry, but her sarcasm was unmistakable. She took his five one-dollar bills with the tips of her blood-red nails.

The wheel ticked to a stop. "Loser," she said, drawing it out. The crowd laughed.

THE CAMPING area a few miles from the hotel didn't look like it held many kids. Instead, it seemed to be filled with more old people, gray-haired ladies in Bermuda shorts and men with fishing caps. Jerry drove through the stalls, until he found Max's van parked at the back of the lot where a wire fence separated the dusty campground from some sort of adjacent junkyard.

Jerry parked next to the van. Max was busy doing something in the side-hold of the van and when Jerry got close he saw that Max was setting up a radio inside. He had his shirt off and a faded tattoo of a mushroom bloomed on his lower back.

"You come to interrogate me some more?" Max said, fiddling with some wires.

Jerry thought about Max with the muscle guy back on the boardwalk. "Just wondering what's going on."

"Pirate radio, in about two minutes."

"Messing with the man."

Max gave him a sideways stare. "My dad was a drunk," Max said. "I tell you that?"

"Never would have figured that one out."

"We lived out in a desert, like around here. Vandenberg. Thought he was real important, working on rockets and shit. He was a murderer and a drunk."

"Lily's a nice girl."

"Your extensive fucking knowledge I suppose. You pick up hitchhikers and fix their lives, like a hobby?"

"You involved in something stupid, Max? Something that makes some remote place in Canada sound good?"

Max reached into the van and switched on the radio. He started talking in the little microphone. "Hey, Amigos," he said, leering at Jerry. "Max here. You wouldn't believe this shit, but I'm standing next to a ghost. Old Captain Trips come back from the dead to pay little Max a visit."

Another stupid idea. If Max knew anything more about Ethan, he still wasn't talking.

"I'll see you later," Jerry said.

"Show up at Havasu and you might meet him too," Max said into the speaker. "Says he done shots with the devil."

On the way back Jerry pulled over under the metal towers near the power station. The river, dark and silent, stirred against the bright sun. The mud suckers were out there too, cruising the bottom, which he imagined as a flat panel of silt and oil. Overhead the electrical lines hissed and the steel girders were peppered with crows. Suddenly he felt awful.

He lit a cigar and thought about what Max said, the part about Jerry being a crazy ghost. It dawned on Jerry that this was what the old timers called a moment of clarity, though nothing seemed very clear in this faded landscape. He thought simply, you are crazy. Go home, old man.

He heard something, a gunshot perhaps, and the crows scattered.

He puffed some more on the cigar. But what about the midnight boat ride with Talia? That had been a moment of normal, a genuine, real moment. And if that was real, well, that suggested he was up to the task of hauling Ethan out of the desert. Didn't it?

He looked at the little Shiva on the dash, waiting for an answer, but all he could hear was the electrical humming from the wires.

IN THE late afternoon, when it was time to check out and follow Max and his band down the road, Jerry went down to the hotel's port-a-chez. Talia stood there already, next to Amber and Jenny's battered Valiant. The porter, a young Latino in an oversized white uniform, had just finished loading her bags into the trunk and she was fishing a bundle of dollar bills out of her leather handbag when Jerry walked up behind her.

Lily spotted him as she sat slumped in the back seat, her

head on Jenny's shoulder. In the front seat Amber saw him in the rear view and held her nails up, wiggling her shiny cobalt fingers.

Snapping her purse shut, Talia turned, nearly bumping into him.

"What's going on?" he asked.

She jumped a little. "You startled me," she said. She tugged him by the arm out of earshot of the girls. "I've made arrangements to drive with the girls," she whispered.

"Because of the woman last night?" Jerry asked.

From behind the dirty glass, Lily kept staring, her eyelids low and cheeks slack. Talia glanced about nervously at her and Jerry followed her to the other side of the plaster column.

"It seems like a good idea," she said. She knit her fingers together as she spoke. "Bonding with the girls and all. It's my best chance. And Lily's getting out and riding with Max as soon as we meet him at the campground."

"So you don't need me anymore?" It about figured.

"I didn't say that."

Jerry sighed, lifted his cap and tried to assess the situation. It struck him as ironic and typical that another woman was about to leave him. So much for new vistas on the old Karmic tour, he thought. "What you told me at the pool? You know, about me not being ready and all? Damned if you weren't right." He started back to the Jeep.

"So that's it? You're just going?"

"Look lady, you were leaving me."

"Leaving you? We had a deal. What do I care if you want to pay for sex?"

"Whatever."

"I left a note for you at the desk. Lily and I planned to wait for you out at the campsite. While Max finishes whatever it is that he's doing. And I've posted notes everywhere on Facebook asking about Ethan."

Jerry heard something distant in her voice. He wondered if she was lying about leaving, not that it mattered.

"We wouldn't have just left you. Anyway, Lily wants you here."

"The little girls over there are probably getting restless," he said. "I knew this plan of yours was a bad idea all along."

"Is that what they preach in those meetings of yours, resignation?" Her voice changed a little. "You quit this easily?"

He wondered if he detected a note of pleading in her voice, if she were, after all, a little desperate.

"Ethan just might show up, you know." Talia waited and then shrugged. "But you're not exactly someone he can count on."

One last cool stare and she turned and walked away.

Before she crossed behind the column and joined the girls, he yelled, loud enough for everyone to hear. "For your information, I didn't pay for sex. I got it for free."

Still standing out of view, Jerry held still and listened. The car door clicked open and shut, then the Valiant lurched out from under the port-a-chez and into the sun, where it turned out onto the busy street.

He climbed back into the Jeep. Max was waiting for all of them back at the campground next to the scrap yards where the greasy hulks and relics from the dharma highway sat and rusted. Everybody leaves Jerry thought, and only some return. It sounded like a song.

He turned the Jeep in another direction.

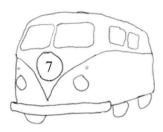

IN THE end, it was his mother who left. She'd met a man who sold second-hand sports equipment and took off for Boise. Jerry had been twenty at the time and he told himself he didn't care. He had his own problems by then.

At her funeral, Jerry's old man showed up. They sat together on folding chairs on another man's porch, drinking cheap bourbon out of plastic cups. After the mourners departed, Jerry asked his father why he hadn't left home that time they were supposed to go camping.

"Men don't leave," said his father.

And, just like Jerry's father said, it was Evelyn who finally left Jerry. He could remember that. As usual, he'd come home late from the bars that night. There was a note written on the paper she used for her legal briefs taped to the refridgerator.

"I'm tired," she wrote. "I've taken Ethan. Andrew will call you."

Andrew was the attorney who checked their taxes and managed to arrange Jerry's long-term leave with the dean.

Jerry read the note and poured himself what was left in a bottle of frozen Stolies, and found the half-gram stashed in his sock drawer in case of an emergency.

In Ethan's room the faded, tape-cornered posters remained on the walls, glowing dimly under a black-light, while the lava-lamp gurgled on the dresser. Whose choice to leave those, wondered Jerry. Well, it didn't really matter. Evelyn wore the pants on that one and had done them both a favor. Sometimes men should leave, and he'd managed to drive away from Talia, at least.

AFTER MIDNIGHT, he was passing through the town called Festive. In the slim light it looked to be a run-down menagerie of wood-frame and masonry buildings. He had gone north instead of east like the girls, and drove under the black mountains off Highway 395.

He was tired and the enclave glided by the window quickly, like the other small towns. He had his eyes on the wide swatch of dark shapes streaming away, when something ducked under his periphery near the right fender, almost too quickly to see.

He felt the impact in his body first, his arms and chest going rigid. Disappearing under the right fender, whatever it was only a shape, black and spectral with two eyes blazing, gone. Before he knew it, Jerry was skidding to the other side of the road, his hands jerking the wheel of the Jeep. A thud stung his fingers.

When the Jeep came to a stop on the gravel shoulder, road dust billowed up in the high-beams. His hands were sweating, but the Jeep was still, the only sounds the mechanical ticking of the engine and the echo of the brakes in his ears.

He sat for a second, then got out and walked back. The night was big and quiet. He found the body fifty-yards back. "Fuck me," he yelled, standing over the dog. "Fuck me!"

He walked back and pulled his Levi jacket out of the car and wrapped the carcass in it, then scooped it off the asphalt and carried it back to the Jeep. It felt heavy, still warm, but definitely dead. He laid it out on the back seat.

The only lights in the small town burned in the window of a wooden barn like structure with all sorts of antennas sticking up into the light. Something about it didn't feel right, but what the hell else could he do? He pulled in front and climbed out of the jeep.

Above the wooden door an old sign covered with dust said: Last Chance Bed and Breakfast. He pulled the screen back and pounded on the door, a distant cadence of crickets coming from the land.

At first there was only silence. Then, just as he was about to leave, the door pulled back.

Low, in a wheel chair, a pallid elderly woman with a blaze of incongruent red hair looked up at him. Behind her the interior of the house was dimly lit. She seemed to Jerry a little over-dressed for the place. What looked like an evening dress draped over her frail chest.

"A customer," she said, a smile spreading in her eyes. "Finally. Welcome to Festive."

Jerry touched the tip of his cap, a lump inside his chest. Damn if it didn't seem she was the only one who lived in this shitty little town.

"Actually, I'm afraid it's something else. Well, I hit a dog. A terrier mix, brown and white."

She looked perplexed, her gaze floating away. Waiting for her to say something, Jerry wondered if his luck could get any worse. Over the spectral line of hills, the strange antennas rose.

"It's brave of you to come back," she said. "He was old. Dusty."

"I don't feel so brave."

"Where are you going?"

"San Francisco."

She brightened for a second. "One of my favorite places. The Bay's lovely. But too far for you to go tonight, surely."

"I'm just passing through."

"But after we're done, you'll want to stay, rest up."

"After?"

"I'm here by myself. I can do most things, but burying Dusty isn't one of them."

She made tea. The house was ornate, with vases full of sweet smelling flowers and racks of little metallic figures. When the pot whistled, Jerry rose from the velvet-covered chair, offering to help, but she declined.

"You live here all by yourself?" he asked.

"Twenty years, since my husband Victor died." She gave him a mischievous look. "I buried him, but not in the yard. I promise you."

"I'm sorry about your dog."

"Your first time? You live long enough, you bury animals. I have a drawer full of collars."

"Once."

"Yes, I can see that. It sticks in your mind. I still remember when Victor and I had to say goodbye to our cat Mollie after twenty years."

Jerry wondered at the irony. In fact, he'd only just remembered burying another dog as he stood over Dusty and wrapped him in his jacket, a vagrant memory of Ethan.

"My boy, Ethan and I," he said, "just a few years ago, helped a fellow."

"I'm sorry to bring back unpleasant memories," she said, sipping her tea.

"A neighbor," Jerry said, picturing the night again. After still another fight with Evelyn, Jerry had stormed out of the house after midnight, heading to the nearest bar, a place called the Groove on Haight.

He was getting tight with a dentist, a red-faced man with fat hands, Jerry remembered that, who cried because he couldn't quit with the drinking. A real pussy, Jerry thought at the time. Turns out the guy had just moved in down the street on Haight, one of the yuppies flooding the town.

Jerry was glad when Ethan wandered into the bar. The man was embarrassed and left. Ethan said that his mother was packing and Jerry should go home.

On the way back they came upon the guy in the bar. He was on his knees, out of his Mercedes, bent over a dog in his driveway.

"My daughter's dog," the man balled. "She'll hate me."

Jerry and Ethan took the dog and buried him in the park. Jerry remembered that.

"More tea?" the woman asked.

Jerry must have laughed a little.

"What?" she said.

"I have a friend who likes tea. I'm more of a coffee guy."

"What about whiskey? I like one now and again," she said, wheeling to a small clutch of bottles set out on a china cabinet.

"Me too. But not tonight."

She nodded, pouring herself a glass from a crystal

decanter.

Jerry pushed the woman in her chair out through the door, rolling her slowly over the ruts of dirt, parking her finally next to a low wooden building. She dangled the lantern in her hand, casting shadows on the wall, making him suddenly think about Talia camping with the kids.

Jerry slowed and looked up at the antennas.

"You a radio nut or something? I know a kid who's into radios."

She laughed. "Heavens no. Those are lightening rods."

Jerry squinted into the night, shading his eyes from the moon. Sure enough, he made out the cables and dead spires.

"I make those," she said. She lifted her glass of whiskey. "It's kind of a philosophy of mine."

Jerry went back to the Jeep and brought back the dog. Still bundled in his jacket, it lay now on the dirt. Jerry pulled back the fabric.

"You'll find a shovel in the shed. The switch is to the right," she said.

Jerry pushed back the door and flipped on the switch. The barn was filled with lengths of metal and scraps of steel. An arc welder sat at the center.

Spading the hard earth with the shovel, Jerry waited for the woman to cry, but she didn't. When the hole came a foot up the handle, he stopped and picked up the bundled dog. Just last night he was sleeping with Katie, now he was burying a dog.

He held the animal low for her. The woman touched its matted head and Jerry knelt to put the animal in the hole.

"That's a perfectly decent jacket," she said.

Jerry thought of the blood on the hind-quarters of the dog. "I need a new one," he said, lowering the animal carefully into the dark hole.

When he finished putting dirt over the small declivity, they stood quietly in the moonlight. The woman held her glass, gazing up at the sheets of clouds that had begun to move past the antennas.

"It's funny the people you meet when you leave your house," the woman said.

"I used to go everywhere," Jerry said. "Me and my boy. Not so much anymore."

"They get older and move on," she said.

"He sure did," Jerry said. "Ran the hell away."

The woman seemed to study his face, making Jerry tense.

"Since you helped me once, I wonder if you wouldn't one more time. I'll make you a deal."

Jesus, Jerry thought. Another deal.

"I need some help with one of my pieces. It won't take long. After, you can have a room. No charge."

"I ran over your dog."

"Don't be silly. I need help, really."

Inside the shed, she drank more whiskey, her hair billowing out of a metal mask. The room blazed now with light. If he didn't know better, she might have been a young woman, one of the crazy artisans back home. Jerry held one of the spires as she welded it to a wrought iron stanchion, the sparks flying.

When she finished, she reached from her chair and turned off the machine, then flipped up her visor. She took up her whiskey glass and admired the chiseled point of the spire.

"You're probably wondering about me," she said. "A crazy woman in a wheel chair bent on welding silly poles and putting them into the sky."

"I'm not taking moral inventories," Jerry said, thinking about the girl in the Riverview Hotel.

"When Victor and I first moved here, I was taking a shower during a storm. I closed my eyes and woke up in a hospital. We have spectacular lightning storms here."

"Traveled down the pipes?"

"Can you imagine? Turns out it's common."

Jerry studied the sections of the lightening rod laid out on the dirt floor. She saw the way he was looking at them.

"After Victor died, I remembered something he told me about facing my fears."

"Seems like you embrace them."

She smiled, her eyes shining in the light. "Why the hell not?"

"I'm pretty tired."

"I don't know why. Maybe it's because I feel we've met before. You look familiar, I think, but I'm going to tell you something."

Jerry waited for her to take a sip.

"Go find your boy," she said.

"How'd you know?" he said. He pushed his hair back under the bill of his hat and she gave him a knowing look. "Guess it's obvious."

"Keep going. Find him."

THE NEXT morning she served wheat toast and apricot marmalade. The sky out the window had filled with clouds, their roiling tops gathering in the blue.

"I can make you a lunch," she said, pouring him coffee. He watched her gaze out the window, first looking at the clouds and then lowering her eyes to the place where the dog was buried. "It's nice there," she said.

Jerry put his toast down on the plate.

"I'm a drunk," he said. "That's the truth of the matter."

She gave him a quizzical look. "I don't know your name."

"Jerry."

"Marion," she said. She wheeled closer, her thin hands whitening on the wheel as she came closer. "Get over it, Jerry," she said, her sharp blue eyes fixing on him. "No one cares what you were. Get back on the road and go do what you have to do."

"Like that, huh?"

"Just like that."

After he got the Jeep started, Jerry rolled down the window. Marion, still dressed in her lace skirt, handed him up a brown bag.

"Road's a strange place," she said. "Say a prayer for Dusty."

"Something tells me mine won't do any good for old Dusty," Jerry said.

"Drive safe," she said, wheeling back towards her door.

WHEN JERRY made the turn back toward Arizona, he thought about what lay ahead. Talia would be awake, sipping tea maybe, no doubt fighting with Lily. And who knows, perhaps Ethan was nearby, his young face among all the other lost faces. The thought brought a heaviness and Jerry closed his eyes for a second, trying to clear out the clutter in his mind.

THE GUARD at the campground gate wore his hair in

braids and had a reflective orange vest, like the guys who worked on roads. He paced in front of the cyclone fence, collecting money and directing cars. A placard on a post declared the place Reservation Land.

Jerry paid and followed the caravan of dust-covered cars onto the wide sweep of tarmac. He rolled the window up. Despite the afternoon heat, he tried to keep the dust out of the cab. It was stifling, and as he wiped his face, it struck him that he was anticipating Talia's complaints, and that only irritated him more. And the hell with tea, too, he thought.

But by the time the pack of cars and vans began to fan out ahead, he reminded himself of the reason for his return. It didn't matter that he was tired or tied somehow to an annoying and seriously repressed lady professor. It didn't matter that Max was an ass-hole. Even Lily with her sad, grown-up face and chipped black nail polish didn't matter. He was here for his son.

The line of campsites appeared hodge-podge and chaotic, reminding Jerry of the old concerts where you put down where you landed, dropped what you had, and waited for what came next. It was hard to imagine Talia out here and suddenly Jerry felt a wave of shame run through his body. She'd stuck with it. The hard flat ran a long way, ending in a knot of campers in the distance, just above a line of blue that must have been Lake Havasu.

He rolled down the window and peered at the camps. The dust burned his eyes. No one looked familiar, or rather, they all looked familiar, leftovers from some other era or some other time in his own life. He knew all these kids, but there was no sign of Talia, Lily or even Max.

Just as he was about to give up, Jerry made out Max's van in the smoky haze, and in a second he spied the Valiant too, both muted with dust, as if they'd crossed the Sahara. When he got closer, he saw that Talia stood alone by her tent, with no sign of the kids anywhere. Jerry pulled in beside the Valiant and turned off the engine. Talia looked back over her shoulder at him. She squinted towards the Jeep's windshield but then turned around with the kind of studied indifference that made Jerry wonder where she learned it.

Talia's tent was a disaster, and Jerry could see the problem at once. She'd gotten the poles screwed up, threaded through the mesh pockets the wrong way. He walked over slowly and stood behind her. She rose up from her knees, holding the pole, trying to pull the pool of blue cloth up into something resembling shelter. The fabric slipped backward and fell on to the ground. But she kept on, pretending not to care. Behind her back, he wiped his forehead with his shirt, nearly overwhelmed by how complex things had become.

"They didn't leave you, I hope," he said.

She kept trying to force the tent pole through the blue canvass. Jerry could tell she wanted to ignore him.

"Of course they didn't just leave me," he heard her say, but then her hands fell to her side and a sigh escaped. "Shit."

Jerry didn't know why, but her frustration cheered him.

"It's the poles. You've got them connected wrong. The short ones go with the long ones."

The dirty look on her face reminded him of Lily. "You're an expert at tents too?"

"More than you are, it seems."

She scowled into the sun. "I told you, I don't care if you sleep with underage whores."

"I didn't come back to apologize."

"Well nobody asked you."

Jerry sighed. Somewhere down below the line of tents a guitar struck up. It sounded out of tune, the broken chords floating on the hot wind. Everywhere he looked there were dirty-faced kids wandering, kids with piercings and slick black hair and silver studs, kids with dirty jeans and beads, and others with hard faces like Max.

"Not exactly a love-in out here," he said.

"Is that why you're here, to provide commentary?"

"You want a hand?"

Jerry could see the blue vein pulsing in her temples and the delicate skin around her cheeks growing redder from the sun.

"If you want to help me, go ahead."

Jerry walked over the folds of tent on the dirt and took up two of the poles at her feet. He was close enough that the rose oil changed the thick odor of dust and when he took the tent loop from her, her sweaty arm brushed his.

"Tents are different now," he said. "Easier."

Talia just stared at him. "We had a deal," she said. "And then you took up with a teenage prostitute. And then you left."

"It was a temporary arrangement. Not a deal." He looked at her.

"Anyway, I'm back."

She shrugged, a bit like a teenager herself. "Whatever."

He snapped one pair of poles together, and then started on the other set. He remembered again why he was here. "I don't suppose you've heard from Ethan yet?"

She took a moment, breathing evenly as she appraised him. Her face softened. "I'm sorry, no."

"It's early."

"Yeah."

He finished with the poles. "You want to hand me the tent?" he asked.

She sighed heavily and came over, shoving the ball of fabric toward him.

"So where's Lily and the others?" Jerry tried again. She remained bent, lifting her hand again. Her nails, painted pale pink were already beginning to chip at the tips.

"Roaming, sleeping somewhere else, I don't know. Not here, okay?"

Jerry ran the poles through the loops of cloth and they both stepped off the flattened fabric dome. He held the tent with his outstretched hand, trying to keep his balance.

"Go on. Go inside and stand up," he said.

He could see from her expression that she thought of complaining, but she got on her knees again, unzipped the flap and slithered under the canvas.

"What about last night?" he asked. She was standing, her muted body just on the other side. She didn't answer and he sensed why. "You weren't out here by yourself?"

She came out. Her pant legs were covered with dust, her hair sweaty on her forehead now.

"It was a beautiful night," she said. "You could see the lights of the boats on the water."

"Jesus."

"I'm perfectly capable of spending the night by myself, if you want to know."

AFTER THE sun went down Jerry made canned chili and corn over the open fire. For the most part, they kept to themselves and Jerry wondered if she'd even eat. But when he finished cooking, he called her and she put down her book and came over. He found some cheap wine in the kids' camp and poured her a glass.

She didn't say anything when he passed her the food, although she gave it a few curious shoves with the plastic spoon.

"You think we can try again?" Jerry said between bites.

She stared glumly at the beans on her spoon.

"Is this the kind of stuff you serve to the drunks?" she asked. "It doesn't seem healthy."

"The drunks at the soup kitchen don't complain. Even though it's not local and sustainable, or whatever you call it."

"There should be a law." She took a bite. "It's not even real food."

After they finished eating he boiled water and made her tea. She sipped it quietly, her face tired in the lantern light. He braced. She'd have more to say to him for sure, about Katie, about him leaving and coming back, about his cooking. But she sipped without a word.

"She'll come back," he said finally. "You think she wants to hang around her mother all the time? You knew the deal."

"I thought it would be different."

"That's what all the drunks say. Anyway, you gave a pretty good lecture about not giving up," he said. "I never bought the line about how those who teach can't do. You need to hang in there."

"I miss her, just like I missed her at home. What's the point?"

"You're asking the wrong guy."

HE WAS asleep when he heard Talia's voice. At first it wasn't clear. There was something else. Watching the moon hang in the mosquito-lined vent overhead, he realized the sound was coyotes. Their distant yelping sounded like children playing. But they came closer, louder.

Then he heard her voice calling him again.

He jumped up out of his sleeping bag and stumbled, hurrying towards her. She'd turned the flashlight on inside the tent and it reeled outward, blinding him.

"Hold on," he yelled, stubbing his toe on the uneven gravel. He focused his eyes in the moonlight. "You're O.K. The tent just fell down."

He got to her and pulled up the poles and canvas. He could hear her breathing hard, but she seemed to gather herself once he got the tent upright.

"Are they gone?" she asked, "the wolves?"

"Coyotes. Just coyotes up in the hills is all."

"I thought you knew all about setting up tents. Mr. Outdoorsman."

Jerry hammered in a stake. "The pole snapped."

She sighed, her shape slack. Jerry went to the supply box and found the bottle of wine, pouring some into a paper cup. The night was clear and the yelping continued to hover over the thin atmosphere above the water.

He unzipped the door of the tent and faced her. Talia sat in her cotton, long-sleeved pajamas, staring at him, the flashlight held limply at her side. She took the cup but kept looking at him, eyes wide, and then abruptly looked down.

Jerry realized he was in his boxer shorts and nothing else. He pushed his hair back, nodded, then backed out of the tent opening.

Talia re-zipped the flap, the long silence mercifully punctuated by the coyote noises settling around them.

"Am I a bad influence?" she said. "Me drinking and all?"

"Wine isn't my thing," Jerry said, feeling stupid.

"You think she's all right out there?" she continued. "And Ethan?"

"It's beautiful out here, like you said."

She unzipped the tent flap enough to reach out with the cup. It took him a second, but he understood. He emptied the last of the bottle into the cup.

"Yes," she said flatly.

"I don't understand. Yes, what?"

"We can resume our deal."

Jerry watched her silhouette. "I ran over a dog," he said.

He scratched his head, waiting. She unzipped the flap again, and Jerry could see her face in the shadows.

"That's awful."

"Me and her owner buried her. A terrier, I think."

"Are you okay?"

"It's the road. The woman who owned her said you never know what to expect on the road. I think that's about right."

Talia hesitated. "I'm not saying I'm counting on you."

"I wouldn't."

"I'm sorry about the dog. You must be sorry too."

"Add it to the list, Talia. Goodnight, okay?"

He heard her yawn. In the distance the coyotes were moving, their small voices somewhere in the hills. "You're certain they're not wolves?"

"No wolves here, Talia."

"I'm really not counting on you," she said.

TALIA LED him through the produce section at a market in Havasu Village, tossing ingredients into the shopping cart. Since she'd discovered a grocery emporium dedicated to yuppie epicureans, she'd been increasingly cheerful, her good will perhaps encouraged by the fact that by early morning Lily had returned to the camp. Their new alliance had proceeded without a hitch, so far. But the day was just starting.

Jerry dutifully slouched over the cart-handle and shuffled after her, but Talia's narrow-eyed inspection began to try his patience. Now she stopped, and visibly took a long inhale above a bin of fresh dill.

"You're sure you know how to grill fish?" she asked as they made their way to the meat counter. "Do you suppose they have a fishmonger?"

"I'll go find some lemons, if you think I can handle it."

Jerry left her, ringing the little bell. She was questioning a poor fellow in a white apron when Jerry got back.

"Are you certain that this halibut was flown in? Not frozen? I mean the ocean is miles away."

"Better go after the tartar sauce now," he said. "I'll meet you by the seasonings."

Jerry edged away. Even her cheerfulness made him wary.

When he finished, he went around the isle and found her pacing near the row of spices with her cell phone to her ear. She smiled at him and turned her back, continuing her conversation in private.

After she hung up, she came over and lifted her index finger to the rows of jars, her eyes searching.

"Is Lily okay?"

"She's fine, I assume," she said. "I wasn't talking to Lily."

She studied the jars of herbs, ignoring him. Jerry felt a flicker of annoyance. She looked pleased.

"Who then?"

"A friend of mine."

"A friend?" Jerry stared at her. "More than a friend?"

"Maybe. A man I see, sometimes. Paul, in the English department." She found the jar she was looking for and plopped it in the basket.

They were walking again. "You didn't tell me you had a boyfriend."

She stopped and stared at him briefly. He kept moving, avoiding her gaze, but in his distraction he clipped a display of sea salt bottles, arranged in the shape of a pyramid. The shiny containers crashed to the floor.

Talia stooped and began snapping up the containers.

"Boyfriend?" she said, reaching for a jar. "What kind of word is that? And I'm a little old for a boyfriend, not that it has anything to do with you."

Jerry fumbled to replace the containers, juggling salt crystals, blue salt, thin bits of dirty gray salt. "Why are there so many goddamn kinds anyway?" He examined the price tag on one container. "Twenty-two dollars for salt? What's wrong with Morton's?"

"French sea salt. Very pure. Not for cooking. You just sprinkle it on the food right before serving." She shrugged. "I'm surprised they carry it here."

The disaster with the salt had shifted her train of thought, Jerry was relieved to notice. And then they turned down the aisle stacked with liquor bottles and wine, and he began to feel light-headed amid the narrow corridor lined with spirits. The feeling had nothing to do with Talia. Since he sobered up, he couldn't help but notice all the pretty colors and labels on the bottles, with names like Cristal and Sapphire. Before, he didn't give a damn about labels and the tints of glass, but now whenever he passed them in grocery stores they possessed a magical aura like stamps from exotic countries.

More like dark continents, he thought, and kept moving.

But halfway home to the registers, the dull shine of a green bottle, some sort of designer gin from Spain, caught his eye. For an instant he could see tawny-hued men smoking small, brown cigarettes at café tables, letting the world go by, before Talia's voice brought him back.

"Maybe you should buy a bottle and go find that girl."

The woman was merciless.

At the cash register she picked up the jar of tartar sauce with disdain. "Why would you ruin perfectly good fish with emulsifiers and fake mayonnaise? It has corn syrup in it too."

"Because I like it."

"You like all kinds of things."

On the ride back to the campground, she played with her cell phone, sending messages, tapping her nails on the dash and overtly ignoring him.

"What's the last thing you remember?" she asked. "About Ethan." She looked, Jerry thought, as if she were preparing to pose a difficult question to one of her many graduate students whom Lily despised.

He turned onto the gravel road, taking up a spot behind a Vespa scooter carrying a dust-sullied boy and girl. They were traveling slowly, forcing Jerry to hit the brakes.

"Those damn kids should be wearing helmets."

"If I'm going to help, I need to know."

Jerry felt a knot of annoyance grow under his breastbone.

The Jeep was inching closer to the gate. The camping area teemed now with cars and kids milling around on the other side of the fence. He wished they could get back to camp, eat his poorly prepared and ill-conceived meal, and go hunt for his son.

"Evelyn blamed me. Said I was too much like his friend."

"I see."

"Not always. I remember a fight with him before he left. We were walking in the park, Golden Gate. I must have been drunk or high. I yelled at him for not taking his future seriously."

"How did it end?"

Jerry looked at her. "A cop came and told us to go home."

"You were that loud? My God."

"He saw me pissing on a rose bush, Talia. What can I say?"

She moved slightly on her seat, lips tight. She didn't say anything else, which suited him fine.

As the Jeep pulled into the camp, Lily and the Hemet girls were just setting out for the evening. Lily stopped, waved, but then kept walking towards the crest leading down to the lake. Watching Talia staring out the window at her, Jerry felt suddenly small and cheap, like a bad drunk.

THE DRUMS started just after the sun went down, a faint wedge of moon lifting above the water. The hollow sounds came from somewhere down near the shore, under the line of scarp that rose and occluded much of the lake.

Talia put her fork down. "You did a good job with the sea bass."

"Amazing, huh?"

"I didn't say that."

They sat for a while in the gathering dark, listening to the dull throb of the drums. Then Talia pulled on a blue sweatshirt and picked up the flashlight. "I think we should go."

"Maybe we should give it a while."

"You have to do this."

He nodded and took up his own light, but when he tested the beam on the tent, his hand trembled on the chrome cylinder. He looked at his fingers. "It's done that since they dragged me out of the water," he said. "Every so often. Figure if it keeps moving, so will my heart."

She glanced towards the festival. "Well, it's understandable. I mean, he might be out there," she said.

They moved towards the line of black and its hazy bubble of light, following their flashlight beams over the hardpan. Halfway to the top of the rise, they angled towards the pounding, knowing the stage would be somewhere beneath. It took a while but eventually they could look down on the platforms, brightly lit and jumping with the dark silhouettes of a circle of drummers. Nearby light radiated on black water; houseboats and sport cruisers glimmered and then shifted in the fragmented night.

Talia stumbled slightly on the steep sand and Jerry held out his hand. He pulled her to the top of the hill. Behind them there was darkness but down on the stage the drummers' silhouettes pulsed. Three skeletal figures danced past them, twisting in and out of the blackness.

The crowd was large — hundreds if not thousands of kids bunching together in small groups, lifting their arms and dancing, beating on drums and what looked to be bongos.

"So, you really got a boyfriend?"

She ignored the question. "What are they doing all gathered around like that?"

"They call it a drum circle. Makes you feel connected, sort of like sharing a heartbeat I guess."

"I'm not sure I'd want to share a heartbeat with some of those people."

Jerry stared into the black. "I can't see worth a damn."

"We have to get closer."

"It's hopeless if you ask me."

"You'd make a lousy art historian," she said. "Sometimes you have to look at a picture for days before you see something new."

She stopped her descent and fetched something out of her pocket, a piece of paper of some sort. Unfolding it, she held it in front of him, waiting for him to shine his flashlight on it. Reluctantly, he offered his light. Beneath the bright bulb, the lines took a second to materialize and he had to squint to see what she was showing him.

Ethan looked back at him. From an old photo Jerry had shown her earlier, Talia had created an almost perfect sketch. Something more though. He appeared older, with more depth in his gaze, shadows running under his eyes, the hair shorter.

"It's just a guess."

Jerry let go and looked away. The lights from the tops of the houseboats cast long green and white spirals on the river.

"I'm sorry. I just thought — "

"No, it's good. You're really good, you know." He bent his knees, squatting, head down. "It just surprised me."

"I posted the picture on the web site too."

He stood there for a few minutes, thinking about Ethan with this new face. Talia waited for a minute or two and then tugged at his arm.

"Come on. They'll scatter soon."

He hadn't really thought about what this would be like, about looking for Ethan and not finding him, and then, maybe actually seeing him. Talia looked at him expectantly. Just do this, he thought. Either that or go back and serve hash, like Saul and all the other wet-brains.

They stopped at the bottom of the hill and Talia shone her beam into the writhing sea of faces, most of them gripped by the pounding beat welling up as if from the ground beneath their feet. Jerry peered too, the deep percussion filling his chest, but all of the faces remained as abstract as masks.

"How'd you make the picture so real?"

"I just imagined he was standing outside my tent."

He thought about her sitting there drawing in the dusty hours alone by the tent. "Sometimes I forget what he looked like," he said. "Hard to believe, but true."

There was a familiar smell of sweat and dope. The dancers remained faceless.

"Jesus," he said, turning his ankle a little. "We're wasting our time."

"You have to try."

He followed her onto the flat hard pan, where she held the sketch out and moved through the edges of the crowd.

"Please take a look — have you seen this boy?" she repeated, holding the picture under the light, interrupting the drumming of a few, before moving onto the next clump. Her voice projected outward smoothly into the crowd and Jerry could picture her behind a lectern, wearing her glasses and admonishing her students. "We need to find him." But no one answered.

After forty minutes they nearly made the stage, where a trio of straggly haired girls with wooden guitars and embroidered tapestry straps over their necks tuned their strings.

Jerry was tired. He wanted to give up, to go back and pull his sleeping bag over his face. Trying to find a face in this crowd was hopeless. But Talia persisted. "Shine your light over there," she said, giving instructions. "Shine your light on those boys near the back."

Both flashlight beams cut through the smoky night, but the boys disbanded, scuttling away. Their beams moved back and forth, then settled on the same face as it tried to back away out of the glare. The boy's eyes caught in the light.

In another instant the face turned away, gone.

"Jesus," Jerry said. "That last one. Did you see?"

"Yes."

"Ethan," Jerry yelled, but by now the music came up,

the three soprano voices echoing in the little valley between the hills and the water. He stood, plunging as fast as he could into the crowd, feeling Talia close behind him. A light jumped near the stage, suddenly deep blue and spindly.

Pushing their way up the hill, they reached the low darkness, aiming their flashlights across the craggy wilderness running towards the hills on the other side of the reservation property. In the distance two boys cut across the dusky beams, but the other, the one who looked like Ethan, kept moving straight ahead and dissolved into the ebony night.

"They think we're cops," Jerry said, breathing hard and stopping.

"Keep going. I'm not afraid of the dark."

Jerry's legs felt thin under him. He gazed up at the stars, his eyes drawn to the Big Dipper, tracing its tail, before once again straining over the dusky field.

"Maybe it's not to be. You ever think about that?"

"Fate," she said scornfully. Talia shrugged impatiently. "The hell with that, Jerry."

She was moving again, scraping over the tight chaparral and scrub. He kept his light on her legs, finally catching up to her side when the blue light drifting over the bluff faded and the music fell away.

They walked for five minutes before Talia's light illuminated something metallic and slick in the distance. She gave him a quizzical glance and they went towards it. A hundred feet closer, they came to it. The aluminum body of an old plane, pristine except for broken wings, glinted against the black backdrop of hills.

"It gives me the chills," Talia said, staring at the oval fuselage.

Jerry thought of the old man's story about the practice bomb being dropped over at the Salton Sea. The whole beautiful desert was probably filled with wreckage and secret radioactive waste.

"Did you see?" Talia said. She pointed her light under the nose, a sparkle coming up in the little windows. Against the hull slumped a young person's body, the face turned and obscured by hair.

The body wasn't moving. In the silence Jerry became aware of his breath, which matched the pounding under his shirt. Talia was looking at him, waiting to see what he was going to do.

"Go on. Look."

Jerry moved closer, keeping the light tight on the boy's chest. Standing over him, he reached down and brushed away the hair.

"He needs some water," Jerry said.

"It's not Ethan?"

"No." Like that it was over.

He heard Talia sigh, then her footsteps. She moved forward with her flashlight, the beam falling onto the boy's face, while Jerry cradled his chin. She pulled a water bottle from her jacket pocket. "He looks dead," she said.

"Just wasted is all."

Jerry stood, suddenly aware of the weight of his body, the pull of gravity. Talia moved closer to help Jerry tug the boy to his feet, when the kid suddenly stiffened and lurched up into the flashlight beams. Talia jumped back, grasping Jerry's arm.

"Just take it easy, son," Jerry said.

"We're cool," the kid managed. His eyes were glazed and he looked at the plane with a confused expression. "You going somewhere?"

"Let us help you," Talia tried.

The boy stared up at the stars. "Nice night for a plane ride," he said. "Fucking nice."

Jerry nodded, but now the kid was staring at him, blinking.

"What the fuck? The Captain?"

"Calm down, son. I'm not him."

The now awake but befuddled boy pointed towards the heavens. "Up there. You come from up there?"

"You're the fucking Captain," the kid said. And then quickly he was stumbling towards the vapor of blue and the voices down by the water. "Like Jesus."

Talia let her flashlight fall against her leg and shook her head. "Another follower. Should we do anything?"

"Get the hell out of here."

They were about to start back when the sound of a motorcycle groaning towards them came up on the other side of the fuselage. Jerry squatted and peered under the belly of the plane, but all he could see was the yellow headlamp winding nearer.

He stepped with Talia into the clearing, both watching the motorbike and rider draw closer.

"Should we be scared?" Talia said.

"It's a small bike."

"Killers don't like small bikes? You're sure about that?"

The bike slowed and approached near the tail of the plane and when it turned to come around the nose, and the light angled away, the clear figure of a girl with thick black hair trailing in the darkness became visible.

When the girl glided to a stop in front of them, she reached under the tank and cut the engine and stood straddling the frame of an old Honda 50. She was surely no more than fifteen, sturdy, with moonlight on her cheeks.

"This is private property," she said, her voice slow and pleasant. She glanced at the hills. "We saw your lights."

Talia clicked off her flashlight. "A boy came up here," she said. "We thought he might be in trouble."

"This is reservation land. My uncle lives up there."

Jerry stepped closer. "We didn't mean to trespass. The boy was just a little drunk. He walked up here. He's gone now and we'll go too."

The girl rubbed her face with leather half-glove, her eyes going past them to the hint of blue radiance. She blinked once, nodding a little.

"My uncle calls them walkers," she said. "The Council isn't going to let them come anymore because of it. No more concerts."

"Walkers?" Talia asked.

"Last year after all them down there left, they found one boy over near a tractor. Over there," she said, pointing to the ridgeline. "Before that there was another kid along a fence some houses down."

Talia shifted. "You mean dead?"

"No water my uncle says. Plus they were wasted."

Jerry felt his stomach churn. "We're real sorry to have bothered you and your uncle. We'll head back now."

"Sure is pretty," the girl said, gazing at the misty blue radiance hugging the ground. "My uncle says it looks like Hawaii from up there. I never been to Hawaii."

On the way back they didn't talk and the low moan of the motorcycle held steady for a long time. Jerry stared at the two beams cutting through the tangles of dry brush. He was suddenly aware he was counting his steps.

Talia finally spoke. "I know what you're thinking. What are the odds?"

They were getting closer to the haze. It didn't look

much like the islands to him. "You ever been to Hawaii?" Jerry asked.

"Honolulu and then the big Island, with all the fancy hotels. I hated it."

"Me too. Evelyn had a conference there and dragged me and Ethan along. Can't remember much except they had some killer dope."

"Great family memories you have. It's not exactly reassuring."

"What about you and Lily?" he asked. "What about your vacations? Besides this one?"

Her head snapped up. "I don't take vacations," she said. "I work."

"Oh," said Jerry. "So no family memories." He felt meanly pleased with himself. "Maybe that's why Lily wants to travel."

When they resumed, Talia walked quietly, as far away from him as she could while remaining in the safety of the flashlight beam. "I'm sick of the dust," she said finally. "There's a hotel at the resort. I'm sure they still have rooms."

"Tonight? Kind of late isn't it, for a change in plans?"

She looked at her watch. "It's barely after ten."

"Right." So much for comrades, thought Jerry.

He was dizzy and exhausted. It felt like the middle of the night. He considered apologizing for the crack about family vacations and then decided against it. The hell with her too. "Planning to head out without me again?"

He waited for her to say that he'd been the one who left. She ignored him once again. Evidently she'd had a lot of experience with recalcitrant students.

"Maybe I can convince Lily or at least one of the girls that they need a shower." She looked at him then. "You can stay here and wait for Ethan."

When they finally reached the edge of the plateau and could look down onto the concert, the whole field of kids undulated in the intense swirl of blue and white light projected from the stage. The mass looked like a single thing, slowly undulating to the eerie electronic strains made by a new band, too far down to see except for the small bodies.

"It's different than I remember concerts," Jerry said. "Hypnotic. We were all fidgety, wild I guess." He could feel the vibrations. He thought about the girl on the dirt-bike and Talia's nervous hand on his arm.

"I'm sure that's fascinating, but I want a bath."

He kept his eyes on the crags and tangles of weeds growing out of the cracks, moving slowly with Talia behind. They'd gone about halfway down into the blue wash when Talia touched his shoulder.

"My God, look," she said.

Jerry lifted his head and saw. Past the festival grounds, way out on the black panel of water, a house-boat roiled in flames, its rectangular top-section engulfed and the fire reflecting on the black water as if the hull were surrounded by candles.

"Looks like there's a life boat out there. That black shape alongside."

"They're just letting it burn?" Talia kept looking at the fire. "Shouldn't we call someone?"

The opaque smoke moved high into the crystal night and wafted against the desert stars, the dullness growing. The undulating crowd kept on, evidently oblivious. He thought about what the Indian girl said, about the walkers, the kids dying in the desert, and about how Talia didn't think it was Ethan.

"This place makes my skin crawl," she said.

"I think Mahatma's right. He says that Shiva rules, the god of whirl."

Talia held her eyes on the kids. "All I know is Lily's out there. We didn't even see her tonight. And Ethan too. You just have to decide to keep going."

"Why do I have a feeling it's all been decided?"

9

MORNING SUN glazed the flying bridges and a stiff breeze whipped the antennas of the tallest boats in the harbor as Jerry stepped onto the dock. The houseboat, charred and skeletal, still redolent of burnt wood and varnish, lingered by itself at the end of the dock.

"Distances are further than they look out here," a man's voice came. "That's quite a hike down that hill. You need some water?"

Jerry stepped around the head-high piling to get a look at who was talking. The man was kneeling, tying a stern line from the boat to a cleat. A blue Harbor Patrol hat shaded his sunburned face as he looked upward toward the campground. "Those kids know how to party. Aren't you a little old for that?"

"I'm sort of here looking for somebody," Jerry said uneasily. "What the hell happened, anyway?"

"Back in my day we tossed eggs and threw water balloons. Bigger and better, huh?"

"You sure? I mean about the kids?"

"Must of looked pretty cool, all the colors, don't you think? We all got to grow up sometimes, right buddy?"

Starting back up the hill, Jerry made a conscious effort to resist his growing suspicions that Max had anything to do with the fire. Max was crazy, but not that crazy, right? Still, shouldn't Jerry maybe share his thoughts with Talia when she got back from the hotel with the Hemet girls, practice the rigorous honesty Mahatma and all his cohorts swore by? What are my responsibilities here, he thought, among the living? He'd come back and joined up with Talia, for better or worse, and damned if he wasn't, well, connected. Yes, as much as he hated the thought, they were in it together. He was no longer alone in his little apartment and he owed her. Damn you, Max, he thought. You and all the other screwed up progeny of screwed up eggs and sperm.

Still, the way he saw it, his main allegiance was to Ethan, right now loose somewhere, and as he trudged up the incline, he decided to try and put aside his uncharitable thoughts and fill his mind with pretty pictures. "Don't live in the down," Mahatma would always say. "Untie the heart, bro. Picture happiness."

Sighing, he tried picturing the dewy grass back at Golden Gate Park, then some sort of silver bird floating above the line of hills beyond the lake, even Talia and the Hemet girls in their hotel rooms, covered with powder in white sheets, or whatever. But it didn't help. No matter how hard he tried, it was all he could do to haul his hopelessly earthbound heart up the hill.

Back at camp, kids wandered about, some half draped in blankets, others in dirty shirts and sweats that passed as pajamas. The Hemet girls' Valiant was gone. At the campsite Lily lounged on an ancient quilt alongside the van, while Max sat alone in the driver's seat above her, behind the little window.

Jerry waved, slightly ashamed at his thoughts, deciding he'd make at effort at amends by making breakfast. "You look like you can use some nourishment," he said, repeating a line he often used on shelter kids.

"Whatever."

He fried eggs, the yolks cooked hard, and made a pot of coffee on the Coleman stove, carrying a plate over to Lily. She was reading a paperback and grudgingly lowered it. She held one eye shut in the sun and took the plate from him and set it down on the blanket.

"What do I look like, one of your charity cases?" she said.

"Just thought you might be hungry." He looked out at the lake. "Things are further away here than they look."

She sighed, folding her book closed, a tattered edition of *Madame Bovary*. "What are you talking about?"

"Ethan made me read that one," he said. "He wanted to know if I thought she was a bimbo."

She took up the plate and poked at the food with her plastic fork. "You ruin the eggs when you over-cook them, you know?"

"You sound like your mother. Maybe she'll take you and the Hemet girls out for a hotel breakfast. Or a garden party somewhere." Jerry liked his eggs cooked this way.

"She hates trailer trash," Lily said. "You think they told her their mother's a heroin addict and they live on food stamps?"

"I can see we're cheerful."

"Maybe she can take them to Europe and lecture them on painting."

Jerry knew he deserved it, her moodiness only reflected

his own. He looked over at the van. Max had his feet up on the dash, a thin line of smoke seeping out the half-open window. Lily was probably high too.

"I bet you had favorites," she said. "I thought teacher's pets ended after high school."

Jerry thought about telling her his version, the sexy coeds who showed up every semester with veiled glances and low-cut blouses, the ones who finally caused the dean to call him in for a talk. "I don't care if you're the closest thing we got to Timothy Leary," the older man had said evenly, "you can't fuck students for a living."

"What about Max?" Jerry he said, looking at the van. "Seems like he's working on his appetite."

"I wouldn't plan on it."

"I've spent the last year around kids like him, sweetheart."

When Jerry walked around the front of the van, Max met his gaze, looking at him indifferently out the window. He tossed the joint onto the dirt. All at once Jerry knew this was a bad idea.

"Meals on wheels," Max said, making an effort to sit up straight. He slipped back again, laughing to himself before getting his balance.

Jerry waited, and Max reluctantly cranked down the window. "Lily already told me I don't know how to cook," Jerry said.

Max took the eggs and dug in, his munchies evidently getting the better of him. With his skinny arms and dirty hair, he made Jerry think of the dogs that sometimes took his offerings of food in the alley, before baring their teeth and running off. Damn you Max, he thought.

By now the lake began to move with tourists, the yellow sun flattening the smooth water near the docks. The burned up boat floated serenely out there too.

"Last night was something," he said to Max. "I keep thinking I'm a fool for believing you, though. About Ethan running with you guys, I mean."

"I eat this shit, I have to listen to you? Is that the deal?"

"Even if you knew Ethan, you wouldn't tell me, would you?"

He wiped the yolk from his mouth with the back of his knuckle. "Eggs are overcooked. I'm telling Talia."

Jerry considered how earlier, when he awoke, the morning seemed almost nostalgic, with no one up, no one requiring civility, just like back at the shelter. Now this. The kid was pushing his fool button.

"I can't help myself, Max. I don't want to, but I got to ask you. Last night did you try to stir things up, start a fire to add a little drama to this whole scene? Seems like it might be stupid enough to fit your style."

"Shit man." Max tossed the plate out the window and turned on the radio. A cowboy song came out of the small wood speakers on the floorboards while he stared straight ahead, biting his lip. All at once Jerry knew he'd made a mistake, but it was too late.

"This is good dope," Max said. "Don't wreck it, old man."

Jerry felt the blood well up along the sides of his neck and there was nothing he could do. Before he could stop himself, he was reaching through the window, his feet coming off the ground.

He took Max by his collar and pulled his face towards him. "I may be old kid, but I can get in a few licks."

With his hands clasped on Max's arms, Jerry realized the kid was stronger than he looked, like most of them. Max struggled free, jerked the handle and flung Jerry back with a shove of the door. Before he knew it, Jerry was on his ass, looking up at the kid.

"I ought to fuck you up," Max yelled. "You put your hands on me, dude."

It had been years since Jerry'd been in a fight, all of them in some seedy dark bar, long past drunk. He could feel his heart race, his body tighten, which surprised him. So much for pretty thoughts.

He was scrabbling to get off the dirt when Lily bounded over. She still had her book in her hand and her dark eyes were glazed in her colorless face.

"What the hell?" she yelled. "He's an old man, Max." She glared at Jerry. "And he's a kid."

Max took a step back. "Fucking says I started some fire," he yelled back. "You think I'm high all the time."

Lily took a deep breath. She shook her head violently, and then stomped off in the direction of the lake.

"Don't get excited," Jerry pleaded. "It's no big deal."

"Can't a girl just read her book?" she said, wheeling, "You make me ill."

"I'm sorry, Lily," Jerry tried. "I wasn't thinking straight."

But she kept going. Max took off after her. "Fuck you and your eggs," he yelled.

"Next time I'll try not to overcook them," Jerry said, sitting in the dirt on his rump.

TALIA AND the girls pulled into camp a little after noon. Jerry put on fresh clothes and threw out the old newspapers and empty cans that littered the camp, and sat smoking a cigar, surveying each new face for a chance glimpse of Ethan. When they got out of the Valiant, Talia's hair was damp and the Hemet girls had on new matching sweaters.

"Looks like somebody's been shopping," he said to the girls. They looked quizzically towards the van. Talia too glanced in its direction, as if they all sensed the fiasco that ended with him in the dirt.

Jerry pointed at the bag Talia carried. He'd decided she didn't need to know about the altercation, or the boat either. Sometimes a commitment to rigorous honesty had to be tempered by a simple need to get by, that was the real truth, in spite of what it might do to his Dharma.

"Lily and Max are down by the lake," he said. "I've already served one set of guests, but I can serve another if you want."

"We ate already at this wonderful organic restaurant," Talia interrupted. The Hemet girls had already begun to wander off. "Goodbye girls."

Jerry looked at whatever Talia was holding. She smiled and slowly unfurled the poster board so he could get a look. It said, "Ethan," in big letters.

"It was the girls' idea," Talia said. "Quite smart, actually."

Jerry puffed on his cigar and watched Talia slip the poster under the Jeep's wiper blades. She nodded to herself, satisfied, then dipped into her tent and emerged with an armload of magazines. After the dust up, his cigar settled his nerves. But having company around when you smoked a cigar always ruined it, and with Talia, though she'd plainly decided to opt for tolerance, the experience was somehow worse.

He stubbed it out in the dirt and looked at a band of scrawny adolescents stroll past their tent. "I've been up since dawn. All the faces look the same to me."

"A little company won't hurt." She sat down and flipped a page. "I did feel a little bit bad, enjoying the hot water and leaving you alone with all this."

The way she'd stalked off last night with the girls, Jerry hadn't discerned the smallest fragments of guilt.

"You seem refreshed."

"What about your night? Did you enjoy returning to your solitary roots?"

"I made eggs for Lily and Max."

"I actually slept better knowing you were out here with her," she said. He could hear the reluctant quality of her voice. She spoke softly. "I counted on you keeping things on an even keel."

"We got along fine without you. I'm not saying it was a love-in." Jerry ran his hand in the dirt along the metal base of his chair, where he'd stashed the cigar butt, and dug it out. Talia stared at one of her magazines. He lifted the butt, hoping she wouldn't notice, and took a draw, but only inhaled dust and the cold foul taste of extinguished ash.

She didn't lift her eyes from the magazine. "If you're going to smoke those repulsive things, shouldn't you at least get a fresh one?"

Jerry ground the stub into the gravel and tossed it into the shadows under the Jeep. Damn if her pleasantness wasn't spoiling his plan.

"Look, there's something I should tell you. I mean, since we're starting over and all."

Talia lowered her magazine and studied him blankly. "Not another girl?" she said. "Not that?"

"You're not going to let go of that, are you?"

"It's not exactly an outside possibility. With your history."

He sighed. "Max and I had a little disagreement."

"Well, is it all right now?"

"Sure. It's over. I mean we worked it out, sort of."

"I told you he was unpredictable. Maybe you'll listen to me next time."

She went back to her magazine. He thought about telling her about the fire, but figured he'd gone far enough down the truth route for one day.

"Can you spare one of those girlie magazines?" he said. "Something to look at, in between all these kids."

She picked up the pile at her feet and shuffled though the stack of *Martha Stewarts* and *Ladies Home Journals*.

"This one specializes in sex secrets for an aging clientele," she said. "It should suit you." She opened her own magazine. "Take a nap. The kids are going to be here a few more days."

"I am a little beat. Anyway, thanks for the company," he said, getting up. "We got to stick together, right?"

"One step at a time."

He couldn't tell if she was being sarcastic, but it didn't matter. He'd gotten through something with her, and that was progress. Better than he did with Evelyn, or Ethan for that matter. Maybe Mahatma was right after all, that the truth can set you free. Or some of it, anyway.

In the tent he watched dust swirl at the top of the mosquito netting before finally cracking open the magazine. The ground felt harder than last night, even with the bag bundled under him.

Before long he dozed off, forgetting what he was reading about, whether it was 'feng-shui' for city dwellers, or second careers for baby boomers, and then dreaming, quite suddenly, about Ethan. He stood on the porch of his old house, the Victorian with the long windows. Rain fell, and the boy was out there in the water, the leather jacket

Jerry bought him at the vintage store drooping, wet.

"Jerry," he heard Talia's voice. "Are you awake?"

Jerry opened his eyes, trying to sense how long he'd been asleep. The sun wasn't in the opening anymore and the shadows lingered in the corner of the tent.

Outside the tent, he found Talia standing next to a boy. The sight of him momentarily halted Jerry's approach, but he wasn't Ethan. Even so, he could sense Talia's enthusiasm before she spoke.

"This young man's name is Jacob," Talia said evenly.

Jerry shook the boy's hand. The boy seemed shy, averting his eyes as he sipped one of Talia's special bottled waters, his neatly cut blonde hair making him look like a young Republican or a Mormon on a mission.

"He wants to tell you something," Talia said.

"I came about the email," the boy said.

"Where you from?"

"Salinas."

"I'm trying to find my son. He goes to these things. Loves music."

"The thing about that guy," the boy said. "Well, he sounds like someone I met last year."

Jerry glanced at Talia. He must have looked helpless, or stupefied. He felt that way suddenly.

"The picture, Jerry," she said.

Jerry regained his composure and dug the photo out of his pocket. He looked at it once himself, and then retrieved Talia's sketch from the workbox on the table. "This is what he looks like now, or something like it." He caught his breath and nodded at Talia, who backed off and sat down in one of the camp chairs near the Hemet girls' tent. "The photo is old."

The kid rubbed the top of the water bottle, considering

the drawing, which Jerry tried to hold still. "I saw it on the web site."

"You certain this is him?"

The kid nodded. "Last year, I'm pretty sure."

Jerry felt something like a current pass up his spine. "What about this year? Don't you guys try to come to these things all the time."

"The thing is, mister, I didn't really meet him around here."

"What do you mean?"

"This place in Sedona, in Arizona, you know." He waited for Jerry to understand, then looked imploringly at Talia.

"It's all right Jacob. You can tell us."

"For kids. Messed up ones."

Listening to the kid, Jerry felt as though the desert had risen up — the lake with it — all the serrated ripples in the small wavelets coming up around his ears, his whole body floating towards the blue sky.

"I shouldn't even really be here," the boy continued. "I'm not using, but this is what they call a low place. We're supposed to make new friends, develop new habits. It's hard."

"It might not be Ethan you met in this place?" Jerry tried to pin the kid down.

"He talked about you. How you took him places and stuff. And about the music." The boy looked at him pityingly. "Good stuff."

"What else?"

"I should be going," the boy said. He looked back over his shoulder.

"This place in Sedona? What's it called?" Jerry tried to keep his voice calm. He didn't want to scare this kid.

"The Lavender House. They come to these things, concerts and stuff, and help kids. Runaways, ones with bad parents, you know."

The boy was still glancing towards the shoreline, where a few chords from a sound check came up. When he realized what he had said, his face reddened visibly.

"It's fine," Jerry said. Fine, hell, it was no doubt true.

"My parents are cool," the boy said. "They took me back, gave me my old room. I just had to get out of there for a while. You know, I'll go back. Just had to get out."

"Was he happy — this boy you knew?"

The kid smiled, his face widening for the first time. "Oh yeah — real happy. He's was doing good when I left."

Jerry didn't know what he was feeling, just the dim beat of blood throbbing behind his ears. "You want a Coke?" he offered, his own voice sounding tinny and strange.

"I gotta go," the boy said, backing up.

Jerry kept holding the picture. Just like that they were somewhere else. He could hear Talia's voice sounding somehow far away, thanking the boy, saying something else, and all along Jerry kept thinking of Ethan, Sedona and his dream about the rain.

OVER THE sun-spirals on the hood the flat mesas became more complex and brightly tinctured, and the reddish buttes and arroyos carved into the blue-white horizon like vast empty rivers. As the vestiges of the desert gave way to the new terrain, Jerry sensed they were heading somewhere different, though there was something ironic about driving full speed towards a dry-out clinic, given where he started.

"You think it's my karma?" Jerry asked. "Him being in a New-Age halfway house? It's weird, you know. Me working at the shelter."

"Given the alternatives, I should think you'd be happy. You said yourself they all have problems. Anyway, you must have had a feeling."

"I wasn't into feeling much when I was walking the streets."

"Well look at it this way. If it is him, at least he identified his problem early."

Jerry glanced at himself in the rear-view. "I could have

told him what his problem was a long time ago," he said.

Talia tipped her tortoise glasses down. She'd been subdued, sitting silently for most of the trip, rifling through her day planner and endless magazines. She'd insisted on accompanying him, against his objections, and though he'd never tell her, he was glad for the company.

"I'm not a spiritual advisor, but shouldn't that arrow be somewhere else?"

Jerry turned to see what she was looking at. Next to the Shiva, the indicator on the glass covered heat gauge climbed steadily toward the far end of the red zone. "Mahatma told me about that," Jerry said. "Said to just pull over and wait it out."

The wide open desert had abruptly given way to drab compounds, industrial buildings, and featureless houses with high razor-wire fences. "Kingman," Jerry said. "I saw it on the map."

Talia sat on the edge of the seat. "Isn't this where that American terrorist is from? The one who blew up that building in Oklahoma? The one Gore Vidal fell in love with?"

"You wanted to come along, remember?"

She sighed. "A deal's a deal."

He pulled off the interstate, made a left turn, and wound up in some kind of abandoned housing project, full of half-built gray stucco buildings without windows or roofs. Mahatma had warned him about the heat gauge, just like he'd warned him he wasn't ready for the trip. Now this, stuck here in a defunct, broken part of America with Talia.

He drove to the end of the block and parked on the dirt near a portable office and a row of empty-looking buildings. On the other side of the parking area spread an abandoned ball field, weed-filled and missing second base.

A tired oak tree straggled near the edge as if trying to reach for clear air.

He turned off the engine, rolled down his window; Talia had barely moved.

"It's hot here in the sun. I'm going to have a cigar and walk around. You can come if you want."

"I bet they all have guns. Machine guns. I saw it on CNN. They shoot watermelons and cans for practice. Those guns are illegal in most states, the civilized ones anyway."

When he got out she leaned over and locked his door, then stretched to crank up his window. He walked around the ball field and the dead lawn, checking on her each time he passed. Twice around she remained sitting there, stubborn, her face looking pink behind the glass.

The third time he came down the road she was behind the wheel of the Jeep and idled alongside him. "Don't look at me like that. It's cooled down."

He climbed in. "You even have a license?"

"Don't be such an idiot. Of course I do. And I've never had a citation, if it's any business of yours."

She pulled the gearshift, glanced needlessly into the big side mirror, since they were still in a parking lot, then drove back onto the onramp to the interstate. Jerry sat there quietly, more or less in awe. "I'll be damned," he said. "You're pretty good."

She seemed satisfied with herself. "You could have turned the heater on," she said. "I read about it in a novel where the hero turned it on to draw the heat from the motor."

"Any other insights?"

She checked the rear-view and spoke evenly. "This is practice. You'll be riding with Ethan after this. You can't take him back to the camp and Max. I'll rent my own car."

"So that's it, then, all this way and it's over."

"Well what did you expect?"

"I don't know."

"Anyway, before we separate, there's something I want to ask you." She shrugged, her voice disapproving. "Did you really smoke dope with Ethan in that Cadillac of yours?"

Jerry cranked down his window all the way and stuck his head into the slipstream of hot air. He leaned back inside before his hat blew off. He counted backwards from ten. He couldn't believe the unending nerve of this woman. "You read my journal? That's private."

"Oh so what?" she said. "Yes, I read your journal back there. What else was I supposed to do, just sit and sweat? And if you didn't want me to look at it why did you leave it up here?" She patted the console. "You were a therapist. Surely you remember your Freud. No accidents, right? You left it there."

"At least I paid attention to him," he finally said. "Maybe not the right kind all the time, but I did pay attention. Ask Lily about your report card."

Talia's jerked the wheel a little to the right. "What are you talking about?"

"She told me about your special tours for the special kids. The weekend gatherings at your house. Between them and that lefty boyfriend of yours, you probably didn't have much time for her."

Talia reared back in her seat. "Are you truly crazy?"

"She might not be so eager to run to another country with Max if you'd given her a little time, don't you think?"

"Like smoking a number with her or whatever you druggies say."

The big tortoise-tinged glasses stared straight ahead.

She brought up one of her pale hands from the steering wheel and smoothed her hair, then pressed her fingers to her mouth for a moment.

Jerry hoped she wouldn't cry. He was starting to feel a little like a bully. "Look, there's nothing wrong with having a boyfriend," he said. "And hell, kids all complain. A blindfolded Ray Charles could see you're devoted to her."

Talia glanced at the heat-gauge as if to ignore him, touching the glass. He saw her take a little breath. "That's redundant. And I told you, he's not my boyfriend. You don't know what you're talking about."

Traffic seemed to be gathering on their side of the road. At least the sky had changed back, the wide-open space again falling around them.

"I don't know what I thought would happen," Jerry said. "Maybe he'd just pull out of it. They all smoke weed. Maybe I should have been smarter."

She sighed and he saw the anger go out of her. "I guess you were the gateway drug."

The traffic slowed. They'd gotten close enough to the obstruction to see the problem. A semi that had pulled a giant trailer was angled into the embankment, the trailer a twisted, overturned mass of splinters and broken glass, still connected to the truck. Jerry could see Talia's concern and put his hand on hers, giving a little pressure on the wheel. "Jeep's heavy to turn. Go slow."

Talia signaled and moved the wheel, following the line of cars skirting the wreckage. When they got clear, Jerry took his hand away.

"A regular car is easier," he said.

"That's good because I'll be driving a bit more." She read his confusion. "Lily's getting restless. I told her I wouldn't hover. That I'd give her a couple of days on her own. She promised to be there when I come back — It's almost a week until the next concert date."

He had almost forgotten the kids back at the camp, worrying about Ethan. He thought about the fires now, and Max and his sinister companions. He almost felt a pang of guilt for getting so quickly to the end of his road. Almost. But what about the agreement and Lily's requirement he tag along? "Lily's okay with you still hanging around?"

"Without the famous Jerry?"

"I'm just asking."

"I'm giving her space. And she'd rather deal with me than any reinforcements I'd call in."

Who was the reinforcement? Her boyfriend or her ex-husband? Not his business, he thought resolutely.

"You'll need time alone with Ethan," she said. "To get acquainted again." She glanced quickly at him, checking to see his reaction. "And you'll want to take him home directly, won't you?"

"You really are a planner."

"Well, he can't be around those disturbed children."

Jerry wondered if she included Lily.

"So that's why I've decided to rent a car. After you two meet up, I've decided I'll run up to some of those famous ruins for a day."

"The Indian ruins you never got to see?"

She gave him a self-congratulatory smile. "Exactly."

"All planned out?"

"Reservations at the Best Western."

He didn't know what to say. In a way, it made sense. And she was right about Ethan. He could hardly go hang out with Max and company. But it was going to be a long drive back across this desert alone with Ethan. Somehow Jerry hadn't pictured that.

It was almost like she could read his mind. She pulled a sheet of paper out of her date book. "You'll have a lot of things to figure out." She held up what appeared to be a list. "School. A therapist, maybe. Call his mother."

He nodded. She'd done her part and more, getting him here. The rest of it — Lily, Max, the Canada deal — it was all her business. And maybe she was right, maybe giving Lily a little space, playing it cool — if she could — was the answer. He sure didn't know.

JERRY HARDLY noticed but the earth was becoming red again. And they were climbing. Rocks and spires materialized, twisting up from the limestone earth. The place was famous for this, claimed Talia. She'd read that in her guidebook.

They were surrounded now with low, pale-toned buildings and by signs promising New-Age therapies. "Maybe I should get my palm read, see how things will turn out," Jerry said. "Or better still, get my colon cleansed."

"This is a spiritual place, Jerry. Everyone knows. Just tell me the directions."

So Talia took such hokum seriously. Who would have thought? He watched her driving, her sleeves rolled up a little on her arms, her sunglasses pushed up on her head, listening to him read the scribbled directions from her day-planner, and thought suddenly that he couldn't imagine this place without her.

The place they were headed for was called the Omstead Hotel. The woman on the phone from Lavender House had recommended it when Jerry called. He leaned back against the seat and watched her weave through the crowded lanes of traffic. "Lavender House. What kind of name is that for a dry-out clinic?" he asked her.

Talia snapped her fingers. "Hey. No negativity." She pointed to a sign. "You are the sum of your own positivity."

"Right," Jerry said. "Then I'm a flat zero."

"Not to mention that positivity is not a real word," Talia continued.

Talia pulled up in front a low-lying concrete and glass structure. "Here we are finally," she said, putting the shifter triumphantly into park. "The Omstead." She put her hands together. "Shall we *om*?

THEY AGREED to dine in a restaurant a few doors down, later, after cleaning up, though Jerry thought the establishment sounded suspiciously nouveau. She met him in the hotel lobby at the assigned time and they walked over beneath a string of decorative lights that stretched along the line of clubs and eateries, through the trees and over the road, where they gathered around a street fair of some sort, which included a small Ferris Wheel and other mechanical contraptions. Jerry thought the scene might have been festive if you forgot the circumstances.

At dinner Talia pulled apart the corners of her linen napkin and neatly placed it on her lap. Her copper earrings caught the light.

"What do you say to a peace pact," she smiled. "With luck it's our last night together."

He waved his white napkin at her. "Why don't I just surrender and save time."

"It's pretty here, don't you think?"

It was actually the sort of dining room Jerry didn't know anymore — wood and chrome tables, linen-lined chairs and butter-colored orchids. Music came from the bar, a woman's voice, soft and ethereal. Some technological instrument accompanied her, at times almost flute-like and then chiming like castanet's or small bells.

Outside the window the mineral-like lights from the local fair winked. The Ferris wheel lifted its chairs into the sky, the bulbs on the spokes churning in the darkness and stars.

The woman finished singing and the ringing back-up music started again, louder now.

"You look lost in thought," Talia said. "Not that I blame you given all that's gone on."

"Those bells in the music," Jerry said. "They remind me of something, that's all."

"Oh really?"

"This mission in Mexico. San Miguel Allende. I went there once with Ethan."

"Another blast from the past."

Jerry told her the story of the trip. It was a year or so before Ethan left. Another impetuous seat-of-the-pants excursion, this one conceived after Ethan's mere mention of the great beat icon Neil Cassidy who once famously drove the magic bus down a steep road, high on acid with no brakes. A plane ride, a rented car and God knows how many tequilas later, and there they were, he and Ethan walking along the railroad tracks where the famous traveler died.

When he finished, Talia sipped her wine. "Driving that bus like that is hardly something to brag about."

"It was different back then. He may have died, but at least he lived."

She ran her finger over the lip of her wineglass. "It may surprise you, but I know those bells, too. And I looked up at the very same spires. It's an amazing church, isn't it? Quasi-gothic."

"With some horny professor I suppose."

"Don't be silly. I went down there to look at the museum. Why would I care if some famous hippie died there? Weren't the spires something?"

Jerry shrugged. "I think Ethan might have been impressed with the place. It was all sort of lost on me. Big surprise, huh?"

She gazed out at the slow turning wheel. "There's this beautiful garden too. You probably don't remember that either."

"We counted the railroad tracks. Trying to find the exact place he went down. I remember the dirt."

She shrugged. "I'm sorry, but I still can't believe you did all those things with Ethan in tow."

She had a point. But he didn't like that she kept making it, didn't like the way she tightened her full-lipped mouth and turned away for a moment. The women he'd liked hadn't been prudes, not even Evelyn. At least not in the beginning — she'd been as wild then as any of them. But then, just as he was thinking of a smart retort, Talia turned toward him again and smiled and Jerry remembered that he probably wouldn't see her after tomorrow. She had a pretty smile, anyway.

"I already surrendered, remember," Jerry said. "Come on, it's nice night for a walk."

As they strolled along the dark highway, she dangled her purse at her waist and let her eyes drift towards the gyrating mechanical rides. "You know, you're not the only one. I struggle with some choices, too. And I know sometimes I beat a dead horse."

She stopped and scuffed her sandal in the dirt. "The

journal. I shouldn't have looked at it."

Sometimes she was nearly likeable, he thought. "Quitting booze gives you a terrible sweet tooth," he said, pointing towards the concession stands near the rides. "How about that cotton candy for dessert?"

"I'll walk over with you, but no, I don't think so."

She followed him over the sawdust to the little trailer where a woman wearing a paper hat stood behind the glass and swirled the cones in the aluminum basin. Jerry eyed the pink stuff. He thought it looked better than the small tart Talia had fooled with at dinner.

He held the cone up. "Sure?"

The perfect eye brows shot up again. "It's just cheap corn syrup and food coloring."

"Right. You and corn syrup."

"But thank you all the same."

While he ate, she wandered in the direction of the Ferris wheel, whose engine groaned evenly in the still air. The translucent blinking bulbs arced up into the stars. They watched as the operator, longhaired and cadaverous, tugged on his ponytail and gave them a look as he pulled back the lever, the long stack spewing diesel exhaust against the stars.

Jerry waved the spun sugar at her again. "Sure you don't want just a bite?"

She looked tempted for a second but then shook her head. They stood and watched the wheel turn upward.

"Never would've figured you for a carnival type," Jerry said. "I think you like it."

"I always think about taking a ride, and then I don't. And then I always wish that I had. I mean, not always. It's been years since I've been to a place like this." She laughed a little, embarrassed.

"I thought your ex specialized in theme parks. Didn't you get a few free passes in the divorce?"

"Don't be stupid. This is fun and silly. His parks are over-the-top, like theme-park pornography."

Jerry looked up at the climbing seats. He didn't really like Ferris wheels. "What do you say? It might do us both some good."

"You're serious?"

"Otherwise you might wish you had later. Right?"

As soon as the attendant clamped down the bar, Jerry regretted the impulse. He glanced at the thin cables and filaments running up the great spoke into a cluster of greasy connections. "Try not to think about the drunks and pill-heads who put it together," he said. "Or my Karma."

She shoved him with her shoulder. "This is your stupid idea."

"Another one of our famous deals."

"Shut up, will you?"

As the ride lurched forward and their little seat rose, they could feel the vibration of the engine, the rumbling of the pistons in the cylinders. It clunked upward, unsteadily. Talia moved closer to him, holding her nose at the smell of the diesel.

Slowly the town below came into view. First the glittery outlines of the lights on the rooftops of the restaurants and spirit-parlors and bars, then the larger field of houselights running into the blackness of the hills. With the moonlight, they could look onto the ebbing of the terrain and the glistening corners of some of the famous rocks. Jerry timidly lowered his chin and looked over the edge of the seat, where all the fairgoers had become small, insignificant.

"You all right?" Talia said. "It feels strange."

"When I was sixteen I smoked a bunch of weed and rode one of these with Becky Weintraub. I threw up on everybody. You should've seen them run."

"Great," Talia said, her eyes fixed on the horizon. "Another vivid memory returns."

"I had a crush on her. She couldn't run fast enough when the ride was over."

She still couldn't move her eyes. "Well, I won't run if you promise there won't be a repeat performance."

The ride arced over, gunning low and swooping back up into the sky. After the third time, Talia looped her arm through his, bunching closer. Jerry was almost getting used to the sense of helplessness and it looked like she was too, now venturing a peek over the side.

"You kind of get used to it," he said. "The weightless, helpless part." He turned slowly to get a look at her. Her face was ebullient. "You've having fun. You are. Look at you."

"Look who's talking."

They'd arrived at the top of the arc again, but this time the ride stopped, and Jerry felt the cheer drain from him, as if he'd snorted the last line or took the last gulp of scotch. Their seat swiveled and squeaked, and their legs hung heavily in the air. The motor grunted in the distance, and then stopped. The stars tilted.

Talia was looking over the side again. "That idiot operator's talking to someone waving and pointing. I think he thinks we're lovers."

"I really wish the swinging would stop," Jerry said.

"It's quite a view if you let yourself see it."

Slowly, he peeked down, his sight finally reaching the small gathering at the bottom in the dim arcade lights. Struggling to keep looking, he saw briefly two heads. One of the heads tilted and a face was looking up at them, small but clear. Before he even saw the circular shape and little rimless glasses, Jerry had a feeling what he would see. Captain Trips smiled, the side of his face and his lenses catching the light for an instant, and then waved. His body looked small, but his head, like a doll's, was large and clearly visible.

"That guy and whoever's with him is a moron," Jerry said.

"Carnie fun. They probably think it's romantic."

"They're sadistic."

Jerry felt the seat move under him. Talia was laughing, rocking the chair gently.

"I wish you wouldn't," Jerry said, holding his eyes still on the horizon.

For a second he thought of telling her about Trips, but thought the better of it. Trips didn't exist, or if he did, it was only in Jerry's own fucked up world. She said it already: two carnies having fun. When he looked down again, the attendant stood alone, now evidently engaged in a conversation with two girls, their thin bare legs prominently visible as they waited in line. Trips was gone.

"He'll start again in a minute," Talia said. "Just stay calm."

"I am calm."

"He's just playing with some bolts I think."

"Very funny."

"You're not going to vomit are you?"

"What kind of question is that for a lover?"

"See? We are having fun."

Jerry took a breath. A second later he felt calm again, his heart slowing. And the rocking had almost stopped too. "Yes."

"And we're here now — isn't that what we're supposed to be doing, according to that hippie philosophy of yours?"

He looked at her. She was right. They were in the moment, right here, right now, poised over the Harmonic Convergence in a rattletrap ride that made everything look small, even Captain Trips. Tomorrow seemed like a long ways off, almost.

DUSTY PALMS leaves and overgrown jacarandas scraped the window glass as the Jeep passed under them. The fallen branches crunched loudly under the tires and gnats buzzed outside the window.

"It looks gloomy as hell," Jerry said.

"Breathe, will you?"

"You make it sound easy."

Talia leaned forward to get a better look. "I think it's pretty, a garden of sorts."

"It's a damn rehab, Talia. No matter how the hell you dress it up."

Ahead the dark green Victorian house became visible though the overgrown vegetation. Jerry squinted past the lines of sunlight on the other side of the shadows. The house badly needed painting, the chipped siding and color under the unruly bougainvillea faded and oxidized. But it looked comfortable, a place where you'd sit in your room and watch the light play in the leaves, or sip coffee on the balcony and listen to the silence. It reminded Jerry a little of his old house and he wondered if Ethan had noticed. Somehow it made things seem better thinking that his son had perhaps ended up in a place that would feel familiar. It was strange to see green suddenly in the midst of desert.

They found a single car parked in front, a well-preserved Volvo wagon with a prominent "Practice Peace" sticker on the rear bumper. Jerry pulled in next to it, but something wasn't right. The scarcity of cars tugged at him, no kids either.

"That boy was a liar," he said. "I should have known. All addicts are liars."

Talia calmly tugged down the sun-visor and re-placed a piece of her fallen hair, which she'd gathered and clipped smoothly in the nape of her neck. She clicked up the visor and held her brown eyes on him.

"We managed the Ferris wheel, didn't we? That was pretty scary too," she said. "I'm ready if you are."

Jerry's arms and legs were heavy. "I wouldn't want to see me, if I were him."

"Will you give yourself a little credit? Anyway, you're not him."

"Credit? I'm a day late and a dollar short when it comes to being a father."

"You might've looked for him sooner. But you almost died. And you're here now."

Those words again, thought Jerry, here and now. Talia started to get out, but stopped. "Last night. I enjoyed it," she said. "And you needn't worry about me out there when this is all over. Lily's coming around."

She walked to his side of the Jeep, giving him a funny critical glance he couldn't figure out, then shook her head, tugged his cap off and tossed it through the open Jeep window. He waited for one of her rebukes, but she simply lifted her hand and pushed his hair from his eyes, her soft fingers tracing his forehead.

"Time to get your kid."

"You think there's a chance?"

"Of course I do."

She stayed close to him while they traipsed over leaves on the walk. He rapped on the oak and wrought-iron door and her proximity couldn't help make him think about the Ferris wheel ride, the stars, how everything looked so small and far away last night, not up close like this. He wanted to thank her for that, but before he could the door pulled back.

"Please come in. I've been expecting you," the woman said.

She looked to be his own age, older even, but the way her impeccably tailored pants clung to her body as she waved them inside gave her a kind of youthfulness. A diamond broach was pinned discreetly upon her lapel. With her translucent, glowing skin Jerry figured her as a wealthy vegetarian, with a propensity for high-end facials.

"You weren't much help on the phone," Jerry said.

Talia grazed his arm. "But we're so glad to be here with you now."

They followed the woman into a spacious entry room. "I'm terribly sorry I couldn't give out information," she said. "You see, it's been our policy to protect children."

Jerry chest tightened. It was that word — protect. He heard Talia saying "breathe" again, then wondered if she'd even said it.

The cavernous paneled walls that rose around them didn't have any pictures, which made the furnishings seem even more impoverished. Just a marble desk and two stuffed chairs. He thought he was prepared for the emptiness, but the still air in the vacant room was thick, hard to breath.

"Not much going on," he said.

To the right a large portal gave way to a sunroom of some kind, with plants and potted trees, but the other doors opened into what looked to be more barren rooms. Talia reached for his hand and squeezed gently. "It does seems quiet," she said.

The woman gestured toward two stuffed chairs. "Sit down, please."

Talia put her purse on the wood floor next to the chair and sat down. Jerry was about to sit too, when he heard the sound of boys — what age boys? — echoing through the open doors of the adjoining glass room. He looked into the room, dense with greenery, but saw nothing.

Then came the voices again, this time one of them lingering distinctly inside, and he was certain it belonged to Ethan.

"Excuse me," he heard himself say.

He walked over to the door and looked in to the sun lit room. Talia kept talking, lifting her eyes uneasily as he passed.

"As he told you on the phone, we're looking for his son," she said. "We've driven quite a ways and have reason to believe he's here."

Jerry heard Talia's voice drift away behind him. So this was what it feels like, he thought, tooling down the dharma highway. He was hard on the gas now, barreling straight for wherever he was headed. Just keep walking, he thought.

But the sunroom was vast, running the entire length of the house, the dense indoor plants and flowers as unruly and overgrown as the outside vegetation, a maze, blocking any clear view of the solarium. His legs felt weak. Finally, in the rear corner, he made out two young men talking behind the fronds of a potted banana plant. It was cooler here, smelling of lavender and mulch, of other plants too. By now the boys had stopped talking. The coolness stayed still enough so he could feel the blood in his arms. He brushed past a rubber plant blocking the path.

"Ethan. Is that you?"

No answer. The two figures were still now, the visible pant legs and shirts frozen as he walked towards them.

"It's me, Ethan. Dad."

With just the giant spears of the banana plant left between him and the boys, Jerry stopped and looked back. Talia was watching him from beyond the valence of light and broken shadow. Did he look as desperate as her face suggested?

When he tugged the fronds away, the two young men stared back at him. They were ordinary boys, both of them much too young to be Ethan.

He started to speak but his voice caught. Just like that he'd gone upside down into a ditch, the wheels spinning above him, gas leaking down the windows. "I'm sorry," he told them, "I'm mistaken."

Neither said anything. They watched him, their eyes holding on him before looking at one another. Without his cap, his hair fell into his eyes. The cool air was somehow warm and sweaty on his forehead and he knew at once he looked ridiculous. "Don't mind me, fellas. I'll be going back."

Talia was waiting for him in the doorway and she took his hand and walked him back into the living room, squeezing gently. The woman motioned again to the chair and sat down herself behind the desk. She dangled her reading glasses from her fingers and appraised him.

"Your water bill must cost a fortune," Jerry said,

steadying his voice. "All the plants."

The woman spoke evenly. "I just finished a biography about Nietzsche, the philosopher. Near the end of his life he saw a man beating his horse in a field. Horrible, really. All Nietzsche could do was hold the animal. It was his final act really, before madness."

"What the hell is that supposed to mean?" Jerry said.

Talia still had his hand and he could feel her gentle squeeze. The woman looked up at him.

"I'm sorry for your suffering," she said. "It must be difficult."

She put her palms together and rested them on the table and smiled at Talia. "We were just talking, your friend and I. Since my husband died and all the children are gone, I don't have much meaningful conversation. Forgive me."

"You were saying a moment ago that Ethan might have been here," Talia said.

"As I told you, our records are gone. After my husband's stroke, we cleaned the place out and sent off the children. Adolescents. Most of them were nearly young adults really."

Jerry pointed towards the sunroom. "What about those two boys?"

"My nephews." She waited and continued. "It was very difficult, but we did what we could. Even if we had the records, it probably wouldn't help. We kept that sort of thing minimal, first names you know?"

"It's all written in the stars anyway, right?" said Jerry.

"We have a photograph," Talia said, giving him a gentle nudge.

He tugged the picture from his pocket, pressing the corners flat on the marble. "We were a loving environment," the woman said. "Not as unorthodox as it seems."

She took up the picture and gazed at it thoughtfully, her eyes glistening behind her glasses. Jerry had no idea how much interest he owed on the credit Talia talked about, but the bill seemed overwhelming about now. When she finished, the woman took off her glasses and stared at him.

"I remember your son," she said.

Her voice was flat. Jerry didn't know what to say. He wondered even if he heard her right.

Talia hesitated, then shifted in her chair. "That's very good news really. It's a start, anyway."

Jerry didn't say anything still; he probably couldn't speak if he tried. He closed his eyes. More than anything, he felt grateful for Talia, for her hand on his. When he opened them the woman was narrowing her eyes at him quizzically. "You knew about his addiction issues?" she asked, sounding as though she knew the answer.

Talia glanced at Jerry. "I'm not sure…we understand."

"Ethan… yes," said the woman, her gaze turned thoughtfully for a moment to the wall. "A lovely boy. Very well read. Poetry I recall. Blake — so many of the artistic ones liked Blake."

"Poems. He writes poems," Jerry said finally, his voice wavering.

"This is strange," the woman said, and paused. "I'm remembering that we notified you. That we called you. Not me, I'd remember. But it's our policy to call and I'm sure my husband would have. Are you certain you didn't know he was here?"

Jerry could feel Talia's fingers tighten. In the next room laughter from the boys sounded like children playing in a park somewhere. Suddenly the ditch had given way, opened up into a crevasse, dark and bottomless. He closed his eyes again and tried to remember, but nothing to him came but a narrowing blackness he couldn't see through, an abyss that made his body feel weightless.

Talia stiffened. "Jerry is recovering from an accident," she explained. "He doesn't remember much from the time before. And in any case, it would have been difficult to reach him."

The woman relaxed back in her chair, taking in the words. She had the look of someone unsurprised by astonishing stories, yet still quietly surprised. Jerry felt Talia's hand again — she'd not let go.

"I see," the woman said. "That's a terrible thing."

"I was a rotten father," Jerry said. "Can you just tell me what happened here?"

The woman adjusted her wristwatch, a stainless steel model, and leaned forward. "They're so many of them," she said. "The usual — all the junk they're into. In our day it was psychotropics and pot. Today it's speed and ecstasy. Pot too, of course. Some can handle it, others can't. My husband and I spent our careers as therapists trying to provide a little light."

"But he was helped," Talia said.

"Yes, I think so. But when we closed, they all left. Some went home, others just moved on. The home life is so important."

"I see," said Talia.

Jerry could see the woman glancing at his hair, and he swept it behind his collar, a wave of self-consciousness passing over him.

"Your home situation?" she asked, her voice hesitating. "Apart from the accident."

"I'm an old hippie," Jerry said. "What can I say?"

Now her voice was measured. "And your own

experiences? With any pharmaceuticals?"

"Like I said, I'm an old hippie."

"Have you talked to anybody yourself?"

This was enough, Jerry decided. He'd dealt with deadbeat parents at the clinic and thought: Don't kid a kidder. He knew damn well what she was asking. "I'm not a dry drunk, if that's what you mean."

Talia released his hand and the woman nodded solemnly. "Well then, that's a good thing. When you find Ethan, that's a good thing."

"You can't give us any more information?" Talia said, putting her elbows on the marble counter top. "Any possible leads to where he might have gone?"

"I'm sorry, dear," the woman answered after a moment, shaking her head wearily. "It was chaos when Herbert got ill. It all ended too quickly. And as I said, we always kept everything quite confidential. Very few records. We were not a state agency."

Talia sighed, gathering up the handle of her purse. "I guess we won't trouble you further."

When they stood, the woman brightened, her face abruptly changed by a thought.

"Come with me," she said, standing. "With any luck, we'll find something I want you to have."

She led them out the front door and around the porch to where a stand of climbing rose bushes gathered against the house, their perimeter rimmed by a circle of flat shale rocks.

Jerry stood next to Talia, watching the woman search among the muddy beds, cracked and dried, hunting for something. At first it looked as if the bed of the garden brimmed with clods hardened mud, but then Jerry saw that they were shapes — dirty clay shapes the size of coffee plates.

The woman peered for a moment, then said, "Yes — here we are."

She bent carefully and pulled at one off the clay pieces, brushing the surface with her hand before presenting it to him.

The handprint was smaller than his, but the dull pressing clearly visible. The name Ethan had been scratched into the surface beneath with a stick.

"They all did them," she said. "We emphasized returning to the child within. It sounds silly, but you'd be surprised. He'll want that when you find him."

Jerry held on to the handprint.

"About the water? You're absolutely right. It is expensive. But Herbert was a romantic. He planted the gardens for me when we were first courting."

TALIA DROVE, her eyes steady on the road. They hadn't gone very far before she pulled over and parked in a tiny lot fronting the small town's first set of buildings.

"You hungry?" she said, touching the clay impression on the seat between them. "I'm not, but I thought you might be."

Jerry stared out the window, his eyes settling on a liquor store next to a donut shop a few buildings down.

"I'm trying to remember but I can't."

"You mustn't give up. Isn't that what you told me?"

"I don't know what I'm doing here."

She gazed at the road. "Yes you do. As much as I know what I'm trying to do with Lily."

"She's back at the camp. With crazy Max, but she's there."

"And Ethan's out there somewhere. We'll search every clinic, every commune if we have to. You'll find him."

He thought of all the little shacks where kids gathered, their camps by rivers, their hide-aways in old busses. "It's a hole Talia — a giant black hole. I wish I would have drowned."

"Stop it."

"Well I do."

She gave a quick turn of the key and the engine started. Reaching to the column shifter, she bumped the Jeep into gear, but kept her foot on the brake. "I want you to do something for me," she said. "I can't believe it, but I do."

THE SANITARIUM was in Los Gatos or maybe Marysville, one of those places an hour or so from San Jose, the city where Jerry's family lived before his father moved them to the brick house in the city. The ride took more than an hour, squirming on the sticky plastic seats in his mother's Bel-Air. Jerry liked it though because he got to ride in front, stretching up to see over the high dash. He was six years old.

Before his mother helped Jerry up into the seat, his father and mother fought in the living room, in the haze of his mother's cigarette smoke.

"He's your brother," his mother said. The white drapes were closed and his father paced in the dull light. "You don't have a choice."

"I'm done."

"But you can't say that, Walker."

"He's disappointed too many of us."

"It's not his fault."

"It sure as hell isn't mine."

The building's steel girders and air ducts reminded Jerry of his erector set. His mother spoke to the man in a uniform and he pointed to the tall white building with all the windows. They had drapes too.

Walking up the stairs, his mother held his hand and her voice echoed off the concrete.

"Uncle Jim is sad. But he's your sad uncle."

"Dad's brother?"

"There's a lot of sad men in your father's family." She leaned over and straightened his shirt collar. "Let's hope you don't grow up sad."

Uncle Jim held his mother's hand and smelled the flowers she'd brought. He rubbed Jerry's head and promised to take him fishing.

After that Jerry's parents never talked about the fact that his Uncle Jim was sad. Jerry remember hearing years later that Jim had died in a car wreck on Route 66, somewhere near Kansas.

Jerry forgot he had told Evelyn the story once, probably when they used to talk and take long walks through the park. After they separated he asked her why she wouldn't try and work it out, maybe go to therapy or start over. "You're all so fucking sad," she told him coldly.

THE JEEP'S old springs jostling over the rough dirt road woke him. He'd been out for a while and now the sun crept low in the window. The land was different too, the red hues deepening into brown ridges and wide mesas, still empty.

He pulled himself up, embarrassed, aware suddenly that his hat was dislodged and his shirt hiked up. He tidied himself and tugged his hat on, surprised at his self-consciousness around Talia. A roadside merchant drifted past, selling rugs and pots under a bare tent frame draped with little hanging dolls, squatting down on the dirt shoulder on Jerry's side of the car.

Talia pulled up to a hand-plastered building surrounded by dusty pickups and battered cars, old Chevy's and Fords. The last of the sun reflected brightly orange against the large windows, which had been taped halfway up on the inside with tin foil to keep the heat out.

"I heard you snoring," she said.

"Where are the hell are we?"

"A clerk at the gas station said they have the best tamales on the reservation."

THEY SAT in front, the sun only partially blocked by the cheap foil. He watched two men in cowboy hats talk over open pick-up doors in the parking lot. One of the men had a boy with him, ten or twelve with a cowboy hat too, who sat on the bumper waving his boots in the air.

While they waited for their food, Talia smiled at the fat, black-eyed children and nodded at the women bowed down with the weight of silver beading and turquoise. She tackled her meal with a gusto Jerry had not yet seen from her and chewed happily on a piece of fried bread.

"What's next, French fries and donuts?"

"Don't be silly. Anyway, I'm going native." Talia pushed an escaping lock of hair off her face.

"So to speak." Jerry turned again toward the parking lot. The boy was on the roof of the truck now, obscured by the silver strip of foil. He looked directly at Talia. "You don't have to baby sit me."

Talia sighed. "Do I need to remind you again about our

deal?"

"Fuck the deal."

"Just eat, okay? You've had a shock."

"You don't really want me along to see the damn paintings."

"I'm disregarding everything you say today. I am. But first thing tomorrow, when we get to Canyon de Chelley, I mean it. Only positivity."

Jerry'd almost forgotten. They were headed into Indian country, where Talia had come with the other professor. For what must have been the millionth time Jerry acknowledged his own foolishness. Had he really consented to this insane side-trip just to see some stick men scrawled on some old rocks? As if it mattered where he went now.

Outside one of the men lifted the boy off the roof and twirled him around before putting him into the El Camino. The car trailed a plume of dust as it bounded over the dirt road.

"Why the hell are you so big on seeing the walls?"

"I may never get this close again."

"And you're not worried about Lily?"

"I told you, she promised me that as long as I was with you she'd forgo her excursion."

"She really said that?"

"She said I was driving her crazy by hanging around all the time. Sitting up waiting for her to get back. Or hanging out with the girls."

"And Ethan? What if he turns up?" He knew it was a stupid question.

"Then we'll hear about it." Her voice had become even and reassuring, like a parent.

He sipped his coke and chewed on the end of his straw.

"I know what you're doing."

"And what's that?"

"I'm not one of your dumb ass students."

"You're a professor, a dead rock star. Whatever."

He started to tell her what she could do with her smartass observations, but she cut him off by tapping the little date window on the face of her watch, smiling broadly at one of the children sitting across the aisle in a booth. Jerry didn't have much appetite.

IT WAS dark by the time they got off the dirt road and back on the highway again. But with nightfall even the paved road seemed desolate, with very few headlights breaking up the vast envelope of darkness.

He thought about how Ethan was still out there in the blackness, about how the chances that he'd ever find him were slipping through his fingers, although Talia — true to form — had already made a list of rehab centers, and group homes, and had flooded the Internet with messages. She'd made flyers too that she insisted on handing out everywhere they stopped.

He felt weighed down by the uselessness of it all.

Talia planted herself in front of the steering wheel again, which irritated him. He felt better, certainly well enough to drive, but she wouldn't have it. They'd been driving for an hour and after numerous forks and right-hand turns on little roads, he was sure they'd very likely returned to the stretch of road where they started.

"You don't know where we are, do you?"

"The roads aren't marked. It's just so black. We could have passed it."

"Or taken the wrong one."

"It's hard to tell where we are. I can't tell one turnoff from the next." She fumbled to find the map again that lay on the seat between them.

"You're lost."

"We'll if I'm lost then you're lost too."

"There was a rest stop back a couple of miles. I think we can find it. You can have the back seat."

She took her eyes off the road and glared at him. "You're not serious?"

"Look at the gas gauge. We don't want to run out on the road. Maybe even get eaten by wolves or bears."

He didn't exactly know why he tormented her. He knew she wanted to make him feel better, to energize him somehow. He knew too that she wanted to prove something to Lily.

In the darkness of the twisting roads, Talia slowed to a crawl and it took nearly an hour to find the rest stop. Under a few dim lights, empty benches and a dog run sat next to the cinderblock rest room.

He saw her stare at the bleak building, starting to say something, and then changing her mind and biting her lip. No more smiling now. She looked tired and afraid.

While Talia took the flashlight and changed inside the small building, Jerry sat at the picnic table and had a cigar. The blue smoke hung in the sky. He didn't dare say a word to her as she scuttled past, getting into the back seat and doing whatever she had in mind to make the night bearable.

He took one last puff, then ground the cigar into the dirt and walked to the car. Neither of them spoke for a while.

"It feels cold," Talia finally said. Her voice hung in the darkness. He'd just managed to deal with the steering wheel, which wedged against his thigh, so long as he kept the back of his head still on the armrest.

"What, you never slept in a car before?"

"Excuse me if I don't have practice being a hobo."

"There's nothing to be scared about."

"I'm not scared," she said tightly.

"It's your deal," Jerry said.

She sighed. She was silent then for a long time and Jerry almost thought she'd gone to sleep when she finally spoke. "The ancients are out there."

"What are you talking about now?" He wasn't in the mood for any new age bullshit.

"The Anazazi — the old ones. They disappeared hundreds of years ago. No one knows why."

"The ones who painted on the damn walls?"

"Some people think they still are out there."

"It's just an empty sky, Talia. Close your eyes. It's late."

Jerry watched the stars glimmer. Ethan and Captain Trips were both out there somewhere too. Far away, the sounds of coyotes came up under the cricket noises and the whir of the wind grazing the scrub alongside the restrooms. Out on the road the muffler of a passing car passing droned, finally fading.

"I'm the only ancient one around here," he said, but she'd already gone to sleep.

13

HALFWAY INTO the valley, Jerry wondered what the
hell he'd signed up for. They were headed towards a place
called Canyon de Muerto — an off-shoot of the famous
Canyon de Chelley — and numerous placards warned of
something called the Hantavirus, some sort of rodent-born
death sentence, which struck Jerry as more than ominous.
The radiant slants of sunlight, initially striping sections of
the smooth rock, gave way to dull shadows, and thick black
clouds loomed overhead at the edges of the receding
canyon walls.

Hightower, their Navajo guide, was a lanky man who
seemed to take pleasure in striding ahead. His gray ponytail
and long Bowie knife swayed rhythmically with each step
over the uneven terrain. Jerry had offered him a cigar as
they started into the valley, hoping to slow him down, but it
didn't seem to help. Hightower puffed away, with Talia
following determinedly behind.

Jerry should have known it would be a forced march.
Back in the parking lot, Hightower had spotted Jerry and

Talia readying their packs alongside the Jeep. The hike down required official guides, and Talia had been reading a flyer about the rule, squinting her eyes when Hightower approached them. "Hey old man. You've been gone for a while," he said to Jerry. "You can come with me into the valley, if you keep up."

"We need an official guide," Talia said.

"I'm a genuine, made in the USA Indian," Hightower told Talia, when she asked him about his qualifications. "My people own this place."

"I want to see the drawings," Talia had said.

"But can you really see?" Hightower's voice was nearly mocking.

With his chiseled nose and flat green-gray eyes, Hightower had the fierce but amused look of some of the Indians Jerry remembered hanging around Haight after the Vietnam War, before they all went back to the reservations to learn about the old ways.

When the bottom of the valley finally came into view, the salty humidity rose up with the sweet smell of the old earth. They could see parts of the stream snake towards reeds and an open swatch of sand and gravel.

"We got a garden down here," Hightower said. "Sounds like bullshit, but it's kind of sacred."

"I can almost feel it," Talia said.

"A little herb might go a long way in that direction," he said to Jerry, grinning.

Jerry didn't have the energy to disabuse Hightower. Besides, he liked him. Hightower winced towards the sky and tugged on some water from a bottle, telling them to drink up too. Jerry hadn't noticed until now that the clouds had deepened, a thick knot above the jagged ridges marking the plateau.

"Coyote may wash things away today," the guide said. "Better drink up so we can get a move on."

Talia's voice tightened. "Flooding? Are we in trouble?"

"Aren't we always," Hightower said to Jerry.

As if I don't have enough to think about, thought Jerry. Now Coyote and the goddamn rain. It occurred to him that since driving into the Southwest, his life was cursed by Indians of all stripes and the vast realm of the unseen. He figured he should blame Mahatma for this at least.

As they plodded through the thin water, Talia tried to step from sandbar to sandbar, but water eventually spilled over her shoelaces. Jerry waited for a gasp, but none came. Progress of sorts.

The riverbed opened up around the next bend and they came to a cluster of tourists huddled around a stand of vegetation closer to the cliffs. Hightower looked exasperated, then dropped his pack and reached for the big knife.

Jerry and Talia watched as Hightower marched over, pushed back the crowd and knelt down at a cluster of thorny vines. He lifted the knife theatrically, causing murmurs, then cut off something and pulled it up, a squash or pumpkin, from the looks of it.

The guide in charge of the group laughed a little uncomfortably, but a couple of the tourists looked horrified. An elderly lady, with one of the dolls that Jerry saw for sale back on the road, nearly tripped as she moved quickly out of Hightower's way.

Hightower holstered his knife and started back. "This here's a family garden," he said. "I wouldn't touch it if it weren't mine." He handed Talia the squash.

"My offering," he said to her, grinning, almost bowing. "Left-over. Last of the season."

"Why the honor?"

Hightower was plodding again. "Maybe because you're an artist." Then he winked at Jerry. "Or because you're making time with a minor God."

Jerry shook his head again, but couldn't help being slightly pleased at Talia's discomfort. Her cheeks had reddened, the way they did when she was about to launch into a lecture, but she sighed and kept walking.

"Besides," Hightower called back. "We don't get beautiful ladies down here every day."

Jerry figured there was no point in trying to correct the man's misconceptions. Anyway, he didn't really care. Jerry figured he had his own problems and he walked with his head down, not noticing that Hightower had stopped ahead until Jerry nearly ran into Talia.

She was gazing upwards to the rising cliff. Amid the gentle striations on the greasy rock face, the pictures loomed clearly. A couple of four legged creatures, the clouds, the sun, and what looked like a little man at the center. Talia couldn't take her eyes away, stepping slowly back in wonder.

"Kind of blows you away, huh?" Hightower said, glancing up.

"Where did they go?" Talia asked. "Some people say they just disappeared — the older tribes."

Hightower set his pack down. "They're here," he said, smirking. "They're the old ones. You just need to know how to look. Right Jerry?"

"Whatever you say."

"What about that little man? What does he mean?"

Hightower squinted up at the picture. Jerry reluctantly looked again, this time noticing the little stick figure's resemblance to the Captain. He dropped his eyes and dismissed the idea as a symptom of his own pathology.

"Maybe you should draw him," Hightower said. "It might speak to you."

But Hightower became distracted. On the other side of the valley, in the direction of the garden, one of the yellow Humvees filled with tourists plodded over the sand, its tires kicking up dirt. The driver had his arm out the window, waving at Hightower

"Something's up," Hightower said, heading off. "Give me a second."

Jerry pulled his pack off and sat down, while Talia continued to stare, transfixed, at the drawings.

"Hell, I could draw it," Jerry said, failing to check his irritation.

"Stop it."

"Yeah. Well, I could."

"That's what people said about Picasso and Jackson Pollock. Just try it if you're so smart."

"Drink your water," said Jerry, handing her a bottle. She sipped, still looking up. Jerry could only think about all the coed tits and ass the wall must have brought her old professor. The stick figure was something sacred all right.

By the time Hightower got back, the skies had opened up. Rainwater sluiced off the edge of the cliff above, the veil of drops making it hard to see.

"Coyote's pissed," he said, blinking towards the skies. "The yahoos said they'd come back and get us, but I told them I'd take you."

"Take us where?" Talia said. She had pulled her sweatshirt up over her head and was trying to shield herself from the rain by hunching under a feeble looking tree. She didn't look happy.

"I live here, remember?"

"Here?" Talia peered into one of the caves with alarm.

"I got a trailer on top. Let's get a move on."

The hike didn't take as long as Jerry thought it would. Hightower led them through a series of narrow pitches, over-flowing with muddy rainwater, paths that Jerry didn't really see until they were in them, some secret route probably ancient. On the steeper slopes, where the thick mud made it slippery, Hightower held out his hand to Talia and pulled her up. He let Jerry struggle upward on his own, and twice Jerry stumbled and swore, thinking he was going to slide down the canyon wall.

When they got to the top, the deep shelf of clouds loomed as far as they could see over the plateau and valley. Hightower had brought them up the other side and they could look back down into the labyrinth of watery canyons, with the muddy stream swelling below. They were miles from the parking lot, and they were soaking. The pathways and car tracks ran with red water.

"This was your idea," Jerry whispered to Talia.

She wiped her cheek with the back of her hand, her jaw tense. "You're the one with the stupid Dharma, or whatever you call it."

Jerry wanted to argue, but knew she was right. She was always right. Besides, her cheek was rubbed red.

"Come on," Hightower yelled, waving them forward. "Got to get out of this gully. Then we're home free."

The trailer, when they got there, was skinned with aluminum like the ones the old astronauts had to stay in before they were allowed to go home. It sat on the edge of what looked like cropland of some sort. Hightower led them towards it, arriving at a barbed wire fence, which he lifted for them to cross under.

"We don't use her much," Hightower said, as they got to

it. He glanced to the far end of the rain swept field, where a large wood ranch house lingered in the distance. "Me and the old lady come out here to get away from the kids. Some wild times."

Inside Jerry and Talia stood dripping, a puddle forming under them, while Hightower disappeared into the front cabin, returning with a pile of clothes bunched under his arms. He tossed them on the dinette.

"Got some games in one of those closets over there. Get dry — it could be a while. No one's going anywhere in this."

Talia's face was incredulous. "You're going to leave?"

"Kind of romantic," Hightower said, bending to give a look out the little window.

"Thanks for the hospitality," Jerry said.

"One for old times, right man?"

Before the door shut, Hightower thought of something and yelled through the rain. "Got some beer in the fridge. Some Chablis in there too."

They changed into dry clothes and sat quietly at the dinette, Talia shivering still and brooding, her hair a glossy tangle. Without sunscreen or a hint of make-up, she looked younger, the contours of her face iridescent.

Jerry went to the little fridge and poured her a glass of wine. He slid it in front of her. "I'm learning if you don't have a solid destination, you can end up anywhere."

Talia glared at the glass. "Any other mystical revelations? To go with the cheap wine?"

"I was thinking maybe we should play a game."

"Did you get into the wine yourself over there?"

Jerry opened a few of the little closets, finally coming to a shelf filled with disheveled games. He found a box he recognized. He remembered playing the game with Ethan when he was a boy, a dice game with a candy cane road and bad sticky stuff you tried to get around.

Talia winced as he spread out the board on the table and handed her the dice. "See where the magic road takes you?" he said.

"Why do I get the feeling you're enjoying this?"
The rain pounded on the metal roof. "You think we're safe?" Talia asked.

Jerry peered out the window and looked out. He could hear the water rushing along the ground. "Sure," he said. "Just a little rain."

Sipping her wine, Talia reluctantly spilled the dice on the table. They'd played for a half hour when Hightower pounded on the door.

Jerry held the door open, the rain sheeting down around Hightower. He was sheeted in a black plastic windbreak. Jerry leaned forward into the rain.

"Gotta stay 'til tomorrow man. Road's flooded."

With the door open the rain was so loud Jerry could barely hear him. He turned and quickly read Talia's glare. "She wants to know if we're safe."

"Man, you know I wouldn't let anything happen to you and your lady." Hightower reached through the falling water and patted the trailer. "You're fine. Right as rain." He winked in the dark. "Have fun, kids."
Hightower waded back toward the house.

Jerry closed the door and came back inside. His face was wet and he picked up a towel. "Says we have to wait until tomorrow."

"I can't believe this." Talia looked stricken.

Jerry took her glass and poured some more wine, batting around the idea that Hightower probably had a stash hidden somewhere in the trailer as well. Bet the Indians know how to grow some dope, he thought. Talia's hands hadn't moved and he put the glass back into them.

"It's damn near dark, and it's a swimming pool out there. Flooding. We're stuck here," he said. "I'll bed down here, near the table. You can have the room up front. You want to finish the game?"

Talia's eyelids lifted. "Go to sleep and not reach the end of Candy Land?" She shook her head and sipped. Jerry took it as a good sign.

Jerry had found a can of Dinty Moore and a box of crackers in the cupboard. After Candy Land they switched to Hearts. Around nine o'clock he heated up the food. Then they switched to Gin Rummy.

"Did you play cards as a kid?" Jerry asked, mostly to make conversation. "Too busy being the smartest girl in the class?"

She shook her head, "I don't think so." She made a face at him then.

Later, lying on the hard, linoleum floor, Jerry listened to the rain, which went on unabated. Talia had retired quietly, the wine working to settle her nerves. She even gloated when she won. "Next time I'll teach you poker," Jerry had promised.

From the direction of Hightower's house, he could hear dogs barking, their yowls keeping pace between the claps of thunder. He thought about the poor animal he'd hit back on the road, feeling a hollowness inside.

Talia's voice behind the little door sounded faint over the rain. He pulled off his blanket.

In the little room, with no more than a bed really, the kitchen nook turned into a mattress, a small nightlight burned in the corner. Talia had the blankets around her, her face peering out of the canopy of dim light.

"It's too hard on the floor," she said. "And cold. There's plenty of room."

"It's just dogs."

"I know what they are."

Her body felt warm beside him, almost too hot. He still had on his Levis and had a hard time tugging the blankets over the cloth. He couldn't see, but figured she still had her clothes on too. He lay quietly, his face up like hers, pondering the lightening flashes outside the window as the thunder sent shudders into the frame under the mattress.

"Sorry if I smell like a cigar," he said, feeling awkward.

"I don't mind."

"This is sort of weird."

"Yeah."

"I can't remember the last time I slept next to someone — a woman, I mean."

"I guess what you did with the little girl, wouldn't be called sleeping."

"Yeah."

"You really think it was stupid?"

"The girl?"

"No. My wanting to come here. Just to look up at a wall?"

"You smell like roses."

At first her lips didn't move and he instantly thought, shouldn't they move? But then the wetness parted and she was kissing him back. Just like that, the car had veered into the darkness, leaving the road, not falling downward, but hurling into space.

"You sure about this?" he managed.

"I'm not sure about anything," she said softly, but kept kissing him.

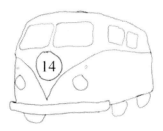

14

THEY'D MANAGED to drive for a long time without talking about what happened in the trailer. As awkward silences went, he'd had worse. What was there to say anyway?

He sat up straighter, straining to hold his gaze on the highway. He watched Talia in the driver's seat again, wondering if she was really as confident as she looked. It was still raining.

"You got this?" he asked.

Talia's hands gripped the wheel evenly and she pressed the accelerator. "I'm fine, really."

I'm not fine, he thought, really.

In another minute or two they were on the other side of the cloud burst and it felt as if they'd pushed into a resplendent region of clear earth and sunshine. Jerry sat back again, running his eyes over the country, puzzled at how different it looked going back.

Talia studied the asphalt road, running thick as glue beneath them. The wipers cut clear swatches on the glass, and through the clean spaces Jerry could make out the weeping, dark line of clouds that blurred the horizon. Talia didn't seem to care about the rain today.

He wondered if her new-found confidence had something to do with what happened, or if it was all bluff, the way she'd act around an infatuated student who got the courage up during office hours to touch her remote and tender hand.

But of course he'd more than touched her hand. He'd touched her soul, or whatever bullshit the poets called it. He couldn't stop thinking about her skin, the rose scent that hung in the air all night, her breasts and the way she was so, well, present.

With Evelyn it had been different. Wherever she went when they made love, it was somewhere else, as if she'd slipped out the screen door and returned for the big finish, the wild black eyes and stiff spine, the obligatory "I love you" before the long toke on a mellow joint, before sleep.

Just thinking about it, Jerry felt a spasm swell under the bridge of his nose. He looked at his shoes, hoping to ride the feeling out. In meetings the old timers always went on about a year. A year this. A year that. For God's sake, whatever you do, a year before a woman. Not counting Katie, who hardly counted, it had been more than a year.

"I want to see them," Talia said. "It looks fun."

Confused, Jerry looked up to see they'd pulled into some sort of roadside emporium, an old gas station flanked by wooden-frames draped with chicken wire and glass. A little wooden sign hung down from one in the front: Reptiles.

"The canyon walls I get," he said. "But, I never figured you for white-trash stuff."

"Lily had a chameleon once," she said. "They grow on

you."

"Jesus."

They got out and walked towards the enclosures. Apparently there was no fee to see such an auspicious collection. The owner, or manager, or whoever he was, sat in a webbed chair with a crossword and bottle of beer, and waved them past. With his bald and sun burned head, the man looked a little to Jerry like a lizard himself.

"You get what you pay for," Jerry warned.

The old cages were tilted here and there on the dirt, with a few perched on picnic tables and rusted drums. Jerry felt for the creatures as yet unseen, shanghaied by the coot and boxed up out here. Watching Talia wade among the rusty cages, Jerry knew that she must have preferred the musty walk to a conversation about last night. Jerry figured she was right. Better to contemplate sun-bitten reptiles.

Talia gazed into the rain-wet, chicken-wire containers as if she were shopping for jewelry. Most of the cages were empty, filled only with broken twigs and rocks, and desiccated feces. Eventually Talia stopped, lowering her sunglasses. When Jerry got to her he saw that she was inspecting a turtle on whose shell someone had painted a peace sign with red nail polish.

Talia was amused, "One of your compatriots."

Jerry looked away and stepped back. Behind Talia, storm clouds formed a solid line back in the direction they came, thick enough to cut. The gloominess was powerful. Soon they'd be back at Sedona, then back on the trail for Ethan.

"So are we going to talk about it, or what?" he said. The words sounded stiff and distant. Just saying them made his temples throb.

"Let's just leave it alone for right now." Talia inspected

another cage. "I'm beat and so are you. It's best to talk about serious things when you're rested, don't you think?"

Jerry kicked a rusted can near his foot, wishing he had a cigar. Talia turned away, running her finger over the mesh of the turtle cage, hooking her sun glasses over her collar. He tried to figure if she were being coy or covering for some sort of revulsion, which was more likely, but he honestly couldn't tell. Plus, his objectivity-meter was dialed down to about zero.

He cleared his throat. "We should probably say something."

"It's really never good to discuss these things when you're worn out."

"So you regret it?" He couldn't believe he sounded so stilted and stupid.

"I know you want me to be horrified," she said. "That's my hunch. That you'd feel better if I was sorry. But the truth is, I don't know what to think."

Jerry took his hat off, wiped his forehead, and felt something desperate moving through his whole body. Even with Evelyn, he hadn't felt this. "I'm kind of working without a net here."

"Some trip, huh? My girlfriends back at school won't believe it."

Jerry could see the hint of a smile. The rain had made her hair more curly. She looked like Lily — like a smart aleck kid who knows she's got you.

"I couldn't brush my teeth or read a paper when I got sober," he said. "I'm up to the comics now. I even floss."

"Why do I get the feeling that this is your way of asking about how it was?" She smiled a bit more.

"What I'm saying is it's been a long time and it's like starting all over again."

She fiddled with her glasses and finally gave him a hard look. "Except for that other girl."

He'd almost forgotten and all at once lost his nerve, or whatever electricity was pulsing through his arms and legs. Suddenly he felt weak, stupid.

She moved away toward another row of cages. "I have an idea," she said. Her voice was mercurial again, almost sly.

An idea again. "Get a drink?"

"You're hopeless. Keep an eye on the geezer."

Jerry gave her a quizzical look, then dutifully turned towards the old man who still held his newspaper. A bottle of beer sat on the armrest beside him. Before Jerry could stop her, Talia yanked open the lid of nearest the cage, grabbed up the turtle, and buried it under her sweatshirt.

In the Jeep she unraveled the pathetic creature and set him on the seat between them. She sat in the passenger seat now and Jerry drove, glancing with disbelief at the shell and the little peace sign.

"Didn't know you were a liberation terrorist," he said. "You could go to work for Max."

"It's criminal. He should be free."

"Wait till I tell Lily her mom's an anarchist."

They drove for a couple of miles, the turtle and everything else between them, surrounded by the wide desert and its silence. In spite of this momentary diversion, Jerry's heaviness still lingered. When he pulled onto the gravel shoulder, a truck swept past, sending a wave of wet dirt. But mostly the road was still, the rain stopped except for occasional dripping. They waited for the glinting rear panels of the truck to grow dull and small before Jerry got out.

Twenty feet in front of the Jeep he set the animal down

in the gravel along the road. It sat by his feet, inert as a flat chunk of rock, but then slowly its wrinkled head emerged.

In the second or two that it took him to get back in the Jeep, Talia had become frantic. She'd risen up, pointing.

Jerry turned and saw that the turtle was already in the road, halfway to the yellow line at the center. He jogged, snatching it up just before a car horn blared and cruised past, the driver flipping Jerry the bird above the dash.

This time he traipsed into the ankle-high scrub and sticker bushes, setting the wretched creature in a coarse thicket away from the highway. When he got back, he and Talia sat quietly, watching. Sure enough, the turtle waddled slowly towards the road.

"I guess he doesn't want the good life," Jerry said.

Talia clearly didn't appreciate his attitude. She reached back and pinned her loose hair into a bun. The corners of her mouth turned down and she was no longer the prankster who had stolen a turtle. As quickly as that, the charm had gone out of the adventure, and whatever they'd shared had evaporated in the desert air.

"Maybe he needs some kind of cultural training, a chairman Mao camp or something."

Talia shook her head, and gazed out the window. "Just drive, okay?"

"I could try again."

"It's stupid. We're almost back anyway, aren't we?"

"And the other thing?" He waited, listening to the metal ticking under the hood. Her voice was as distant as the horizon out the front.

"I told you, I really don't think we should talk about it just now."

The earth started to look red around them again. They were almost back to Sedona.

IT WAS night by the time Jerry sat down at the bar, and from his stool it didn't look like Jupiter would have a chance to align with Mars, not even close. The light was dim, but from what Jerry could see, the mechanical arm near the ceiling was screwed up. The drooping arm held a model of a sagging planet Earth that fell somewhere below Pluto. The globe was a battered sphere that barely hung above the heads of those on the dance floor, a harbinger of destruction like some doomed earthbound comet.

The establishment was called the Astral Plane. The first lights Jerry saw after he walked away from the Sedona hotel, and away from Talia too, were the beckoning lights of the bar. Out the window the night sky had cleared and was replete with stars, real ones, not like the fake splotches of neon paint and glitter that loomed around him in the bar. "Welcome to our planetarium," the hostess had said when Jerry walked in.

He was sitting on a chrome stool, with his hands around a cold glass of club soda. The inky wallpaper depressed him, or would have if it was possible for him to feel worse. It was a papered-over sham of a universe.

He heard Talia's voice again, as she stood at the door of her room. "I'm sorry you want me to say something about us. About what happened. I can't. Not right now."

On stage a trio of retreads played what they called cool-jazz, elevator music with no hard edges. Lily would love this he thought, conjuring up her sarcastic sneer. Even Max was better than this. He might be an asshole but at least Max was real.

Jerry was minding his own business, when he sensed a murmur coming back off the dance floor in his direction.

The guitarist at the mike, an anorexic looking fellow with wispy hair extensions and a French beret, was saying something to the crowd. Suddenly Jerry felt the glare of the spotlight and found himself in a glow of tinsel light emanating from somewhere around Mars. "Let's just say we're in the land of miracles," the guitarist said into the microphone. "Enough said."

Mercifully the spotlight overhead dimmed and Jerry huddled over his drink.

A middle-aged woman, swirling a drink with an umbrella sat down next to him. "You alone?" the woman said, sounding like she'd seen too many bad movies. "They want you to sing," she whispered.

"Bar Keep," Jerry heard himself say.

At the shelter Jerry had listened to all sorts of drunks and addicts talk about falling of the wagon, their stories filled with lurid details about the first drink tasting like a continuation of the last, no matter how long before, and that they'd jumped back onto the cart and found the exact same seat they had before. He didn't know if they were right, but for the first time in a long time he started to feel like himself.

He was through his third glass of scotch before he spoke to the woman.

"Any idiot can see it's all wrong." He pointed at the paper-mache planets.

"Excuse me, darling?" She put her hand on Jerry's arm.

He pointed toward the mobile. "The goddamn cosmos. A retard would know."

He noticed how shiny the fabric of her dress was, as she moved away from him in the darkness. Now the guitarist with the too obvious hair extensions was bending into view, his face catching the light in Jerry's glass tumbler. Jerry saw that his glass was dangerously close to empty, and he banged on the table a little to alert the bartender. He hoped the man with the bad hair would go away, but the guitarist lingered, staring.

"Look asshole," Jerry said, "I'm not the rock star, so go play that shit you're parents paid for with all those afternoon lessons. Got it?"

"You don't remember, do you?"

The way the guitarist bent over his glass of cheap Chablis reminded Jerry of an old lady at a brunch. "I don't remember a lot of things, sport."

"The sessions down at McCellroy's joint, back when? You don't remember? I did a session with you. We rocked."

"How much they charge for that hair," Jerry said. "Isn't it a fire hazard?"

"You're bitter, old friend."

"Pound sand, Frenchy."

The guitarist went away, or at least he seemed to fade into the haze. The bar-keep brought him another drink, and Jerry started to like the place.

But at some point the room got smaller, the dark ceilings closing in around Jerry as if a storm door were being shut down over the stars. There'd been no news about Ethan, and Talia was somewhere else, both of them locked out behind the thick wood of the bar.

The music, if you could call it that, started up again, and Jerry squinted toward the stage. It looked blurry, a spangle of blinding lights and electronic distorted words coming from the tower of speakers.

He heard laughter, someone saying, "We don't want you around anymore anyway."

He held still, trying to see who was talking, but all he could see were a swarm of glistening faces. Were they leering?

"Messing with a little piece of heaven," the beret seemed to say. "Go back under a rock, Mr. Big Shot."

Jerry turned back to his drink and took a slug of scotch, wondering if he'd heard correctly. Something hot welled up in his chest. Before he knew it, he'd waded into the crowd, his numb hands clutching the replica of the planet Earth. In a moment of lucidity he marveled at its fragile surface and improbable lightness. A cheap thing, he thought, all paper and glue.

THE INDUSTRIAL tile was hard and cold on the back of his head, and the odor of ammonia stung his nose as he breathed. His right nostril didn't seem to work either. Pulling himself up off the floor, Jerry let his eyes wander over the place. He'd seen worse.

The Soma station, for one, over on Bryant, before the gangs took over. Almost everyone in there seemed to be sleeping off a jones, cranky, waving fists over a pack of cigarettes, bodies twitching on the hard metal benches. And there was a psychiatric joint somewhere; he remembered that one too, with its blue and yellow Miami colors on the outside, but the inside was grim concrete and dull whitewashed walls.

In fact, Jerry saw that wherever he'd ended up this time, was close to pleasant, kind of like the day care center where he used to take Ethan.

As near as he could tell, the color of the walls above the scrub-worn, stainless-steel toilet were a Romper-Room blue. Blue was a good shade, he thought, a pastel hue, meant to soothe the nerves and instill lethargy among the doomed.

He lay still, waiting for the therapeutic color to take hold. Back in grad school he'd read about the effect of color on the addle-brained, but then he'd also read about the newfangled treatments for dipsomaniacs and degenerate dope fiends too. Fat chance, he thought. Better probably to go out a four-story window or jump from the Golden Gate, like some of his friends had.

"Some coffee?"

Jerry felt a nerve in his neck catch as he turned. He expected to see someone older.

The kid wore a pristine uniform with tight creases, as if he were a Cub Scout who had just pulled his uniform from a clean package provided by his mother.

He sat at a desk on the other side of the bars, tapping a pencil on the phone with fingers that probably never held a razor, or a drink.

"I got a kid older than you," Jerry said. Just saying it tugged at him.

"Coffee's fine today. And we got the flavored powder stuff for cream. Hazelnut's pretty good."

"No thanks."

"You got in a bad one."

A bad one, thought Jerry. You could say that again any way you cut it. But he had no clue what the kid was babbling on about.

"A fight," the Boy Scout finally explained. "And other stuff."

Jerry didn't hear anything judgmental in the kid's voice — nothing like the tone of the two Mormon boys with ties and matching glasses who always showed up at his door at the house on Haight Street and lectured him on knowing

Jesus.

"You don't remember, huh?"

The boy rose and stood on the other side, up close against the bars, his cheeks red with acne and his breath smelling of spearmint gum. The spearmint breath brought back the belligerent bartender and the thin-shouldered aging musician and his imitation jazz.

"I've been dragged kicking from better establishments." Jerry tried to sound tough but it was a failure. After all his good intentions he'd been locked up again. He didn't even know where he was. He gingerly rubbed the sore place on the bridge of his nose. Lucky thing it wasn't broken at least.

"Not in a bar or anything. Actually Sergeant Kowalski arrested you in the cemetery over on Beardsley."

"A cemetery?"

The boy ambled back to his desk and consulted the report. He read slowly, lifting his brows, as if sounding out the words to himself, Jerry figured.

"Says you went crazy."

"That's what it says?"

Down the hall Jerry heard one of the metal hinges creak. The boy glanced down the corridor as if he expected someone, then back. "You were sort of sparring with yourself," the kid said. He peeked at the paper again. "Then you got into it with Walt Steadman, the night man."

"Another fight?"

"Walt said you were talking to someone near the headstones."

"Jesus."

"No sir, not Jesus. Someone named Mr. Trips. You can't blame old Walt. He felt sorry for you. Thought maybe it was a relation."

"Sure hope I didn't hurt old Walt."

"No, sir, you couldn't hurt old Walt. It was you that could've been injured. Walt runs a tow-truck and changes tires all day. Says he used his shovel on you. You slept all night after he whacked you."

Jerry hung on to the bars and then slumped back on the steel bench, "Perfect."

The kid sat up stiffly and nodded at someone who walked in through the outer door. Jerry heard him stammer out a greeting.

The middle-aged officer was more like what Jerry expected, as wide as the cell-door. He scratched his sideburns, gray where his dye job had faded. "Thanks, Kyle. I'll take it from here."

The boy stared for a minute more and then went out through the double-doors. Keys hung out of the officer's pocket. He shook his head and opened the lock. "We're going to pretend this never happened, fellah."

"You're letting me out?"

"Not all of us are storm-troopers like you think."

Jerry stood up, his legs wobbly. No point in looking a gift horse in the mouth.

"Listen, man. It's a disease." The officer held Jerry's coat. "And you've been through some tough stuff." He ushered Jerry down a long corridor. "They hold meetings up and down the street in this town," the man said. "You know. A.A. Even the star-gazers and guru types go."

Talia stood in the small processing room, across from a desk.

Dressed smartly in a black shirt and pants, she snapped the latch shut on her purse as Jerry walked into the room.

She gathered the pink papers from the countertop and turned toward Jerry. "We'll talk in the car," she said and then walked out.

Things kept getting better and better.

"She's quite an advocate." The officer cleared his throat. "The thing about your son is tough. But man, you got to pull yourself together." The officer kept his eyes on Talia's backside as she went back out the door.

The officer kept talking, telling Jerry how hard times just show our true metal, continuing even when Jerry shook hands silently with him and followed Talia into the clean air outside. He saw the light turning brightly on the hard facets of the surrounding rocks and spires.

Jerry sat down in the passenger seat, head still spinning. "So are we going to talk?"

"I don't talk to drunks, Jerry. Not Max or Lily — and certainly not you." She jerked her head, indicating Jerry should take the back seat. He got out and then climbed into the back, noticing his bags sitting neatly next to hers in the rear hold.

He pulled the door shut and the Jeep clunked forward. "I had a bad night. It happens."

"So it would seem." Her posture was ramrod straight and she didn't meet his eyes in the rear view mirror.

He tried to sound normal, conversational. "So what's the news?"

"I spoke with Amber. Lily's nowhere to be found. The girls were quite concerned. They were looking for her." She looked over at Jerry then. "I didn't have the heart to tell them about Ethan."

"Lily gave her word. She'll be around."

Talia pulled into traffic, heading under an overhang of rock that blocked out the sun. The closeness and the hum of the engine filled his head.

"She gave her word," he said again, leaning his head down on the backrest. The coarse stitching hurt his cheek.

"You gave your word too." She ignored him then and Jerry slumped back into a bumpy half sleep.

AT A gas station Talia strolled back to the Jeep, sipping from a bottle of cranberry juice. Jerry had gotten up and clambered into the front seat. His head felt swollen. He squinted into the light. Even in his state, he detected an ominous resolve in Talia's crisp steps.

She pulled the sun-visor down as the Jeep left the shade of the overhang and looked at him askance. "One day at a time," she said, curling her lip a little "Right?"

He knew he had it coming, whatever it was that she was going to say. He was vaguely aware too now of his body odor and the bitter stench of booze in his shirt. He rolled down his window and closed his eyes, letting the sun warm his cheeks. But his head still pounded.

"The kid said I gave as good as I got," he said, the words out of his mouth before he stopped them. He winced before he finished speaking. Stupid, he thought. Really stupid. But he couldn't stop himself.

"I'm sure he was impressed."

"I said I was sorry."

"For God's sake, Jerry. You sound like Lily. I don't care."

Her words felt like they hung in the cab, hovering over the sound of the tires whirring on the highway. The hills widened, Lake Havasu somewhere ahead in the hidden declivity on the other side of the burnt earth.

"What about us?" he asked her.

"One out of control teenager is enough, wouldn't you say?"

"You're relieved."

She stared at him. "Excuse me?"

"I can hear it, Talia. You're off the hook. Don't have to deal with it now."

"It seems to me you're the one not dealing with anything," she said.

"You have an excuse now. Break it off before you feel anything." He stared at her. She even looked like an ice-queen.

"And what about Ethan? How can you help yourself?"

"My head doesn't hurt enough, is that it?"

"Poor Jerry," she said, her lips pursed.

They pulled into the long dirt road heading towards the gate. The concert was over and the swinging doors unmanned. When the water came into view, the charred hull of the burnt-up houseboat rocked quietly alongside the dock.

Jerry sat up straight. Talia's expression hardened, her eyes fixed on the disbanding campsites. In the distance, alongside a couple of flattened tents, the Valiant sat alone.

"Oh God," Talia managed.

"She's around, okay."

She steered carefully over the ruts, taking her eyes off the road long enough to glare at him. "Just don't," she said. Her voice was short.

"What are you saying?"

She hesitated. "I think we should go our separate ways, Jerry."

"I stumbled, Talia. It happens, you know?"

"This isn't working."

"So that's it? Just walk away?" He felt his heart in his chest again and started to say something more when he caught another whiff of his shirt. It's a disadvantage, he thought, to argue with a woman while smelling of vomit.

He started to say something and then gave up. The hell with her too.

"Just don't upset the girls. Can you do that at least?" She wiped her face with her sleeve.

They'd arrived alongside the Valiant. Amber and Jenny were folding up their tent and they stopped and stood up when they heard the Jeep stop.

"She's gone," Talia said, shaking her head, getting out. "Isn't she?"

The Hemet girls were dressed in white pullovers, and dirt-stains covered the bottoms where their knees had been on the dirt.

Jenny got to Talia first, giving her a big hug. She hugged Jerry too, who grew suddenly self-conscious about his own disheveled appearance, let alone the stench.

Talia stood head bowed, hands pressed to her face. Dark was setting in again. "I should never have left her."

Jerry wanted to say something to her then.

"I knew better."

"She promised," Jenny said.

Amber came close and put her arms around Talia. "She said she'd meet us at the next stop."

Talia rested her face on Amber's shoulder for a moment before releasing her.

"It'll be O.K." Amber kept hold of one of Talia's hands.

Jenny looked up at Jerry. "Did you find Ethan at least?"

Jerry looked out at the boat. A man stood on the deck, tearing off a piece of charred lumber, tossing it onto a pile on the dock.

"No," Jerry said.

Talia sighed, and then shook her head at Jerry.

"Got room for one more in the car?" Talia said, addressing Jenny.

The girl looked confused, her eyes searching out some answer first from her sister and then from Jerry. He lifted his brows.

"I'll get the bags," he said.

"You sure?" Jenny said. Her voice was weak, tentative.

"I'm sure," Talia said. "Sure as I am about anything."

16

THE SIGN said "Tits and Cocktails," the words blinking brightly in the brim of a neon pink martini glass against the gray wood of the shotgun shack.

Jerry slammed on the brakes and tugged the wheel, skidding on the gravel shoulder. He circled back on the dirt and parked next to the faded eucalyptus trees that surrounded the place. Out front, whirligigs made from chrome turned in the wind, their little propellers catching the thinning light.

Jerry stared at the sign that had actually once announced Tee shirts and Cocktails, before someone had monkeyed with the letters. The afternoon had turned humid, a thin veil of high clouds over the desert holding in the heat, making his shirt stick to his chest as he walked to the door.

The bartender was busy stacking beer cases, bent halfway into the cold locker behind the bar. When Jerry walked in, he had to sidestep around the only customer in the place, a woman in a terry cloth robe dancing slowly between the pool table and the jukebox. She stared at him dreamily, her far away eyes fixed on something she imagined. Damn near his own age, she dangled a cigarette in translucent fingers, her skin a little flaccid and leathered from too much sun. She floated to the Hank Williams song.

Jerry put two dollars on the counter. "Cell won't work. You got a phone?"

The barkeep stood up slowly as if his back hurt. He was an old guy, with a tight gray goatee and a too-bright and over-sized fake diamond stud in his ear. He couldn't quite stand straight and kept one hand on his ribs as he talked.

"Drinks are two dollars," he said. He looked over Jerry's shoulder and gave a disgusted glance to the woman. "Doris there is free."

"Just change for the phone."

"Dee, honey," the man said wearily. "Stay away from the window, will you? We don't want any more accidents."

Jerry found the phone by the emergency exit in the back. The bar was dark, and the carpet welled with the sweet smell of vomit and beer in the tight corner. He watched Doris do slow turns as he dialed.

Mahatma answered on the third ring. Jerry had hoped he wouldn't, but he did. "Talk to me, brother."

Jerry rested his head against the pay phone and closed his eyes. When he opened them, his face looked back at him, twisted and distorted in the chrome. He couldn't help but think of Talia back at the fair, their twin shapes in the funhouse mirror, the slow revolution on the Ferris wheel above the sea of lights.

"You were right. What can I say?"

Mahatma sighed. "You pushed the fool button, didn't you bro?"

"I thought it would be easy. Just climb in the Jeep and

go look for him. Fuck."

"Drunks like to tell each other easy does it. Ain't nothing easy about it."

"My head hurts."

"And the woman left."

"How'd you know?"

"What's that music?"

"You knew all along."

"For a while I pictured you out in the hot sand with the pretty flowers — chasing the kid. I knew better, because I'm a drunk too. What is that?"

Jerry watched the woman twirl. "Dee's doing a slow grind."

"Shit bro, a bar? You got get out of there, buddy. Jump back on the horse."

"That's what Injun Bob says."

"I don't like the way you sound."

"Relax, all right? I'm coming home."

He heard Mahatma tapping something, probably a cigar on the little Buddha by the phone. He pictured him staring at the small piece of blue ocean he could see out the window, or else staring at the sweat-coated body of the little guru in the picture on the bookcase.

"You want my opinion, bro?"

Do I have a choice, thought Jerry. He stayed quiet, letting his eyes focus on Dee. She stumbled, almost losing her balance, and her robe parted as she nearly went to her knees. Her thin breasts reminded him of the ducks hanging in the Canton restaurants in Chinatown. She was pathetic and sad, a chum.

"Hold on," he told Mahatma. He let the phone dangle its chord and went and helped her sit in a booth.

"What's she drink?" he called to the bartender.

"About a quart and a half."

On the way back to the phone, Jerry plopped down a ten-dollar bill. "This should last a while," he said, trying to give Dee a smile.

"Where'd you go?" Mahatma said.

"I bought a lady a drink."

"Shit, bro."

Jerry heard Mahatma clear his throat and then there was a loud sound of static. A recorded voice demanded more coins. For a second Jerry thought about just hanging up the phone and walking away, but he quickly dug out four more quarters and plunked them into the slot. He knew Mahatma too well.

"Go on and say it," Jerry said when the chimes in his ear stopped.

"I want to go fishing."

Jerry saw that Dee had perked up, a bit of color flowing into her cheeks. She lifted the glass at him and winked.

"Fishing," Mahatma said again.

"You're kidding."

"You told me you'd take me, remember? Bro, you may never leave this place again."

Jerry remembered the conversation. It was after his meditation destination, the place he trained his mind to go when Mahatma made the drunks practice mindfulness after some of the meetings. A lake in the Sierras, with a towering glacier reflecting silver water, the first place Ethan had ever caught a fish.

"Convict Lake?"

"It's on the way, bro."

Jerry closed his eyes and tapped the receiver against the bill of his ball cap. A couple of weeks ago his biggest concern had been the lumps in the pancakes and the nasty comments of the morning drunks.

"I know what you're doing."

"Just one more stop."

"It's too cold to fish. And it's not really on the way."

"Just get in the Jeep and drive. I am leaving in an hour."

"Why are you doing this?"

"Don't forget to check the oil climbing those hills."

Jerry studied his eyes in the chrome, bottomless and round. "You didn't ask me," he said finally. "About Ethan."

"Get in the Jeep and drive, bro. I'll see you soon."

Jerry started to say that he wasn't up for this, but the phone had already clicked off.

IT WASN'T long after he left the main highway and turned towards the lake that the streaking halos and buzz of the road vanished, leaving only the still eeriness of the big moon, which hung in the windshield. The dash clock read, 2:20 am and it was all Jerry could do to point the nose of the Jeep up the desolate strip of rising road. The land appeared as shadows.

Even though he couldn't see it clearly yet, Jerry could sense the vastness of the region, the impossible distances of the mountain tops that rose up around him and the terrible receding valley below. It was a sense that registered as a low buzzing in his chest, the way he felt when he looked at magazine pictures of galaxies and planets, vast impossible regions you could never touch.

His room back home was different; he could run his fingers over the walls and feel the carpet under his feet. Talia had been different too. He touched her. Damn you to hell, Mahatma, he thought.

He had his side window up, and the reflected light from

the gauges partially cut off the blackness. He was climbing quickly and the air felt clean as glass, but the road still tugged at his abdomen, the volcanic ridges and deepening valley coming clear and turning slowly in the mercurial light, the deepening cleft on the other side of the guard rail an unremitting abyss.

He downshifted, tightening his grip on the wheel, keeping his eyes centered between the high beams. Just keep climbing, he thought.

He'd been here before with Ethan, ascending this very road in the sunshine. He remembered how they had spotted a wreck down there in the ravine when they'd first come up this road — a panel van, as he recalled, whose broken cab was imbedded in the rocks. Jerry figured then that the highway patrol or rangers had left it there as a warning to kids about the dangers of drink and drugs. Ethan spotted it first, pointing at the heap of rusted metal.

"I know what you're thinking, buddy," Jerry said.

"Dead, huh?"

"Don't worry so much."

Now, closer to the crest, the engine shuddered and seemed to fade. Fuck it, Jerry thought, imagining himself slipping closer to the edge, or just stuck in some empty space of darkness. He stepped down on to the gas and the Jeep kept going, crawling almost, until the shadowed shapes of the trees leveled off and the incline softened. He felt better. Not good, he thought, just better.

In spite of spotting the wreck on their first day, the trip with Ethan had actually been one of the more successful excursions in the Hippie Home School curriculum. He remembered he'd been on the wagon, intent on teaching Ethan about fly-fishing, something his own house-bound father failed to teach Jerry, even after all the promises.

Ethan didn't like catching the fish that much, flinching at the touch of the cold body when he unhooked it, but he loved the lake and tall peaks. Eventually he quit fishing altogether, clearly just happy his old man wasn't acting crazy.

Maybe all fathers fail their kids, Jerry thought as he reached the top of the incline and the entrance to the camping area. One way or another, they all fucked up and either didn't do something or did the wrong thing. Still, he could picture Ethan's big-toothed smile, a boy not quite grown into his bones yet, standing in the shallow water making casts with his pole.

Jerry tried to hold the picture of Ethan in his mind, but the tall evergreen shadows and glacial peaks seemed to swallow it up, like the way they consumed the big moon and the radiant sky.

The log cabin bait shop, its small windows dark, looked the same as it had years before. He pulled in, parking in front of the shop, and cut the engine. When he rolled down the window, the sound of the river was loud. No use trying to find a camping site at this hour, he figured, so he tugged the blanket from the backseat over his shoulders and closed his eyes. He was getting used to this.

IN THE MORNING when he woke up, he lifted his head from the bench seat and saw the shapes of men in waders slinking towards the lake. Smoke from a campfire drifted over the road and hung in the still air.

A tapping at the side window startled him. When he turned, he discovered Mahatma leaning against the passenger door, a glowing cigar dangling from his mouth.

Jerry drew up the blanket and stared at him. Mahatma,

his head under a cheap straw cowboy hat, tossed the cigar onto the gravel. "Bro, you drunk?"

"Do I look drunk?"

"High?"

"Fuck no, all right?" Jerry studied Mahatma again. "You gone native or something?" He got out of the Jeep and the cool air hit him full in the face. "Shit it's cold."

They ate in the coffee shop attached to the little souvenir and bait shack. It was a solemn meal, in spite of Mahatma's wide-eyed ogling of the emerging lake out the window as the sun came up.

"Bro, I know you're not a morning person, but will you look?"

"I've been here before, remember?"

"Be that way."

"And you shouldn't smoke cigars before breakfast."

When they finished eating, Jerry led Mahatma into the adjacent tackle section of the establishment and picked out a couple of inexpensive fly rods. They stood together then, quietly considering the display case of flies. Mahatma squinted at the revolving rows of feathered lures, nodding as if he had a clue about how to fish and pushed his hat back. "You sure these won't hurt the fish?"

"Seven, eight hours, we could be home." Jerry pictured the cool fog of San Francisco. He picked out a garish fly from the trays and held it up for Mahatma to examine. "You really never been fishing for real?"

"My mom took me to a pool where an old man hooked me up with worms and charged a dollar, that's it."

"I'm no expert so don't get your hopes up."

"You got to hope, buddy."

"I'd settle for a duffle of reefer and some scotch."

Mahatma held his eyes on him.

"I'm kidding," Jerry said, trying to smile. "Let's just get this over with."

After they packed a Styrofoam ice-chest with cokes, potato salad and sandwiches, they rented a skiff at the docks and set out on the lake. Mahatma sat forward with the gear while Jerry worked the tiller on the little engine. Their breath hung in the air. The sun still hadn't lifted above the tall peaks, some of them still touched with snow, but a bright line of light touched the highest reaches. The water, black and still, stretched in front of the bow.

Out in the center of the lake, where the clear surface blued into the inky depths under the boat, Mahatma gestured for Jerry to cut the engine. Jerry obliged, throttling down as the skiff glided to a rest.

Mahatma lifted his hat and looked up at the icy peaks. "Kind of takes your breath away, doesn't it?"

Jerry sighed. "Why don't you go ahead and ask me whatever it is you want to ask me."

"You sleep with her?"

Jerry watched the far shore where a lure caught the sun and went away. "Is that why you got me out here? To talk dirty?"

Mahatma squinted into the sun just coming up behind Jerry. "I'm asking in a professional capacity, my man. This whole business reflects badly on my guru status."

"So now you're a guru?"

Mahatma fiddled with the tip of the rod, which he bowed and released. "Woman are rough, that's all. You got a lot on your plate."

Jerry dangled his fingers in the chilly water, remembering the story of how the lake got its name after some fugitives tried to swim across, but grew hypothermic and drowned. Their waterlogged bones doubtless were still down there in the black depths. He shivered a little and zipped up his jacket.

"The girl Lily's mixed up with this kid Max. They travel around to the concerts, like Ethan. And Ethan was with the group, or nearby earlier."

"Attachments," Mahatma said philosophically. "I feel you."

"I think Max deals drugs to pay for the trips. And he's spooky. A loner. He wants to haul Lily to some place in the Canadian Rockies."

Mahatma fingered the eyelet on the rod. Jerry knew the look; he had something on his mind. "Something in the guru manual prevents you just telling me what you're thinking?"

Mahatma ignored the question. He sat up straighter and gazed towards the shoreline where the whitewater streamed under the pines. "Come on, let's fish."

Jerry fired up the engine. When they reached the shore, he nosed the skiff into the white rocks and sand, while the estuarial currents stirred past the hull. The stream cooled the air, a scant mist floating off the rumbling cascade of water flowing into the lake.

"Take the line and tie it off on that tree," Jerry said.

Mahatma climbed over the gunwale, then waded gingerly over the rocks, dragging the bowline over his shoulder to a scrub oak. He tied the line off and then tugged the hull onto the sand.

After they unloaded, Jerry sat on a rock and rigged the poles. He noticed Mahatma looking at the gray surface of the lake.

"Took guts, you going across that after all you been though with water, bro."

Jerry handed Mahatma his pole. "Stay close."

"You're talking to a veteran of jungle combat."

"I don't want to haul your ass out."

They started up but Mahatma stopped and jogged back to the grocery bags, slinging them over his shoulder and joining up again. "You ever see that movie where they had to eat each other in the Andes?" he said.

"This ain't the Andes," Mahatma said.

The hike up the rocks took time, with Jerry forging a path over the flat granite slabs protruding from the smaller boulders and slag. He could hear Mahatma breathing behind him over the rush of water, but didn't look back. Eventually they moved past the thick green pines, into the sparser trees whose gray trunks and mottled branches hung down overheard. The cascading water made Jerry think of Talia and their adventure with Hightower, but he tried to just keep walking.

At a deep pool churning with thick water, Jerry stopped. The sun had moved behind them, filling the stream with white light trapped in the eddies and swirls.

"Looks as good as any place," Jerry said.

"I'm a vessel," Mahatma said, waving his pole at the water. "Show me." He patted his chest. "Catching some altitude, man."

Jerry unfastened the fly from the cork handle on his pole, then let the line fall. As the line dangled above the currents, he tried to remember his father's instructions about casting, delivered in front of the T.V. He liked the part about hammering nails, the part he told Ethan about.

Jerry's first cast looped out, then back and out again, settling finally in the still center of the pool. "Pretend you're a carpenter," he said to Mahatma, who was staring at him.

"Like Jesus." Mahatma nodded.

His first cast was amazingly good, and Mahatma's line

too found the tranquil section of water beneath the logs of a fallen tree near the curve of the river.

"I don't know about you, but I feel better already," said Mahatma, sticking a cigar into his mouth.

Jerry looked up at the rocks and the steep glacial chute above them. Past the steep section he spotted the plateau area up in the thin trees where Ethan and he had hiked. The terrain shifted up there, becoming vastly steeper where the river moved up towards the ice sleeves that drooped down.

"I'm going to go on up a ways," he told Mahatma.

"What if I hook one?"

"Give a yell and I'll come down."

"Why you want to go higher?"

"I just do."

He was right about the difficulty of hiking up and wished he hadn't started. Picking his way over the shifting rock, he felt that his footing might give way, sending him headlong down the mountain.

When he got high enough he could look over through the bare trees and see the shelf and little pools. He carefully traversed the loose ground and ended up at the plateau. Exhausted, he slumped on the same flat boulder that Ethan had sat on when he caught his first fish.

Across the swirling water, where a patch of brambles bowed out among the rocks, Jerry thought he could still see the filament and fly from Ethan's cast. It looked faded, but it was still there.

Down below, Mahatma waved his pole beneath a haze of cigar smoke, and past that, the lake spread out like a bowl full of ice water.

"You all right up there?" Mahatma yelled.

"I'm fine," Jerry called, unable to take his eyes off the tangled fishing line. "I'll be down in a minute."

"Is it pretty?"

Jerry took a breath. "Yes."

Going back, Jerry went slowly, but slipped, and rode a wave of rock down for fifteen or so feet before digging in his feet and stopping in a cloud above Mahatma. The fall left him breathless, and he stood there, gasping as if parts of him still hadn't caught up. After he regained his composure, he saw that Mahatma hadn't even noticed.

"I got one," Mahatma shouted suddenly. "Lordy, I got one."

"Sheet it in with that other hand. Easy," Jerry said, sidestepping towards him.

"This ain't how them stockers in the fishing pond felt. Woo wee!"

Jerry reached him and put his hands on the pole. "Nice and smooth."

While Mahatma tugged the line, Jerry watched for the fish. Eventually it edged towards the surface, its copper body ebullient under the gelid water. Jerry slid his hand underneath and cradled the body, the sentience of the creature heavy in his palm.

Mahatma stared at the feathered lure in the fish's lip. "I guess they got small brains."

"Like us. He's fine, okay."

Jerry reached down with his free hand and tugged the hook from the lip cartilage, then dipped the fish back under the surface. When he released it, the fish darted into the depths, and disappeared.

"Can we go home, now?"

"What about you? Don't you want to catch one?" Mahatma asked.

Jerry shook his head no.

"Your attitude is starting to wear thin, buddy. You

ought to think about it."

Down below they sat against a log in the sun and smoked cigars, while Mahatma spooned potato salad into his mouth.

Jerry eyed him, through the smoke. "You better slow down on that stuff," said Jerry, but Mahatma kept eating.

"So she's an art professor, huh?" he said.

Jerry knew Mahatma would just keep on until he answered. "She wants to paint, but I think she's scared."

"And she went with your crazy ass to hunt down Ethan? Must be some woman."

"That stuff you're cramming down your mouth, it's nothing but chemicals and warm mayonnaise."

"I like that bro, this new concern. The body's a temple."

"It's going to get dark as soon as the sun goes behind the peaks. Cold too." Jerry could already feel it.

"You going to meetings? You don't sound like you been going to meetings."

"Come on. I'll let you steer."

Mahatma took the wheel and the trip seemed uneventful, then halfway across the lake, the engine sputtered, and died. Jerry had been lost in thought at the bow, watching the docks get closer, but when the engine cut out, he suspected Mahatma was playing a trick. Jerry gave him a long look, but Mahatma had a "not me" expression as the hull glided quietly to a stop.

"You're fucking kidding me," Jerry said. "Tell me it didn't quit."

Mahatma fitfully jerked the engine chord but finally gave up and slumped on the stern cross-plank. "Somebody will come by," he managed.

"I deserve this." Jerry shook his head.

"You can't fake karma, dude."

"That's not what I meant. For coming out here, I deserve this."

Mahatma started rubbing his belly, under his shirt. "Just relax, enjoy the view."

Then he grinned and dug in the bags between them and retrieved a cigar. Jerry closed his eyes amid the glacial silence. They floated, not talking. Mahatma sprawled out, staring over the gunwale into the inky water.

"It's a bottomless mystery."

Jerry looked at the water, imagining the bones of the convicts settled in the muck.

"I hate water."

"I was talking about women."

They floated quietly. Jerry dragged his fingers over the side. "I forgot the softness," he said finally.

Mahatma blew smoke. "The smell too — like flowers, huh?"

"Sometimes she'd look at me and my legs would quit. Make me feel stupid, or important — alive I guess."

"That's their power, like fucking General Electric."

"So what am I going to do?"

Mahatma shifted his weight, unsettling the boat. "Be your own lamp."

Jerry regarded him wearily. "You ever get tired of talking like Kung Fu?"

Near the docks, the boats remained close to shore, gliding distantly along the rocks where the bait fishers lined up like small birds. Jerry regarded Mahatma closely. "Back when I was down and out, I ever say anything about Ethan coming home?"

"You remember something?"

"The lady at the rehab said something about Ethan calling home. As hard as I try, I can't remember."

Mahatma bit off some of his cigar and spit into the water. "You didn't make much sense back then. You talked to yourself. Your shoes were always untied. You fell down."

"And now I'm better?"

Mahatma threw his cigar into the lake, then clambered to his knees on the cross-board. This time when he tugged, the engine started, and he momentarily lost his balance as the boat surged forward. Mahatma shouted over the engine. "It is a fucking mystery."

THE TENT felt cramped with Mahatma wedged in beside him. The starry sky shivered above, the wispy strands of the Milky Way floating behind the fly netting at the top.

Mahatma lay in the corner of the tent, moaning, both hands massaging his gut. "I told you not to eat that shit," Jerry said.

"No one asked you, bro."

Jerry lay on his back, the sleeping bag and the extra blanket pulled up to his chin. They were a couple of little boys, Jerry thought, staring up at the night like a couple of Cub Scouts.

"I feel lost," Jerry said finally.

Mahatma struck a match that flared orange. He touched Jerry's shoulder and handed him a cigar, then held up the match and lit his.

"You smoke too much," Jerry said.

"I could say likewise." Mahatma smiled into the dark.

"I just told you I was lost."

"I'm thinking about something else," said Mahatma. "Sidewalls, bro."

"What in hell are you talking about now?"

"Maybe it's time we let go. Go modern. Haircuts, I'm thinking. When I was a kid, twelve or thirteen, I'd get a woody when the lady barber'd put the clippers to my head. She looked like Della Reese."

Jerry blew smoke into the dome of the tent, momentarily blurring the stars. Just ignore him, he thought. "She's probably got her nose right in one of her stupid magazines. Or in some book."

"Talia, huh?"

"And that jackass Max lurks around, pushing his shit. Poor Lily."

Mahatma sighed. "One day my mom and me walked in and Della was gone. My heart sank. A Marine with thick fingers stood behind her chair. On the drive home I begged my old mom to go somewhere else. No more hard-ons."

"Max and those damn fires. He's going to hurt someone."

Mahatma stared. "So what are you going to do?"

"Go home. What the hell else? Start over. Devote myself to feeding my sick brothers and sisters."

Mahatma reached back and flicked his ash outside the tent flap. "Today when you climbed up high, you didn't even fish. Why you go up there, if you weren't going to fish?"

"IT STILL kind of looks like it used to," Jerry said, pushing back against the leather chair. He was trying to ignore the antiseptic smell of the comb the barber was dragging through his hair.

Mahatma lifted his eyes and considered the other side of the street across from the barbershop, where the hazy brown sky rose above the line of old storefronts that ran along the base of the mountains. "I wouldn't know about that bro."

Mahatma sat under the broad mirror lining the barbershop wall in front of him, shuffling through the stack of old magazines on the chrome and glass table. Mahatma was just trying to help. Jerry repeated this to himself. But his irritation at Mahatma was growing. Focus on something, Jerry thought, anything, and he concentrated instead on the main street outside the window.

The stuffed deer atop the Sportsman Lodge across the street really hadn't changed much in the years since Jerry was last in this town. Condos and strip centers may have encroached, along with spas and business parks, baseball fields and big-box hardware stores, but the buck still gazed proudly at the big sky.

Not that the animal hadn't taken some licks; it was held up there with bailing wire and duct tape, while one of his broken antlers twisted in the breeze as tractor-trailers sped by underneath. But the buck's glass eyes still gazed with conviction at the barren ski-slopes, suggesting an old-boy holding strong against the passage of time, no matter how stuffed and gone.

Jerry turned away from the animal and considered his own dismal reflection in the mirror. Mahatma, evidently still sick from the look of his sallow complexion, wasn't much to marvel at either. His blonde-gray dreadlocks may have been gone from under the scroungy hat, but it didn't seem to matter. He had his head buried in a *Sports Illustrated*, one of the special issues featuring models with skimpy bikinis in the surf. A Pepto-Bismo bottle poked out of his pocket.

Jerry thought about the buck. He wished he could say the same for himself — that he'd held up against the merciless procession of seasons, the sun and the snow, the good times and bad, but he knew better. Moreover, he doubted Mahatma's insistence on getting haircuts before heading home would do a damn bit of good.

"I can still taste the boysenberry cobbler, in that place across the street," he said to Mahatma, gesturing toward the diner. "It was warm. Ethan and I ate some with ice cream and then we went and got out of the heat in a movie theater. Sean Connery."

Mahatma peered over the blonde on the cover with the wet legs. "You can't go back, bro."

"And you need to have caught a fish without losing

your lunch to have attitude like that."

"I caught one."

"Whatever you got to tell yourself."

"I'm just saying, is all."

Jerry looked at his shorn head in the mirror. "I look like a Republican."

Mahatma shifted in his chair and let the magazine drop in his lap. His face had grown tense and Jerry could tell he had something to say. He tugged out the medicine bottle, unscrewed the cap and gulped.

"I should've told you on the water." Mahatma said when he lowered the bottle. "I got some amends, bro."

The barber, thin and gangly as the hat rack in the corner, stepped between them. He jammed the tissue into Jerry's collar, made him wonder if the Republican crack offended the barber. Jerry waited for him to move, then sighed. "Go on."

"You get excited he might draw blood. It happens, bro. My mom busted me once trying to sneak a mouthful of Bazooka at the barber's, and when she raised her hand, I almost lost an ear."

The barber in the mirror gave Mahatma a dirty look. He sported a crew cut massaged with grease, and an oversized cowboy belt. The buckle pinched into his waist, and was embossed with an image of John Wayne sporting an eye-patch that must have impressed all the sheep farmers and cowboys who hadn't sold out to the condos. He looked like he about had enough of the city boys.

Mahatma's eyes went clear. "Your lady, Talia — she called me."

Jerry felt the heat of the clippers on his ear. He closed his eyes, the buzzing filling his head, "Jesus Christ," he didn't care now what the barber did to his hair.

Outside, Mahatma handed Jerry his baseball hat. Jerry tossed it into the trash. Even though you could see still the glaciers up on the high peaks of the sierras, it was warm here in the valley in the sun.

"So what'd she want?"

They were walking over the broken sidewalk towards their cars. "What do any of them want?" Mahatma said.

Jerry gave Mahatma a dirty look and stopped at the traffic light. While they stood there, a gas tanker rolled past, its polished hold exploding with glare.

Mahatma waited for the truck's engine noise to abate before trying to explain. "She said she was going to get you out of the hoosegow. Wanted to know if it was the right thing to do. You know, not enabling."

"That's it?"

"Pretty much."

Jerry stopped walking. "She's not my lady."

They had gotten to Mahatma's white pickup in front of the Jeep along the curb. "You gassed up?" Jerry asked.

"Negativity is a toxin, bro."

"I want to drive straight through. No sight seeing or dallying. You got your fish, now we go."

"Feel any different without your freak flag? A thing like a haircut can give you new eyes. Make you see a new world."

Jerry squinted at his dim reflection in the bakery window; he could see the ears, the sheen on his cheekbones, his neck. He looked more like he used to, before the accident. Younger, maybe. But no, he didn't feel any different. He faced Mahatma and gestured toward the buck towering overhead.

"Wonder if he was thinking about a new world when they popped him?"

"Serious negativity, bro."

"Just keep your foot down and don't stop. Got it?"

"You the man." Mahatma climbed into his own car.

THEY HADN'T gone sixty miles, headed north up 395, before Mahatma signaled and pulled off the interstate. He stopped at the off-ramp and waved Jerry up. It was boondocks.

On one side yucca covered sand and shale, and on the other, past the concrete overpass, some sort of dish antennas, whose huge convex shapes glinted under the sun. Jerry pulled alongside and rolled down the window. "Don't look at me that way," Mahatma said. "It's just the fuel pump. I was going to have it fixed, but I forgot. It's a simple job."

Jerry didn't have to push Mahatma's truck with the Jeep, which he feared. The vehicle limped steadily down the narrow side road towards the small hotel and service station near the grove of antennas. But the gas station was further than it had seemed and soon the highway was a distant strip in the rear-view.

Jerry didn't get out when Mahatma parked under the overhang and went inside the little office to find the mechanic. A moment later he exited, followed by a small-boned man in a blue jumpsuit. He said something to Mahatma, went into the garage and brought out a little board with wheels to slide under the truck, then rolled under.

When the mechanic finished, he slid out and said something to Mahatma, who glanced dubiously at the Jeep. Will this ever end, thought Jerry.

Mahatma walked over and leaned into the passenger

side window, his hat nudged crooked.

"You look stupid with your new haircut," Jerry said. "Maybe it's that shit-kicker hat you're wearing, I don't know."

Mahatma's reached in and stroked the statue of Shiva. "He says he'll get the pump and put it on in the morning."

"Who says? Shiva or the mechanic? I'm barely holding on here."

Mahatma ran his finger over the painted head as if it were a pet. "I told you, shit happens."

"You and your friend Shiva there."

"Why don't you split, bro? You can make it back on your own. I'll follow tomorrow."

Jerry took a deep breath. The air, tinged with sage and dust, felt heavy in his lungs. "Get in, we'll get a room."

"I get the bed," Mahatma said, climbing in to the Jeep.

"You sound like Talia."

"Your lady."

Jerry gazed out at the antennas, a picture forming in his mind of the invisible microwaves floating into the atmosphere, never stopping. Captain Trips was probably out there too, grooving to the intergalactic noise, twirling his arms like a doped up fool.

He pushed the Jeep into gear and circled back to the motel, a quarter mile or so back. The road was filled with potholes and the Jeep bucked, seemingly objecting too.

After they checked in, they wandered into the café for something to eat. The booths held seemingly morose men in beige uniforms who picked at their string beans and roast beef as the evening sun set in the windows. Locals, Jerry guessed, losers who worked at the antennas. Mahatma stuck cheerfully with toast and eggs, his stomach still an issue, while Jerry ate a double-cheeseburger and fries, in spite of the fact that his own stomach felt sour. His meal was an act of rebellion against the absent Talia, he realized, then felt stupid and childish. As if she cared at all what he did, anyway.

Neither of them talked much when they went back to the dingy room; they spent most of the evening propped in their single beds, tossing the remote control back and forth until Jerry said he was going to sleep.

"You should watch this, bro. This is good." Mahatma kept the TV on, watching something about knights and the Holy Grail on the History Channel.

He fell asleep almost immediately, leaving Jerry wide-awake, listening to tales of damsels, church bells, and the emergent cult of love. It didn't exactly take his mind off of Talia.

Mahatma's after shave permeated the air and when the T.V. finally went silent, his congested breath came with small grunting sounds. The clock radio chirped. This was what he was reduced to. Talia might have been a prig but at least she wasn't a mouth breather.

When Jerry had enough of watching the clock's luminous hands creep in the dark, he pulled on his pants quietly and slipped out the door.

As he walked towards the red lights of the closest antenna blinking in the darkness, he unwrapped a cigar. The big moon was out again, less effulgent than in the mountains, but still bright enough to cast the valley in contours. He carried his jacket but he didn't feel cold.

Arriving at the bulwark of the enormous dish, a concrete slab at the base of the sheet-metal room housing the mechanical workings, he hopped up and gazed into the vast dome of night. Above, the antenna creaked, its conical shadow moving imperceptibly in the darkness. The night was quiet. He could hear the sound of the metal cooling, small ticks and mechanical twitches.

He'd barely begun to rid his mind of thoughts of Talia, when a flicker of orange light bounced over the sand from the direction of the motel and then sharpened into two headlights.

In another minute he recognized the Jeep as the two orbs moved steadily towards him, then the silhouette of Mahatma's newly shorn head clearly visible behind the wheel. Jesus thought Jerry, there really was no escape.

When Mahatma arrived, he got out and hopped onto the concrete base. He pulled out a cigar and popped it into his mouth, then lit it. "Kind of reminds you of clear nights on the bay, huh bro? All that blackness and the stars."

"Maybe a little, I guess."

"Mind if I ask you what you have in mind coming out here?"

"I was thinking about jogging out there in the sand until I couldn't go anymore. Then I'd lie down. No one would find me. Except maybe the coyotes and vultures."

Mahatma exhaled heavily, the thin margin of red light from the apparatus above shone on his cheeks. "I guess I should of told you I talked to her."

"It's not that."

"What then?"

"I keep having bad thoughts. About Ethan."

Mahatma took a long drag on his cigar as the antenna above hummed a little in the wind. "After I got back from the jungle, after Nam, I thought I could get it together again. The dope, the night sweats, the migraines — all the shit. I thought I could put it behind me."

"The way I see it, one step at a time just takes you longer to get where you're going. Why not run?" Jerry puffed on his own cigar.

"When it ended, Miriam left me and dragged little Sunny with her across the country to her parents. I fell hard and long." Mahatma made a gesture across the sky. "Miriam and I had been married ten years and she left me just like that."

"It's not the destination, isn't that what you say? It's the journey. Sounds like a bummer of a trip." Jerry concentrated on breathing.

"You're suffering, so I'm not going to get pissed."

"Sorry."

"When I finally got clean and spent all those days in India with the yogi, I got the idea that I could go home, try again — you know, still thinking I could put it back the way it was."

"No ready, huh?"

Mahatma slid off the abutment and scraped over the sand, smoking. Jerry let his tongue linger on the damp cigar. Suddenly it tasted bitter. He tossed it into the darkness, watching it explode into sparks on the hard dirt. Behind him, from inside the metal room, he heard the mechanical sound of the gears kick in again, and then the dark shape above them lurched and rotated slowly against the stars.

They both stared up until the machinery stopped, the dome of stars once again frozen.

"A few days ago I saw Ethan," Jerry said. "Clear as the Big Dipper up there. In a dream. It was raining and he was standing on the porch of the Victorian. His sweater hung down from the rain. He was pounding on the door and I just let him stand there."

Mahatma was still looking up at the dish, his head cocked back. "I heard the old TV shows bounce around out there in space. That's what these deals hear. One big endless cycle of I Love Lucys and Gilligan's Island. Think that's true bro — it's all the shit just coming back at us?"

"There's not a god damn thing wrong with the fuel pump, is there?"

Mahatma lowered his gaze and chucked his cigar without answering.

Jerry looked past him to the scrub and yucca shadows protruding on the horizon. He knew better than to underestimate his friend. Since waking up in the hospital bed, when Mahatma spooned Jello into his mouth and watched Giants' games with him on the overhead T.V., Mahatma was really the only person who understood him. Everybody else was either dead or crazy or gone, except maybe Captain Trips, whoever the hell he was.

"They've probably made Death Valley by now," Jerry said after a while. "For all I know, Lily's in a fucking van headed for the border."

"You won't know until you find out."

"What the hell makes you think Talia would have me?"

"I heard something in her voice, bro. Love or hate, I can't say. But I heard. Besides, you know as well as me she needs you."

Jerry sighed. "There's Ethan too."

"Yes, there's your boy. You can't forget him."

Jerry jumped off the concrete casement and they walked far enough so the utility light on the other side of the housing illuminated Mahatma's face. With the haircut, though, his face looked different, and Jerry couldn't tell what he was thinking. But he could probably guess.

"I thought I wanted to remember," Jerry said. "But I don't know."

They reached the Jeep. "You knew all along, didn't

you?" Jerry said. "That I'd go back."

Mahatma opened the car door.

"It's a long walk back to the hotel, bro. It's lonely out here, so get in will you?"

THE WINDING road above Death Valley allowed a view onto the entire desert floor — from the dusty humpbacks close by, all the way down to the expansive salt flats and foothills. Where clouds drifted over, dull shadows appeared, bunching up on the higher slopes of the Last Chance Mountains.

Jerry told himself not to look down. A bluebottle fly that had buzzed around the cab for the entire drive finally lit on the face of the little Shiva. The fly paused, wings ruffling the air slightly. Jerry could hear Shiva whispering. "Get out while you can," the god advised the fly. "This is one bad trip to nowhere."

Jerry opened the wind-wing and shooed the fly out, watching it whisk away into the gray nothingness above the canyon floor.

With luck, the fly might find some shade, Jerry thought. Then again he might perish in the wilderness thanks to goddamned Shiva and his ideas. It had been a long time — decades — since Jerry and his friends had hidden from the

sun out there like box canyon cowboys and desperados.
Years since the all night acid parties spent howling at the
moon, followed by long days recuperating at the edges of
the sulfurous pools, wondering if they had seen God. Two
or three days, he remembered, they'd stay back in the
cooler folds of the canyons, cooking over open fires,
stripping down to skin and bone, waiting and hoping for
something, anything.

Mahatma's cell-phone, stuffed away in the glove box,
startled him. Jerry clicked the lock, fumbling with the
phone, trying to keep the Jeep on the narrow road.

Jerry didn't wait for Mahatma's greeting. "You trying to
kill me?" he yelled.

But there was only silence. Then a girl's voice, distant,
weak. "Where have you gone?"

Jerry pressed the phone harder against his ear. "Lily?"

More silence. "Nobody listens to me," she said. "Not
even you."

She sounded wasted, like when they first met way back
at the Salton Sea, but then her voice fell away behind the
static.

"Can you hear me, Lily?"

By now he'd arrived at the summit turnout; he tugged
the steering wheel and slid to a stop against the boundary
fence. He got out and ran to the edge, breathing hard as he
got to the rim overlooking the smooth folds of clay that
rolled slowly down to the dusty basin.

"Lily, are you there?" he shouted. "I'm coming Lily.
Did you hear me? I'm coming to meet you."

She was gone.

He was still panting. Under him the wide sweep of
bleached earth reached as far as he could see on both sides.
Halfway across the basin an executive jet glided silently

into the bowl of dusty blue sky. The serenity suddenly struck him as pure distance, further than any he'd yet experienced. He was supposed to be getting closer, but what if he was getting further away?

The thought made his calves weak. That and the idea that something might be wrong with Lily, besides a bad joint or fight with Max. He could barely think of Ethan.

He realized then, standing and staring into the void, that something else was moving, directly under him.

At first it registered as only the smallest of shift in the dun-colored sand, a shadow or gust of dust. But then he saw the bodies — one, no two — naked. They were covered with tanning oil from the looks of it, squirming on a blanket set out on the slant of rock.

He blinked and edged backwards, trying to remain inconspicuous. Flushed with a sense of guilt, he quickly glanced at both sides of the railing, relieved to find only a distant pick-up parked at the far end of the overlook.

But when he ducked his eyes down for one last look, the girl was standing and waving her finger at him, her oiled breasts glowing in the sun.

"Take a picture," she yelled up at him. "It'll fucking last longer."

Jerry couldn't take his eyes off her. The guy was still lying down, obscured by the girl's body. Jerry had to say something.

"Some view," he managed, cringing at his own choice of words.

She was sneering up at him. Her hair was cut like Talia's, the sun glinting on the lighter strands, which caused him to linger longer than he might have, but now she abruptly stepped out of the way and the body under her came into plain view.

Like a baby on his back, Captain Trips lay naked on the smooth rock, his stomach and erect penis framed by sunlight. A grin spread over his mouth, his teeth gleaming, a joint pinched in the corner.

JERRY FELT a restlessness settle into his bones as he drove down the incline towards the tourist center. He was going back, but he wished he knew exactly what it was that he was signing up for. He'd tried telling Mahatma back when they were fishing that it was a bad idea. Talia had wanted him to leave, and he could only imagine how she might take his reappearance.

"Just open the door," Mahatma had insisted.

It wasn't as if he wasn't trying. But was there really any chance Talia would greet him as a lover? Much more likely she was going to see him as a seedy drunk who managed to grope her at a low point, and who didn't quite get her hints about getting lost. She had an argument, really.

He ran his hand through his cleanly cropped hair. It was like being in high school, this stupid lost feeling, which historically called for a few lines or pills and or some other form of self-medication. Now all he had were Mahatma's cheap cigars, so he unwrapped one and lit it up.

The campground wasn't crowded. Like all the other desert sites, this one too seemed to be popular with gray-haired retirees and a handful of skinny kids in jeans and dirty shirts.

He drove slowly, eyeing the campers and tents, but found no evidence of the kids or Talia either. Something about the prehistoric rock, the chalky sand, and the limitless expanse of salt flat left him now feeling utterly small and insignificant. He passed a bent-up park sign with the words, "Lowest Point in the US." No arguing that.

He stopped in front of an enormous R.V., fully equipped with a dish T.V. Except for a blonde child strumming a kids' guitar in a desultory fashion, no one else was around. No Talia. No Max or Lily. Maybe she wanted a bath, Jerry said to himself. She's so clean. He turned back out on to the highway.

He hadn't driven far when he needed to slow down and look. Fashioned out of rose-colored desert rock, the hotel rose upward from the desert floor. Jerry saw it long before the turn-off. The Moorish walls stood shrouded in oasis-style palms. Jerry stared. No question, if Talia was anywhere in this forsaken place, this was surely where she'd be.

With the evening light dwindling into pink and charcoal shades, he parked outside the hotel and watched the last sliver of sun move past the cut in the Last Chance Mountains.

After ten minutes the sun was gone. As the palm fronds rustled against the layered rocks of the building, he bent the rear-view mirror and took one last look before going inside.

The concierge didn't look up from his papers until Jerry got to the desk. A coolness hovered in the room and the young man wore a heavy white uniform decorated with gold buttons and epaulets dangling off his shoulders.

"I'm here to meet someone." Jerry hesitated. "Talia Price. Here maybe with her daughter, Lily."

"Room sir?"

"I'm not sure yet. I have to find out about Talia."

The concierge rustled his papers. "Sir, without a room number, I'm not authorized to say if she's a guest. Security issues."

"Do I look like a security risk, kid?"

"It's not personal, sir. But we ensure privacy. You can

wait if you want. Perhaps she'll pass through."

"I should just sit around?"

"You can go to the bar. Our bartender makes a good cocktail."

"Trust me, you don't want me to do that."

The boy seemed to be enjoying himself. "Perhaps you'd like to buy a spa pass and go to the pool. The lights are pretty in the evening."

"I'm not big on party lights."

The boy shrugged.

Jerry gave up and paid. The concierge handed him a terrycloth towel and key. The prospect of waiting around depressed him, but what choice did he have?

"Those doors there," the boy said, pointing across the lobby. "We have a changing area where you can rent pool clothes" His eyes twinkled. "And massages are available. Sheila's on tonight. Patrons swear by her hands."

"I look that desperate, huh?"

After changing he sat heavily at one of the mesh tables in the pool area and watched the elegant patrons stroll past the blue flood lamps and palm trees decorating the hotel entrance. Even in the night, the breeze here was still warm and dry. The trunks of the trees glittered with spiraling ornamental lights that gave the odd impression of a holiday, which only made him feel worse.

People stared at him over the low rock wall. After twenty minutes, he'd had enough and reluctantly took off his shirt and slid into the rock encrusted Jacuzzi, taking refuge in the chlorine bubbles.

Sitting in the roiling water turned out to be a mistake. The tiredness in his legs seemed to spread to his torso, but thankfully stopped at his neck.

Above him, the dizzying firmament turned slowly

around a wedge of a spring moon, seemingly promising something more, just at it did in the old days. But this time he wasn't waiting to see God or glean some cosmic insight in the Milky Way — he only wanted Talia.

It must have been an hour before he gave up and hauled himself out of the pool.

After he dressed, he looked across the wooden-slatted floor at the massage room. On the other side of the window, Sheila was busy kneading someone draped in towels on the massage table, her cleavage and veined arms slick with perspiration. She looked nothing like Talia. But seeing her still gave him a carnal pang of hunger, reminding him suddenly of how pathetic he'd become.

Deciding some food might help, he walked across the lobby and into the restaurant. The dining room swirled with candlelight, but possessed a cavernous darkness, which made it hard to see much besides the torsos of the diners and the occasional glinting of raised wineglasses or the sparkle of earrings.

He sat alone at one of the booths and ordered a steak, but when it came he could only pick at it, the rare meat suddenly repulsing him, its juices pooling red and shiny in the middle of his plate.

From his pocket he dug out the paper on which Talia had scribbled her cell phone number so many days ago.

The phone rang repeatedly; he was ready to hang up when she finally answered. He hesitated. "It's me," he said.

She sounded startled, remote. "Oh. Hello."

"I've been doing some thinking," he said. "I guess I miss you."

Again a pause; her voice came, again very distant. "Well, yes, it's nice hearing from you too, Jerry. But, there's no sign of Ethan."

She sounded distracted. "Where are you?" he asked.

"Death Valley, Jerry. And you?"

His stomach churned but still, he felt undeniably brightened. "I'm at the Inn. Furnace Creek, with a big chunk of meat in front of me."

"That's, well, remarkable."

"Meat is murder, right?"

"No." She hesitated. "I am too. The same establishment. This very moment. I'm actually having a spinach salad."

Jerry stood up, allowing himself to believe for an instant that Shiva had his back, that Mahatma was right. He placed a hand on the table to steady himself and looked over the room full of table lamps, the black forms hovering around them. Near the window on the other side, he found Talia's face, shadowed from the candlelight.

Across from her sat a man.

Standing in full view, Jerry couldn't do much but go over to the table. Talia waved now, and the man with her lifted a glass of dark wine toward Jerry.

Boyfriend or husband, Jerry thought. It figured. He couldn't believe that he'd called her, and he blamed Shiva and Mahatma, thinking if he ever recovered from sheer embarrassment he'd strangle the both of them. Even if one of them was nonexistent.

When he reached the table, Talia said, "I hardly recognize you with your hair cut." She hesitated. "This is odd."

Remaining seated, she looked over the candle at the man, who buttoned his jacket as he stood. Taller than Jerry expected, he wore a striped cotton shirt under his tailored blazer, expensive trousers, and carefully parted hair that fell artfully into his eyes.

Husband, thought Jerry.

She glanced up at him. "Morgan, this is Jerry. He's the one I told you about who's looking for his son."

Jerry shook hands, suddenly drained of strength. Morgan's grip was angular and firm, and he held on long enough so that Jerry could feel the warmth of his palm.

"Jerry, this is Lily's father."

When he let go, Morgan ran his hand through his thick black hair, his signet ring shining in the candlelight. The way he examined Jerry gave the impression he was choosing a vase for his office or a shrub for the office entranceway. He was strong and handsome and looked like he could still run a mile or row a shell across the bay — or whatever his types did. Jerry glanced at Talia, but she couldn't quite look back at him.

Morgan said, "In our day it was all-nighters down at the docks or seeing how many travelers you could guzzle roaming the bars with fake IDs. The world's gone goo-goo."

Jerry pictured Lily, heard her voice on the phone. She was probably speeding towards the tundra.

"Pretty crazy," Jerry said to Talia. Her hair was different, more tapered where it crossed her cheek, shiny.

Morgan kept on, "Your kid's come off the handle too, huh? That's a shame. Driving around and raising hell is the new moonies."

"Something like that."

"Well, at least we got ours in the cross-hairs. She's a wild one, though. I guess you know that."

Jerry studied Talia for any sense that she might've known about the phone call he received from Lily, but her face remained impassive. "She's a lovely girl, Lily."

Morgan gave a derisive laugh, one Jerry couldn't read and which he suspected was perfected for business meetings and conference tables. When he sat back down, Morgan lifted his wineglass to his lips and gave a wry, conspiratorial glance towards Talia, who allowed a muted smile. Jerry wished he were back in the jacuzzi staring at the empty night.

Talia finally turned to speak to him. Her voice was as controlled as if she were talking to a disgruntled parent calling about a failing child. "Morgan's come here to help with Lily. She didn't make it to Death Valley after all. We're getting pretty desperate."

Jerry pondered her choice of words. We. "And the others?"

"They left earlier. Supposedly they're all meeting up the road at a place called Lassen." Talia crinkled her face for a moment. "It sounds awful. All lava pits and volcanic ash."

Jerry considered telling her about Lily's call, but now clearly wasn't the right time. There were the fires too, Max's drug peddling. He could only nod.

"What about your plans?" Morgan said. "You going to stay on the trail to the next shindig?"

"I'm not sure," Jerry said, looking out at the dunes rising on the dusty earth beyond the tinted window. "Maybe."

"If I can be of help, let me know. I have resources."

"I seem to remember Talia saying something about fiberglass Pyramids."

Morgan let a grin pass over his lips. "Don't kid yourself, Jerry. It's a rough business."

He whisked an imaginary piece of lint off his jacket sleeve, a sleeve that even Jerry could tell was made of expensive cashmere. Don't react, Jerry told himself.

There was a sudden sound of synthetic music — Morgan's cell. He retrieved the phone from his inside breast pocket and glanced at the screen. "I gotta take this one. Damn Persians are killing me. A thousand years of rug grinding and you get pretty good."

He reached down and touched Talia's shoulder, his ring disappearing in her hair, and then strode off toward the lobby. He didn't think to give Jerry another look.

As soon as Morgan was out of earshot, Jerry said, "I need to talk to you alone."

Talia sat immobile, her expressionless face turned toward the gray window.

"He's a cartoon," Jerry said. "You can't be serious."

She glared. He could tell she didn't want to show emotion, but couldn't help herself. At least that was something.

"You're not in a position to point out cartoon characters, I'll tell you that."

"What about us?"

She stared pensively across the dining room, then reached out and fingered the glass vase in the center of the table. He watched the impassiveness overcome her like a trance. "There is no us."

"I came back. For Ethan, but Lily too. And you."

Her eyelids fluttered, then clamped shut. "I really can't do this."

Jerry looked across the dimly lit room to the alcove where Morgan went. He was still inside, his dark frame blackening the space except for the slow movement of his luminous cell-phone. "What the hell did you tell him about us?"

"Stop it, will you."

"I have things I have to say."

"I can't."

"Look, I know I fucked up, okay?"

She gazed again towards the black curves of the dunes. Her voice had a resignation he hadn't heard before. "I'm leaving. With Morgan." She shook her head as if to herself, but didn't look at him. "Try not to make this so hard, Jerry."

"I don't believe it."

She sighed. "It's true. A private jet in a couple of hours." She gazed towards the alcove and spoke in a melancholy voice. "I wish there was another way."

"I thought we were supposed to be helping each other."

"Why are you doing this? It was finished."

Jerry didn't know what to say. Morgan had clicked off his phone and had begun to move among the tables towards them.

When he spoke Jerry heard his own desperation, but it hardly mattered. Nothing really mattered anymore. "Get away. Not now. After dinner. Walk out to the dunes out there."

There was no time for more. If he continued talking, he'd have to converse with Morgan, which seemed unbearable. Actually, it was all pretty much unbearable.

Morgan hadn't arrived yet, and Jerry strode away, pretending not to notice him. He walked straight to the door and when he got past the reception desk considered turning around, but didn't. In another second he made the door and stepped into the evening air, which stirred gently with salt and mesquite odor. At least he could feel the clear air in his lungs again.

Once past the stone patio and the ambient light of the crescent window, he kept walking. The receding haze behind him and the emerging stars above gave the impression he was walking into the sky, floating like the old days. But he felt heavy, hopelessly earthbound.

A while further, he realized he'd gone a considerable

distance and had already reached the beginnings of the massive dunes. He peered back towards the hotel. In the small cubicle of light he could still see the tiny figures of the diners, in particular Talia and Morgan, a prick of candlelight between their silhouetted heads.

Jerry wondered what she was saying. Telling him maybe more about Jerry, or worse still, telling Morgan about herself. That she missed him or wanted him back. Reminding him.

HE TRUDGED up the shallow face of the dune, finally making the narrow crest. On the other side, he sat first, then lay back against the warm sand.

Looking up, he lay still, suddenly aware of the beating of his heart. Overhead the entire cosmos drooped down on both sides, a silent, distant tapestry.

After an hour, he got up and lumbered down the dune. When he got close enough he saw that most of the window tables were empty and cars were turning out of the entrance way.

The concierge gave him directions to the airstrip, which was only a few miles away.

Ten minutes later he approached the perimeter fences and strip of landing lights, their brightness tracking out into the desolate blackness. He pulled over on the dirt shoulder, turned off the engine and lights.

The jet taxied from behind the small hangar in the distance, then crept into the blinding light. It remained obscure for two or three minutes, and then the low rumble of the engines came up, disturbing the absolute stillness of the night. When it rushed past the jeep, the jet's engines roared and the buffeting shook the cab. The aircraft stayed low, then arced up.

Jerry thought for an instant he could make out Talia in the window, but then the fuselage turned and bent sharply upward, its blinking lights merging with the stars above the Last Chance Mountains, gone.

THE MARCH wind howled against the cinderblock outhouse. A bare light bulb gleamed thinly against the outer concrete wall. Perched sideways on the stiff front seat, Jerry opened his eyes and stared at the little Shiva. The night was dark but the stupid statue seemed to command the only slant of illumination coming through the Jeep window.

Jerry had slept poorly and could feel his collar rimmed with sweat; he was getting tired of waking up on the front seat, never mind the shithouse smell.

"This is your fault," he said to Shiva. "You and fucking Captain Trips."

The little statue stared back. Jerry had made tree country, and the tall pines shivered up high in the windows. Jerry glared. "And fuck your friend Mahatma, too."

The rest stop was deserted, except for a single car in the moon shadows at the far end of the parking lot. He thought he could see the outlines of a driver, but wasn't sure. He might have suspected that Captain Trips was behind the wheel, but for the fact that he'd just paid Jerry a visit while he slept.

Jerry closed his eyes and tried to conjure the dream again. He and Captain Trips were driving somewhere in the old Cadillac, cruising into a sunny glare.

Captain Trips, sitting behind the wheel, wearing a Hawaiian shirt and aviator shades, tapped the dash with his free hand to something that sounded like Pine Top Perkins, the ocean on the other side of the car, the beach somewhere.

Jerry could still feel the seats of the Caddy, big and warm on his back, their soft buttery leather stained with the smell of Jamaican grass. He'd always liked those seats.

As he sat there and tried to summon the rest of the dream, he became aware of some sort of racket outside the Jeep. He looked out the window and saw the man at the end of the lot had left his car and was now dragging a trashcan towards it.

Jerry closed his eyes again.

Captain Trips laughed and patted Jerry's knee soothingly and he passed the joint to Jerry, its soft paper clinging to his lips. They were somewhere that seemed like Mexico, driving through warm rain.

"You gotta remember the dance, kid. I keep telling you." Captain Trips spoke lightly, drumming his hand on the dash. A little skeleton man dangled from the rear view mirror.

Jerry pointed at it. "What's that?"

"Just something I picked up." Captain Trips began to sing. The rain melted into blue light.

A gust of wind roared through the pine trees and Jerry pulled the sleeping bag up over his shoulders. He closed his eyes again and waited.

He and Captain Trips floated on a river, the water wide
and greeny-brown, the Cadillac gliding gently between the
banks of two shores, going out to sea. Jerry had an oar in
his hands and rowed on one side out his window, while
Captain Trips, the big joint in his mouth, paddled on the
other.

"Looks deep," Captain Trips said, his glasses white
with glare. "Real fucking deep."

He was laughing, his small glasses bouncing up and
down on his nose.

In the Cadillac's rear-view, Ethan's face appeared; he
sat there in the back seat with Lily and Max. Out the wide
windows, magnolias and roses lined the banks of the shore,
the thorny vines spilling down, the yawning gray sea
merging with the horizon.

Further down the river, a church, like the one down in
San Miguel, appeared along the banks. The plaster walls
were cracked, the big golden bells up high gonging out the
side windows.

Again, Captain Trips slid Jerry the enormous joint. He
took a long drag and held the cigarette over his shoulder,
waiting for Ethan to take it.

Then the big hood of the Cadillac floated up towards
the moon, the sky darkening. Out the window, from down
toward the water, Lily was reaching up, her thin hand
coming toward Jerry. Behind her, Max and Ethan, all
connected to her like paper dolls holding hands, all the way
down to the sea.

The bells tolled.

Sitting still, Jerry could feel there was more, but he
couldn't see it. He sat quietly, breathed evenly, but nothing
materialized. Even if it did, he thought, what the fuck did it
mean other than the fact that Captain Trips took pleasure in

torturing him?

For an instant Jerry thought about calling Mahatma and reporting his dream. Since waking up in the hospital, Jerry didn't really dream. The shrinks said he should talk about his dreams when they returned. Mahatma had always been asking, but lately he'd given up. Until this one, the only dream Jerry had managed to remember was one in which he succumbed to drink, ruining his sobriety. For a while it was enough to wake up sober, but it got old. Now this.

What could Mahatma add, Jerry thought. Besides, Mahatma was partly to blame for the damn thing anyway and if he called him, Jerry would only tell him to go to hell.

THE MAN by the Ranchero was stoking the can fire with the last of a handful of papers when Jerry got to him. Jerry kept his hands in his jacket and said, "Hey." Up high behind the trees a faint trace of dawn hardened the edges of the boughs.

The jumping flames in the can sharpened the man's chin bones above a three-day beard. Jerry stretched his fingers over the fire. When he'd walked over, Jerry thought the guy might be lonely; now it struck him that the man could be his double. Whatever was going on with the dream, it still churned Jerry's stomach.

"Long night," he said.

The man dug into his sweatshirt pocket and pulled out a bottle, holding it out to Jerry.

Jerry tried to look appreciative. "I better not."

"That's funny, cause I better."

Jerry watched him tilt the bottle and recalled all conversations he'd ever had over such fires. They all went the same.

"Cold as hell," Jerry said.

"Wind does that."

"You from around here?"

"Summerville — up past Lassen a ways. I left from there a while ago."

"I'm headed to Lassen myself. To the park. How far do I got left?"

"A ways further I guess. Figure the further I get from my old lady, the better." He held out the bottle again. "You sure?"

Jerry smiled. The man reached down and plucked up a scrap of paper caught under his shoe. He held it over the flame, dropping it into the drum when it caught fire. "There goes the fucking house," he said.

Jerry didn't understand but smiled.

"Catalogue plans. Drawn-up by an architect-guy. Thought that would impress her. So what's your sad song?"

"Everybody's got one I guess."

"Most star women."

As the man lifted the bottle, Jerry suddenly was struck with a strong image from his dream again. Its clarity startled him.

Jerry and Talia were going at it in the front seat of the Cadillac, her hip bones writhing under him as he moved on top of her, the wall of the cave drawings out the window, with the little shadow man watching. In the back seat, Captain Trips sucked on a joint, the back of his curly hair bouncing rhythmically up and down.

Jerry pushed the picture away. "Just a little while more to Lassen, huh?"

"Had a fire when I went through. Made a hell of a traffic backup."

Neither man spoke for a while, and the dull sound of

the wind against the trees rose and fell. After a while, Jerry looked up from the sooty drum and could see the light coming up in the trees, their massive trunks taking shape in the dawn. The very last part of the dream came back to him, blotting out the man and the fire and his lost wife.

Talia sat at a table in a tiled room. Jerry stood below her, near a pool, and then the bells sounded again and he gazed upward. Her pale face was swathed in light. She lifted her finger to her lips and the scene faded and then at last there was only Ethan as he'd been that night long ago, standing in his sweater in the rain, the water pooled dark around his feet, the street gleaming wetly.

Jerry rubbed his eyes and watched the man finish the bottle.

"Time for me to go," he told the man. "You take it easy."

The man lifted the bottle as if in salute. "This here does all the taking care."

IN THE cab Jerry watched the tree line gain shape in the morning light. He sat for a long time, until the out buildings on the other side of the road came clear, before picking up the phone and dialing.

After three rings Mahatma answered. He sounded sleepy, as if Jerry might have awakened him.

"You going to tell me what happened to him?" Jerry said.

"Say you're not drunk or high on dope."

"I had a dream."

There was a long silence. He could hear Mahatma pop open a medicine bottle and turn on the faucet, then take a drink from a glass. "I'm taking aspirin bro," Mahatma finally said. "It's still dark out the window."

He could hear Mahatma sip more water, then sigh and pull a chair across his wood floor.

"You going to tell me what happened?" Jerry asked again.

Mahatma coughed again and then sat silent for a moment. "Tell me what you dreamed."

He was standing out in front of the house. Ethan was. It was pouring rain so hard, a river ran down the street. He stood outside on the porch.

"Where the hell are you?"

"The deal is, I just let him stand there Mahatma. I was high."

"Drunk dreams, man. Let it go."

"Out on the streets, all those nights before I went into the water, I said something. I know I did."

"Come on man, the seagulls aren't even out yet."

Jerry leaned his head against the glass and watched the man drag the can fire away from the car, readying to move out.

"I'm asking you, Mahatma."

"What do you want me to say, man?"

"Just answer my question."

"Your question?"

"Yeah. What happened?"

"Don't ask me to get between you and your Dharma man. Don't do that to me."

Jerry cracked the window and took a breath. The man from the parking lot drove past in the Ranchero, steering out onto the highway.

"Jerry, listen. If I knew that, I'd know everything."

"You sure?"

"You're the only one who knows what happened."

Mahatma was quiet for a while. "I'm sorry."

Jerry pictured Mahatma back in his house, sitting in his boxers, waiting for the seagulls to appear over the water. "It's not your fault."

"Shit. I'm your friend."

"She's gone, you know."

"What do you mean?"

"The other night I watched her get on a plane and fly away. What am I even doing here?"

"You miss her?"

"I'd forgotten what that felt like."

Mahatma didn't say anything for a time. Across the road the tops of the trees up high were tiered with light.

"The birds are dancing over the bait boats," Mahatma said. "It's a nice morning. That must be it, huh?"

"I'm not following."

"What you're doing, bro. Nice morning. That's all there is."

Jerry thought about it. "I'll see you around."

THE TOPS of the trees held blue smoke that clung to the leaves like violet cotton, and the burnt scent of soot from the fire still floated in the cool air. This is how the end of the world will smell, he thought.

At the outskirts of the wooded park Jerry stopped at a mini-mart for gas. A couple of kids counted change on the counter as he searched the magazine rack behind the clerk for a local paper, hoping to see something about the fire.

The top two racks held plastic-wrapped magazines and Jerry found it hard to look past the pictures — alluring pink skin in leather, a round bottom, a bare arm and an ankle with a snake marked on it. His hesitancy to shift his gaze from the tattooed biker chicks suggested an emerging depravity he didn't want to think about just now. Besides, one of the airbrushed faces looked like Talia's and the flesh tones reminded him of the smooth skin above her breasts.

On the bottom rack he found a local paper with a single headline: "Will the Mountain Blow?" He'd forgotten he was in volcano country.

He handed the clerk a twenty. She was middle-aged with a graying ponytail poking out the back of her baseball cap, and he sensed she didn't like the way he was looking at the pictures.

"You know anything about a concert going on?" he asked.

"Aren't you a little old for that action?"

Jerry thought of Lily and her phone call. "I'm looking for my daughter," he said, trying to sound indignant. "She's a runaway."

"Not in the park. It's not allowed. Try Miller's Road, about a mile more. They turn in there."

Jerry glanced at the newspaper headline. "You think it's going to blow?"

"They been saying that for years. Volcano's ten thousand years old."

"My luck it just might," he said. He tried to sound casual. "Hey, you hear anything about a fire?"

"In the park. All out now. Some jackass lit up one of the observation docks."

Jerry pointed at the magazines. "That one there on the end, with the brunette," he said. "I want it." He avoided the woman's contemptuous stare.

The traffic was sparse. A mile or so later, he guided the Jeep into a pine-needle covered patch off the main drag and parked. He kept a lookout back towards the road while he peeled the plastic cover from the magazine, then found the picture.

The Talia look-a-like stared back at him. Mostly naked, she wore big black boots and red lips, legs wide, standing there in a leather collar, hands on her waist, like, well, an angry college professor.

He clutched at his crotch, hoping for some electricity,

but only a sense of foolishness welled in his loins. He tried some more, then the gleam of a car flashed in the trees. He let go of his Levis, finally giving up. He swore he could see Talia's eyes in the bimbo's own, laughing at him. "So much for your Dharmic path," she'd say.

This is what it's come to, Jerry thought. One jerk at a time.

Back on the road the light in the spaces between the trees grew dim. After the openness of the desert, it felt like he'd crawled into a cedar chest and pulled the door closed. Then again the gloominess probably had something to do with Talia.

He found the girls' tent and their flag, billowing from one of the poles, in plain view, erect near one of the trunks of an enormous pine. Amber sat alone in dirty pajamas, staring at the ashes in the fire pit. She coughed a little and clutched a bottle of orange cough syrup in her hand.

Jerry gently disengaged her fingers from the syrup. Her face was smudged with dirt.

"Robitussin. That's what my mother gave me," he said.

"You look different." Her voice was whispery.

"It seems pretty quiet around here."

"Lily got burnt." Amber looked at him with big eyes but then shrugged. "I think she's O.K. Jenny took her to the nurse by the lake."

"Jesus, Amber. What about Max?"

"He's gone."

Jerry drove with his foot pressed hard on the accelerator, and once on the highway had to fight to keep the big-hubbed wheels tracking. The speedometer needle bounced to seventy, the cab humming and vibrating. It struck him, as keen as the rushing asphalt, he'd blown it here. Talia was last seen disappearing into the sky, Max was gone, and Amber had taken to cough syrup. God only knew about Lily.

HE MADE out the Valiant sitting at the far end of the lake parking lot, near a row of cedar outbuildings. It was getting dark, but he could see the two girls sitting near a pier that extended out over the gray water.

They gazed at him evenly when he walked from the Jeep. Above them a haze of smoke swirled, and they puffed home-rolled cigarettes, clove from the smell. Lily's hand, bundled in gauze, rested on Jenny's leg.

Lily didn't wait for him to get there before she called out. "If they love you, they come back," she sang to Jenny in a loud voice.

"She's on Vicodin," Jenny said. "It makes her kind of crazy. You look different."

"Republican," said Lily.

"What happened to you?" Jerry stared aghast at the gauze.

"Like you care," Lily said, pouting. "You left us."

"I'm sorry, okay? Anyway, your mom told me to go."

Jenny interrupted, puffing on her cigarette. "Talia said you had a fight. We asked her. After you dropped her off back in Havasu." Jenny took another puff. "Divorce is hard on the kids, you know."

"I got drunk," he said.

"Nurse Ratchet only gave me a few pills," Lily said. "I'd give you some but I took them all."

"You going to tell me what happened?"

Jenny lifted Lily's hand from her leg and shook her keys. She flicked the cigarette away. "Amber needs me," she said. "You two are meant for each other."

After she drove away, Jerry sat down next to Lily. They

sat quietly and watched two children sitting on the dock, dangling their legs into the thick water.

"They got leeches out there," Lily said. "Lots of leeches around. Know what they call leeches that suck the blood out of your heart? Jerry is their name."

"You can beat me up all you want. But I want to know."

She pulled on her cigarette, rolling her eyes. "I fell in the water. It's hot."

"You got burnt in the water?"

"That's what I said."

"Sure it wasn't one of Max's fires?"

She dropped her shoulders and gave him a long stare. "You don't know anything."

"I know he's been setting things on fire."

"Come on, you're just so lame, I'll show you if you don't believe me."

On the drive Lily stared at the darkening trees, but at least she calmed down.

"You know Amber and Jenny's mom was a drunk," she said. "Lost their trailer and disappeared. They live with their grandmother in a trailer next door. Spend all their days doting on the old lady, changing the oxygen bottle she drags around. It was hard for them to leave her, even for a while. They know what she's done for them."

"Why are you telling me about this?"

"They don't forget people."

He followed her up a long hill somewhere in the rough terrain of the park. The air was tinged with the smell of sulfur, the residue of all the volcanic heat under the tight rocks and low scrub. A small stream, first muddy, then deeper, trickled at their feet.

When they crested the hill, Lily stopped, clutching her hand. She gazed down over a network of planks that led to the bottom, a large pool of seething water, turquoise at the edges bluing into a dark center. Jerry pictured the magma and red hot earth just below the surface.

To the right along the bank, the burnt timber of a dock stood out like a charred house. The pitch of burnt wood came up and blended with the sulfur smell of matches.

"What happened here?" he asked.

Lily massaged her hand, pondering the debris. "Max and I ended up down there. We were hiking. Fighting."

"And he lit the fire?"

"Not like that. I got pretty mad at what he told me. My hand slipped into the water."

"He lit it, didn't he?"

"Later that night. He got pretty fucked up and went a little crazy."

"Shit, Lily."

"Maybe he just wants people to listen to him. You're the psychologist."

"He's trying pretty hard. Fires have been following us the whole way."

She was staring at the pools, not looking at him.

"What the hell were you two fighting about?" Jerry nudged Lily a little.

"His big plan. He went to Arizona to buy drugs."

"Jesus."

"How do you think he pays for everything? He doesn't exactly work at McDonalds."

"Let's get out of here."

Darkness settled in over the park; the trees blackened the inky night, hiding most of the stars. They'd almost made it back to the campgrounds.

"I'm sorry about Ethan. Mom told me," Lily said.

"I'll find him."

"I should have said something sooner."

He pulled in alongside Jenny's Valiant. A light played in the girl's tent, but there was no sign of Max or anyone else. The embers from the fire glowed in the little fire ring.

He turned the engine off. "I don't know if I should tell you," he said.

Lily's face was vacant and she was looking at the tents.

Jerry wanted to shake her. "Your mother went and got your father."

"What?" Lily's cheeks reddened.

"I told her it was a bad idea."

Lily was shaking her head and hit her knee with her good hand.

"Come on. Don't make me regret telling you."

"My dad. Hell no." She turned on him "You have no idea what he's like."

Jerry thought about telling her about Death Valley, but didn't. "He's just a father, I guess. Worried."

"Yeah, well you guessed wrong. Like I said, you have no idea."

She sat down in a chair and Jerry could see tears in her eyes. "It'll be O.K.," he said. He started to walk back to the Jeep.

"Can you put some wood on the fire," she said finally. "Maybe stay up and talk?"

THE RIVER was a black torrent turning darkly under the streetlamps. It ran down the asphalt and spilled over the curb and across the lawn, flooding all the way up to the rose beds and porch steps of the Victorian, from where Jerry watched the channel of foaming water move downward toward the sea.

Captain Trips and Ethan straddled the fenders of the Cadillac, which floated like a raft on the river, moving on the water in the direction of the house. The gray rain fell through the lights, this time drenching not just Ethan, but old Trips too. Both paddled hard against the black water, but the square body of the flooded convertible just slowed. Ethan was yelling, "Are you inside, Dad?"

But they kept moving, drifting past. Trips reached back over the window frame and laid on the horn. Ethan waved his paddle over his head, still shouting.

Jerry just watched it float past, Trips honking.

Suddenly Jerry was stirred from the dream by the realization of an actual horn blaring. He stared at the mosquito-netted aperture above him and slowly gathered himself. Some idiot was actually honking. Though grateful to be spared this latest vision of Ethan in the rain outside the old house, something told him that the racket outside the tent was no bargain either.

He tugged his pants on and watched the tent's zipper flap peel open.

The figure darkening the opening wasn't Talia. Jerry fumbled with his belt buckle and stared back at the guy, who wore thick black horn-rims and a five-o'clock shadow. A cheap wool suit, green and vaguely Irish, fell over the bulge on the hip. Maybe it was the smell of cheap aftershave, or the dead-pan stare through the heavy lenses, but Jerry knew instantly the guy looking at him had something to do with Morgan.

JERRY DUCKED under his arm. "No donuts or coffee?"

Sure enough, Morgan was standing on the dirt lane in front of the tent. He raised his hands in appraisal of Jerry and set them on his hips, his black turtleneck and pants obviously chosen for effect. He looked slim and treacherous and might've scared Jerry except for the fact he was the Pyramid King.

Behind him, Talia leaned against a black town car parked under one of the tall pines. Jerry wanted to laugh at Morgan and his dramatic entrance, but Talia was in black too, a happenstance that Jerry found all at once heartbreaking.

Morgan took in the pines. "Nothing like a little geologic time and space to give a man perspective," he said. "Makes everyday problems seem so small. I could market this shit,

I kid you not."

"You know what time it is now, Morgan?"

"Wake-up time."

Jerry looked across the camp at Talia. "You okay with this?"

She folded her arms and sagged against the side of the town car. It was impossible to read her, and even if he could, he was likely not to like the plot. Morgan raised his hand to his second-rate Irish thug.

"This here is Roy Willis, a man I use sometimes. For some reason, people listen to him."

Willis wandered over to the Hemet girls' tent. He jerked back the flap, poking the bridge of his glasses to keep them from falling off as he bent to get a look inside. He stood and gave a thumbs-down gesture to Morgan. The girls were gone, but Jerry still wanted to break Willis' dirty fingers.

While Willis continued rummaging through the camp, Jerry couldn't look at Talia, dressed to match her ex-husband and standing there just watching. But he knew he deserved it — all of it. It didn't matter.

"They went to hang out. One of their friends, her father has a camper somewhere around. I heard them talking." Jerry watched Morgan coming towards them. "At least she's not heading north yet."

Morgan studied him. "A camper, huh?"

In fact, Jerry didn't know where Lily had gone. After they talked last night and he went to bed, he heard her whispering to the Hemet girls, followed by crunching footfall on the pine needles. Something about the campground up the road, Lily had said, voice muffled. But wherever she had gone, he thought, anywhere short of being on her way to Canada, had to beat this scene.

"Doesn't sound like you've been much of a guardian

here, Jer. But then, we all know that isn't exactly your strong suit."

Talia shifted uncomfortably and came away from the town car. "She's here. That's all that matters."

"I told you she'd be here," Jerry said.

Roy Willis strolled around them, his interest now directed at Lily's pink backpack, which stood by the fire-pit, the knitting needle and yarn protruding from the side pocket. He popped the button and rummaged through the contents and then let the bag fall to the dirt.

Talia shook her head at Morgan.

Willis bent and fished something out of the ashes in the fire pit, Amber's charred cough syrup bottle.

"You like your jailbait hopped-up?" Willis said. "A little dreamy, maybe."

"Roy used to be a cop," Morgan said, laughing. "He did some checking and a few bells went off."

Jerry glanced at Talia. "You sign off on this crap?"

"Come on, Jerry, we don't need to remind you of your personal failures. If we do, Roy here has them all written down in a little book."

Morgan was enjoying himself.

"Stop it," Talia interrupted.

"I thought we talked about this," Morgan replied evenly. "He's a perv."

"You talked — like you always do. I listened. And I've had enough."

"Enough, huh? That's not the tune you were singing when you called me. A girl needs her father," her voice growing irritated.

"Well, there's no plan and you're not helping. At least Lily's here."

Morgan scanned the girls' camp skeptically. "I don't see

her. You think your friend Jerry there has some special new insight now?"

"Just tell him what you found out."

Morgan looked pained; Jerry wanted to believe this outburst suggested some sort of personal triumph for him, but he understood it had more to do with Talia's irritation with Morgan than any feelings for Jerry.

Morgan dragged his shoe through the dirt and spoke grudgingly. Jerry took small comfort in the fact that Talia was able to exert her special power over him as well. "It seems our boy Max has some legal issues in Arizona," he said. "Me and Willis here are going to do some poking around, see what happens, maybe get a little leverage in case we need it. It's not a hippy concept, leverage, but you understand." He looked at Talia. "There, I told him. You happy now?"

Talia put down her purse on the picnic table. "You go with Mr. Willis. I'm staying here," she said.

"Here?" Morgan pointed at the trees. "In the woods? In the dirt?"

"Just go, Morgan. Do what you want, but go."

Morgan looked at Willis. "She wanted me to come, now she wants me to go. Always was a capricious little thing."

Talia scowled now. "You're right. I should never have called you."

Morgan breathed in the vanilla-scented pine-sap and sighed philosophically. He seemed amused. "You want to go back to the garden, Talia, be my guest. It's probably best I don't see Lily just now anyway. My mood's bleak. Even for a capitalist pig."

"If the shoe fits," Talia said.

Morgan stood up. "Willis and I are going to go find our boy Max." He adjusted his jacket and then reached out and brushed a piece of hair out of Talia's face. "But I am on top of this, Talia."

Talia stepped back angrily and Jerry felt his own skin prickle.

Morgan waved to Jerry from the open window as the car slowly spun around. "Try to stay out of the liquor cabinet while I'm gone," he said, rolling it up.

Jerry watched the tinted windows wind through the trees and get smaller until the car finally turned onto the highway.

"Don't say anything," Talia said. She clenched her jaw, her mouth tight. "Really, I mean it."

The quiet had returned to the camp. He could hear her breath sounds.

"I missed you."

She shook her head. "God, not you too?"

"Not me too what?" Jerry tried to think of what new error he'd made.

"Are all men incapable of hearing?"

Jerry thought about Lily's hand and the fire, about warning her about Morgan. He sat for a second, even in his misery enjoying the faint scent of Talia's perfume.

"You always smell like roses," he said.

"What?" Talia scowled.

He knew that was a mistake. Anyway, there was no way to avoid telling her the bad news. "Lily burned her hand in one of the hot pools in the park. First degree."

Talia stared at him.

"She went to the nurse by the lake and it's fine now. I know I should've said something. It's crazy, but I felt a little protective with Morgan around."

"God, is there not one responsible adult male left? First you get drunk and now you tell me this. It's unbelievable."

"Not fair."

She held out her palm. "Are you going to stand there or give me the keys?"

"What are you going to do?"

"Get drunk and drive off and leave you, what do you think I'm going to do?."

"Maybe it's not a good idea, you driving like this." Jerry wanted go with her.

"You're not the best person to give advice on finding lost children. Just give me the keys so I can go find her." Her black clothes made Talia appear ominous.

He deserved it, he thought. Talia knew the truth — and maybe Captain Trips and Ethan did too. What kind of responsible adult was he to let them float by, out into the unseen darkness of the sea, even if it was only in a dream? What kind of adult would side with a kid against her own father, regardless if he was a first-class jerk?

He looked up and watched the sky, trying to memorize the shade of blue made deeper by the trees. Jets had left a line of white trails.

He handed her the keys. "I think she's at the next camp up the road. With the other kids. Either there or just across from it there's a grocery store with a grill where the kids hang out."

She didn't wait for him to stop speaking. The Jeep squeaked to a stop a foot from the base of a redwood, and then a second later the rear tires spit dirt as Talia hit the gas. He waited, but her eyes never came up in the rear-view.

HE'D GROWN tired of waiting, of staring out at the trees like a hangdog loser — which he surely was — when

Max's van rattled into camp.

The other improvised sites among the misty larches had recently awakened from their comatose afternoons; kids milled about with water bottles and breakfast bowls filled with cereal, preparing to go listen to music in the forest. They waved their bottles and spoons at Max, who flashed a peace sign from behind the rectangular front windows.

Jerry sat in a folding chair by one of the tents. He'd been reading a tattered mystery he found in one of the deserted campsites, a story with a dark-haired heroine and a tired British counterspy. Just seeing Max made the nape of Jerry's neck get hot. He could feel the redness creeping along toward his throat. Lily wasn't in the van. Jerry could see that much. What else did Max load up on — bushels of dope, assorted pills, gasoline, firearms?

Max parked and climbed out of the van with the nonchalance of a rock star arriving at his own concert. He sniffed and peeled off his tee shirt and set about tinkering with something in the hold behind the seats. In the distance, the sound of guitars started up.

It was about all Jerry could take. He set the book down on the chair and walked over to the van. Max had just stood up out of the hold and was tugging a pair of strippers across a speaker-wire.

"Fucking copper leads are old and brittle," Max said, eyeing Jerry. "Like everything else around here."

"I saw her," Jerry said.

"Hey, you got your freak flag cut."

Max kept twisting the wire, not looking up, so Jerry wrapped his hands around Max's fingers to stop them from moving. He was surprised by their strength. "I saw Lily's burn, Max. I'm not playing around anymore."

Max jerked his hands away. "You got some bad dope,

man. Get some more or sleep it off, dude."

"You want to sell me some, now that you're back from the Arizona score?"

Jerry pushed past him and started rifling through the junk in the cluttered hold: an old pillow, a duffle full of electronic parts, dirty clothes, a grease-stained mattress.

Jerry gave up. "Maybe it's in the wheel wells, huh Max?"

"Like in one of those 6o's movies. Is that how you did it Jerry? Cool."

"Lily told me all about your plan. And about the fire you lit."

Max threw down the wire leads and paced back and forth, his pallid chest flushing red. Finally a nerve.

"God man, you are really seriously fucked up. I had nothing to do with them dumb ass fires."

"I think you're a liar. Or maybe you're so gone you don't care anymore."

Max picked up the wires again, and began twisting. He'd grown subdued, which surprised Jerry. "Marysville, dude, I went to Maryville. Picked up some parts for the show."

"Nothing's going to happen to Lily anymore. Do you understand me?"

"You know what, you're crazy. Why don't you just find your kid and leave me and Lily alone?"

Jerry considered telling him about Morgan and his goon, just to rattle him, but realized at once that would be really stupid. He'd figured warning Lily might push her enough to break it off, but that had been risky enough. Besides, Max was pathetic.

"Why don't you just tell her to go home with Talia? Maybe do the right thing."

Max slunk down on the edge of the cargo hold. He twisted the wires and squinted up at him, his black eyes suddenly rimmed with shadow and his bare shoulders slumped in a hint of resignation, which approximated to Jerry an understanding between them. It wasn't much, but it was a start.

"You don't even know the girl," Max said. "I love her, and I don't even know her."

"Maybe I don't."

"You think she listens to me anymore than Talia listens to you?"

"You're dragging her down."

"You should know, dude."

Jerry started back for the Hemet girls' tents. The kid had a point, but Jerry sure as hell wasn't going to admit it to him.

HE HEARD the Jeep before he saw it. Lily rode in the passenger seat and before her mother finished parking she'd bounded out the door and run over to Max, wrapping her arms around his shoulders and burying her face in his neck.

Jerry had set up Talia's tent just a few feet away from his own. He knew Talia might take one look at the sleeping arrangements and bolt to the nearest four star hotel, but he figured he'd give it a try anyway.

She looked calmer, getting out of the Jeep, head up, moving smoothly — not too fast but not slowly like she was shell-shocked, facing away from Lily and Max. A leather bag that reeked money hung from her shoulder. She didn't look like she was thinking of leaving. But really there was no telling. She stood in front of the two nylon domes.

Jerry thought of telling her it felt like old times, the two of them like this under the big sky, but thought the better of it. "They got bears around here. Probably pretty smart to stay together."

She sighed. "We might as well be in Canada."

At least she was speaking to him. So then, Jerry had to say it. "I told Lily about Morgan," he said, squatting down to pound in the stakes.

Talia gazed gloomily towards the other camp. Max had spread a bunch of gear out on a tarp near the van — black speaker boxes and shiny electronic components, a microphone on a stand — and Lily was running her bandaged hand over the parts as if she were touching flowers in a garden.

"She told me," Talia said. "She says she trusts you." Talia shifted her bag. "I didn't much feel a lecture was appropriate."

Lily took up the microphone and pretended to sing a song to Max, dipping and slithering around the equipment on the tarp. Talia watched her with an expression of wonderment, as though Lily were a stranger. Lily pranced to Max and held the microphone to his lips and he mouthed something too, a private pantomime. Jerry thought about Lily's contention that no one listened or heard.

"You all right?" he said.

"I was thinking."

"About what?" Jerry persisted.

Her voice was slow and distant. "After he made his big transition to the private sector, Morgan seemed to take pleasure in ridiculing all the things I loved. God knows she won't admit it now, but she loves some of those things too."

Talia turned and watched Lily singing again. She shrugged. "It's silly to think of now, but I keep remembering this time when I brought her home a box of

crayons. All new — the big box, you now? The one with a
hundred colors. She was only six but she loved green, the
color of green. She sat there, a baby really in her little sun
dress and read the names for green — chartreuse, sea foam,
teal, jade, forest green." Talia looked up at the forest
around them. "This color of green."

"But Morgan just laughed. He said in the real world
there was only one green — money. And I was wasting it,
buying fancy crayons for a baby. He started yelling. If you
asked her about it, I bet she still remembers that."

"He enjoys being an ass is all."

She slumped down in the folding chair and took a long
sip of water. "I'd like to think it's all about him. That Lily's
angry at him. But he's just part of it. The rest is me, I'm
afraid."

"It looks okay between you two. She came back with
you, after all."

"That's because of you." Talia looked at Jerry.

"Me?"

"She thinks you need us. With Ethan. That's what she
thinks."

"That's ironic because I kind of thought you guys
needed me."

"I don't need you." Her voice was cool, detached.

He looked into the empty tent. "So where do we go
from here?"

"She wants me to get rid of Morgan, and keep driving.
She says she needs more time."

"And you've agreed?" Jesus. This woman and her deals.
She made Morgan's wheeling and dealing look shabby.

"Yes. The same arrangement."

It amazed him how freely she assumed he'd do what she
wanted. She was right to be sure of herself though because

he knew he'd capitulate to any demand. "That's good."

"I'm glad you approve, Jerry. I mean coming from you, that's a real comfort."

She unzipped the tent and went inside. Somewhere far off in the thick green forest the ebbing chords of a guitar music drifted through the pines.

"Do you mind," she said from the other side of the canvas. "I really want to be alone."

22

IT WAS Jenny's idea. The impromptu meeting of sober kids took place at the other end of the encampment. Jenny, dressed in pajama bottoms, led him over the pine-straw through the towering trees. He'd have preferred to lie in his tent, but she dragged him out by the hand.

"You can't just mope around and feel sorry for yourself."

"You sure they want a relic like me around?"

"They're tweakers and K-hole kids, Jerry. They won't care. Besides, you're an inspiration."

The meeting was going on alongside a clutch of tents. Jerry propped himself on the dirt against the base of a thick tree and tried not to be rude, while Jenny sat on a log next to him.

Jerry listened but was having trouble concentrating. The bark was rough and sharp, and he thought he could feel ants scaling his skin under his shirt. He nodded at Jenny, trying his best to appear attentive. The kid talking, a nervous boy whose eyes barely looked out of a mangy haircut, was saying something about secrets, his fingers tapping the top of a wooden guitar he'd brought along.

Jerry glanced at Jenny and smiled. She was sweet, and the kids were sweet. What was he, but an old man with his own secrets.

While the boy talked, the light drained from the trees on the other side of the campground. Jerry pictured the magma seething, unspoken truths the earth held in until it finally blew. Maybe they were already consigned to hell but wouldn't know it until the hard crust exploded and the red-hot cauldron swallowed them all.

When it was his turn to say something, all the kids stared at him. Jenny stared too, the hood from her homemade sweater drawn up around her blonde hair.

"I know a little about keeping things bottled," Jerry said. "I'm a drunk mostly, though God knows I've done it all. The thing is, I got things inside too."

Jerry focused on Jenny's face, cheeks still apple round with the sweet legacy of baby fat. For the first time he seemed to notice what a child she was.

"I'm in love with a woman I have no business loving," he said. "And I see ghosts. One really. And I have the feeling I might have killed my kid, or close."

On the way back to camp Jenny walked quietly. The trees shone with flashlights, and bodies blackened them as they moved past.

"You know I won't say anything," Jenny said. "I think you were brave to go."

"Thanks for taking me there."

"Maybe you'll find him tonight." Her baby voice was sweet.

"I don't think so."

"Come on, you never know what you'll find." Jenny

patted his arm.

When they got back Lily was standing in the camp. She dangled a bottle of wine from her left hand.

"Where did you guys go?" she asked.

"Just for a walk," Jenny said.

"Look. Max brought a peace offering," Lily said, raising the bottle. "He says it's good, if you like wine, which he really doesn't." She poured a glass for her mother, and Talia, opting to be a good sport, smiled and nodded.

A blue scarf held Talia's hair out of her face. She'd changed from the jacket and black pants that matched Morgan's, and stood ready to go now in jeans and sturdy hiking shoes. The brown shoes, their surface as slick and mahogany brown as dates, looked to be recently waterproofed. He wondered if she'd waxed them herself, thinking maybe of another storm, and the rain at Canyon de Chelley. She must think about it sometimes, about the rain on the windows, about him, no matter what she said.

She lifted a battery-operated lantern and looked through the gray light at him. All business. The thin air made the night cold, totally different than the ambient desert air of Death Valley, and her mute eyes gave no clue to her mood.

Lily was easier to read. She stood there in bare feet, the hem of her levis mud-soaked. For such an intelligent girl, she worked hard at making things difficult.

Jerry took the bottle and poured Talia another glass. She handed him the lantern.

"It's not awful," she said after a sip. "Not at all. I guess I should really thank him." She looked at Lily. "Please. Thank him for me."

Lily crossed her arms in front of her and aimed a satisfied glance at Jenny. But Jenny was watching Jerry. She looked sad, he thought, probably the residue of their earlier conversation. He was a louse to burden a child.

"I wish you'd put on some shoes," Talia said, her eyes on Lily's bare, dirty feet.

Music started up again. Lily looked into the dense blackness of trees where a small chink of light blinked and the music played.

"Can't you just have fun?"

"It doesn't seem like much of a party," Talia said.

"Stupid boys mostly," Jenny said. "Boys thinking they're cool or something. They park their cars in a circle and turn on the lights." She shrugged. "A few people sing and stuff. I might not even go."

Talia took a sip of wine and looked at Lily. "What about Max?"

"Why are you bugging me?" Lily said.

Talia leveled her eyes at her. "Just a question."

"I don't know where he is, all right? He left."

Jerry lifted the lantern a bit, as if to signal them both to stop. Their breaths issued gently in the cool night

"I'll get my jacket," Talia said.

She backed out of the tent on her knees, carrying a large chrome flashlight, evidently acquired since her meeting with Morgan. It was nearly the length of her forearm, and she had to work to lift herself up while pointing her finger at the trees.

"Let me get that," Jerry said, holding out his hand.

She jerked it away, stumbling a little before regaining balance. "I'm okay."

Lily grinned at Jenny. "You aren't drunk are you?" she asked Talia.

"I leave that to the experts," she said.

Jerry expected to find meanness in Talia's glance, the professorial appraisal he'd grown to hate. But her thin face offered no more than a gentle, grudging smile. "We have quite a few around here," she added, looking at Lily.

Jerry handed Lily the lantern and followed Talia out into the forest. Jenny and Amber hung back with Lily. Before long, the dim light behind them disappeared and they fell into thick knots of branches and rising bark, the floor underfoot littered with mulched needles and broken leaves, and the flashlight beam bounced in and out of hollows around fallen logs.

Talia crunched steadily ahead, oblivious to his mood.

"Jenny dragged me to a meeting in the trees," he said. "A bunch of kids doing the best they can."

The glare of Talia's big light came up in his face and blinded him momentarily. When he opened his eyes her dark figure had already turned away, pressing onward into the gloaming like a conquistador.

"And you're trying too," she called back. "That's your meaning?"

"You better slow down," Jerry said, watching Talia. She was almost running now, her gait uncharacteristic.

"What did you talk about, you and your friends?" Talia was smiling.

"Secrets."

"Drunks and their secrets," she said, still bounding onward. "And I'll bet you have some doozies."

"Are you all right?"

She pointed the flashlight at the stars in the opening of the canopy. "Look at that moon. We walked on it. Not we, actually. Unless you count Hightower's trailer." She laughed a little, not meanly, but in amusement.

Jerry hung back a little, now letting her lead. Maybe it was the wine and altitude, but she was acting strange.

Talia stopped, the beam of her light unsteady and

shining again too brightly into his eyes. This time he got his arm up in time, shielding his face from the high wattage glare. They'd come to a large fallen tree, wedged between a cluster of unruly saplings on one side and large pine on the other. Spider webs and lacquered bugs moved in the spray of light.

Talia waved her fingers at him. "Give me a hand," she insisted.

He took her palm, feeling a twinge at the contact, perplexed by her newfound exuberance.

She got an awkward foothold on the coarse crumbling bark of a log and climbed up, balancing on top. She released his hand. Jerry looked at her. Her arms were spread and she had the triumphant look of a child performing at a dance recital.

"I have secrets," she said. "You think you're the only one, but I have them too."

She was looking towards the low glow. They'd gotten close enough that they could make out the kids sitting amid the headlights. It looked dismal, only three or four boys and a handful of girls. One of the girls was singing with a boy, both sitting cross-legged in the dirt. From this distance, no one looked like Ethan.

"What did they say when you told them?" she asked.

"Pardon?"

"When you said you loved me?"

She bobbled, nearly losing her balance. She let the flashlight fly and almost fell, but regained her balance just as Jerry reached up and steadied her leg. He kept his hands on her as he reached for the flashlight.

He raised the beam, letting it graze her face. In the haze he could see her black irises floating in the liquid pupils, as unmoving as the stare of an owl.

He felt a surge of heat well up in his belly. The look was unmistakable and he knew all at once he'd been a damn fool for letting her drink Max's wine.

"Shit," he said.

She looked down at him. "It's pretty up here."

He reached up to offer her a hand down but she ignored him. She stood standing on the log, head back. "I think the altitude's getting to you," he said. He tried to take her hand but she batted him away.

"Look. I'll just say it. You were right. Morgan's an ass. I was wrong to invite him on our little trip. Why spoil the fun?"

"Come on down before you get hurt."

"I mean it. I thought it would be different. You know — that he'd help. I mean, my God, he's her father. But he's become ridiculous."

Jerry thought about Morgan, with his leather coat and his perfect hair, and his pathetic sidekick, Roy Willis. It made him faintly sick to think about him with Talia.

She was looking down now. "The thing is, you shouldn't let him intimidate you."

"I don't care about Morgan." He had to get her out of here, and off the log before she fell and broke something. "I think we should go back."

"Back? We have to go look."

Jerry gently tugged her hand. "He's not there."

She let go and jumped down on the other side, crunching loudly when she landed. He shone the light at her.

"Don't just stand there. Come on."

Jerry reluctantly stepped up on the hard scrabble of the log, and then stepped down to Talia. They stood for a second, looking at the sky, and then Talia took up the flashlight again and they walked toward the crowd.

"So you were what, fifteen or sixteen when you started drinking?" she asked.

"Yeah, so?"

"That's your age then — fifteen or sixteen. I read about it in a magazine. Like one of those icicle men they thaw out of a glacier — frozen in time. Icicle boys."

"You learned all this from a magazine?"

"When you come back you're the same age you were when you left."

The clearing was on the other side of a line of trees and the long beams from the headlights protruded crisply over the flats, past the outlying trees surrounding the performers. "Take my hand again," Talia said, holding it out. "Maybe it's the altitude, but you're right, I am a little dizzy."

"It's been a long day. Maybe this isn't such a brilliant idea."

"Don't be silly, just for a minute."

They stayed at the perimeter, watching the music. Jerry instinctively searched the dark shapes for Ethan, but his heart wasn't into it. Three waif-like girls with stringy blond hair, wearing long gauzy dresses and thick paisley headbands, strummed guitars. They looked like they belonged in front of a teepee on a commune.

"They're beautiful," Talia said, staring at them. "Like the old days for you."

"You sure you're all right?"

"We must be high up. Wait a minute — Woops."

Suddenly her legs folded under her, and she slumped on the ground. She laughed a little and let her fingers play with the dirt. Her laughter was pitched a half tone higher than usual.

She tossed a handful of pine needles into the sky.

He moved in close, careful to take a hold of her gently around her ribs. When he did, his nose grazed the softness of her neck, the rose-oil caught up in the smell of the sulfur and pines for an excruciating instant. A horn sounded, and the car engines started up, moving, sending their lights askew over the barren rocks, before other cars took their places. Talia shivered a little.

"Just relax," he told her. "We need to head back."

"Why all the fuss? Those girls are like angels. Don't you see? And we have to find Ethan."

JERRY TURNED her shoulders so she faced toward the camp, catching her when she stumbled a little.

"I'm fine," she said again. "Just a little dizzy."

He ushered her back through the trees towards camp, clasping her shoulders and walking slowly.

"Stop for a minute," Talia said. She wrapped her arms around her own shoulders and stared upward. "I have a secret too." She smiled up at the moon.

Goddamn you, Max, he thought. "Come on. We should keep moving."

She rose, obediently.

"Maintain," he told her, again the goddamned words coming back. "Stay cool."

She looked at him crossly. "Whatever are you talking about now?"

"Just keep walking, will you?"

He clasped her arm and pushed onward. He wanted to look at her face again, into her eyes, to examine those enormous and dilated black irises. No doubt about it, she was tripping. There was no way of knowing what sort of acid Max put in the bottle. Jerry only hoped it was the sort you could move with, not the kind that left you immobile and fixated, a quivering mess that would doubtless leave scars. Someone as uptight as Talia could spend years trying to sort it out after. But right now it hardly mattered. The main thing, as every acidhead knew, was to stay calm.

They'd nearly made it back to camp, when her head fell back. For a second he thought he might have to bear her entire weight, but she steadied.

"No more moon," she said. "It feels like rain."

He kept trudging, managing a look up. Sure enough the ragged black shapes went up into thick gauze that had darkened into an impenetrable sky. This new weather seemed, right about now, some sort of celestial comment on how dismal things had become. He pictured Max soaking the little blotter of acid in the wine, laughing to himself at the thought of sending Talia over the edge. Well, Jerry was about to go over the edge too. Plus, he'd managed to drag Talia into his own Dharmic nightmare.

He pulled his windbreaker off and tucked her shoulders under it, and kept moving. Just keep moving, he thought.

"I'm floating. Are you floating?"

"We're almost back. Just keep walking."

"Not that old song again."

SHE INSISTED he sit with her in the tent while she undressed. The drizzle muted the light and the trees and the only light came from the Hemet girls' tents, which glowed and buzzed; as far as he could tell Lily wasn't inside. Max's van, black as a pirate ship, sat behind it.

"Some romance," Talia said.

"Time for bed."

"Do you want to read me Dr. Seuss?"

"It's been a long night."

"Have you been drinking again?" Now she was enraged.

"I need to go."

She had some trouble crawling into her sleeping bag. He held the end out so she could wriggle her feet in, then pulled the covers around her. The flap was still open; the rain felt electric on his cheeks.

"You have to come back. You always come back." Her voice had grown dreamy.

"Sure, Talia."

On the way to the van he stopped by the Hemet girls' tent and bent an ear to the canvas to see if Lily was inside. But it was just Jenny and Amber. Jerry could hear them whispering together and giggling, the tent fabric exuding the smells of clove and pot. No Lily.

He approached the van from behind, trying to get a look past the rear drapes inside. It was dark between the cracks of the material, and he was tipping forward, trying to see, when the engine fired up, sending him on his heels.

The lights stayed off, so he crept around the driver's side, his steps muffled by the engine, each slow step imagining what he'd do to Max after he jerked open the door and got him on the ground.

He stopped halfway and peered into the tiny mirror, trying to see Max's face. But it was Lily's eyes that met his, barely lit by the reflected light from the Hemet girl's tent.

She rolled down the window.

Jerry approached cautiously, waiting to see Max in the black compartment. He made himself unfold his fists and breathe. Beating the shit out of Max wouldn't help Talia, even if he could. But the passenger seat was empty.

"He's in the back," Lily said, "sleeping off whatever. I

got him to rest."

"I notice you have the engine running Lily. You going somewhere?" Jerry kept his voice controlled.

"Look, he's a fucking jerk, I know. He does stupid things sometimes."

"Like dosing your mother. That's sort of off the charts."

"He's remorseful." Lily shrugged.

"Take if from me. Remorseful doesn't count for much. She could have had a breakdown."

"Don't be all moralistic on me, Jerry. It's not like I'm down with his deal." Lily stared to roll up the window.

"You still haven't told me why the engine's running."

Lily raised her chin. "Talia's tougher than you think."

"Don't go."

"I have to do this my own way." Lily gunned the motor.

"Aren't you even a little concerned? I mean, she handled it pretty well, but you never know what can get broken when you mess with your head."

"Tell her I'm sorry. It's probably better this way."

"Tell her you're sorry? What about where you're going? What should I tell her about that?"

"Tell her she'll like the Russian River. I'll keep my word, okay. Just tell her."

He wanted to yell into the quiet campground. "You made a bargain, remember? A promise?"

"We're cool," Lily said. "I'll see her in a day or two. Tell her not to worry."

"So no concerns, huh?" He understood Morgan now, wanting to grab her and damn the consequences. "Maybe you want to wish her a good trip." He knew he was being childish.

She reached down and brought up a canvas bag from under the passenger seat, then slung it to him out the window. Jerry didn't even want to look. He peeled it open slowly and peered into the black folds. Inside sat a revolver nestled in a bunch of pills, like a cup in flour.

"I'll do it my way," Lily said.

"Don't do this, Lily." He placed his hand on the door handle.

She bumped the floor-shifter. "You can't stop me," she said, and the van lurched forward and lights came on, the beams cutting through the drizzle.

HE KEPT the tent flap unzipped, partly for air, partly because the gentle drizzling rain striking his cheek kept him awake. He'd propped her suitcase under him. He intended to watch Talia all night, but the gray rain kept falling.

He closed his eyes. The light blowing drizzle touched his face.

Out of the blackness he could feel Captain Trips beside him, the unmistakable odor of sweaty whiskey and pot right there too. Even before Jerry opened his eyes he could see the yellowed beard and round face.

They were sitting in Jerry's old living room, surrounded by all the books on the wooden shelves. The rain fell past the slats beneath the streetlamp. Trips lifted a bottle of bourbon and poured it into a tumbler and set it down in front of him.

An old letter was on the table next to the line of coke chopped up on a picture. Jerry took a gulp and kept his eyes on the blinds, waiting for the shape to appear.

The boy looked the same as he always had — it was just Ethan slumped under the yellow porch light. He knocked.

Trips grinned. He struck a match and lit a joint, then yanked up a broken guitar and began to play a song. Again he heard knocking.

Jerry reached down and read the letter. Ethan was fine. He was trying very hard. Staying sober. He was coming home. So much for the bum's life, right Dad?

The joint flared between Trips lips. He kept playing. Jerry took a long pull of the hot bourbon.

The door knocks finally stopped and Jerry glanced at Trips, seeing a twinkle in the round eyes in the round face.

Then Jerry was at the shutters, watching his boy walk away.

Trips hand was soft, his fingers like Talia's, but fatter. He opened the door, walking Jerry onto the porch. The sun was out now and it was a fine San Francisco day, the green blue fingers of the bay visible, the leaves on magnolia trees shimmering. Music played in the background.

Jerry woke enough to feel the hard ground underneath him. Just a dream, he told himself, but he wasn't sure. He heard the trees rustling outside the tent. It seemed very dark and he slept again.

THERE WASN'T much more to remember. The small ceremony was just a week later. The black shapes stood around, most of the faces too dark to see, although Jerry knew Evelyn was around somewhere. A big hearse parked near the crowd. Trips and Jerry stayed back, hiding behind a stand of bushes in the memorial park. Behind the charcoal lenses, Jerry tried to see Trips' eyes. His beard had gotten grayer.

Jerry had stayed out with Trips until everyone, even Evelyn, was gone.

Back inside the house the Captain poured more booze. Jerry snorted a line. It would be night soon again, time to get out of the house, time to roam the bars, time to sit in the Cadillac and wait for the music.

THEN IT was raining again, the tiny drops stinging his face and his back hurt. Talia sighed, her face as slack and pale as a baby's. She rolled over in her sleeping bag, murmuring something indistinguishable but unmistakably gentle. No matter what Max had done, she wasn't the one on a bad trip.

THE FIRST rays of sun came through a crevice in the volcanic hills and settled on the surface of the lake. Dark shadows still draped the canyon walls, and the sunlight formed a patch on the water, golden and candescent. Any other morning, thought Jerry, it might have been beautiful.

The canvas bag with the drugs and gun sat on the seat next to him. He turned the ignition key to off and waited for Mahatma to pick up on the cell. He answered on the third ring.

"I know ex-drunks are early birds, but do know what time it is?" Mahatma said.

"You're my friend, right?"

Mahatma stayed quiet for a time. "I hear that voice again, bro."

"My only friend, not counting Talia. I don't even know what she is. Friends are supposed to be honest with each other."

In the silence the shadows seemed to lighten on the banks and the end of the pier shone. The rain was gone, and least for now. Jerry heard a match fire up and Mahatma draw on a cigar.

"Hell bro, the doctors at the clinic said it could happen fast. I'm sorry, man."

"How the hell could you let me do this?"

"Come on man, you didn't forget all that psychology you read along with everything else did you? It had to happen like this."

"You couldn't tell me? I went to the goddamn funeral, hid in the bushes like a dog."

"You were suffering, bro."

"Well, it feels like home."

"It will get better."

"What the hell do you know about it anyway?"

"I been there, remember. Not the same address, but the same part of town."

Jerry sighed, remembering Talia back in the tent.

"So what was I, some charity case to you? Bet I told great stories wandering past the clinic — real sad case."

"You weren't exactly coherent, bro."

"Must have been real entertaining to listen to my pity party every night. I imagine you thanked Buddha when I drove my car off the cliff."

"It wasn't like that." Mahatma spoke too quickly, Jerry thought.

"Oh yeah."

Mahatma took a deep breath.

Jerry waited, not sure if he wanted Mahatma to say anything. The sun was almost up now, a blinding glare like fire between the red hills.

"What the fuck am I going to do now?" Jerry finally said. He dragged his wrist across his eyes and looked away from the light. "You should have told me Ethan was gone.

Not let me going out looking like this." He hardly noticed he was holding the revolver.

"How the hell do I know," Mahatma said.

With his free hand Jerry broke the Shiva statue off the dashboard and held it close to his face. What do you think motherfucker, he thought, half-expecting the tiny mouth to sneer back at him.

"You okay?" Mahatma said.

"I appreciate your honesty," Jerry said.

"What about the lady, bro?"

"I don't know."

"It's not over."

"I'll be seeing you, buddy."

Mahatma was mouth breathing again on the line. "The thing is, bro, you did know. You just needed to not remember for a while."

"Thanks for nothing." Jerry clicked off the phone.

He shook his head at the plastic figurine, and then decided to wedge it into the ashtray along with a wet cigar butt and refuse. "You probably like it in there," he said to Shiva.

He stared at the gun for a long time, too long. Then he grabbed the canvas bag and got out of the car. It really was, otherwise, a fine morning.

The wooden pier over the lake tilted gently when Jerry walked to the end. He had to squint to keep the sun out of his eyes, their wetness stinging again.

He dropped the gun into the sack, tied the top into a knot, and tossed it as far as he could and walked back to the Jeep. When he turned to look, the bag had sunk into the black water.

HE'D GOTTEN some toast browned in a skillet and the eggs were going by the time Talia crawled out of the tent. Her hair had a bouffant quality, all piled up, and her pajama top was buttoned wrong, which might have amused him another day.

The rain had cleared out, but a few clouds still stuck to the tops of the trees. Talia blinked towards the other camp and yawned. He handed her a cup of tea when she clambered up.

"You all right?" he said.

"I had nightmares."

"They must be going around." He didn't feel like talking.

She sipped, but her gaze eventually moved to the other campsite. Her eyes narrowed.

"Where's Lily?"

"Why don't you get some food in your stomach."

"Were you ever able to hide your feelings at all?"

"Last night Max played a little practical joke. His idea of one anyway. You want to hear it?"

"I can't wait."

Jerry flipped the eggs and set the spatula on the edge of the cast iron pan. He put his hand on her shoulder and she gave it a stare.

"You're fine, so we'll stay cool, right?" he said.

"Just tell me."

"Seems our pal Max fortified your wine with a little something"

Talia moved the teacup away from her lips. Her eyes were big. "I'm assuming you're not talking about vitamin supplements."

"A mild dose. Hell, I used to take more to get up for a class." Jerry tried to minimize the facts."

"My God."

"I know. You had a good time, in case you don't remember."

"That's your trick. I remember everything." Talia straightened her shoulders. "And for the record, I don't find it amusing."

"I'm not laughing."

"That's it?" Talia sat back.

"No."

"No?"

"This may be worse."

She shook her head at him in disbelief, waiting in silent indignation.

"Lily split with Max."

Talia seemed to bite on whatever she was thinking, but no words came out of her mouth. She held her cup rigid, her glare going out into the trees. She might've stayed like that but the Hemet girls were thankfully coming out of their tent, waving over to them.

"I can't believe it," Talia said. "We had a deal."

Jerry pinched her shoulder again and smiled over at the girls. "She said she's keeping it."

"And you believe her!" Jerry banged his spoon on the table.

"Calm down. There's no reason upsetting the girls, right? Yeah, I do believe her."

"That's it, right? All of it? And it didn't occur to you to stop her?" She slumped down into the folding chair, trying her best for the girls, who were walking over.

Jerry sighed. "Yeah, that's it." Turning to the girls, who wore matching pajamas dotted with elephants, he said with false cheer, "Anyone want some eggs?"

They ate quietly, watching kids breaking down camps

among the trees. The sulfur odor returned, the temporary
reprieve from the weather abating.

"The Russian River is pretty," Jerry said, looking at
Jenny. "I used to hang out there myself in another life."

Jenny gave a conspiratorial glance at Amber, who
pursed her lips silently. Jerry wondered if the girl would
ever learn to speak her mind.

"We're not going," Jenny said.

Talia had been straightening up the camp, loading paper
plates into a grocery sack. Jenny's comment brought her
back to the chairs where they were eating.

"You don't have to disrupt your plans on our account,"
she said, sagging a little. "It will work out with Lily."

"It's our grandmother," Jenny said. "She's not doing so
good. We're family I guess. Right, Amber?"

Amber nodded solemnly.

"You girls were looking forward to the big
rendezvous," Jerry said. "Sure it can't wait?"

"She's pretty sick."

Talia took their plates dejectedly. They'd barely
touched the eggs.

"It wasn't supposed to go like this," Jerry said.

"We know," Jenny said, again glancing at her sister.
"It's just best, you know."

The girls packed ragged towels and silverware into a
cardboard box and when Amber carried it to the car Jenny
looked again at Jerry. "Things aren't so fun anymore, you
know?"

He nodded.

After he helped them take down the tent he loaded up
all their remaining gear into the Valiant's trunk and waited
by the car while they said their goodbyes to Talia. She
hugged them both. "We can do the spa again," she called

out before they got back to the Valiant. "Don't worry about Lily."

After she got the car started, Jenny rolled down her window and looked at Jerry. "I had a teacher once," she said. "Mrs. Payne — remember her Amber? For Spanish. We had a lot of Mexican kids around the trailers where we lived. I should've done better, I guess. I got an F on the final and she let me do it again. She said we all need a do over sometimes."

"Drive safe."

"I hope you find him, Jerry. Remember, Mrs. P was right. We all need a do over."

Jerry tapped the top of the roof and stepped back. The Valiant coughed smoke and rattled off though the trees and the two girls raised their arms out their windows, a trace of exhaust the only evidence they were ever there at all.

THEY'D JUST gotten to a large meadow, still inside the national park, with spring flowers beginning to grow, when Jerry couldn't drive any further. The stench of sulfur pervaded the wet field, but Jerry just couldn't stand continuing any longer.

Talia studied his face. "What is it? It's the thing you wouldn't say back at camp, isn't it?"

"Not Lily."

Jerry looked at the Shiva head poking out of the ashtray, still riding shotgun with him. Right off another cliff, thought Jerry, straight to the bottom.

"I don't even know how to say it."

Talia popped the glove box and dug out one of his cigars. She made an effort to smile and held it out for him.

"No thanks." He hated the sound of his voice, the way he was polite, the way he trained himself to behave.

"There is something else, isn't there?"

"I need to move." He checked the laces on his shoes. "I'm going for a walk."

"It's about Ethan, isn't it?"

The marsh was soft and sticky underfoot. Talia kept pace with him, looking back sometimes over her shoulder at the Jeep, but not saying anything. Pretty soon they'd gone so far that the Jeep looked like a toy. But she stayed beside him.

"You're not complaining," Jerry said finally.

"Stop it."

They'd come to the meadow's edge where the reeds fell away into a crevice that looked to be a secret dumping ground of sorts. Most of the junk was indistinguishable, rusted metal and wood scraps and garbage bags filled with old clothes covered over by vegetation, but there was something else in there too, down low in the festering mud — a beat up sedan buried up to the door handles. Jerry peeled back some of the reeds and peered in the window.

"Look at that," he said.

"What are we doing out here?" she asked.

Jerry bit his lip hard enough to taste salt. His insides were balled tight. He didn't want her here — didn't want anything anymore. All their deals were just so much noise, the whole errand useless since the beginning. End it, he thought. Now. Before everything's even more fucked up.

"I can't do it, Talia. I can't take you to the Russian River."

Talia found the Jeep and held her eyes on it for a long time.

"Last night those things I said. I meant them." Her voice was as clear and lovely as a flute.

"You were high."

"Not really. But I didn't tell you everything."

"Oh yeah?" Jerry just felt tired.

"Well, I think I love you too." She smiled but she knit

her fingers at the same time. "I know. It's odd and unexpected, and I have no idea what it means." She held out a white hand toward him then. "But, truly, I do."

Jerry felt the knot inside his stomach let go and kicked the side of the car and had half a mind to put his hand through the muddy windshield.

"Now you say it." Typical, he thought. "Before last night, that's all I wanted to hear."

She grabbed his hand. "At least I'm not afraid to say it."

He pulled away. "Ethan's dead."

This morning those irises were wide and focused. He thought at first she was astonished, but they softened into something else. "You remembered," she said after a while.

The volcanic air tasted bitter in his mouth. "The way you say that makes me think you're one step ahead of me."

"Morgan's idiot goon hinted as much. When he looked into your past." She took his hand and held it in both of hers. "I'm so sorry, Jerry."

He wanted to rip his hand away, to run into the razor-edged plants and just be finally, blessedly done with it.

Her eyes were clamped shut, wet. "Morgan didn't have any real details and I didn't want to believe it, didn't believe it. I thought he didn't really know. But other times I think you've known all along."

"What else did he say?"

She opened her eyes. "The detective said Ethan had been gone — dead — for over a year. And that you knew. You were there later."

Jerry let go of her hand. He was trudging back towards the Jeep. She ran to catch up with him, tugged at his arm to get him to stop. He pulled away. "Sounds to me like you knew more than some vague details."

They stood in the middle of the parched meadow and

she pointed to the long trail of footprints heading back to the Jeep. "That's it? Just follow your tracks all the way back to your little empty room as if none of this happened?"

"You got any other ideas — maybe find another cliff to drive off?"

"Stop it."

"Or maybe another one of your details. Where you play along so I do what you want." He kicked at the dust and old bark bits.

"You know that's not true."

He closed his eyes. He saw Ethan at the door in the rain again. Jerry had been fucked up himself that night, embarrassed and afraid because if he opened the door he'd have to talk to Ethan about it. Talia was right. He'd always really known, deep down, what happened.

He thought about how white and bony Ethan had been when he'd come home from the clinic in Sedona. He'd gone to live with his mother for a few months and then drifted back first to drugs and then to the streets. When Ethan had stood dripping in the rain that night Jerry had known why he'd come. He'd needed Jerry to help him, but Jerry hadn't even made it to the door.

"It's over, Talia."

"And Lily and me? You can't just close your eyes and pretend we don't exist."

"You're better off rid of me." He could picture Old Trips laughing at the line. "Tell your friends back at school about the crazy drunk you met on your bohemian travels. The guy who hid behind the curtains when his son came home for help. About how his son O.D.'d while the guy lay on the floor, stoned, listening to blues. And the really trippy part, don't forget that. How your traveling companion eventually drove his Caddy into the water and couldn't remember any of it."

He started walking again, but she grabbed at his shirt. "Look at me. I need you. Lily needs you. This is real too."

"You've seen too many movies, Talia."

"I need you."

"I'm lousy in a fight."

"Can't you see? Whatever this stupid trip has been about, it's not nearly over."

He turned and started back again. The muck collected on his shoes as if they were scaling the moon. She trudged beside him, keeping pace, not talking. The walk back seemed to take longer. The bad air didn't help, either. But by the time they got halfway across, he recognized something had shifted inside.

Closer to the Jeep a breeze pushed away the edge of the stench. He opened the tailgate and they sat down, stripped off their shoes and wordlessly began pounding them on the hardpan.

"Got your new hiking boots dirty," Jerry said. "Time to buy some new ones."

"I ruined them."

Jerry wondered if she'd gotten the joke. "They got all kinds of expensive tourist shops along the Russian River."

She banged the soles of her boots together. "I'm truly unspeakably sorry about Ethan, Jerry."

"Yeah."

"But you know I'm right. This trip — if it's about anything it's about not running away."

His head hurt. He noticed again how white her hands were and hated the thought. Hated how she believed everything she said. He was petulant. "I can't think about anything."

"But you know I'm right?"

"Aren't you always?" He saw the tears in her dark eyes again then. Her eyelashes were sooty and wet, and there were small lavender shadows in the sockets. Her shoulders were narrow as a child's. Even with the weight of Ethan on him he wanted to push those strands of hair out of her face.

"I can't promise you I'll be any good."

She brushed her boots off once again and dumped out the remaining sand. She put one boot on and tugged at the laces. "The river ends up in the ocean, doesn't it? God, I want clean air. Anything but this."

Jerry got his own shoes back on. "I know a place. I used to go there before it all got so dark."

"Take me there," she said, helping him lift the tailgate up. "Before it goes dark again."

25

THEY WALKED on the beach, barefoot in the crisp tidal surge spilling over the urchin and muscle-encrusted rocks near shore. A storm had gone through and the sand was strewn with the flotsam of passing boats, seaweed and broken timber. The water lacked pattern and they walked through a hodge-podge of irregular wavelets, weaving through the muddy fingers, trying to keep their feet out of the icy water.

After they'd arrived at the old inn — really just redwood and glass cottages set on the cliffs near the roar where the Russian River emptied into the sea — Talia insisted they leave the bags on the bed and walk down along the beach.

They'd almost reached the steep rock cliff that divided the sand when they came upon a suitcase floating in the surf, its broken cardboard shell tumbling in the briny water. Talia dangled her shoes in her hand and pondered the container.

She was doing her best, Jerry saw that. She wanted him

to still believe in the possibility of moving forward, but he
wasn't so sure. In fact, he'd pretty much given up on
everything, except that now seeing her standing, shivering a
little in the cold, refusing even to accept loss, still curious,
he thought she was the bravest person he knew. Brave, but
almost certainly mistaken.

She pushed at the case with one bare foot. "I wonder
what's inside."

"Lingerie, diamonds." Jerry said.

"Maps to a new world." She rubbed her arms with her
hands. "A warmer one, too. It's freezing."

The next wave turned the suitcase over and the carcass
of a dead seagull covered in oil spilled out. Talia screamed,
and then retreated from the edge of the water.

"So much for my luck," Jerry said.

They stood near the bottom of the steps that led back up
to the hotel and watched a ship moving on the edge of the
horizon.

"I'm almost home," Jerry said. "Just a few miles down
the coast."

"I can't even think about home," Talia said, in her old
prissy voice. "And I'm a college professor. A responsible
person."

"Unlike me."

"All I really think about is Lily."

He pretended he didn't mind the implications.

She pressed his fingers. "Besides you, of course. I mean
my old life is gone."

"You and Lily still have a chance," he said.

She stooped down and took a handful of sand and let it
trickle out of her fingers. "I never asked you about it, what
you remember. How it feels now. It must be hard. What
about a happy one? You got any of those?"

"We saw Kubrick's 2001 on a rainy day at the old theater. I let him stay home from class and I blew off a seminar. We ate pesto pizza on Ashbury Avenue and argued half the night about the ending."

"That's nice."

"Don't get your hopes up," he said. "I'm barely holding on."

"Let's watch the sun go down from the room," she said, pulling herself up. "I'm turning blue."

HE STEPPED from the bathroom and discovered her in the bed, a four-poster in front of the picture window. She had the covers pulled over her stomach, but her bare breasts were bathed in the caramel light coming through the glass. On the other side of the bed the ocean was a gray line with half the sun resting on top.

He slid in beside her and the softness of her skin made him stop thinking.

Her belly smelled of talc and flowers and when he kissed her skin there, it tasted sweet and slightly medicinal from the perfume. The sun had moved lower and a line of shadow moved across her white skin in the hollow below her belly button. He lingered, his mouth following the sunset.

Before, in the trailer at Canyon de Chelley, there had been the tug of the unknown, something dark and primordial as the place itself — but this was different. He lingered down there, her breath sounds distant, her thighs warm on his temples. He was conscious; he was here, now.

Finally she dragged him up, pulled him tight in her arms and kissed him, her legs hooking his close.

She climaxed in shudders, her whole body going rigid

before she pushed him away.

When he looked at her, her eyes looked black in the dim room, almost desperate.

He rolled over and stared at the window. The light had gone out of it and the night over the sea had become gray and thick.

"What was Morgan like?" he asked.

"What do you mean?"

He propped himself on his elbow. Her face was still flushed and her hair hung in wet strands on her cheeks.

"Hell, not sex. Being married."

She sunk her head into her pillow. "I thought I detected jealousy before."

"Is he really dangerous?"

"He's a businessman. Is that dangerous enough?"

"I'm serious."

"He was a good husband. A good father. In his way. He just sort of lost his imagination, which is why he acts like he's in a B movie now."

"And you think I'm any better?"

"There's a difference between being crazy and inauthentic. Everything's make-believe to him."

He pulled on his boxers and climbed out of bed, then walked over to the small refrigerator atop the bureau. He opened it and took stock of the row of miniature liquor bottles on the door. He saw Talia scrutinizing him dubiously as he twisted the cap off a bottle of soda water and took a gulp. She may have slept with him, but she was still a smart girl.

"A washed up psychologist with a dead son — you're not exactly moving up the food chain."

"Literally washed up."

She elbowed herself up against the headboard and

stared at the ocean. The ships they'd watched earlier were pricks of isolated light and he couldn't tell if they were moving.

"Do you remember your name — your real one?" she asked him.

The question surprised him. "Is this a test?"

"Morgan told me. Elliott Jacobs."

"Have you forgotten? I remember everything."

"Well, I know it's none of my business, but I like Jerry better."

He nodded, suddenly too weary to answer. He opened the little refrigerator door again, taking out another bottle of soda. In the polished chrome cover of the icemaker he saw his own face lit from the interior light, metallic and distorted. Without the long hair, the face looked almost amiable, the harmless visage of a stranger perhaps — a responsible guy you'd pass on the street, with a job, a wife, a kid even. Alongside, still there on the door, was the row of tiny liquor bottles, old friends he recognized perfectly.

THE OLD Guerneville Bridge still looked like a child's train set, a single span structure set across the banks of the Russian River. It had been here for a hundred years. Men in white overalls were painting some of the girders a dark pungent green and Jerry could taste the fumes stirring over the water.

They sat in a line of traffic waiting for the cars to move through the intersection. From here they could look through the steel girders. Jerry pointed down the wet riverbank.

"High school, we'd hitchhike here on weekends. It was pretty wild. We used to get high and jump off at night. You'd just kind of hold your breath and wait for the water."

"I'm sorry if that doesn't impress me." She pursed her lips.

He reached from the driver's seat to pinch her shoulder. "Prig."

Her smile was half-hearted.

"Once I climbed to the top. Big show off. Seemed like forever waiting for the bottom. Sort of like now."

Jerry remembered the time he brought Ethan here when he was fourteen or so. He'd bragged for years about jumping, and then one day Ethan said he wanted to make the leap. They hopped into the car and drove away from the city, up the coast and then turning inland and winding through the redwoods until they reached the little resort town.

But Guerneville had changed — not the buildings or the little main street he was looking at now, but the feel. All the hippie kids running around had been replaced by busy families with Suburbans. Cops were everywhere.

He'd waited with Ethan until the scene looked clear. It was dark and fog drifted over the river. Ethan followed him out onto the spans, nodding and smiling, and then they both jumped. Like that. Flying out over the wild black water. Just remembering made Jerry's lungs feel empty.

He thought about telling Talia but decided not to. She had enough on her mind.

"Turn at the fire station. We're looking for something called the Sunrise Place." Talia crinkled her brow and read the scribbled directions. She'd made reservations for them to stay at an old inn just outside of town, but before they went there they were meeting Morgan and his stooge.

Jerry didn't like the idea and he'd felt a weight pulling at his belly ever since they left the sea and come into the rain-soaked forest. "Why didn't you tell me before?"

"Tell you what?"

"Sunrise Place, huh?" Jerry recognized the name from the fliers decorating Mahatma's bulletin. "I know it — a runaway shelter. Morgan's a real funny guy." He didn't know why they had to meet him again anyway. They'd all had their say already. But Talia'd taken his call.

The halfway-house turned out to be down one of the

side streets off the main road. The clapboard building was adorned with a garish picture of a sunrise and the black town car sat on the dirt lot alongside. Jerry pulled over and parked along the curb. Maybe Morgan had gotten religion. "You up for this?" he said.

"What about you?"

Morgan sat at a counter drinking a bottle of Coke. A sallow-faced kid with hollow cheeks stood behind him; Roy Willis was in the corner and when they approached he saluted them sarcastically with his soda. Then Willis puffed a cigarette and placed it in a plastic ashtray, glanced at a newspaper.

"This place should make you feel comfortable," Morgan said.

"I told you on the phone, this is stupid," said Talia. "Can't you just go back to your pyramids and let me handle this?"

"You and your boyfriend, you mean."

"Not that again."

"I don't give a rat's ass about you and your drunk friend, or what you see in him," he said. "I care about my daughter and this crazy notion that she's going to live somewhere in a hut in the Rockies raising god damned turnips."

"Sheep," said Talia.

"Whatever."

"You really think strong arming will work? That it's ever worked?" Talia's face flushed. "If you're not careful you'll really lose her."

"Screw careful." Morgan said. He pointed the mouth of the bottle at his companion who was tapping a rolled up newspaper on the counter.

"Roy here has dug up some information. Turns out Max's got a warrant issued in Arizona — something to do with drug peddling. They got a sheriff back there who thinks he's a cowboy. Likes to lock his prisoners in tents and make them dig holes in the desert. They piss in paint cans. I think maybe it would suit that little bastard running around with my daughter."

"She wants to leave him," Jerry said. "She just needs the chance to think it's her idea."

Morgan sipped his coke and gave a wiseass grin down the counter. "Roy found out something about you, too. Did Talia mention it?"

In the adjoining room near a small pool table, a bearded man came in and sat down in a folding chair at one of the tables, with a young man, wearing a down vest. Talia was watching them, her gaze detached.

"I know what happened with my boy," Jerry said. "You'd be wise to leave him out of it."

"So the veils have been lifted," Morgan said, tipping his bottle, sipping. "I'd buy you a drink but they don't serve anything here you'd much care for."

"How many times do I have to say it? Canada's a joke." Talia fiddled with her purse. "A way to talk about wanting something else. It's not about the mountains."

"What did we used to call them — hippie dreams?"

"You said it yourself he's trouble. He'll snap if you push him." Jerry made himself breathe, counting to himself — four counts in, four counts out. "So will she."

"I keep forgetting you were a therapist."

"I think we all want the same thing here, Morgan."

Morgan stood and pushed back the stool. "Roy here's authorized to make an arrest and that's just what he's going to do."

Talia slammed her daybook down on the Formica counter. "For Christ sake, Morgan. Think about Lily. Don't you even know who she is anymore?"

"She ran away from you too, don't forget."

"Don't you wonder why?"

"It's a waste of time."

"I lie awake wondering. And you know, I think it's because we're fakes. Don't look at me that way — it's true and you know it. Me and my art talks and you and the damn theme parks. We're what she hates."

"I listen to a talk therapist on the radio sometimes, too. You can't be her friend. Ask the hippie about that one." Morgan slipped his arms into the sleeves of his leather jacket. Talia held herself straight and her eyes were big.

"For God's sake, we don't even know if she's here."

"Well if she is, I'll find her."

"So you're going to chain her up and drag her home?"

"Whatever it takes."

"She's nearly eighteen. You can't hold her. And the next time she'll leave for good."

"There are establishments that deal with little girls like her. She won't go anywhere." Morgan reached out and put his thumb under Talia's chin. "Trust me."

Jerry felt something hot in his legs and stomach. But Talia tossed his hand away. "Keep your hands off me."

"Sure thing. But I will find her."

"Great idea. Find some place where they lock up women. That must appeal to you."

Her voice was tight, controlled, but Jerry noticed that her hands were shaking a little.

He made eye contact with Morgan. "I told you. Just a little more time, O.K.? We'll deal with her like a human being."

"Fuck that. I get our little girl back and the firebug she's running around with goes to jail."

"What fire bug?" Talia asked.

"You're saying you haven't noticed the fires following Max around? It's the kind of performance art that can get you shot these days."

Jerry took Talia's arm while she stood there staring incredulously at Morgan. "Come on, let's get out of here."

They sat in the Jeep for a few minutes before Jerry started it. Talia seemed dazed, her sullen stare fixed on the airbrushed picture of the Sun and its starburst spangles in front of them. Clouds had come back, and the curve of the window held the dull light in the corners.

"You asked me what he was like," she said. "He's deranged. Absolutely deranged."

"Give me a minute," Jerry said, opening the car door.

"You can't reason with him," Talia said. "Don't even try."

"Just hang tight."

BACK IN the café, Roy Willis had slid over next to Morgan, who was now sitting. They both were eating tuna sandwiches over paper plates.

Morgan wiped his mouth and blinked at Jerry. "You again?"

"Look, there's something I didn't want to say in front of her," Jerry said.

Roy Willis bit into a pretzel and adjusted his glasses with the back of his hand. "This should be good," he said to Morgan.

"I took a gun off of Max," Jerry said.

Willis stiffened as if his back hurt. Morgan's eyes darted to him, then back to Jerry.

"You got the gun?" Morgan asked.

"No."

"That's good."

"Let Talia do this her way and you can all go home. She'll keep everyone calm."

"You think this new information of yours is real persuasive?" Morgan chuckled.

"He's desperate."

Willis ate another pretzel, licking the salt off before popping it into his mouth. "What about you, pal? Isn't it time you went home and cooked for the wet brains?"

"Morgan, don't listen to this clown. He'll blow it all to hell."

Morgan was biting into his sandwich and had mayonnaise on his lips.

"Chronologically at least she's almost an adult. This grabbing her won't work. You're making her think Max is right."

Willis stood up, and Morgan dabbed at his face with a napkin.

"Trust me, Jerry. Go home. Roy here really wants to earn his money."

THE ROAD up to the inn wound through old grape vines. Clouds had moved in, falling over the hillside, and the heavy gray air blanketed the rows of small trees as the Jeep ground up the incline towards the dull shape of the house at the top of the hill. Talia stared pensively out the window.

"What Morgan said about the fires," she said finally, "do you think it's true?"

"I wouldn't listen to what he says."

"So that's it huh? We sleep together and you don't answer my questions."

Jerry glanced at the dead trees and pictured the houseboat looming with flames on the water, the sack with the gun and pills Lily handed him the last time he saw her. Be careful what you ask for, he thought. "She'll call."

Talia glanced at the wooden structures ahead for the first time, where the chateau style farmhouse with several outbuildings lurked in the fading gray light. Apple trees rose alongside them, barren and claw-like against the night.

"It would make a pretty painting," Jerry said.

"It's depressing. Anyway, they say the vines out there date to the time of Christ — they were brought from the old country."

"It's desolate for sure." He shrugged. "Want to try somewhere else?"

"Even if it's depressing, a fool could see it's romantic, Jerry," she said, not really attempting to hide her tone of disapproval.

That's me, he thought. A fool for sure.

They got one of the upstairs rooms overlooking the orchard, complete with an antique brass lamp burning a yellow candle. But the gray gloominess of the orchard seemed to seep past the thin drapes and collect around the thickly covered bed, draping the thick oak furniture, and floating up into the dark slats of the heavy beamed ceiling.

"At least there's a fireplace," Jerry said. "Beats the old days when we used to live in a tent."

He left her sitting on the bed punching her cell phone frantically and went down to get their bags. He figured he'd be a porter in his next life. When he came back in she'd switched on a small light over the desk and put on the heater but the room still felt cold.

"The woman downstairs swears by their game hens," Jerry said. "She mentioned some famous French recipe."

Talia held up her cell and shook her head.

He took one of her hands — ice cold. "Come on. I can watch you get drunk."

She stopped after two glasses of white Bordeaux, whose buttery electric bouquet she described in detail to Jerry. He let her talk — even though it always bored him to listen to people talk about wine, made him think that you didn't need all the words to get fucked up. The china plate in front of her still held most of the bird and sauce-covered vegetables when she put her linen napkin on the table.

"You need to eat," he said. But she pointed at his own untouched plate.

"You want to go see the wine Jesus drank?" he said. "I'll make a fire after. Before it starts to rain again." Act cheery, he thought, even if you aren't. He remembered Mahatma saying that somewhere. Act cheery and after a while you'll feel that way.

"I should be trying to call her."

"The fresh air will do us good."

The rows of trees in the scant light looked like ravaged figures traipsing over the hills. Against the black valence above the line of hills the shapes arced toward the private apple orchard a few miles away where the concert was being held the next night.

Talia stayed close. Neither spoke. They walked over the hill, the cold air thick with the pungent scent of the earth and old vines. From here they looked down over the river where the low sounds of the rushing water came up. Standing there he could recall a time of color here, a bright summer exploding with yellow light and the smell of apricot Schnapps, one of those summer days when he came here during high-school.

He never knew her name, but even now he could recall the way her tongue tasted of licorice candy and the hot tincture of the booze. After one of his dives off the bridge, she led him back to her car — a pink Dodge. She had the little Schnapps bottle in her glove box along with the candy. They drove up here on one of the fire roads above the water and fucked in the back seat, ending up bunched on the floorboards, covered in sweat.

That night they had stripped off their clothes and

walked in the hidden currents of the river. He held her hand and they tiptoed over the rocks while the water tugged at their calves. They walked so far they could barely stand. He slept with her in the car and when they woke, they had bruises on their feet, but the sun off the dash was hot on their faces. They ate waffles at a little café before he hitched-hiked back home to his house.

Even now, standing there with Talia in the moist, gray night, he could feel the brightness of that morning, the way the water looked electrified, the whole time caught in a yellow haze that seemed impossibly distant. He was with Talia now, but he was in the darkness. It was if he stepped out of the sun-scented day into the empty night, this orchard of clouds and dead vines.

"What are you thinking about?"

"Something from before. Where we used to go by the bridge. A place to hang out where nobody can see you. Not Lily, but Max. It's worth a shot."

"Can I come?"

"I'll make you a fire back at the room. It might be dangerous. Not to mention wet."

When he got the logs going, she sat in the bed leafing through one of her books. The firelight illuminated her bones and made her eyes shine. She waited until he got to the door to say anything.

"I won't blame you."

"For what?"

"For not coming back."

"Don't be dramatic, okay?"

THE BUILDINGS alongside the bridge were dark except for their neon signs, but the men who'd been

painting were still working under a giant arc light that cast
shadows over the abyss above the water. Jerry parked along
the narrow boulevard and got out. If Max were anywhere,
he thought, he'd be down there along the river.

There were a few groups of kids up top, near the
opening to the bridge, smoking cigarettes and talking, but
the street was quiet. He passed by the faces — stopping
long enough to check them out — and skirted around the
side of the steel girders and concrete abutments, near the
workers who followed him with their eyes, before he got
under the footing and made his way down the wet grass and
loose dirt.

The river was loud and higher than he remembered, and
the rising mist prickled his cheekbones as he picked his
way carefully over the gravel and rock shore, away from
the cloud of light above the bridge. If there were kids down
here, as there had been in the old days, they would be
further along the shoreline of the river, huddled near the
concrete ramparts around the first bend and out of sight. He
dug out a cigar, lit it and kept moving.

Through the high-power lights shining above the
bridge, a silver mist fell into the roaring blackness, until he
finally made his way around a small tree-filled protrusion
in the bank, which blocked the light. Simultaneously, he
spotted the small glow of a fire against the black backdrop
of the riverbank.

He tossed his cigar into the roar of the river and walked
slowly towards the fire, soon close enough that the shapes
began to harden. There were six or seven of them — boys
from the looks of the hoods and sullen slumped figures —
but he needed to get closer before he could tell.

Green and amber bottles flashed. The smell of pot and
cigarettes drifted closer. Loud voices fell off. Then one of

the hooded shapes turned slowly, and Max's long nose and black eyes faced him in the firelight.

Max lifted his beer bottle, but even before he spoke, Jerry knew it wasn't just the beer that would be talking. Max moved his eyes slowly, laboriously.

"We have a major dude here. Fuck."

Jerry looked at the faces, then back to Max. All of them seemed the same, subdued and slack. "I need to have a word alone, Max."

"Wow — Is Talia okay, man? I get carried away."

"Alone. I want to talk." Jerry kept his voice calm.

"Of course, of course." Max rose and stumbling, made a mock bow. "A fucking legend. One of the old dudes. Travels in fucking disguise."

"You'd be doing yourself a favor to take a walk with me."

"Calm the fuck down, dude. I don't care if you are a fucking legend or whatever."

They left the hoods and somber eyes at the fire and walked back towards the bridge, Jerry leading the way until the fire was once again obscured by the outcropping. Jerry stopped alongside the water and waited for Max to trundle up.

The river was dark at the middle and rumbled over the deep parts, but trickled around their feet. Max circled in slow motion and sloshed in the wet gravel and pebbles. He was as high as Jupiter, Jerry could see that.

"Where's Lily, Max?"

He spoke slowly. "Around."

"You got any more guns, or bags full of pills?"

"No."

"You sure?" Jerry asked. "Sure?" he said again.

"You don't believe me?"

Max had his hands balled in his sweatshirt. He didn't look up and kept scuffing at the wet rocks. He started to wade out and Jerry caught him by the arm. "You got a warrant out on you from Arizona," Jerry said, holding him tight. "Why don't you just get out of here? Leave Lily and go?"

"I don't want to."

"Max, it's over."

"What are you doing here, man? Shouldn't you be gone? You leave — that's your deal."

"People are after you. You, not her," Jerry said, ignoring everything else.

"Everybody knows about you." Max laughed. "You don't stick."

"You could get free."

Max shrugged. "That's you. Well, I love her, man."

Jerry could feel the hard muscles in Max's arm tense. He kept his grip on his forearm, letting him circle in the shallows. Jerry imagined he was walking a broken animal, the way he'd read about how they walked that racehorse in a pool to keep him calm after surgery. But Max was no horse, he was more like a skinny wild bear, the kind they had in the Canadian Rockies. "I'm staying," Max said again.

"People won't be happy they find out you've been lighting fires, either," Jerry said.

Max was staring at his footsteps, but looked up at the river, near the middle. "Fuck man, you're so messed up."

Jerry tried to lead him out of the shallows, but couldn't. The water, cold as ice, spilled up around his shoes. Max kept walking him.

"You should get some help," Jerry said.

For a second Jerry thought about telling him about the

clinic, about Mahatma, and then got a hold of himself. He was just a kid. They were all just kids. But Max was beyond even Mahatma. And tomorrow Max would be back to his usual self. Jerry knew better. "Keep moving," he told him.

"Fucking legend, man."

Jerry thought about Morgan and Willis out there in the darkness. "Can't you just pack up that van and go? Just drive on out of here across that border to Canada or wherever the fuck you want to run to and leave it? Some place where you can build a house out of tires or whatever it is you want to do."

"I ain't like you."

Jerry sighed. "You want me to take you somewhere?"

In the half-light Jerry could see his grin. "Don't try to trick me, dude. Lily ain't here."

"Shit, Max."

Jerry tried to pull him away from the water, but Max slapped his hand away and started traipsing back in the darkness towards his friends. "You'll catch cold," Jerry yelled.

Max lifted both arms. "Don't feel a fucking thing."

HE OPENED the door quietly. Talia was standing at the large window overlooking the orchard. He'd hoped she'd be asleep, but knew better than that. Holding still for a second, he watched her. He could hear a voice on the TV.

The brass lamp on the desk cast a reflection of her torso and face against the window. She stood there, then hooked her pajama cuff over her palm to wipe away the fog. It looked like she was trying to erase her own image.

He closed the door quietly. She gazed at him.

"It's going to rain again," he said.

"It will be like that pig farm."

"Yeah."

She came away. "You missed the show," she said.

"Lily was on the radio."

The wooden doors of the antique cabinet hung open. Jerry looked at the old piece of furniture, trying to comprehend what Talia had said, then slumped down, sitting on the edge of the bed and staring at the electric wires in the tubes atop the old fashioned hi-fi radio inside. A single speaker buzzed faintly in the back of the cabinet.

"The fire went out. I couldn't sleep and was hoping for Puccini or something. I didn't even think it would work."

"You're sure?"

"What do you think?"

"Max was down by the river — wasted. She must've been filling in I guess."

"She's here at least. Or somewhere not too far away. God, I almost don't care. We've driven around and around only to come to this. A dead orchard and Lily's voice in the dark."

"What the hell did she say?"

"Listening — she talked about listening to each other. It was actually rather sweet."

"It's almost over, Talia. I think Max will do his show and let her go."

She bit her bottom lip. "You got that impression from Max, did you?"

"Sort of."

"He's crazy, Jerry. Impressions don't count."

"He loves her."

"The big expert on love suddenly."

"I'm still here, Talia."

"Yes you are."
"You want me to hold you?"

HE WOKE pressed against Talia's naked back. Her skin touched him everywhere, its softness still and warm on his shins, stomach and chest.

He slithered out of bed, relieved to pry himself away from her softness, relieved to be free — to what, make tea and coffee in the little percolator, just as he did back at the shelter?

She pulled her pajamas on and wandered to the window. Jerry poured the hot water over one of her teabags. Hibiscus tea, he guessed from the fragrant scent. Watching her looking over the orchard, he thought about how many mornings he spent gazing out onto the street, not knowing until now how good it felt to be disconnected from all the men in suits walking along the boulevard, the kids in their tattered clothes and stuffed backpacks — the dogs too, that roamed free in the alleys near the shelter.

He walked over and handed her the cup. Out the window the rain deluged the vines, cut thick furrows coursing with water that ran down the hill, towards the river. Talia watched it intently and sipped her tea.

"I don't even want to get dressed," she said. "What will happen?"

"Maybe I can warn them. Scare the kid before Morgan finds them. Max might just leave?"

"Love might play a part."

Jerry sipped his coffee. "What if it wasn't Max who set the fires?"

She turned and looked at him. That faint sheen had gone from her skin. Her brown eyes were opaque and miserable. "Why would she do it?"

"She talked about listening. To get heard."

"Setting fires for attention. God, I can't hear this. It's all endless."

"What difference does it make? You know she's screwed up. She has to get free is all."

Talia had taken the throw from the couch and wrapped it around her, letting its fingers of brown fringe trail on the floor. "It's so cold. Even here."

"Maybe I can get her attention." Even he knew it was a ruse.

But her dark eyes opened up, hopeful. "So why are you still here?"

He sat down and laced up his boots. When he got them on he reached into his duffle and pulled out his Levi jacket.

"I never thought it would be like this," she said. "I had this idea she'd like me again. I'd take her home and make things better." She laughed a little, without smiling. "Take her shopping. You know. Get her hair cut."

"Things don't always pan out, Talia."

"You think it will work?"

He grabbed the cell and put it in his pocket. "I'll call you as soon as I know anything."

"You're sure?"

"Try not to think about it, okay? Read one of your books. Draw the trees."

MUDDY RAINWATER, choked with broken limbs and debris, came down out of the hills and flowed across the road, so Jerry drove cautiously. Shiva, still up to his neck in ashes in the tray, stared at him while he steered against a steady stream of headlights going east, towards the apple orchard. Shiva didn't have to say anything. There was little chance Lily or Max would be in town. Jerry wasn't proud of the fact, but his blood stirred a little, now that Talia was in the rear-view, back in the cold room.

But by the time he reached the stop sign in town near the bridge, Jerry's chest felt as though his heart was barely moving, much less sending blood to his limbs. The town hardly resembled its nearly cheerful appearance of the day before — rain now slewed off the roofs of the shops, cascading onto the crowded sidewalk and onto the lank-limbed adolescents wearing little more than shorts and tee shirts. Jerry tried not to look at the girls in their clinging now flesh-toned tops, nipples more evident through the thin fabric.

He tightened his jacket and got out of the Jeep, wading across the flooded street to get to the sidewalk, the section nearest the bridge entrance still roped off and busy with painters working under a scaffolding and tarp. He knew there was little chance he'd find either Lily or Max up here. More likely they were already traipsing through the muddy orchard, stoned on whatever new stash Max secured to buy his way to Canada and his house made out of hay. He heard his own words spoken earlier, "I love you," and kept on. It's what you're supposed to say, he thought.

In quick order he dipped into the pizza joint, coffee hut and various sundry shops, all packed with kids. No luck. He bundled his jacket tighter, made his way around the River Rat bar and headed down the muddy path alongside the bridge.

At the bottom, the river sounds were much louder than just last night, a low moan like a freight train going down the tracks. He blinked into the rainfall, watching the currents knife up and explode, the whole wide channel of dark water sliding towards the sea.

From here he tried to get a look down-shore where he talked to Max, but the river was swollen, rising over the rocks and sand, all the way up to the banks. In his mind he could see Ethan again, side by side on the fender of the Caddy with Trips, in a river like this, floating away and thought, "Go, boy."

The River Rat Tavern smelled of wet wood and hot dogs, which sat in a tray atop the end of the bar. Standing in front of a couple at the far end of the padded bar, the bartender watched Jerry peel off his soaking jacket and waited until he put it by his feet to ask what he was drinking. From where he sat, Jerry could look out the side window at the bridge, heavy with kids standing along the railing.

"Soda," Jerry said.

The bartender looked like a tired hippie, somebody left over from the old days. His tie-dye shirt and thick curls falling from a bald spot seemed at odds with the fiberglass kayak shells and river tubes hanging off the walls. Beat-up baseball caps and visors with insignias from different locales hung from the ceiling like bats. Jerry contemplated the places people had come from — towns like De Moines and New York. He doubted that many alumni of the hippie home school had dropped by to hang out with the old sculls and broken sports equipment.

"Find the one you're after?" the guy asked, sliding the soda and a napkin in front of Jerry, who regretted glancing upward.

"Haight Ashburry," Jerry said reluctantly. "The purple haze."

The man lifted his gaze a few feet to the left, rolling his eyes at a cap with a peace sign. "Ain't like it used to be," he said. "Heart's gone out of this place. Will you look at the cha chas on that one."

"Yeah."

Jerry watched the rain fall through the spans of the bridge, trying not to appear rude while he waited for the barkeep to move away. Under the tarp, a fat man in white overalls waved his paintbrush at a kid spinning on a skateboard.

Jerry stared at his soda, trying not to think about all the booze on the rack. He kept his eyes on his ice cubes and didn't notice Morgan and Roy Willis flank him on either side, both sliding their stools out quietly. Then Morgan called for three Johnny Blacks and pointed his finger down the line.

Jerry let his eyes run to the bridge then back to the small dark chinks of mirror behind the rows of bottles. Morgan was wearing a red field jacket. Going fox hunting, Jerry wanted to ask. But he knew the answer.

Morgan waited for the barkeep to disappear before he lifted his glass in toast.

"Here's to finding the son of a bitch and making Canadian bacon out of him," he said.

Roy Willis pulled on a cigarette, his glare at the

bartender almost begging for him to say something. Jerry stared back at his soda.

"You don't like the good stuff?" Morgan said. Jerry looked at him. His ring was prominent and the way he held his drink to show it off gave Jerry the impression he practiced.

"What are we doing here, Morgan?"

"The question is what are you doing here."

Fuck, thought Jerry.

"But I guess there's no question." Morgan turned back and studied the bottles. "Why do I get the feeling you're shirts and I'm skins in this game?" He looked at Willis. "What are you?"

"Skins."

Jerry took a sip. "I never liked football."

"Yet here we are, in the fucking mud. Rolling around. No pads, Jerry. Somebody's going to get fucked up."

"You're wasting your time."

"I have to be honest here. How long do you think it'll be before you pick up a drink, just like that one, and end up right back where you started? It will be different this time because your kid's really gone — but I'm guessing not that much different."

"What did Talia see in you?"

"Christ buddy, look who's talking. You're in way over your head with that girl, let me tell you. Not that I don't sympathize." Morgan took another drink. "But I have a sneaky suspicion you don't want to be here much anymore."

"Shut up, Morgan."

"She's a difficult girl herself, my ex. And you can see the writing on the wall."

"You don't know anything about how I feel."

"I know you killed one kid. Isn't that enough?"

Jerry could see Roy's face in the mirror; it seemed to redden with each drag on his cigarette. Suddenly it was over.

"Fine," Jerry said. "You win."

Morgan turned in his seat and stared hard at him. His eyes widened.

"I said you win," Jerry repeated.

Out the door Jerry turned left, walking into the stream of headlights peeking out of the gray haze and spattering rain. He kept his head down, but the rain stung his cheeks. When he got clear of the crowds on the sidewalk, towards the end of town, he lifted his thumb and kept walking, vaguely aware of the passing lights. A car honked, the low rumble of the river swallowing it. He kept walking.

He hardly saw the car pull over and nearly reached it before glancing up at a pale blue Impala, ill-kept and sun-bleached, angled off the asphalt. It was the kind of car the cool types drove in high school. Perfect, he thought, the rain pelting his face.

Walking towards it, Jerry made out the ponytail of the driver resting on the backside of a leatherjacket above the low seatback, the head still.

He reached the car and was about to climb in the front seat, when he made out the figure of someone else slumped in the front seat, a serape covering him. The driver glanced sleepily towards the back, his eyelids veiled.

Jerry popped the rear door and jumped in, enveloped by the smell of skunkweed and dope that stayed in his nostrils. The driver kicked the column shift up and crept out into traffic, not turning to greet Jerry.

Once underway, the half-moon eyes came up in the rear-view. He stared at Jerry, then the eyes smiled, narrowing into slits. He pulled up a roach from between his legs and held it over the seatback. "I'm pretty tired," Jerry said. "Afraid I might go to sleep like your pal up there."

The man scraped his ponytail out from his collar, pushing it sideways beneath the dirty rubber band, then took a long drag. He talked without letting out a breath and squeezed the words out.

"Ain't staying for the tunes?" he said. "Old Buttercup Blues Band are getting down tonight."

"I'm trying to get back to the city."

The guy reached out and punched the weatherworn blanket with his knuckles, waiting for a response. "Could be dead," he wheezed, finally exhaling. "He wakes up we might score some and get back up here later."

The serape shifted, and it came away from the body enough to reveal a swatch of gray-black hair. The driver coughed and glanced indifferently at the joint, his eyes widening.

"Used to be wild — a wolf. Now look at him."

Jerry was beginning to feel the pot swim in his head and the thought occurred to him that if he yanked the blanket off, Captain Trips would be underneath, thumbing his nose, laughing at him. Suddenly he thought of the little Shiva, still buried in the ashtray back at the Jeep. He thought of Talia too, waiting above the muddy field.

"I got to get out," he said.

The eyes came up in the mirror. "No place to turn around unless you want me to put you in the ditch," the guy said.

"Just stop."

The car slowed and squeaked to a stop. Jerry jumped out, waited for a car to pass, and jogged to the other side of the road. Looking back over his shoulder, he could see a finger of the ocean, gray and black, in the direction of the shelter. He pulled his collar up and put his hand out, walking back towards town.

The car hadn't pulled away. The window came down and a thin vapor of smoke rolled out. "Fuck man, you crazy?" the driver yelled. He held the joint out and beckoned him back with a wave.

"Peace and love, brother," Jerry said.

He lifted his hand and the blue Impala sputtered off, its tailpipe rumbling and vibrating in the cold rain.

TALIA DIDN'T say anything when he came in, just stood struggling with the bent belt buckle on her coat, silhouetted and drawn in front of the night-soaked window.

She looked ready for business. She wore thick black pants tucked into rubber-soled boots, her hair tied back. On the bed, she'd placed her big metal flashlight and an umbrella.

Jerry walked over and examined the bent prongs on Talia's belt. The water coming off his clothes stained the wood floor. She stood still, close enough he could smell rose oil and the canvas of her jacket.

She gazed out at the rain falling through a utility light near the shed. Then she slowly turned and looked at him again and seemed to catch her breath enough to speak. "I didn't think I'd see you again."

He thought about trying to explain about Morgan and Roy Willis, the Impala, Shiva in the ashtray, Trips — and love, there was that too, but what was there to say anyway?

When he cinched the belt, he got his fingers caught under the strap.

"It seems you're stuck," she said.
"Where else is there to go?"
"I'm glad."
"You want to go to a concert?"
"I'm scared."
"Some trip, huh?"

RAIN AND fading sun made all the trees dark, and red brake lights moved into the apple orchard in a solemn crimson procession that struck Jerry as anything but festive. Ruined cardboard signs sagged off trees where they'd been tacked. Water cut rivulets in the incline moving inexorably down to the road and river, following gravity. In fact, he thought, it was damn near funereal.

Talia spent the ride looking for Lily through the darkening light, scanning the deluged cars and foot-bound pedestrians. But by the time they reached the plateau looking onto the distant stage, bound by apple trees on both sides and filled with kids, she'd given up. Cars were everywhere, parked at severe angles in the mud, and Jerry saw at once it was impossible to get closer.

But abandoning the car here like others were doing seemed foolish, so he drove left and skirted the crowd. Talia look glazed, fingering the Shiva in the ashtray.

"I just need to talk to her," she said.

"Take a look at that — up by the trees."

There was just enough daylight left to see the cars and trees. Max's van, as dark as a pirate ship on the midnight sea, was parked between the last two apple trees. The stage, strobed with colored light, was still a ways off, with the darkening throngs spread out in a large swatch under the rain.

Jerry angled the Jeep up onto the muddy hill and parked. He kept his distance from Max's van, even though they could see it was empty.

"They could be anywhere," Talia said. "God, it looks like it could all float away."

"We better stay together."

Talia had her flashlight, which struck Jerry as pathetic. She watched his face and looked like she detected what he was thinking so he made a show of gamely pulling his light from the front seat and switching it on. Like a kid, he beamed the light into her eyes, but she didn't see the humor. He knew she'd given up.

Jerry tugged the hood that had slipped down Talia's back and pulled it over her head, tying the cord under her chin. "I'm here with you," he said. "That's something isn't it?"

"If we get separated we better meet back here."

She'd learned, he'd have to give her that. He wondered what knowledge he'd gained on the trip. At least she was somewhere new. Just now, for him, it all felt a little too familiar.

Talia sprung open her umbrella and dug something out of her pocket, handing him a knit cap. He didn't say anything and pulled it on.

Setting out, they stayed high on the hillside and started for the stage, whose makeshift scaffolding and platform turned under a glaring spotlight. When the glare came around, it touched on pieces of the crowd for an instant before spinning off into the rainy blackness. A trio of young men, still barely visible, strummed wooden guitars on stage and sang what sounded like a folk song. Distorted amplified rhythms echoed over the crowd and came towards them.

As they started, Jerry felt his stomach spread, the sight of the crowd and sound of the music too familiar. It was all too close to their busted hunt for his son. Talia was ahead of him.

She held her umbrella up and sent her beam over the crowd, briefly illuminating a pair of ecstatic looking irises and wan faces frozen in the light, then a clump of bodies, soaked and writhing to the music. Compared to the other gatherings, this one felt closest to the old hippie festival Jerry remembered. Most of those, he recalled, ended badly too.

After stopping and searching three or four times, Talia turned inward under her umbrella.

"Where the hell is she?" Talia said.

"Have a little patience. Just keep moving."

She stopped and looked at him, her face in darkness. He didn't need to see her to know what she was thinking. "I really don't need a lecture now."

Jerry pointed his flashlight and blinked into the rain. "Up there by the stage. Max will be close to it, and maybe Lily too."

They kept on, eventually moving closer to the level of the crowd. The rain kept falling, making their footing difficult. Talia took deliberate steps, focused now on the nearing stage.

Jerry watched the crowd, trying to train his eye onto the circle of light arcing out from the spotlight, and he tried to pick out faces. He told himself to concentrate, but the rain and glare made it hard. Anyway, he knew damn well it was futile.

But she had helped him look for Ethan, probably knowing too how it would end.

Fifty yards from the stage, clear across the field, a figure moved at the edge of the light and caught Jerry's attention. There was something about the lanky gait, the angles of the jacket, that felt familiar and then disappeared into the darkness. Jerry stood and breathed in the dank air and waited for the light to come around again.

This time he got a good look. Roy Willis was in front, wading through the crowd, with Morgan lagging behind, still in his red jacket, like a hunter letting his dog work. Willis' face, framed for an instant in the searchlight as he gazed in their direction, looked like an explosion of ruddiness, his glasses opaque as silver dollars.

Just seeing the two of them made Jerry's blood feel heavy in his arms and legs, worse than when he'd stared out at the crowds and tried to hunt Ethan's face. But whatever he felt, he knew at once he wouldn't let Talia see them.

By now Talia had almost reached the stage. Beneath a fluttering tarpaulin at the far end, a crowd of kids mingled, some with instruments in their hands. Jerry looked for Max or Lily, but didn't see them.

Talia was frozen, squinting through the rain. Jerry got to her and tugged on her sleeve, pulling her around to the other side of the tall stack of speakers stacked on the hill, where they found respite beneath a pile of plywood cascading with rain. From here they could still see a portion of the stage, but the far end of the crowd where Jerry'd seen Morgan was obscured.

"I'm going to find something to stay off the mud," he

told her.

She nodded. He could see in her eyes how tired she was. He quickly scrounged a piece of cardboard around from the back of the stage, nodding to a few kids, then hurried back and put it down on the wet ground.

"It seems hopeless," she said, lowering herself slowly, folding her umbrella. "But I don't need to tell you that."

"How many times did you say it? Don't quit. You can't."

"You don't even want to be here. I can see it your face."

Jerry pulled his cap off and slapped the water off. It was soaked. "Damn it, Talia. I'm right here."

She was gazing at the crowd. The cast off light from the turning spotlight illuminated her eyes and the wet sheen on her smooth skin. He unbuttoned his jacket and pulled out his tee shirt, leaning forward with it to carefully wipe her face.

"What did we learn?" she said. "I mean what has all this been about?"

In his mind Jerry ticked off all the stops on the road, all the detours and dead ends. She'd picked a hell of a time to turn philosophical.

"Maybe this is it, right here, right now." He forced himself to sound confident.

She almost smiled, a hint of upturned recognition registering on her lips. The music stopped and the night was consumed by the hard patter of rainfall all around them, the thick guttering sound of the water pooling and then running off the stage.

They were both watching the crowd turn under the rain when Lily's voice came from behind.

Talia gave a breathless gasp and turned to look. Lily, a cipher in her black clothes, knelt and gave her mother a hug. Her eyes were nearly closed, squinting against the rain and her hair was flat and soaked with water. She looked at Jerry over her shoulder and pushed Talia away.

Her voice was fearful. "Just let Max do this. It will be over and he'll go. Alone. I told him," she said.

"You're not making sense, sweetheart. What are you saying?"

"I promise, all right. But you have to listen. Why don't you ever listen?"

"Catch your breath, Lily," Jerry said. He made himself sound calm and matter of fact. "Start over. Just tell us what you mean."

But then Max's voice came out of the speakers and fell over the audience. Lily looked up at the crowd and then dropped her eyes back to her mother, her face creased and desperate.

"The last one — a stupid film. Before the real bands. Just let him do it and he will go."

Talia tilted her head up toward the stage, trying to comprehend, to listen. Max was saying something about the festival, the old days, his words distorted enough that Jerry couldn't understand. They could see his legs and the bottom half of the microphone stand, but not his face.

"He wants me up there," Lily said, rising suddenly. She stepped out from under the overhang into the rain. "I'll find you after. You have to believe me."

"Lily, no!" Talia reached for her, but Lily had already bounded around the speakers and was gone. Jerry rose quickly and pulled her up, both of them moving clear enough of the stage to see.

Still a hundred yards or so from the stage, the unmistakable shapes of Willis and Morgan moved towards the stage, slowly at first and then beginning to run. Jerry tried to think what to do, but suddenly felt the glare of a spotlight touching his face. He squinted into the bright light, coming from the other side of the stage.

Lily had joined Max, he could see that much, and Max seemed to be pointing down at him and Talia.

Talia turned and buried her head against him. "So the dead rock star's returned," Max said, or at least that's what it sounded like to Jerry. He could see Lily tugging at Max, pulling at his arm to make him stop. Jerry hoped he hadn't found another gun.

The crowd laughed, held up their cigarette lighters and cell phones in the rain, and booed. Beneath the fluorescent haze Morgan walked a few steps behind Willis, who used his broad shoulders to push toward the stage.

"Stay here," Jerry shouted at Talia.

He ran up the metal steps leaped up on to the stage. The crowd cheered louder, laughing, and Max recoiled, the skull ring on his hand catching light as he reached towards the lapel of his leather jacket.

Lily stared at him, big eyed. "What the fuck are you doing?"

"You don't have a chance, Max." Jerry had to yell to even hear his own voice over the sound of the crowd. "It's all coming down here. Let it go and come down with me before it's too late."

But Max jerked away and took Lily's hand. In an instant they'd bounded off the stage, the crowd cheering, and parting for them as they ran.

Roy's fist knocked Jerry to his knees. He heard a swell of raucous hoots, the crowd evidently thinking that this was a part of some act. Roy's breath still smelled of tuna when he leaned down and spoke into Jerry's ear.

"I ought to cancel your ticket for real," he shouted.

"Make you a real dead rocker, you fuck."

But Morgan was down at the edges of the stage already, following Lily and waving for Roy. His red coat was so drenched it looked like he'd worn it into a shower. He flipped Jerry the bird, bringing more cheers. Jerry used his fingers to clear some of the moisture off of his face, and when he looked again, they were all gone — Max and Lily vanished into the night and Willis and Morgan in pursuit. Jerry touched his forehead again and his hand came away bloody.

He found Talia standing at the steps. The spotlight was still on them and Jerry tried to ignore it, turning his back, but the crowd hissed. Talia was crying. She let her umbrella fall into the mud, clutching him desperately.

Jerry took her by the sleeve and pushed through the kids at the edge of the crowd, pulling her finally to the clear on the embankment.

She slipped him a handkerchief and with one hand he held it against his head and with the other pulled her back to the hillside, finally clearing them from the light.

He grabbed her shoulders and yelled into the rain. "We have to get to them first. Can you do this?"

She nodded and swallowed. This time Jerry led, tugging Talia by the hand.

By the time they arrived at the cars, Max's van was already moving, Lily's face like a white orb pressed against the side window. The van lurched into gear, spouting muddy water behind it.

"Why is she doing this?" Talia said.

"Maybe she doesn't have a choice."

"What do you mean?"

Jerry started for the Jeep. "Come on."

When they reached the muddy descent down to the

road, Max's van turned onto the asphalt. Seconds later the headlights of the town car came clear of the lot and it fell in behind the van, the lights bouncing onto the wet roadway.

JERRY COULD feel his tires slipping on the mud, but he hit the gas anyway, throwing Talia back. "Hang tight."

When they finally reached the pavement, the taillights from both cars were almost invisible, almost gone in the mist and rain.

Jerry tried to concentrate on the road as the roaring engine and rattling chassis made him think the Jeep might fall apart around them. He'd reached out once to put his hand on Talia's waist but when he felt the rear tires slide and the rear end fish-tail, he'd pulled back to keep two hands on the wheel.

Talia had to yell to be heard over the engine. "What did you mean when you said there wasn't any choice?"

Jerry kept his mouth shut, but Talia tugged his jacket sleeve.

He didn't look at her. "I got a situation here."

"Tell me!"

They were drawing closer to the red taillights in the rain. If Jerry could keep the Jeep on the road, he might even catch them. After that, he couldn't figure.

Talia interrupted his concentration, pulling at his jacket sleeve again.

"Goddamn it," Jerry finally said. "He had a gun. I took a gun off Max, all right?"

The drone of the engine filled the cab, and the wipers clacked manically, but Talia's silence felt profound.

Jerry tried to make it better. "He doesn't have it anymore, Okay?"

He didn't have to look at her to know what she was thinking. She stayed quiet as he held the accelerator down, watching the rear bumper of Morgan's car get closer.

"You should've told me," she said. "That's what people do who care about each other."

"I know."

Just ahead the sedan was weaving though the falling water, the conical beams of its high-beams flashing luridly on the panels of the van. Roy Willis clearly detected by now that they weren't just another pair of headlights. Weaving in and out of view, sliding wildly in the mud, dipping almost out of sight and then rising again, Max kept pressing ahead, periodically sending plumes of water onto the hood of the town car.

"Morgan's going to kill those kids," Jerry said.

"Do something."

Jerry jumped on the accelerator, not thinking, cranking the wheel hard to the right. In an instant Roy Willis was glaring through his spattered window at them both, while Jerry struggled to get the Jeep past.

Talia clenched the edge of the dash and Jerry kept the accelerator down, his left wheels climbing up on to the shoulder of the narrow road, until the black shape of the car pushed back in his periphery. In a fusillade of jumping light and water, he turned the Jeep until it held the center of the highway.

Willis laid on the horn.

Jerry jammed the shifter into second and stomped the brakes, while the van sped ahead. Willis was going crazy, his emergency lights flashing, as Jerry kept maneuvering back and forth to keep him at bay.

"Get going, Max!" he yelled. "Go, kid."

"Please Lily, please," Talia called too, squinting back at

the town car, and then squaring her shoulders and looking resolutely forward. "Just go." They slowed; the Jeep slightly angled in the center of the road.

The crash was deafening. Tossed hard against the seatbelt straps, Jerry had to scrabble to get control of the Jeep, which lurched towards the muddy declivity alongside the road. He was still carrying enough speed so that when the front wheel caught the gully, the Jeep ground headlong into the foliage and the front window exploded with the leaves and branches.

The engine was still running, but they were stopped, nosed into a thicket. There was a rush of noise, horn and mud as the town car roared by up on the road.

Jerry looked into her eyes. "You all right?" Talia's jacket was torn and her arm looked twisted.

"Just go."

He got the Jeep backed out and on the road, which slowed his pulse. But the sight of the lights coming up from the town car up in front made him feel as if wires hooked to a battery were connected to his heart. He glared at the Shiva.

"What?" Talia said.

He rolled the window down, fetched the figurine from the ashes and tossed it into the rain. Then he focused on the car lights, glowing above from the next bend.

Before they reached the stop sign near the bridge, Jerry reached down and switched off the lights, letting the car roll so that even the brake lights wouldn't flash. Talia gasped and they crept in blackness until they edged into the light from the bridge.

At the dark end of the town stood the bridge, still lit by arc lamps. Black water, silver under the streetlamps, coursed between the curbs and around yellow sawhorses set out where the road flooded.

Jerry breathed in, trying to slow down and look.

The town had a sleepy, washed-out quality about it. The kids were gone — the concert just vanished into the wet, and the shops closed. The workers were gone from the bridge, which rose up in the rain and fog.

He let his gaze draw closer. Red lights blinked. "There — by the truck. Jesus," he said to Talia.

On Willis's side, the town car was pulled alongside a delivery truck. A trail of smoke rose from the muffler into the rain. Just ahead, a few yards short of the bridge, Max's van sat with its lights out, a black shape barely visible in the glare of the arc lamps.

"What are they doing?" Talia said. "Oh God."

Before Jerry answered, Willis's door opened and he stood in the narrow crease between the loading van and the delivery truck. Morgan was yelling something out the window on his side, covering his eyes from the rain with his arm.

Willis lifted his gun over the doorframe and pointed it towards the van.

Talia gasped, covering her mouth with her hands.

"What does the goddamn fool think, Max is just going to let her go?" Jerry said.

"Do something, Jerry, please."

Then the van's small headlights shone in the rain and glare, flaring brighter from the engine as Max slowly began to idle, turning away from the water slightly, moving almost in a circle, towards the road leading out of town. Even with the windows closed Jerry could hear the river, the loud noise of the flooding water tearing at the banks and the stanchions of the bridge. Willis stood in the rain, mouth wide, his voice barely discernable above the movement of water.

Jerry hit the gas. He waited until the last instant to pull on the headlamps and then, swerving, slammed his palm onto the horn. Willis's glasses sparked like mirrors in their direction before he dipped back inside the car. Peering over the Jeep's hood, Jerry could see Morgan, his hands up as if he were being robbed, his face distorted with surprise or fear as the Jeep plowed hard into the side of the towncar.

For a single instant the conflagration of shattered glass and wrenching metal seemed to settle, leaving only the hissing of the radiator in the rain and steam billowing out of the hood, and Jerry thought his plan might work, that Max would have the sense to drive on out of there. The towncar with Morgan in it wasn't going anywhere.

But then Talia screamed, pointing in the direction of the lights on the bridge.

Jerry turned. Out the Jeep's window, he caught the last glimpse of van as it spun out of control and crashed through the barricades set out by the workmen, through the railing of the bridge, and then was gone.

Morgan had gotten out of the car and stood yelling, pounding on the disabled vehicle, his rain-blurred face somehow still loud and hysterical. Roy Willis slumped over the wheel.

Jerry jumped from the Jeep and ran through the flooding street.

By the time he hit the rampart of the bridge, Jerry had stripped off his jacket. He let it fall and kept going. Talia's voice was behind him, no more than a faint echo as he jumped headlong over the railing and into the silver spangled light above the whitewater. He closed his eyes, a kid again, showing off, falling. But then he opened his lids, and the ledge of water came up, and he slammed into its rushing thickness, swallowed whole by cold and black.

He tugged and thrashed. Trying to breath.

When he finally broke the surface he could see the dull shape of the van frozen above the water. He flailed, trying to keep his eyes fixed on the vehicle, aware suddenly that the van must have been caught on something, a tree or rocks maybe.

Two hard pulls in the direction of the shore and he was bouncing directly towards the van in the icy waves, moving until he hit the paneled side, the cold pressing his chest and legs into the metal. For an instant, the swirling water provided him with a reprieve. He could crane his neck enough to get a look at Talia. So this is it, he thought, where the road leads.

But then he thought of Lily.

Spitting water, he clawed for the roof-seam with his fingers and slowly began to pull himself around the back, to Lily's side. Once there, he saw, in the shadows, the huge trunk of a tree knifed into the side of the van. The van tilted and moaned, palpable against the loud current, its metal exterior beginning to give under the weight of the water. The tree wouldn't hold it for long. Jerry scrabbled over the tree trunk, pulling himself to the window.

Getting a foothold with his feet against the wheel-well, Jerry slid his hands down to the glass and tried to peer inside. The water pressure pressed him against the door, so he could free his hands. It was dark and water spilled over his face — but then he saw. Lily was inside, toppled onto the motionless Max, her pale face still above the rising water. She was reaching up for Jerry.

He slammed his elbow into the little window. The rushing water muffled the sound of the broken glass. Water breeched over the window frame. Jerry broke off the remaining shards of window glass.

"Come on, girl. Give me your hand. Give it to me, Lily. Let me help you!"

She reached up and he got her wrist. "Max," she screamed. "I can't leave him."

"I know, baby. Just give me your hand."

He tugged, grabbing onto the tree and leaning back against the rush of water. She came free, floating through the bent window frame, arm up toward Jerry.

And then the van was gone, its round body slipping off the branch and floating like a boat into the blackness until it was beyond the sphere of light.

In that moment Jerry saw that they were both somehow still attached to the slippery tree trunk — an act of Shiva or what the drunks called a higher power, or goddamn whatever, and he got a hold of a limb and kept his other arm around Lily. Do this, he thought. You've got to do this.

"He's gone, Lily." Jerry shouted into her ear. She looked toward the white ripples and rolling waves erased into receding darkness. "You've got to get over to shore — it's over now."

On the riverbank he could see Talia's flashlight beam floating in their direction. Morgan and Roy Willis were still on the bridge caught up in some sort of pantomime of despair, with Willis' angular shape leaning over Morgan, who'd gone down to his knees.

Jerry saw something else too, closer to where the log pushed onto the sand. Two shapes stood in the dim illumination on the high ground near the trees. It looked like they were holding hands, watching.

"It's not going to hold," Jerry shouted to Lily. "We stay here, we end up in the Pacific." She didn't move. "I've already done that, Lily."

Lily face was turned from the bright arc lights coming off the bridge and it was in shadow. Her face was blank and she gripped his hand hard, the way Ethan used to when he was little and afraid. She turned and held her eyes rigidly on the slick tree trunk.

"Don't think, Lily. One hand at a time. I've got you."

She reached her fingers out tentatively at first, while he held her waist, and then began to scramble up from the floating fingers of branches on to the stripped, bent tree trunk. Jerry inched forward, using his body to block her from the current while she pulled her legs up and slid along the wood. The tree arched above the water. Squinting against the rain, he could see that she only had five feet more to go, but the tumult of water cascading underneath would take her if she even got her feet into it.

He kept his arms under her, fighting off the current with his elbows, bracing his feet against a wedge of root. She'd moved halfway across the branch when Talia got to them. Her flashlight gone, she waded into the shallows, close to the cleft of black water channeling downstream.

"Stay there," Jerry yelled. "The current's too strong. Let her reach for you. She's got to reach."

Lily ticked her head towards him, not turning, but hearing. She inched forward, her arms outstretched on the log. Talia waited, her own arms extended.

Their hands met, and then their arms, as Talia reached around her daughter and dragged her off the broken tree and over to the sand.

Jerry tried to catch his breath, watching the two women collapsed together on the shore, Lily's arms still around her mother's neck.

"Take her home," Jerry yelled, his face down against the wet log. "Just take her home, will you."

When he looked up again, Talia was sitting up, her face shining a little in the muted light. She nodded at him, gently. Above her, on the bank, the two figures turned away and their shapes came clear — the rotund outline of the Captain walking away with Ethan, fading into the glistening leaves stirred by the rain and wind.

For a heartbeat Jerry wondered if he'd even seen it — and then he was gone, the tree splintering off loudly and crashing into the rushing water, his body surrounded by cold and black again.

Epilogue

AN INDIAN summer light broke over Alcatraz and illuminated the jagged edges of the Island. You'd never guess it was late October from the way the sun blazed down, warming the passengers on the boat so that a few of them even removed their jackets. The rugged island outcropping rose off the stern, beyond the thin vapor of diesel fumes. All around the bay, the sea had blued and hardened and shafts of light went deep into the water.

Mahatma stood at the stern's curved railing. He raised his saltwater rod toward the seagulls and flicked the line. The kids watched dutifully. "Dudes, you got to let it happen. The fish comes to you. Like every other thing in life."

"Do you fish a lot?" asked one of the boys.

"I have been taught by an expert," Mahatma replied. "The man of fishing."

Willy stepped away from the others. His adolescent face was hidden by an oversized baseball hat that sat over his ears. He buried his hands in his leather jacket and nodded. But he didn't lift his eyes.

"We're kind of hungry."

Mahatma rested the pole on the railing and blinked his eyes. "You want to end up in the lock up? You got to slow down, dude. Learn to relax."

Willy nodded and shuffled back to his friends — five others that Mahatma had dragged from the shelter. They tossed bread and watched the seagulls swarm.

Jerry put his hand on Mahatma's shoulder. "Not as easy as it looks, the Hippie Homeschooling."

"Bro, you should be able to reach them. I mean, what the hell good is your certificate?"

"I haven't passed yet."

"Some fucking therapist."

Mahatma turned the handle on the reel and studied the line. He smiled at a new thought.

"You aren't afraid anymore, are you? That's something, huh bro?"

"Of the water? I guess not."

"But all the other, huh? It takes time."

"I guess."

"You saved that little girl, bro. And those boys? You're teaching them. Shiva would be proud, brother."

"Yeah."

When they got back to the dock, Jerry sipped coffee at a small café while Mahatma took the boys to look through the telescopes set out on the wharf. Over on the docks three massive sea lions lay on their sides, not bothering to move as tourists walked past. Jerry knew how they felt — oblivious and sleepy in the sun. He still envied their lethargy, but knew he had to fight such impulses. Welcome to the world of the living and the breathing, he thought.

Back at the shelter, Mahatma waited until the boys went

to their rooms to grab Jerry by the shoulder and march him around to the loading dock. He didn't say anything until they got over to the dumpster.

The Jeep, its dented fenders pounded out and newly painted, sat in the shade.

"Figured a professional needs a clean ride," Mahatma said. "I had her towed back and fixed up. Consider it a graduation present."

"Like I said, I haven't graduated from anything yet."

"What about women? Think they want to ride around in a junk heap? Or on the bus?"

"You're crazy." Jerry grinned.

"Take a ride. Got her tuned up, ready to cruise."

Jerry hopped in and saw a new Shiva on the dash, this figurine painted and larger than the previous one. Jerry rolled down the window and gave Mahatma a stare.

"Circle keeps turning, bro," Mahatma said.

"I'm sure Mr. Shiva won't mind if I get off the ride."

Mahatma pounded the roof and started towards the back door of the shelter. When he opened it the smell of hamburgers cooking spilled out. "You haven't learned a damn thing, have you bro?" Mahatma was laughing. "Only one way off."

Mahatma was right, but Jerry didn't want to think about the endless road that always brought you back to the place you started.

BUT, of course he drove the Jeep down the long avenue and turned in the direction of the old house. Past all the rooftops, the bay still looked as blue as a sapphire.

He slowed when he got to the old Victorian. The yuppie owners had added a marble birdbath under the big elm, but everything else still looked pretty much the same. The house always showed well on sunny days, and today was no exception. A thin woman with a blue bandana and a garden spade came through the front screen door. A small boy holding a plastic shovel bounded down the stairs behind her.

Jerry nodded pleasantly and kept driving. It was too early to go back to the shelter. If he went back now he'd have to help Saul with the dinner, or else go sit in his room, read a magazine or watch TV. Or, worse still, start packing up his things, worrying about the North Beach apartment he'd just rented, or the new job he was about to start. Instead, he turned the Jeep in the direction of the bridge.

He parked on the road, right before it wandered toward the Presidio and the Bridge, and he walked down a path that skirted the ice plant very near where the Cadillac skidded into the Pacific.

The ice plant had come back thickly on the steep hillside. He studied the wet-looking tangles for some sign of his tire tracks, but saw nothing.

Nearing the bottom of the hill, where it all started, he remembered something Mahatma said once: "Everything disappears except for what's left inside the duffle bag of your heart, bro."

"Go to hell," Jerry said out loud.

On such a fine day, with the sun out and the water and hillsides across the bay so clear, he knew his friend was right, though he'd never admit it. If he did, he'd have to think about what was left inside his heart, and he knew better than that.

The grass was warm under him when he sat down. Off the bay, the musty briny smell turned on the wind.

The shallow water under the pier was translucent and

ran slate gray under the shade at the end, where a few crabbers sat smoking, staring down at their strings.

The boardwalk was busy, the sun having brought out all sorts of people. He watched mothers pushing strollers, old people arm in arm, joggers in their bright suits. They all walked past; it all kept turning, held there by gravity, but turning.

"Quite a nice view," came the voice. "You should have reminded me how pretty it was."

She was standing in the sun, her hand over her tortoise-shell sunglasses, staring out at the water. Her hair was pulled back and a canvas daypack fell off one of her shoulders, with something rolled up sticking out of the flap.

She turned slowly and surveyed the hillside above him like an explorer studying landfall. "Mahatma said you might be here. Look how steep it is."

"And what brings you here?" was all he could think to say. He got up, aware suddenly of his face reddening from the sun, and from his own stupidity. Right back where he started.

"Quite a fall you had." She tilted her sunglasses onto her hair, considered the grassy incline, and then reached into her pack. She enrolled a canvas.

Jerry stared at the painting — the dancing skeleton man, the image of the wall from Canyon de Chelley.

"At least I tried," she said, frowning a little. "But it's not perfect."

"Trying has to count for something," he said. "At least that's what I keep telling myself." But the painting was good, he could tell.

After he kissed her, Talia held her eyes shut for a moment, then opened them slowly and blinked out towards the spangles freshened by the breeze, as if waking up from an afternoon nap.

"Look at us," she said. "You'd think we were a couple of teenagers. You've been a horrible influence, I'm afraid."

She moved a few inches away from him, her eyes on him. "How are you Jerry, really?"

"Been leading a group of kids at the shelter," he said, gazing at Alcatraz. "And working in a clinic under another guy. At a clinic in Berkeley. Thought I might try and get my license back."

"Really?"

"More than thought, I guess. It's sort of in the works — official in about three weeks. I'll be working with kids — adolescents."

She considered this, nodding to herself as she squinted out towards the water.

"You have blue in your hair," he said.

Still gazing out at the water, she smiled, blushing a little. "Impetuous, I know. Lily dared me. She has a radio show at her school. You know, she's started back." She made a little face. "Communications major."

He placed his fingers on the single shot of electric blue.

"And it's just a touch."

"I miss you."

She wrinkled her nose again, then reached back and loosened her hair. "I had this idea," she said. "I was thinking it might be fun to go for a ride in the Jeep. I mean, if you have time."

He reached his arm around her and pulled her tight, her ribs pressing against his.

"Don't you have to teach or something?"

"I took another leave. To think about what I want to do." She looked at him. "To paint, maybe. Or something."

"You're serious?"

"I'm always serious," she said, but she smiled.

"A ride, huh?"

She lowered her dark glasses. The breeze off the bay blew her hair, and carried the scent of rose oil. She hoisted the backpack over her shoulder and started up the hill toward the Jeep.

Acknowledgements

Any road trip requires help along the way. A novel is no different. I've had a lot of assistance on this trip, forever in need of the spiritual equivalent of a spare belt or serviceable tire. My mom, dad and sister have been eternally supportive. So too Samantha, Josh, and Ben. Scott Miller has always been "here now" with some sort of Dharma wrench. Bob Driscoll too, was always good for an inspired laugh. I can't forget about Paul Rohrer's dinners. I'm in debt to Trish and Rick Cornez. Michael Measures and Bob Kizar provided editorial assistance. And a number of intellectual roadhouses appeared at the right times–Larry McCaffery's parties, and Alville nights with Tim and Serena Powers. Of course, this novel would not have found print without Mark Smith's enthusiasm and desire to establish Blue West Books. I am eternally grateful to Emory Elliott. And I can't help but think always of my favorite Irish novelist, Brian Moore, and his encouragement in my creative writing classes at UCLA, way back at the beginning of the trip, but not so very long ago.

CPSIA information can be obtained at www.ICGtesting.com
Printed in the USA
LVOW08s0435200715

446845LV00001B/55/P